# Whale-Sized Heart

## by
## C.J. Love-Jones

© 2025 C.J. Love-Jones

www.cjlovejones.com

Published by: English House Publishing

Developmental & Copy Edit: Nicole Hartney:
www.letter-eye.com

Cover & Interior Design: English House Publishing

ISBN: 978-0-9863042-8-6

Content Warning: *Whale-Sized Heart* includes fictionalized depictions inspired by historical events involving orca captures in the 1970s, specifically the Penn Cove incident, and other violent scenes addressing the treatment of orcas in the wild, including a discussion about a real-life 1950s event in which the U.S. Navy killed wild orcas to control fisheries in Iceland. While these events are included to reflect historical practices and the attitudes of some individuals at the time, they may be distressing for some readers. They are included to present an accurate and impactful portrayal of the challenges faced by these animals. Without these scenes, the story would lose the depth and authenticity necessary to honor their history and to fully explore the issues that continue to affect orca populations today.

**A Note from the Author:** I've dedicated a significant portion of my life to animal welfare—from farm animals and companion animals to habitat conservation. As a sensitive reader on these issues, I crafted this story with your heart in mind, aiming to handle it with the same care I'd hope for my own. While some events in this story are tragic, they reflect real history and carry a purpose—to take you on an emotional journey and leave you with a sense of optimism for future generations.

For the whales—who bring out the best and worst in all of us.

When a man drowns in the Salish Sea
he is escorted into the village of the deep.
There, he is transformed into the great killer whale.
Every whale is an ancestor.
These are the Qwe 'lhol mechen—the people under the sea.[1]

# Chapter 1

All the easy things had been done.

It was the hard things that were needed to save them.

The whales were gone. No one had seen them in more than a year, not even a distant flicker of a shadowed fin. Only three individuals remained in the once-great family where hundreds foraged and roamed.

Voluntary speed limits and fewer plastic straws were progress, but they didn't bring back the salmon—or silence the noise pollution. The ancient giants who lumbered beneath these waves since the islands were nothing but kelp and sand had vanished from the only waters they'd ever called home.

A deep sadness lingered now.

The sea was dying.

And Raymond believed that what happens to the sea, will happen to all of us. He also believed that what was left of his life, could be an offering, a last chance at redemption for what he'd done.

Ray sat under the moonlight every night for a year, waiting for the angels to come and take him home. But Ray's angels wouldn't fly down on light feathers and wings—his would rise from the deep.

If he was lucky, they'd accept his life as one final apology.

If he was lucky, they'd come tonight.

By day, the Salish Sea stretched out in calm ribbons, winding through islets, rocky crags, and reefs. From the jagged cliffs of the San Juan Islands to the mist-veiled shores of Vancouver, its waters wove through a maze of fjords and estuaries. Four hundred miles of craggy shoreline, hidden coves and sandy beaches. Most uninhabited, a few accessible by ferry.

At night, the islands rose up, casting long shadows that kept watch over the deep channels carved by glaciers long ago. Here, the sins of the past still clung to the beaches. Once-lively bays where orcas hunted and the Chinook ran thick were now suffocated by silence. From Portland to Victoria, the estuaries sat empty.

The sea was silent—once a sanctuary, now a graveyard.

Six decades passed, yet the chaos of the capture era still lingered. Gone were the helicopters and seal bombs of the seventies. And gone were the cargo ships and the paparazzi flash of whale watchers that came in all the decades after. Scars remained, etched into the bones of the sea. The oldest family faced extinction, their absence haunting the silent shores.

Ray traced the rope with his fingers, testing the knot before pulling it tight around his waist. His hands, rough from years of salt and sun, trembled as he unbuckled his boots, rolled up his pants to above his knees, and lowered himself onto the platform. Ray dangled his legs in the dark water, the cold bite of the Pacific was a shock, but it slowly numbed the arthritis in his knees.

A small mercy. One last gift from the sea.

The mooring line floated in a thick coil between his legs, and the anchor sat heavy in his lap—it's long silver shank and flukes jutting up. The old fishing boat rocked slightly—waiting, like everything else, for what came next.

The sea was calm—deceptively so. Moonlight bathed its surface, stretching a silver path to the edge of the horizon where the ocean fell into the sky.

A perfect line of shimmering light, inviting him home.

If the legend was true, the people under the sea would forgive him if he gave all of himself. And if ending his lonely life could bring back one of theirs, it was worth the cost.

Just one female could save their bloodline.

He'd done everything he could to bring them back, heal their home, and ask for their forgiveness. Ray understood the orcas and their world better than he understood his own. He was their greatest admirer—a citizen scientist, devoted to their survival. As much a part of their world as any human could be, he understood their clicks and calls, and their haunting cries.

He could recognize every scar, saddle patch, and notch on their majestic fins. And he dreamed of their epic return. But now, there were too few left, and no food for them to eat. And now he too, had nothing left to lose.

Ray's breath was slow and measured as he lifted the cold metal, the rope trailing from his waist, and held it over the water. His shoulders trembled as he stared down, hoping his angels would come and take him home.

But even if they didn't, he knew that tonight—his time was up.

Ray felt the pull of the water, the soft sway beneath him. He let himself believe that the ocean might accept him. Ray pulled air deep into his lungs, taking one final breath, when he felt a shift in the water—a swell rolling in from somewhere deep.

His eyes snapped open.

A ripple.

Small, almost imperceptible.

A subtle change that wouldn't have been noticed by an untrained eye. But Ray was a man of the sea. He understood the language of water, how it moved, and where to look for the behemoths living beneath. He'd spent a lifetime reading their signs, taken thousands of photographs, spent countless hours drifting on the sea—watching, cataloging, mapping their routes.

The locals had laughed at his efforts at first, ridiculing the recluse who lived at the edge of the islands. No one could save the orcas simply by taking their picture and tracking where they swam.

Now it seemed, they were right.

His efforts weren't enough.

No one could save them from the men with money controlling the industries that were more powerful than the will of the people.

Not even Shephard—the little boy from the other side of the island, who held the key to their survival and loved the whales as much as Ray—could act in time to save them.

What had been stolen from those whales in the summer of 1970 could never be returned. Some wrongs can never be made right. Never be forgiven.

Ray had given them everything he had.

Silence was the price.

Until now. Until tonight.

A soft breath broke the surface.

Kawoof...

Ray froze, eyes wide, heart hammering in his chest. The mist from the whale's breath hung in the moonlight like a halo, shimmering against the still water.

Then, slowly, a dark shape rose from the depths, and Ray found himself staring into the eye of a giant. Her fin cut through the light as she hovered beneath the surface, watching him.

Ray let out the breath he'd been holding.

He whispered her name into the mist. "Ocean Sun."

He hadn't seen her in so long, now here she was—staring back at him with eyes as old as the sea itself. Eyes that had seen the same horrors he'd seen. Eyes that had witnessed what he'd done—to her, to her daughter, to her family.

"Thank you. For coming to escort an old man home."

The whale seemed to blink. Her black eye glossy in the moonlight as she stared at the harmless man.

Ray felt his chest loosen. His soul untangle.

This was his redemption.

"For what we took from you, I owe you what's left of my life."

She blew out another breath.

Kawoof…

Then slowly slipped beneath the surface, her shadow disappearing into the deep.

# Chapter 2

Kassidy Karlson pulled down her sunglasses, squinting as she stared out from the passenger side of the black SUV with dark tinted windows. A crowd was gathered outside the gates of the closed amusement park.

"Why are there people here? They look angry." She snapped her head toward Billy, who kept his eyes fixed on the road. "I thought they were closed. Billy? Answer me. Why are there people here?" Her voice was sharp, demanding.

Billy didn't flinch. He never did. That was the thing about him—he had been handling her life for years, smoothing over problems before she even knew they existed. If anyone could fix this, it was him.

"The park is closed. I don't know who those people are—maybe disgruntled interns or something. I'm sure it's nothing. Relax, everything has been taken care of. No one knows you're here," Billy said, barely glancing at her as he pulled into the empty parking lot.

Billy took out his phone and pressed it to his ear. "We're here. Mmm hmm. Okay, got it." He turned to Kassidy with a casual shrug. "They're protesters."

"Protesters?" Irritation flared in her eyes. "What exactly are they protesting, Billy?" she asked through gritted teeth.

Billy barely glanced at the crowd. "I don't know. People protest over every little thing these days." His tone was light—too light—as he shifted the car into park. "We'll be fine. They'll open the gates when we get close."

Kassidy frowned. Something in his voice—casual, dismissive—felt off. She turned back to the chanting crowd, her gut twisting. This wasn't some random protest. It felt... personal.

Billy leaned over, placing his hand firmly on her knee. "Kass, I always have your back, don't I?" His voice softened, coaxing. "You worry too much. Just have fun today. You deserve this. *We* deserve this. It's what we've been dreaming of."

Billy was right. They'd been dreaming of landing a mega sponsor like Capri Son for years. There were A list celebs having their agents call in trying to land it and Billy had gotten it for them.

Her stomach still churned as the chants grew louder. "You know how much I hate confrontation. Can we sneak in the back?"

"They're sending someone out to get us." Billy's voice was smooth, reassuring, but his grip on the steering wheel tightened as if betraying the calmness he was trying to project.

Kassidy's eyes darted to the protesters.

They were holding signs, their voices rising in angry unison.

"There he is." Billy stepped out of the SUV and grabbed a duffel bag from the back. He moved with a forced confidence. Then opened Kassidy's door and interlocked his arm in hers.

"Maybe we shouldn't—"

"Don't even finish that sentence. Do not let those drama-demons get to you. This is not going to get you canceled. All you have to do is swim around in a giant tank and look beautiful like you always do. And get paid a bazillion dollars to do it. Everyone's going to love you. Trust me. This is going to be easy breezy."

She hated controversy.

Walking into a protest was the last thing she wanted to be doing.

People like her got canceled every day for supporting the wrong business, liking the wrong tweet from 2012, or wearing the wrong shade of green on Earth Day.

All it took was one off-the-cuff joke. Or a five-year-old Halloween costume someone decided was problematic in hindsight. That was enough to spark a social wildfire—one that would engulf her career in the cancel-happy culture she never thought would come for her.

Just last month, megastar June Poppi got canceled for posting a selfie with a plastic straw. How was anyone supposed to stay on the right side of every cause, every trend, every hashtag?

It was exhausting.

But the money Capri Son paid her for this gig… No one would turn this down. And she needed that money.

It was already spent.

Kassidy clutched her oversized Vata weekender, given to her by Marlys Vatafurstenburg herself, and bravely strode forward.

"Your ticket keeps her in jail!"

"Free. The. Swift!"

"Bring. Keelah. home!"

The chants from the protesters stuck to her like wet leaves as she approached the entrance. Kassidy tried to shake off the unease crawling up her spine, but something about the whole scene felt off.

These protesters didn't look like RippleHub drama-demons who didn't really care what they were fighting against, they just thrived on the fight.

These people were...passionate and determined.

"What are they chanting about?" Kassidy asked as Billy escorted them closer toward the gate. A man waited for them on the other side.

"It doesn't matter. It has nothing to do with you," Billy said, his hand gently but firmly guiding her through the crowd, his arm wrapped around her like a lifeline.

"What's the Swift? Who's Keelah? That name sounds familiar."

Billy ushered her forward. "You overthink everything, Kass. Let's just get inside."

The crowd stared at them with accusing eyes. A hundred silent judgments in their glares. Kassidy could feel them searing into her skin.

She heard a woman whisper, "Is that Kassidy Karlson?"

Kassidy cringed. Recognition was the last thing she wanted in the middle of a protest she knew nothing about. Her throat tightened. She couldn't afford to make a mistake.

A tall woman with two long, dark braids and fierce eyes stepped forward blocking their path. Her voice sliced through the chants.

"Qilalugaq belongs in the Salish Sea," the woman said. The words landed like a verdict, like a prophecy. Her gaze fixed on Kassidy— sharp as shattered glass.

"The sea does not forget," she intoned, voice a rasp of wind over water. "A debt will be paid—in blood or in sacrifice. You decide."

Kassidy flinched. The words struck like a lash.

"Kee-la-loo-gak?" Kassidy repeated, stumbling over the syllables, chasing meaning in a language she didn't recognize. The name sat heavy on her tongue—foreign, ancient, like it had crossed oceans of time to reach her.

"I—I don't know what you're talking about."

The woman didn't blink. Didn't move.

She lifted her chin, her voice a rasp dragged from the deep. "Not what," she said. "Who."

Kassidy's feet kept moving, but her head twisted back toward the woman—like her body hadn't caught up to the knowing that had already begun.

They made it through the gates, the grounds manager locking them in and the protesters out. Kassidy's heart calmed as the barrier grew between them and the angry mob.

The manager barely glanced toward the crowd, as if they were nothing more than a daily nuisance. "Jonah's waiting at the new exhibit. Follow the signs," he said, pointing. "You can't miss it."

Without another word, he turned back toward the entrance, his attention already elsewhere.

Ahead of them, the empty amusement park loomed like a ghost town. The rides sat motionless; concession stands shuttered. The silence was eerie, yet somehow louder than the noise of the past.

"Is it just me, or does this place give you the creeps?" Kassidy muttered, her arm linked with Billy's. "It feels like we're walking through the set of a horror movie."

"It's not just you." Billy let out a low chuckle, running his palm down his tailored suit. "But it's just because usually there's a million screaming brats. Come on, this way."

A sudden gust of wind whispered through the empty rides, making the rusted metal on the Ferris wheel creak. Their footsteps echoed against the concrete as they passed lifeless attractions and darkened gift shops with rows of stuffed animals.

Thousands of eyes stared at them from behind the glass, unblinking, locked in their cages. Watching. Waiting for the screaming children—and their parents—to come back.

Kassidy's nerves buzzed like static.

"What if I lose people over this? If those people are protesting, I'm sure others are too," she said, her grip tightening on her tote bag.

"Your followers worship you. You could sell them vomit-flavored jellybeans, and they'd eat them up and be like 'Kassidy Karlson rules our lives. I don't eat, sleep, or wear anything she hasn't recommended.'"

"Exactly. This is so off-brand for me."

"Your brand is evolving, Kass. This is the next step," Billy said, brushing off her concerns.

Kassidy lowered her voice, more determined to get through to him. "After this, I'm done taking whatever comes along. I want my brand to stand for something more meaningful than boob tape and make up sponges."

Billy snorted. "Kass, after this paycheck, you can promote hemorrhoid cream for all I care and both of us will still retire gorgeous and rich. Just get through this gig and you'll have carte blanche. The world will be your clamshell."

Frustration tightened Kassidy's chest. She felt trapped in the world she and Billy had created. "It's oyster, not clamshell. And no more sponsors who see me as just an object to sell their products."

Billy laughed. "Honey, I hate to break it to you. But that's what you are. You get paid a bazillion dollars to smile and sell lip liner. You know I love you, but you really shouldn't be complaining about this."

Kassidy turned away, jaw tight. "I know," she drug out the word, "I just don't want to look back and see that all I did was push women to buy makeup and shapewear, or tighten their thighs and skin or get their lips filled."

Billy stopped, eyes sharper now. He stood in front of her, gripping Kassidy by the shoulders. "Listen to what you're saying. You want to make an impact—but avoid all controversy. You don't want to promote fluffy products—but you also don't want to lose the platform you built on those fluffy products." He shrugged his shoulders. "Got it. Now that I know what color unicorn we're looking for, it should be easy to find."

Kassidy glared at him.

The truth stung.

Yes, she'd built an empire—but somewhere along the way, she'd become trapped within its walls, locked behind the gate, staring through the bars at a world she could no longer reach.

She'd kept her opinions buried to protect her business. But this would be the last gig where she played the beautiful face with nothing behind it. No more superficial endorsements. No more selling products that made her feel like a puppet. No more pretending her world revolved around how she looked and what she wore. No more pretending, no more being a pawn in someone else's game. After this, she'd only take work that mattered, that reflected who she really was.

As soon as she figured that part out.

Billy's tone changed, he knew her, and saw she was struggling inside. "Kass, whether you know it or not, what you're about to do is going to make a huge impact. Every girl already wants to be you. Now they're going to want to do this. You're selling the dream," Billy said, leading her down the path toward the exhibit.

His hand stayed firm on her back, guiding her forward, but Kassidy's feet felt heavier with every step. "And what's with all the negativity today?" He lowered his voice to a playful whisper. "After this gig, we'll go on the hunt and find you a man to spend the rest of the month with, okay?"

"There are no men. I've looked. They're all trophy-wife seeking tools."

They stopped in front of a sign, arrows pointing in every direction—Cheetah Encounter, Primate Planet, Dragon Island, Oceans Alive...Mermaid Metamorphosis.

"This way," Billy said, escorting her.

The park stretched out before them, unnaturally quiet, surrounded by cornfields and dead soil. Like so many amusement parks, Capri Son was forced to re-invent itself when the federal ban on keeping captive Orcas came down.

The park stayed closed while building new attractions, before emerging into the public eye with a fresh mission—one that offered a fully immersive experience, far beyond sitting on rides. It was an attraction unlike anything else in the world. At least that's what Billy said it was and why he booked it for her.

Kass didn't know all the details, only that Capri Son had something no other park did. Something that would draw people not just from across the nation, but from every continent on the globe and all she had to do was swim around in a mermaid costume.

This was the biggest gig of her career, but her mind drifted back to the woman's words.

*"Return her or everyone who has kept her hostage will be cursed."* The words stuck, looping over and over, intertwining with her growing discomfort.

Qilalugaq?

Must be a sea lion or walrus.

Since the ban on keeping orcas, a movement had risen to keep those animals out of anything deemed an amusement park.

Kassidy couldn't shake the feeling that something deeper was happening. Her steps slowed, the air around her suddenly thick. Every empty ride, every angry face outside the gates… She hated that she didn't know exactly what she was walking into.

But she trusted Billy.

He'd never done wrong by her before.

At least, not yet.

# Chapter 3

Capri Son's new exhibit was poised to be the most breathtaking architectural wonder on Earth, slated to open in a few months. Conceived by NASA's top engineers—pioneers in crafting worlds within worlds—it defied imagination, achieving what once seemed impossible.

Kassidy and Billy stood outside the entrance, her breath catching at the sight. She'd been around luxury and extravagance, but this was otherworldly. And Capri Son was banking on Kassidy, one of the most prolific influencers on the planet, to lure spectators from across the globe. Her face on their campaign would sell millions of tickets.

Kass and Billy stared at the opulent stone statue that marked the entrance. Towering thirty feet into the air, the ethereal woman's black hair flowed in every direction over the wave-splashed rock she was perched on. Her tail was adorned with thousands of shimmering scales in shades of blue and green. The sign above her head, written in opulent flowing letters, read: Mermaid Metamorphosis.

Beyond that, an enormous, shimmering dome rose like a dreamscape, spanning countless city blocks. Its iridescent surface glistened under the light, revealing a mesmerizing world within—an aquatic paradise teeming with vibrant marine life that swirled and danced in an endless ballet of color.

"Oh my God, they even modeled the statue after you," Billy said, mouth agape as he stared up at the monstrosity.

"Okay Billy." Kassidy cocked her head to the side marveling at the sight, a reluctant grin breaking across her face. "Maybe you were right. Maybe this is…"

She stopped, locking eyes with her childhood friend turned business confidant. They stared at each other, then their faces lit up like sparklers. As if on cue, they clasped hands and exploded into a flurry of spins and jumps, their laughter ringing out like bells.

"The most incredible thing ever!" Billy shrieked.

Kassidy's long black waves flew wildly as she bounced, while Billy—all sharp edges and perfection—barely moved, not a hair out of place. But his uncontainable grin said it all, even as he jumped alongside her, boots thudding, every motion was precise.

"Did I call it or what?" he crowed between jumps. "I told you this was off the hook!"

Their feet thumped against the ground like kids who'd just found out that school had been canceled forever.

Kass clung to Billy's arm as daylight faded into a velvety black, their steps muffled as they walked down a long, sloping hallway that led into the unknown.

At the end, was a luminescent glow—a giant porthole that held back the water world on the other side. Kassidy pressed her palms and face against it, peering into the aqua wonderland teeming with life.

She couldn't help but feel a strange mix of wonder and trepidation. She could swim just fine—splash around, play the part of a mermaid without a second thought. That wasn't the issue. But this? This wasn't some enclosed, controlled tank where she could kick off the bottom or grab onto the sides if she needed to.

This was vast, open, endless.

The water stretched beyond what she could see, dark and shifting. It felt too deep, too real—too terrifying.

"This is nothing like that mermaid tank in Dubai," Billy said, eyes wide with wonder. "That was a fishbowl. *This* is epic."

She felt the excitement of it—the once-in-a-lifetime rush—tangled with the real possibility of danger. A rare opportunity. One that had landed in her lap instead of going to the dozens of celebrity faces vying for the job.

It was exhilarating. And terrifying.

A bend in the long, dark hallway opened into a gigantic dome of glass, a terrarium under the ocean floor. It felt as though it held back the whole ocean itself—keeping the air-breathing world safe and separate from the saltwater ecosystem.

The floor beneath them was gritty, like sand, an exact replica of the ocean floor itself. Even the air had a hazy blue hue, blurring the line between where the air-breathing world stopped, and the water world began.

Kassidy stood frozen, mouth open, clutching onto Billy's arm as a Jurassic-sized manta ray, wings stretched wide, glided over their heads, casting a rolling shadow. Kassidy craned her neck upward, watching as it disappeared into the deep blue.

"Everyone on the planet is going to want to see this," Billy said, eyes tracking the schools of neon fish. "And your face is going to be on every billboard in the world promoting it."

Kassidy's smile widened. "It's magical," she whispered, as she watched the nurse sharks that slumbered and the sea turtles that tumbled. A bait ball of silverfish hovered in the turquoise stillness; there wasn't a single space untouched by mystery. It was a sensory masterpiece.

Then, something big caught her eye.

A flicker of movement far off, a blur in the distance. She stepped closer to the dome, cupping her hands around her eyes. The water stretched outward like the edge of the universe, endless, indifferent and towering over her, shrinking her to a speck.

Kass pointed, finger touching the glass. "What is that?" she said, just before a voice from behind pulled her attention away.

"You must be the mermaid."

Kassidy turned to find a woman in a sleek Versace business suit, sharp gaze fixed on her, inspecting her with careful precision, head to toe. A small, knowing smile played at the corners of the woman's lips.

"Yes, this is her. Kassidy Karlson," Billy said, stepping forward, announcing her like she was royalty.

The woman didn't so much as glance at him. Her appraising gaze remained locked on Kassidy, taking in every detail with an intensity that made every hair on her neck stand at attention. This woman was cool, calculating in her evaluation.

"Well… I think our marketing team was right. You'll do nicely for this," the woman said, reaching out her hand. "I'm Jonah Thorne, CEO of Capri Son Industries." Jonah looked up as a giant eagle ray glided over their heads. "It's like stepping into another world, isn't it? A world where we don't belong, but here, in this exhibit, for a little while, we get to pretend."

Kassidy's throat tightened. Something felt off. She chalked it up to that primal instinct—the one that knew humans didn't belong underwater, that this world wasn't hers to step into no matter what. But unease wouldn't change anything now. She was in too deep; locked into this contract more than any before. At least, that's what Billy had said. And she was committed to this, in more ways than she cared to admit.

So Kassidy did what her grandma taught her to do—smile and be polite. Complain later in private.

"It's incredible. And it's nice to meet you. I'm very excited for this opportunity."

"We're very excited to have you. Follow me," Jonah said, waving them forward. "Today you'll be in the big tank, the Orcaverse, I like to call it."

*Orcaverse?*

Billy plastered on a grin big enough for both of them, mouthing, *the big tank*, before nudging Kassidy ahead.

Jonah, leading the way, strode confidently through a series of dimly lit employee-only hallways that formed a complicated maze. Jonah stopped in front of two oversized metal doors and turned to Kassidy.

"When little girls see you swimming in here, they're going to beg their parents to bring them so they can feel the magic of this place. It's going to bring back an entire industry," Jonah said, voice light and almost wistful. "The white shark arrived just in time for the shoot today."

"Wait...*WHAT?!* As in, Great White Shark?" Kassidy blurted, the words spilling out before she could stop herself.

Jonah turned slowly to face Billy with an annoyed, tight-lipped grin. "That's right. It seems your agent hasn't fully briefed you," she said, her tone calm, yet with an edge of dismay. "It's all in your contract."

Jonah stepped closer to Kassidy, her face catching the dim light, and in it her features twisted into a grotesque illusion. It was a contrast to her soft voice, becoming lovely, even complimentary.

"You're...stunning, Kassidy. When girls and women see you swimming like a mermaid, next to all of the apex creatures in the sea, they'll feel...inspired. They'll feel longing, like they want to become you. And they'll want to come here and experience the wonder you represent. You're doing these creatures a great service.

"Their tickets, their price of admission—that's what keeps these majestic animals alive. Otherwise, they'd be made into soup. Tossed back into the polluted waters they came from.

"All of the creatures here have been saved from death, rescued. This tank was built especially for them, and as you can imagine, it wasn't cheap. If tickets don't sell, there will be no one left to care for them. No one left to fight for the beloved ocean creatures.

"Every marine animal here has no other home, no future in the wild. And I'd hate to think of what would happen to any of them if we hadn't taken them in. Only a place as big as Capri Son can afford to take care of such enormous animals the way they deserve. Here, they have the best care in the world.

Jonah's tone was firm, leaving no room for argument.

"We have an entire team dedicated to each of our assets—specialists who've spent their lives working with marine mammals. Veterinarians run full health assessments constantly—bloodwork, hydration checks, ultrasounds, you name it. If there's even a slight change in their breathing patterns, we catch it.

"Our marine mammal nutritionists calculate their diet down to the calorie, ensuring that each one of our beauties gets exactly what they need. The ocean's a war zone. Pollution, noise, a collapsing food chain. In here? Everything is thriving."

Jonah stepped forward, closing the space between them. Kassidy met her gaze, unease curling in her stomach. Jonah pressed in like a current Kassidy couldn't swim against.

"This is bigger than an endorsement, Kassidy Karlson. You have the power to make people believe in what we're doing here. Something wonderful. Something good. Imagine what that will do for the animals. It'll secure their future. Here, with us. Those fanatics have no idea what we do to protect these animals—if they did, they wouldn't be outside our gate. Now, you're part of the team that saved them too. Imagine what that will do for you? You're already loved. This will make you beloved."

Jonah's features smoothed back into the polished mask of a practiced PR professional. With a joyful, professional smile, she waved them forward.

"Come!" she said brightly. "I want you to meet your safety team. Then I'll walk you to your dressing room. The costume team is waiting for you."

As they stood at the top of the lake-sized tank, Kassidy felt lightheaded, weak in the knees as she looked down into the crystalline water. They must have been ten stories above the ground, and it made Kassidy feel like she was standing on top of the water, looking down into a bottomless ocean.

She forced herself to focus as they stepped onto a system of walkways that divided the man-made marvel into sections. The water beneath them was eerily still, its surface hiding the depths below. Blurry, shadowy shapes glided silently through the blue abyss, their movements ghostlike and hypnotic.

"None of the predators can hurt you," Jonah said, her tone crisp as she turned to Kassidy. "You won't even be in the same tank with them. Per your contract, you'll be perfectly safe."

She gestured toward a man in a sleek wetsuit standing nearby.

"This is Eli. He's leading the safety team who will be in the water with you."

Eli stepped forward, extending his hand. Kassidy shook it automatically, but her focus drifted back to the tank. The water glimmered under the artificial lights, a vast and surreal expanse of shimmering blue—a sprawling, cavernous creation far beyond what she'd imagined and far outside her comfort zone.

Eli began detailing the tank's cutting-edge features and safety protocols. This wasn't just some swimming pool. This was a man-made ocean. Separated into sections by invisible walls so undetectable it was as if they weren't even there.

Eli continued, "The predator sections are completely separate from the others to maintain harmony among the species. Sharks occupy one area, rays another. Keelah has her own space of course. The dolphins too. They can all swim side by side, but the transparent walls keep them apart."

Jonah interjected, her voice softening. "All of their years in a sterile, silent, chlorine pool are over. Here, these marvelous creatures can finally communicate with other marine life. Here, they're all safe."

"You'll be in the main tank," Eli said. "The separation is a state-of-the-art design, nearly undetectable to the eye, but it's there. It's what makes this the safest swimming experience in the world. You'll be next to everything in the ocean, but not in any danger. The illusion is seamless—no one will be able to tell that you're not actually sharing the same water."

She moved on instinct, but unease coiled in her stomach.

What exactly had she agreed to?

Pretending to be a mermaid? Sure. That had been part of the pitch.

But swimming beside a great white?

That was never part of the plan. Or at least, she hadn't known about it. She'd left all the fine print up to Billy. He handled the contracts. The details. The risks. The problems.

She just showed up and did the job.

Maybe she should have read the damn fine print this time.

It took three hours and an entire team of special effects make-up artists, but the metamorphosis was nothing less than spectacular. They'd turned the already stunning Kassidy Karlson into the fantasy that every girl and woman has dreamed of being.

"You look amazing," said the wig master, a boisterous woman in an oversized strawberry red wig of her own. "I follow you on Ripple, by the way. Loved that bit you did about cutting in half your boob tape to use as kinesiology tape for your tendonitis and saving a fortune— who knew, right? You always look beautiful, but when your twenty million followers see you like this, your page is going to blow up! And this place? Total sensation. Eeek!"

She clapped her hands and beamed a wide smile.

Kassidy forced a small, strained smile in return.

The whole team pulled and cinched the tight, faux scale-like material around her body, tugging her this way and that while Kassidy stared at herself in the mirror.

Her grandma would be proud at the sight of her, successful, in control of her future—so far from the small-town girl she'd raised. The Iowa State Corn Princess had transformed into something phantasmagorical.

She could almost hear her grandma's voice, reminding her she was beautiful in more ways than just her pretty face, long before the world noticed.

Beauty had propelled Kassidy to social media stardom, but the figure staring back at her now was a stranger. Long, dark hair cascading past her hips. Painted lips, overfilled just enough to blur the memory of her real smile. Laser-perfect skin. Venus dimples. Countless hours sculpting her waist and thighs into an hourglass at the gym—and even more hours spent under the bright, sterile lights of a med spa. Botox. Filler. Threads. Peels. A face so precisely tuned it didn't flush, didn't move—just sat there, molded on like a mask.

Even without the makeup and the costume, she had built this image, crafted it carefully, but now it belonged to someone else. Even her eyes—once deep, liquid, alive—looked like polished glass, reflecting back a woman she didn't recognize—not anymore.

Her career had taken off so fast, she couldn't even remember choosing this image she'd created.

When she emerged from the changing room, Billy and Jonah were waiting, their eyes lighting up.

"Stunning," Jonah said, circling her like a predator inspecting its prey. "You're going to sell this experience better than anyone else could."

Kassidy's heart thudded against her ribs, loud and relentless. She had made herself into a doll—dressed up, positioned for display—and she had no one to blame but herself.

Billy stepped forward, tugging at a wrinkle in her costume. "You look gorg, doll. You ready?"

"Maybe?" she said, the word came out in a desperate whisper.

Eli gestured toward the tank, his tone reassuring. "We'll help set you in gently."

They moved toward the edge of the water, where a sleek platform extended over the tank. The surface was still, its hypnotic blue hue shimmering under the lights.

The thought of going underwater in this elaborate, weighted costume felt like the lid of a jar sealing shut around her.

She turned to Eli, her voice wavering. "You'll swim beside me, right? Just in case? This…" she looked down over her intricate mermaid tail, "is heavy."

"We'll get some preliminary shots while you're adjusting," Jonah interjected, her clipped tone leaving no room for hesitation.

"We have a whole team of divers and camera crew nearby," Eli added, his smile tight, professional. "But you won't need us—you'll be fine. The water will do all the work."

The cold water lapped at her ankles, and the costume tugged at her body, its weight pulling her down.

All eyes were on her—Billy, Jonah, the divers, the makeup artists— every one of them waiting, expecting her to perform. Her pulse quickened as they lowered her into the water.

It stretched out below her like an endless ocean, vast and deep— but in that moment it didn't feel like the ocean. It felt like a cage—like she was confined in a tank for the entertainment of people.

Kassidy wasn't the only one bound by forces beyond her control. Near the arctic circle, in a place she'd never seen and with a man she'd never met, another kind of cage existed—one built of steel and expectation.

And a thousand nautical miles south, on a lonely boat, an old man cinched the last knot, tethered to choices that had been tightening around him for decades. He also left behind a trail—one he hoped Kassidy would follow, that might bring everything he loved and cared about in the world—together.

Three separate worlds were unfolding—moving like unseen currents, each driven by passion, duty, and fate.

And the tide was rising, ready to pull them together.

# Chapter 4

The air in Alaska wasn't like the air back home. Maybe it was the absence of wind, or maybe it was something deeper beneath the surface—something pulling at the tide. Shephard couldn't explain it, only that nothing felt the same there.

Ray used to say the sea knew things. Shep never understood what that meant. Maybe he'd figure it out here, a thousand miles from home—where the water was quiet in a different way, like it was holding its breath.

Resurrection Bay meandered from the coastal city of Seward to the open waters of the Gulf of Alaska. Flanked by snow-capped mountains for eighteen miles, the fjord was a pristine wilderness, guarded by peaks that lined up shoulder to shoulder, like the Moai of Easter Island. For Shephard, everything about Alaska was a stunning, visual feast.

It was late fall, and the tourist season was over. Only locals or the ultra-wealthy ventured this far north with winter looming, and Shephard was no local.

A lone sea otter floated lazily in the marina, belly up, and using his body like a dinner plate for his crab. The crab's shell was no match for the hungry otter. He smashed it with a rock, and all ten legs went stiff then spread apart in a slow surrender. The tiny traveler floated and feasted until nothing was left of the crab but fragments of shell.

"You little savage," Shephard Maddox muttered from where he stood at the edge of the pier watching the otter devour his dinner.

Shephard buried his hands deep in his pockets, fighting off the chill in the air, as his breath came out in small, cloud-like puffs. Neither Shephard nor the otter were aware of the danger lurking underneath.

The otter sensed it first.

It rolled and dove under, but surfaced a moment later—already limp between the razor-sharp teeth of a killer whale. The attack was so swift, so close to the pier, water splashed over the concrete. Shephard hopped back, momentarily stunned by the proximity and the stealth of the black-and-white predator.

A creature that massive, so adept at blending into its surroundings, was something to be both admired and feared. The way it struck without warning—precise, unstoppable. The orcas moved with a quiet mastery Shephard understood all too well.

"They never used to come in this far," a local fisherman called out from where he was tying up his boat.

The man walked over to Shep, his face weathered and lined from years spent on the water under the sun. He wore thick gloves and a coat warm enough to withstand the creeping cold.

Together, the two men watched until the pair of orcas disappeared into the calm fjord.

"Used to be they only ate the seals and sea lions," the fisherman said. "But there's less and less of them around so those whales are hunting smaller prey now, even the otters. Hope they don't wipe out the otters or the whole damn gulf will die."

Shep furrowed. "Yeah? How's that?"

"It already happened. In California. The otters were hunted for their pelts," the man said. "Once they were decimated, the purple urchins took over. Ate everything on the ocean floor. Destroyed whole kelp forests. The otters were the only thing that ate the urchins.

"You wouldn't think it, but those otters are the keystone. Without them taking out the worst troublemakers, the whole ocean will die. And without the ocean—well, let's pray it never comes to that."

Shephard raised an eyebrow. He wasn't the praying kind. He was the doing kind.

"Who knew the otters could save the world," Shep offered, an easy charm in his voice. "Guess we all have our role to play."

Shephard was something of an otter himself—a man who exuded warmth and optimism, but who was also a keystone for an entirely different ecosystem.

Back home in Washington State, most people saw him as a charmer with a handsome face, too good-looking to be taken seriously.

But to the few people who knew the real man behind the polished charm, they knew what he stood for—a man who embodied resilience and purpose—a beacon of hope in what many feared was a dark and uncertain future.

Shephard was born from the DNA that built the industrialized Northwest—a man capable of creating worlds, or tearing them down.

"First time in Alaska?" The fisherman's voice broke through the silence.

"Am I that obvious?" Shephard asked with a self-deprecating smile, glancing at his expensive, barely broken-in adventure gear.

"You one of those big-game trophy hunters," the man asked. "Here to tag a grizzly?"

Shephard shook his head, amused. "No, nothing like that. Just enjoying the scenery."

"These mountains have a way of showing you how small you are now, don't they?" His gaze drifted toward the looming peak of Mount Marathon. "The wild here doesn't discriminate. Stick around long enough, and this whole place will remind you that we're not the apex predator. Not here anyway."

Shephard turned to the glossy row of yachts docked nearby, each one gleaming in the fading light. The boats displayed their names proudly on their sterns.

"That one yours?" the fisherman asked, nodding toward the largest, most obvious boat in the marina.

Shephard chuckled. "Nope. It's my grandfather's."

The fisherman whistled a long flat note, his gaze sweeping over the yacht that was too large to fit into a single slip.

"Looks more like a cruise ship than a boat."

Shephard's eyes settled on the name scrolled in gothic letters across the stern: *The Reckoning.*

The yacht was excessive in every way, an obnoxious display of wealth and power. It was exactly what Gunter Amon would own. Predictable in business, yet the most tempestuous man alive. Now elderly but no less dangerous, Gunter's power had grown sharper with age.

"Shephard!" Gunter hollered. His grandfather's booming voice stilled the air.

Shephard excused himself from the fisherman, making his way toward the yacht. When Gunter called, Shephard answered—some alliances are better managed up close.

Gunter sat in the opulent parlor, cigar in hand, surrounded by his navy buddies and their stumbling laughter. Shephard stepped inside and was immediately enveloped in the warm, suffocating air of smoke, and wealth and excess.

The room was decorated with modern yet classic touches. Plush chairs, polished wooden tables, and walls adorned with expensive art that only Shephard bothered to notice.

Gunter sat with a cigar firmly between his teeth, the smoke curling around him like a poisonous halo. His two retired pals lounged nearby, sipping drinks and laughing as a portly crew member scurried about, delivering their bourbons and expensive salted meats.

"Do you know why I brought you here, Shephard ?" Gunter spoke in a grand booming voice.

"Because I'm the only one in the family who can stand to travel with you?" Shephard retorted, settling unruffled into a seat.

Gunter's companions remained silent; their loyalties clear. The tension remained thick, every breath hanging on Gunter's reaction.

But he didn't react to the jab. His ego was too thick to be punctured by a lightweight insult from his grandson.

"No, boy! We're here because it's your birthday, and I want to give you a gift."

Shephard chuckled, leaning back in his chair. He knew how to play this game. "Now how many times do I have to tell you, I don't need any more hookers and blow, Grandfather."

The room went dead silent before Gunter burst into a fit of roaring laughter, deep and guttural, the kind of sound that shook the walls.

His navy buddies followed suit, their aged faces cracking into smiles as they slapped their knees and nodded in agreement.

"Damn it, boy, now that's why I like you! Not afraid to say it like it is. I respect that. Got a good sense of humor. Sharp, too." Gunter pointed at Shephard with two fingers, a fat cigar pinched between them.

Shephard sighed, half-amused and half-annoyed. "Thank you for the offer, though, but like I said on my twenty-first, and then again on my twenty-fifth, and now on my thirtieth, I prefer to work for my women." Shephard politely accepted a drink from the steward then turned back to Gunter. "They taste sweeter that way."

Gunter grunted his approval, nodding. He leaned forward, his expression turning serious. "Indeed, Shephard, indeed. You know when to hold your tongue, when to speak the truth, and you have the guts to disagree with me."

The old man's friends nodded along, their approval automatic, as if their entire existence revolved around agreeing with Gunter.

Shephard, ever the chameleon, slipped into the role he knew they expected—a little *too* easygoing, a little too agreeable. An otter, yes, one with the ability to navigate any type of water.

Blending in with the good ol' boys' club, playing along, didn't diminish him—it was calculated.

"I like the way you think, son. I like your discipline. So that's why the time has come for you to take over DeVille Power."

The room went still.

Gunter's two companions didn't speak, didn't need to. They simply nodded, silent witnesses to the moment.

Shephard's smile didn't falter.

He sat there like he'd been made for this.

"You're the only one I trust to do it," Gunter continued.

His men didn't so much as blink, waiting for Shephard's response. Their presence a quiet reminder that Gunter's word was law.

"That, and this yacht—" Gunter gestured around them, a satisfied gleam in his eye, "is your birthday present."

Shephard stared at his grandfather with stalwart eyes, not surprised but still processing the responsibility that had just been handed to him.

Had he expected it? Yes.

Had he been working for it for fifteen years? Absolutely.

But still, it landed heavy.

Every decision he made from then on carried the burden of his ambition. One misstep could unravel everything he'd built, and the stakes had never been higher.

"I can't accept this yacht as a birthday gift. It's too much. You've given me enough already." Shephard said, though they both knew it was a formality, and that he didn't have much choice.

"Then consider it your sign-on bonus. You've earned it," Gunter barked.

Shephard placed his hand on Gunter's knee, squeezing lightly, amused by the old man's attempts to buy his loyalty. Also, he enjoyed pushing his grandfather's buttons, even if just for sport.

"Goddamm it, Shephard, get your hand off my knee, you pervert." Gunter snapped, swatting his hand away. "I didn't raise you to be a queer."

Shephard smirked. "You didn't raise me, Grandfather. My mother did. Your daughter, remember?"

Gunter dismissed the jab with a flick of his hand, his expression already shifting to something colder, sharper. The subject was a dead end, a locked door Shephard rarely dared to open. Talk of family—of Shephard's parents, siblings, and niece—wasn't forbidden, but it was met with a disdain everyone could taste.

Shephard was the last thread connecting Gunter to their fractured bloodline—everyone else in the family had disowned the man over a decade ago. But Shephard understood his role and recognized that staying in Gunter's orbit offered the potential to save a family that needed saving even more than his own.

Shephard leaned back, letting the silence stretch just long enough to remind Gunter that some wounds never fully close.

Then, with a practiced calm, he changed gears. "So, what's the next move? Me, into your office?"

It sounded crass, but that kind of egoism was what Gunter respected.

"Exactly. You'll start in two months. The lawyers are working on the paperwork as we speak. And you'll run it like I have, no bending to the green regulations and eco-tax bullshit. You hear me, Shep?"

Shephard leaned back, nodding, though inside, his mind was already moving the pieces around the chess board.

This was what he'd been waiting for, though he had no intention of running the company like Gunter did. He'd been planning his own path for years, strategizing, plotting the long game.

"I've seen how you handle yourself with those activists and tree-loving politicians. You've got the guts to stand your ground, and that's why you're the perfect one to take the helm." Gunter's voice lowered slightly, almost paternal, but the sharpness of his words still hung in the air like a threat. "I'll stay on as your right hand of course, your...*advisor* for a few years...while you transition."

And there it was...the catch.

Shephard had expected it—had even planned for it—but hearing the words aloud still set his nerves on edge. He knew this moment would come, but until Gunter was out for good, his hands were tied, and the clock was ticking, there was no more time left.

Shep wasn't sure if Gunter would ever fully relinquish control, not while he was alive anyway, not even to his own grandson. The man's need for power was insatiable, even in his old age.

Just then, the young captain entered the parlor, dressed in crisp whites, his posture straight as a rod. "Mr. Amon, if you're ready, sir, I suggest we head out. Halibut fishing has been great this year. We're at the tail end of the season so might I recommend—"

Gunter cut him off with a wave of his hand. "I don't want any goddamn whitefish."

The room fell silent—again, the way it did every time Gunter raised his voice or his hand, even a little. The captain, who had likely dealt with his fair share of high-strung clients, even looked taken aback by the outburst.

"If you want to try for salmon, Sir, we're allowed one Chinook," the captain offered, trying to smooth things over.

Gunter's eyes narrowed. "One King fish? Can you believe that? One?" He spat. "There used to be millions of them in these waters. Big ones too, fifty, sixty pounds. Now all you get is one puny thing not even enough for a meal."

"I'm afraid the salmon fisheries are in decline here," the captain said, "like they are in Washington. And we'll need a permit."

Gunter snorted. "I don't want no goddamn pink fish either! And I sure as hell don't need a permit to fish in these waters. Let the DNR come aboard and try to stop me."

The captain hesitated, clearly uncomfortable, then nodded, and walked away.

Shephard watched his grandfather with a cool, detached expression. Gunter's defiance of authority was nothing new, but it still grated on Shep's nerves. The old man was a relic of a world where his name, money, and bravado could bend reality to his will.

Gunter still believed that, too—believed he could dodge accountability, buy his way out of anything—even buy immunity. Maybe he still could, for now. But cracks were forming, the winds were shifting. The old-world Gunter clung to was collapsing, and when it did, not even his money could hold it together.

The captain expertly maneuvered the yacht through the marina, its engines humming as they glided through the still waters of Resurrection Bay and past the Spring Creek Correctional Center. A maximum-security prison surrounded by national parks. Aside from the crew, Shephard wondered if Gunter or anyone else on the boat even knew what the lit-up compound was.

The fjord stretched out before them all the way to the gulf, framed by towering mountains capped in snow, their jagged tops cutting into the gray sky. The water was a perfect mirror, reflecting the picture so clearly it was difficult to tell where the sea ended, and the sky began.

When they reached the open waters, everyone gathered on the starboard deck, bourbon in hand. Shephard followed them outside, leaning against the railing as the cool Alaskan wind whipped through his hair. The sea stretched out in every direction, an endless expanse of cold blue.

"Well, well, look who showed up," Gunter said, pointing toward the water. "The only color fish I have any interest in hunting. There's your culprit, right there, Shep!"

Shephard squinted into the distance, following his grandfather's gaze. Three towering dorsal fins sliced through the water, the unmistakable black-and-white forms of killer whales breaking the surface.

The sight was awe-inspiring—these creatures, these apex predators, were a rare and majestic presence in these waters. But Gunter's reaction was far from admiration, and Shephard knew to keep his cool about this—*especially* about this.

"Each one of them is a ten-thousand-pound problem," Gunter muttered, his voice full of contempt. "Bastards cost me more money than the goddamn IRS. Greedy and fat, eating and eating until the whole ocean is empty. That's why the salmon are gone! Not because of fishing, but because of them."

He waved his hands and elevated his voice.

His obedient disciples nodded along, mumbling their agreement.

"And those goddamn Greenpeace fanatics would rather see the human race starve to death than deal with the real problem!" Gunter continued, his voice rising with each word, feeding off the support of his devoted audience.

Shephard watched the whales move through the water with effortless grace, their sleek bodies carving through the waves. He admired them in silence, unwilling to voice his thoughts aloud.

Those whales were survivors—adaptable, relentless, and powerful. They had ruled these waters for millions of years, long before humans ever set foot on this earth.

They were meant to be revered and learned from. Gunter's hatred for them was rooted in something Shephard didn't fully understand, something primal, or perhaps even...evil.

The captain walked out on deck. "What a surprise," his voice carried his smile. "It's unusual to see them this time of year." His eyes were wide with awe as he watched the whales glide by.

Shephard felt a chill run down his spine. He couldn't tell the captain to shut up, but he tried willing him to stop speaking.

He glanced at Gunter, who was already walking back into the parlor. Thank God.

A long time ago words might have gotten through, but he was more hardened than ever these days.

"Three too many, if you ask me," one of Gunter's friends said, menace in his voice.

Then, without warning, Gunter reemerged. Shephard didn't hear him. Didn't sense him. Until it was too late. The cold kiss of steel grazed his shoulder, slipping past like a whisper of death. The shotgun.

Gunter's hot musty breath.

The moment closed, crushing, suffocating as Shep realized what was happening.

The captain moved to act.

Then hesitated, frozen, as if some part of him refused to believe Gunter would actually pull the trigger.

The explosion came a heartbeat later.

Deafening.

White-hot in Shephard's ear.

The world splintered into a shatter of sound.

His body recoiled, ears on fire, skull vibrating as if the bones inside his head had become tuning forks for the blast.

The shot ripped through the air, tearing through the stillness, leaving nothing behind but its echo, bouncing off the water and mountains.

Instinct took over and Shep threw his hands over his ears and his body tensed. The pain wasn't just sharp in his head—it was everywhere, flooding his senses, shaking his vision.

# Chapter 5

Gunter had one in the chamber and two in the barrel. When he released the trigger, a casing flew out and landed on the deck, automatically loading the next shell. Three blasts rang out in succession.

The sharp cracking sound of the shots shattered the surface as explosive sound waves rippled through the air. Shephard took a step back, head between his hands, stunned by the sudden explosion that went off inches from his ear. His head rang and a sharp pain pierced the back of his eyes. He could smell the gun smoke and feel the vibrations ringing in his ears and teeth.

Where the bullets pierced the surface of the water, a plume of spray shot up. As it settled, Shephard saw blood spreading across the surface.

Gunter's eyes were filled with a vengeance that seemed to come from somewhere deep, and his head and neck were shaking with rage. As if those whales embodied every frustration, every challenge, every obstacle he'd ever faced in his long agonizing life. He stopped to reload, leaving desperate wails coming from the water in his wake.

"They're a menace!" Gunter howled, fumbling to reload his shotgun. "They've been stealing from me for decades. Taking what belongs to me! To us! It's time they learned their place!" Gunter turned to his grandson, his expression hardening. "The world belongs to those who take what's theirs Shephard! Don't you ever forget it!"

The crew stood frozen, powerless to intervene. This was Gunter Amon—after all, his only loyalty was to mayhem, and no one dared stand in his way.

He had money, power, and entire industries in his pocket. A lifetime of handshake deals, and backroom agreements had built his empire, no matter the cost. Gunter could set a building ablaze with people inside, and his cronies would call it a stroke of bad luck—then collect the insurance payout on his behalf.

Shephard's head was still ringing and gurgling as if his brain turned into liquid from the proximity of the blasts, but he stepped forward and stood next to his grandfather. Shep knew he was the only one who had a chance at stopping the madness.

"What have you done?" the Captain said. "They're protected... there's a fine...jail time...they're endangered."

"I'll pay the goddamn fine." Gunter shook out more shells from his coat pocket, dropping some on the deck while his elderly hands struggled with the gun.

Shephard stepped forward, his gaze locked on his grandfather—a man with whom he shared blood, a man whose DNA was etched into his own, into the core of who he was. He'd spent a lifetime rejecting that truth. There was another man who deserved the title of grandfather more. Shephard swore he'd never walk the same path as Gunter. He'd made promises to himself—silent, unbreakable ones. The kind no one else could know. Not yet.

How could he be so cruel. There was blood in the water. Whales holding up their wounded to the surface so they could breathe. Their cries, their desperate pleas for help was beyond heartbreaking.

Shep had a urge to grab Gunter and toss him over the side of the boat. Gunter lined up to take another shot. The captain continued to protest, fear in his eyes for the whales, perhaps for everyone aboard and himself.

"Sir, I can't allow this. You'll lose your boat. I'll lose my license. Please put the gun down. This makes no sense."

Gunter didn't like the word please—it was a word for the weak, he'd said, a word women used.

The two elderly navy men stood watch behind Gunter, sick smiles pasted on their faces, supporting the massacre.

The whales were terrified, crying out, their tongues and teeth showing, quivering as they called to one another. They didn't swim away from the danger, they stayed together, exposed regardless of the threat.

"Grandfather—" Shephard said, and it hurt to talk, to hear his own voice unbearably loud in his head.

Before the old man could fire another round into the ailing orcas, Shephard set one hand on his grandfather's shoulder and with the other, he placed two fingers on top of the long barrel and carefully put pressure downward.

Gunter allowed it. His grip loosening, as if humoring the idea of standing down. But the wildness in his eyes didn't fade. It sharpened and held a glint of something volatile.

Gunter's gaze swung toward Shephard.

Who didn't flinch. Didn't move.

Shephard's heartbeat raced, but he knew how to adapt. How to stay calm. Stay controlled. Give Gunter an inch—just enough to let him believe he was still the one pulling the strings. When Shep spoke, his voice was smooth, effortless, designed to disarm.

"Grandfather, you're about to get my brand-new yacht confiscated. And I can't have that now, can I?"

His demeanor oozed ease, but his pulse pounded beneath the surface of his chest.

"I haven't even taken her out for a maiden voyage yet."

The words landed. A muscle twitched in Gunter's jaw. The flicker of unpredictability was gone. The battle between power and pride had already been decided.

Gunter always got what he wanted.

"Does that mean you'll take the job and accept my gift?"

His voice was gruff. The question wasn't casual—it was a demand wrapped in the pretense of choice.

And they both knew it. "If it will make you stop shooting that damn gun off in my ear, yes, I'll take the job—and the boat. Now put that fucking thing away before you get us all thrown out of here."

"It's done then!" Gunter shouted, leaning his loaded gun against the railing. His eyes turned from black into the deep brown they were before he slipped into a rage. He slapped Shephard hard on the back, "but mark my words Shephard!" he hollered, "you'll have wished I shot every last one of those damn whales and all those protesters too! So help me God if they step one foot on my property I'll kill them hippy ocean-worshiping cunts."

Gunter turned, and with his pals at his heels like obedient dogs, walked back into the parlor.

The captain exhaled with him, rubbing his chin, his movements stiff and tense. The first mate hadn't moved. He looked frozen, jaw clenched, eyes wide. Then both men turned to Shephard, expectant.

"Gentlemen," Shep said, his voice confident as he squared his shoulders. "This is my boat now."

The captain nodded—a small, cautious movement, as if not wanting Gunter to see, and testing the truth in Shep's words.

Shephard stood with his grandfather's gun at his side. His grip firm, but his control absolute.

"That means you work for me. Not Gunter. There won't be any more trouble. You have my word."

The first mate's shoulders sagged, the breath he'd been holding slipping out in a quiet, almost imperceptible sigh.

Shephard wrapped his hand around the rifle, flipping the safety with a smooth click and stretching it out toward the captain. "Would you mind locking this in your safe until we get to port?"

The captain nodded—didn't hesitate, didn't question, just took the gun, turned, and walked away. The first mate followed, falling into step behind the captain.

Behind them, the small family of orcas drifted, their cries lost to the vast, blood-stained water.

When Shephard was finally alone, he gripped the guardrails, his body folding in on itself. Anger, rage, and pain twisted inside him, a reflection of the violent churning waters ahead—for the yacht, for the whales, and for his life.

Everything was falling into place, yet so much else was still falling apart. He hoped it wasn't too late. He'd fought hard to contain the damage, but some things were beyond his reach, and so much had already been lost. The pace of progress gnawed at him. He couldn't stumble now—not after all he'd sacrificed.

Shephard stood up and walked back into the parlor to join his grandfather in celebratory drinks. Gunter would expect nothing less.

The three friends slouched in the oversized leather chairs in the main parlor. Flushed faces and glassy eyes from the copious amounts of top-shelf booze regarded him with dull curiosity.

Smoke from their cigars curled around their fingers, adding to their hazy inebriation. They'd been swapping stories and reminiscing about the good ol' days when they wore the uniform.

Their laughter was loud and raucous, the camaraderie of their shared past blending with the excesses of the night. For those three men, what had transpired outside was nothing more than another moment in time.

Gunter hollered when he saw Shephard walk in, waving smoke away from his face. "There's the future CEO of Deville Power! And the best goddamn grandson a man could ask for. Get over here Shephard and pour yourself a drink."

"Gunny here tells us you're quite the ruthless businessman. Ladies' man too," Frank said, Gunter's most stalwart pal and a complicit, silent accomplice in every ruthless act, every morally bankrupt choice he'd ever made.

Shephard didn't like him. Didn't like any of them. Especially not when they got together.

"I guess the apple doesn't fall far from the tree," Shephard said, agreeing with Frank and pouring himself a shot of whiskey.

Then Shephard stood behind his grandfather. What he wanted to do was to retire to his suite, out of earshot from the blathering braggadocious men and try to quell the loud ringing still plaguing his every thought. But these men were pivotal, their roles critical in his plan, especially now.

"Looks like you'll be able to come with us to Kodiak this year." Frank nodded toward Gunther. "Now that you've named your successor."

"He sure will." Shephard set his palm on his grandfather's shoulder and gave it slight squeeze. "He was just saying how he still had a space in his trophy room for another grizzly."

The trophy room was a monstrosity inside Gunter's waterfront mansion and held every animal Gunter had ever taken down, including Africa's big five. It was every big game hunter's dream.

"You got a blackfish in that room?" asked Rex—a wiry man with thinning hair slicked back, but no less unsettling as the other two oversized men. Rex's troubling grin seemed to do all the talking. Shephard was extra careful when Frank and Rex were around.

Gunter grumbled. "Too many goddamn regulations."

"Too bad we couldn't have hauled a few back from Iceland," Frank grunted, swirling his glass. "Would've been enough for what—a hundred skeletons?"

"One hundred?" Gunter barked out a laugh, tapping ash from his cigar into the crystal tray. "More like three hundred. We wiped those bastards off the map up there."

"That was in '57, wasn't it?" Frank asked, scratching at his grizzled chin.

"No, '56." Gunter corrected, eyes glazing over with nostalgia. "Hell of a week that was. I can still smell the salt and decay."

Shephard moved to sit in a chair at the far side of the room, away from the smoke. And of everything treacherous and cruel he'd witnessed from his grandfather, this story was the worst.

"We took them down like shooting fish in a barrel. Machine guns, depth charges, rockets even."

Frank finished the story the way you'd reminisce about old times over a drink, sharing fond memories with friends. "The navy had a machine gun mounted, and Gunnie here must have let ten thousand shells spray the water that day. Turned the whole bay into blood."

"An orgy of blood!" Rex spouted.

"Dumbest animals on the planet," Gunter said. "Didn't even swim away. They just flopped around, flailing and waling and lined up like they wanted to get shot. So, I shot em. As many as I could while the other men threw in the bomb. Saved the whole goddamn fishery that year and every year after. Those Icelanders would've starved if we hadn't been called in to take 'em out."

The men laughed and grunted as if telling stories about a fishing trip to catch a few walleyes.

"Yeah, we had an arsenal on that ship," Gunter said, a fondness in his tone. "The U.S. didn't pussy foot around back then. We had balls. We took out the threat. None of these bullshit regulations when a man can't get anything done and it's hard to make a goddamn dollar!"

"Those were the good days," Rex agreed. "The Navy spared no expense back then. Didn't have to tip toe around some fucking marine sanctuary because the blackfish don't like our rudder noise."

Frank blew smoke toward the ceiling. The men smiled.

"You know I heard those whales never came back to whatever they call that place, Whale Bay, wasn't it?"

"More like Bloody Bay. But Hvalfjörður, I believe it was called," Rex said.

"Not that there were any blackfish left after those three days anyway," Gunter laughed. Then they all laughed. "We did a good thing. Saved a lot of businesses and families like ours from going under. Just like what I tried to do here today. And back home too. Fisherman around the world can still fish because of us."

Shephard downed the rest of his whiskey in one gulp, the burn doing nothing to douse the fire roiling in his gut. His hands trembled slightly as he set the glass down on the table, but his face stayed neutral, lips pressing together to hold back the anger rising in his chest. These men...they didn't even flinch. They relived it like it was some glory day, a war story they'd tell at parties. Casual. Blasé. Like they hadn't taken part in a slaughter. No remorse. No regret.

Though he couldn't say it aloud, not yet, Shephard believed that any man capable of slaughtering those animals without a shred of remorse could just as easily turn their blade on a fellow human.

Shephard stood up abruptly, pushing his chair back with more force than necessary. The scrape of wood on marble caught their attention, and Gunter turned to look at him, cigar hanging loosely from his lips.

"You're not done!" Gunter protested. "The night's young, boy. We haven't even opened a good bottle yet."

But Shephard *was* done. He could feel the rage boiling beneath the surface, threatening to spill over.

"I've got a big job waiting for me back home," Shephard said evenly, swallowing the bitterness in his throat. "Surely you can understand that I need to be rested." He ignored their calls to sit back down, to stay and drink and smoke and reminisce about their violent conquests.

"Goodnight, gentlemen."

His voice was strained, taut as a wire, and he didn't look back as he walked out. He felt Gunter's eyes burning into the back of his head, but he kept moving. His pulse thudded in his ears, drowning out the braying laughter behind him. The walls seemed to close in as he stepped into the hallway, the thick stench of cigar smoke still clinging to his hair and skin.

He shoved his hands into his pockets, clenching them into fists until his nails bit into his palms.

Shephard opened the door to his spacious private cabin, the soft click of the lock sealing him away from the world outside. As the lights flickered on, the polished surfaces and luxury felt empty, lonely. This life he chose—staying close to Gunter—came at the unbearable cost of keeping everyone else at arm's length. To protect them, to protect himself, no one could ever truly know Shephard. Not when even the smallest crack in his facade might invite his grandfather's piercing scrutiny.

When his head hit the pillow, it wasn't comfort he found—it was the echo of gunshots still ringing in his ears, reverberating like a curse he couldn't shake.

When Shephard closed his eyes, the cries from the water returned—sharper now. And not just the cries of today, but of decades past.

Like Ray, Shephard too was a man of the sea.

He could feel its past and sense its grief across space and time.

Ghosts from families hunted and stolen haunted his dreams—their voices carried back to him on the tide.

He could hear their language—the people under the sea. He could sense their sorrow woven into every wave, mourning all they'd lost.

Ray was right when he told Shephard, "The ocean never forgets."

# Chapter 6

Kassidy floated effortlessly on the surface of the vast saltwater sea, thirty feet above the simulated ocean floor, feeling both ethereal and surreal. The crew had transformed her entire body into a sparkling work of art—glitter-filled paint and luminescent accents adorned her skin. Her scales glistened in hues of aqua, magenta, and iridescent purple, shimmering like a living prism under the light.

From the waist down, her legs were encased in an exotic, flexible tail covered in glittering scales. The tail wasn't stiff or cumbersome in the water like she'd anticipated. When she moved her legs, the fin responded as if it were featherlight, and wisps of enchanted fabric floated through the water as if they were made of water itself.

"How does it feel?" Jonah hollered to Kassidy, her voice traveling easily across the surface of the water.

The silver and lavender shimmer on Kassidy's cheeks sparkled when she turned toward the crew watching and snapping photos from the network of floating docks.

"It's magical," Kassidy said, sweeping her arms through the water and genuinely feeling the transformation.

"Wonderful," Jonah called back. "That's exactly what we want to come across in your photos. We want every little girl, teenager, and woman in the world to feel magical when they undergo this metamorphosis."

Capri Son had truly mastered the art of creating an immersive experience, allowing participants to become part of an underwater world like no other. There were no rubber tails or air hoses, no flopping around on dry sand. For a significant fee, guests would be transformed into their mermaid alter ego and swim alongside all the marine life.

Guests could even go to the website months before their visit and design their costume themselves. Even the extravagant headdress that concealed the oxygen system could be customized, allowing participants to breathe freely underwater without the restriction of an air hose or tank.

There were options for private parties, birthdays, and weddings. For two hundred and fifty thousand dollars, you could say your vows under-water, with all the marine life as your wedding party watching from behind a reef.

Kassidy ducked her head under the water and allowed the world above to fade into a muffled silence.

Jonah turned to the photographers walking along on the network of floating docks.

"Get shots from every angle," she instructed, voice sharp with authority. "I want options—Mantas, Eagle Rays, the White Shark, the reef sharks—everything. Make it look like a dream. And don't just shoot her—shoot through the water, use reflections, light. Make it feel otherworldly."

Jonah's gaze moved toward the deepest part of the tank. "Then, release Keelah." A slow smile crept across her face. "I want the mermaid and Keelah alone. Capture that first moment—before she even understands what she's seeing. Get the wonder, the disbelief. That's the shot we sell. Women don't want to be just mermaids in a lonely ocean—they want to feel like they are part of the ocean— connected to all its creatures. That's what we're selling here people— the magic of being the ocean's most fabled creature, swimming free with all the sea life around her. And, swimming in harmony the ultimate apex predator—the orca."

The headdress and mask Kassidy wore hugged her body like a second skin, barely there, freeing her in ways she didn't know were possible while under the water.

She felt as though she'd truly transformed into a creature destined for the water, not above it. The sensation was surreal—a blend of fantasy and reality that left her feeling nothing short of awe. For a brief, haunting moment, everything felt magical and right, and she knew this was a role she was born to play. Maybe fate had guided her here—to help bridge the worlds between air and sea.

Kassidy let herself sink further under, committing to the photo shoot and to being open to the whole experience. As her body sunk lower, she felt weightless.

The clear mask over her face and nose was made from the same material as the divider between the tanks that kept the marine species separate. NASA technology, indestructible, yet completely transparent. Underwater, it was almost imperceptible. Music that had been built into the headdress played softly—a calming mix of whale songs and soft oceanic tones. Kassidy felt lithe and flexible, her tail an even longer extension of her already long limbs, guiding her down through the clear blue haze, as though it had always been a part of her.

Kassidy twisted and twirled her mermaid body effortlessly and for a rare moment, she forgot the cameras were there at all. She imagined it was just her, and she was swimming free, next to the ocean's most majestic creatures. She swam above the loggerhead turtles munching sea grass. Stretched her arms out like the rays that created shadows around her and undulated her hips and knees faster as she dispersed the silver bait ball of fish. She frolicked and played and discovered and it truly was the most otherworldly experience she'd ever had.

But everyone had it wrong. It wasn't just girls and women who would want to do this. It was every man, woman, and child on the planet who had ever dreamed of breathing under water.

A blacktip reef shark glided toward her, its sleek body slicing through the water with laser precision. A surge of unease gripped her—she was nothing more than an intruder in its world, even with a barrier between them. Maybe—she shouldn't be there. Maybe—neither should they. Then she saw it. The great white.

Its massive form drifted past, close enough that she could make out the rough scars along its flank. Its belly, pale and endless, glided past her. Its head tilted just enough to show her that it saw her, too. Her pulse slammed against her ribs. Its presence was both mesmerizing and terrifying—ancient, untouchable, and far too close.

Kassidy put the proximity of the sharks out of her mind and swam beside the enormous eagle rays and glided among hundreds of species of corals and swaying anemones. Then she dove deep to touch the sand, as real as any beach. Grains of amber and white fell through her fingers and an octopus jutted out from a rocky outcropping. Its giant tentacles held tight together as it swam away from her with its watchful hyphen eye.

Kassidy brushed her fingers along the invisible barrier separating her from the ocean beyond. Underwater cameras clicked and flashed. She hovered there, tail floating below her on an invisible current. She marveled at the illusion. The seamless blend between her world and the one on the other side—teeming with life. It was magnificent. Then she saw the shadow. Larger than the others. Far off in the blue distance, a dark shape moved—enormous and ominous. Her heart raced as it grew bigger, drawing closer.

An immense black-and-white body emerged from the deep blue, gliding through the water. A distinctive white patch curled around one fin like a crescent moon. Sleek, powerful, and majestic. An orca.

Its intelligent eyes locking onto Kassidy's. With a flick of its tail, it passed overhead, casting a massive shadow—a total eclipse.

Kassidy felt her body begin to tremble—part terror, part awe, and part something darker. Betrayal.

Her chest tightened as her thoughts snapped to Billy—then back to the orca. How was this even possible? Was it even real? Maybe it was a hologram? A hallucination? It wasn't even legal. Was it? And why hadn't anyone told her? She never would have agreed to this.

The controversy.

The protest outside.

It all made sense now.

Oh God—her grandma. Ginny would never forgive her.

And Kassidy? She would never forgive Billy.

The giant shadow circled back, its dark eyes—deep, ancient— locking onto her once more, coming into focus as it closed the distance. Kassidy's mind screamed at her to move, to get out of the way. The great white was terrifying, but this creature was twice its size—a force that demanded reverence as much as terror. Yet she didn't move. She remained frozen, in shock, her hands pressed against the invisible barrier as the massive form loomed closer.

Kassidy's heart raced. Her hands trembled as she pressed them to the glass. Almond-shaped eyes gazed into hers, not with malice, but with—curiosity.

The orca hovered motionless, still, except for the slow, deliberate movement of its pectoral fins. Then, a slight tilt of its head, as if considering her, recognizing something.

In its dark eye, Kassidy caught her own reflection—a wavering silhouette against the glass. But there was something else in it too—not just her own unease staring back at her. But a sadness. Hers. The orca's. Maybe it was both—she wasn't sure.

Sunlight pierced the water's surface sending long narrow rays of light down through the water making Kassidy's scaled glow like liquid stardust. Coral gardens swayed in the current beneath them like an audience bearing witness to their connection. Time seemed to pause as though the ocean itself was waiting for what might unfold between these two kindred beings.

Kassidy felt an ache in her chest at the sight of the tall dorsal fin— once strong—now collapsed under the weight of captivity.

A bright flash made the orca blink then turn and swim away from the encounter.

And just like that it was over.

Kassidy didn't realize she was holding her breath until it rushed out in a panicked gasp. She inhaled sharply, but it wasn't enough—the air felt thin, useless, as if she were drowning anyway.

Panic seized her chest. She needed out. Now.

Without thinking, ignoring every warning to surface slowly, she kicked hard, desperate to escape. The rescue swimmers were on her now, hands clamping around her elbow—but they weren't pulling her up. They were holding her back.

No. No, no, no.

She kicked harder, fought against them, twisting in their grip. She needed to get free, to escape the world that wasn't hers. The water was closing in around her, the pressure of what she'd just done, crushing against her. She couldn't be a part of this. It was all wrong. Everything was wrong.

She swam for the surface, desperate to be free.

What Kassidy didn't know was that when she entered the water, the ocean had been waiting for her. It wrapped itself around her—and had no intention of letting her go. It was about to pull her under.

# Chapter 7

As she broke through the surface, she was met with clapping and cheers from the crew.

"You should see the shots they got!" Billy said, grinning from ear to ear as he reached out to help her onto the platform. "Incredible, Kass. You're going to die when you see them. The way that whale looked at you. We got it all on video and still. The shots were so good they wouldn't even know how to enhance them!"

Kassidy yanked at the headdress, her breathing growing shallow. "I just…I need to get this off. Now!"

Billy furrowed his brow as he watched Kassidy struggle to remove the gear with shaking hands.

"Kass, what's going on?"

Eli helped to unfasten the headdress from the rest of her costume and lift it from her head. She gasped for air even though she'd never been without it. Billy crouched beside her, grinning like he hadn't just ripped the ground out from under her.

"You were amazing down there. The shots are going to blow everyone away. This is going to take your career to a level you never even dreamed of before!"

He was acting like nothing was wrong. He was acting like he hadn't just betrayed her. Kassidy's skin felt too tight, the shimmering makeup now sticky and dull. The tank. The orca. The isolation. The loss of freedom. How long had she been in there?

She looked over the vast expanse of water. It had felt enormous to her, but to the orca? It was a bathtub. The wild, bound by panes of glass. A hunter turned into an exhibit.

This wasn't the ocean. This was a cage.

Kassidy's voice came out tight, shaking. "That whale. She doesn't belong in a tank, Billy." Her teeth clenched so hard her jaw ached. "Did you see her eyes? She's not just some attraction. She's…she's—"

Billy didn't let her finish. His smirk sharpened.

"The rocket ship that just launched your career?"

Kassidy's stomach dropped.

She turned toward Eli, searching for backup. He looked away, like he knew he shouldn't be part of this conversation.

Her voice was barely more than a breath. "Billy, how could you not tell me?"

Billy exhaled. "Because Jonah wanted the reaction to be real. She wanted it to be a first encounter. A real one."

Kassidy's arms crossed over her chest. "Or you knew I'd never agree to this gig if I knew they had an orca."

Billy didn't even deny it.

"You're right. I knew you'd say no." His voice was arrogant, like he wasn't even ashamed. "But now that you're here—can't you feel it? This is big. Bigger than anything we've ever done."

He gestured toward the expanse of glass and steel, his excitement spilling out in waves. "This is what you wanted. Something bigger than you. More meaningful than eyeliner."

Kassidy's whole body trembled now. Not from exhaustion. Not from the cold.

It trembled from the gravity of what she'd been thrust into.

"I can't believe it. I can't be part of *this*." Her voice, now barely a whisper, came out as a desperate whimper that tasted like regret.

Billy stepped in front of her, blocking her escape without touching her. "Just...just listen. Hear me out."

Kassidy halted, eyes narrowing. She wasn't convinced there was anything he could say that would make this better.

Billy drew in a slow breath, his gaze flickering between desperation and hope.

"I didn't know about the orca—not at first," he said. "We were already deep into negotiations when I found out. And by then, I couldn't back out."

He hesitated, eyes scanning her face as if looking for a way in. "Besides," he added, "she doesn't do tricks or anything like that. They rescued her, Kass. She's here because—"

A voice cut through the conversation, smooth and confident. "Isn't she magnificent?"

Kassidy turned as Jonah approached.

Jonah's polished smile remained intact. "As long as a city bus and tipping the scales at five tons," she said, as if reciting a fun fact.

Rage seared through Kassidy.

Billy had put her in the middle of this.

Orcas in captivity? What the hell was he thinking? This wasn't just bad PR—this was cancellation territory. Total annihilation.

Her mind raced. She knew enough about the contract to know she couldn't back out. She couldn't even give the money back. She didn't have it. And even if she did, backing out would violate the terms. It would be career suicide because no company of this magnitude would ever sign her again.

But staying? Aligning herself with this? Oh my God. Her grandma was going to kill her. And the fans? A cold wave of panic hit her like a rip current. They'd go berserk. And not in a good way.

She tried to act nonchalant, squeezing her hair with a towel while she figured out what to do next. For so many reasons, she couldn't be there right now.

"I didn't realize you had orcas" Kassidy said, a tightness gripping her stomach.

"Orca." Billy corrected.

"This is Keelah," Jonah said, gesturing to the far-off shadow. "Keeping captive orcas is banned, as I'm sure you know. But Keelah here needed a refuge from the miserable aquarium she was trapped in down in Mexico City. It was a sad spectacle. She was wasting away in a hot tank, with fungal infections and sunburn. Almost dead when we found her. She can't return to the ocean; she's been taken care of for too long. She wouldn't survive, so Capri Son did the right thing and saved her. It's all perfectly legal, of course. The United States and Mexican governments are both involved in the agreement. After what happened to Keiko, they granted us the permit to keep Keelah here, where she'll be safe. She will be well cared for and can live out the rest of her days."

"Who's Keiko?" Billy asked.

"Free Willy." Jonah swallowed and glanced down at Billy's shoes, as if appraising them. "He was released back into the wild when he shouldn't have been, and it killed him. Keelah has made a full recovery from the squalor they were keeping her in. This place is heaven for an orca like her. And this way, the world can enjoy her beauty while she's here."

The whale vanished into the blue haze, but Kassidy couldn't tear her eyes from where it had disappeared. Jonah's voice faded into the back of her mind as she droned on about Keelah's recovery.

How could they pretend this was saving her? Kassidy's mind raced as her grandmother's stories flooded back—tales of orcas, majestic creatures born to roam vast oceans and to swim endless miles of open water, not languish in captivity. This was a gigantic tank for a human—but for a killer whale? It was a prison.

Even if they had "rescued" her, Kassidy knew that most of the world wouldn't see it that way. There were people who would never support a whale in captivity, no matter the circumstances. The uproar over orcas had already shut down entire industries, sparking nationwide outrage. Capri Son's new model of amusement park was born in the wake of that backlash—designed to be above scandal.

But this? This was controversy. This was captivity. This was everything Kassidy wanted to avoid. This wasn't just scandal—it was cruelty, sanitized for public consumption. She hadn't signed up for this—whales, debates, and headlines.

Her lips parted, the words spilling out before she'd even thought them through. "I'm sorry—there's been a mis—"

Billy jumped in, his tone light, almost breezy. "Miscalculation! Clearly, she should've gone with an ash hue in her hair instead of these warm tones. It would've really brought out the blue highlights in the water. I'm sure you can fix that in editing." Billy glanced at the tank, then back at Kassidy, his voice measured, barely audible, so only Kassidy could hear. "Don't forget, they rescued her, or she wouldn't be alive right now. It's not like they're torturing her. She's fine."

"Torture?" Jonah barked. "Hardly. This whale gets treated better than half of America's household pets. She has trainers, biologists, and cognitive researchers with her daily. They monitor her stress levels, track her moods, and reinforce positive interactions. Every breath is documented, studied, and adjusted.

"She's not just cared for—she's protected. Watched over. Nothing happens here without us knowing about it first." Jonah exhaled, shaking her head.

"If you're thinking of backing out now—" it was a clear warning—
"well, let's just say that, per your contract (and I do hope you read all
the fine print) you'll have to pay it back, plus a penalty. And I can't
imagine even you—the famous Kassidy Karlson— can afford that."

Kassidy remembered that part of the contract. The terms were
clear: backing out would trigger a cascade of consequences—legal
action, blacklisting, a public breach that would stain her reputation in
ways no PR firm could repair. Capri Son would make sure of it. They
had the power—and the reach—to bury her career before she could
even issue a statement.

The penalty wasn't just financial—though the sum exceeded her
payment by a number so staggering she could hardly fathom earning it,
let alone repaying it. Besides, it was already gone, spent on a
commitment she couldn't undo.

Her hands weren't just tied. They were shackled. Bolted to the very
floor beneath her that they owned. And now they owned her, too. She
couldn't escape, and even if she tried, the fallout would crush her long
before she reached the surface.

How the hell had she ended up here?

She'd read the fine print. Well...most of it. She'd skimmed the
legalese, trusting Billy to handle the details because Billy handled
everything. He knew this job would be off the table for her—no matter
the payout—and he signed her up anyway.

Billy grabbed Kassidy's arm, pulling her aside.

Over his shoulder, he flashed a quick, apologetic smile at Jonah.
"Excuse us. Just one moment."

Kassidy stumbled as he ushered her out of earshot.

"This is not what I signed up for, Billy."

"Well, it's what we have to do," Billy shot back, his tone clipped,
but his eyes darted nervously toward Jonah, who was watching them
from a distance.

Kassidy scoffed. "Everyone knows what happens when those orcas
are kept in a tank. Trainers drown. People die. Orcas die. That's why it
was banned. There's a reason these places can't keep them anymore.
And it's not just the law—it's cruel. It's wrong. And I—"

"Keep your voice down," Billy muttered, as he glanced over his
shoulder.

Jonah stood a few feet away, her polished demeanor barely concealing her impatience. She crossed her arms, eyes sharp and unyielding. Kassidy didn't need to guess what that look meant.

Billy flashed another apologetic smile, as if to smooth things over. "She's…passionate," he said, turning back to Kassidy, a mix of pleading and warning in his eyes. "Don't blow this. That whale is fine. You heard Jonah. She's got the best care in the world here."

"No, Billy!" Kassidy snapped, her voice trembling with emotion. "You didn't see what I saw. This isn't freedom." Her mind raced as the image of Keelah's sad, soulful eyes burned into her memory.

Billy's face softened. "Kass, I get it. I do. But we're here to sell the experience. We aren't involved with the whale."

"Orca. She's not a whale. They're different," Kassidy corrected.

Billy tried to smooth things over, his tone annoyingly upbeat. "Well you're not promoting the orca, then, Kass. You're promoting the mermaid experience. That's what this is about—being the face of a magical fantasy. Not some animal rights crusader."

Kassidy turned to him, her glare sharp enough to cut stone.

"Don't look at me like that," he said, his smile faltering, revealing the cracks in his usual carefree facade. "You heard Jonah—they saved that whale. Have you ever been to Mexico City?" he added abruptly.

She didn't respond, so he leaned in, his voice dropping to a whisper. "Kass, listen. It's not just about the money—you can't bail, or you'll be the influencer who couldn't handle the pressure. And we can't get out of it, even if we wanted to—"

"I *know*, Billy," she snapped, cutting him off, her voice brimming with frustration and something perilously close to despair.

This wasn't what she wanted. This wasn't who she was. The experience was magical, yes, one of a kind. And she was grateful for it but not at the expense of keeping that whale in prison.

Billy exhaled sharply, forcing his strained smile back into place. "Just play the part until this is over. After this ad comes out, you can do whatever you want. Pick and choose your projects, start a foundation, save every whale on the planet if it makes you feel better."

Kassidy looked past him, her eyes landing on Jonah. The woman was watching them with an icy stare.

Kass couldn't shake the feeling that she was betraying a purpose larger than herself—all the people who had worked to keep those orcas out of tanks. She was betraying them. And she was betraying herself.

Her eyes darted to Billy, silently pleading for a sign of solidarity, of shared outrage. But what she saw in his face wasn't horror or doubt—it was dollar signs.

She swallowed hard, fighting back the tears stinging her eyes and the nausea twisting her stomach.

"How old is she?" Kassidy asked, though she wasn't speaking to anyone in particular.

Eli overheard. "Keelah? Fifty-seven," he said, reeling in a rope from the tank, wrapping it around his palm, then his elbow.

Kassidy's heart stopped. "Fifty-seven?" The word came out in a near whisper.

She was afraid to ask the next question.

Then she didn't have to.

"She's been with trainers since she was four," Eli continued, as if he already knew where her mind was going.

Kassidy swallowed hard. "Was she born here? I mean, in a place like this?"

Eli hesitated. Just for a second. And in that moment, she saw it—a flicker of something unspoken, something he felt too. A quiet understanding. A shared tragedy.

"No. Keelah was wild."

The word hit like a blow to the chest.

Wild.

Captured. Taken. Kidnapped from the sea.

Just like the orcas her grandma used to whisper about. The ones she cried over. The ones she never wanted to talk about.

When Kassidy woke up that morning, she hadn't imagined facing this moral and emotional abyss. This wasn't an evolution of her brand—it was a permanent scar on her soul.

Her heart ached, and the thought of the future, her face, promoting this, seemed like all her life's dreams slipping away.

They were both captives in a way, their every move dictated by forces beyond their control. The difference was stark, though: Keelah had survived her captors for fifty-three years, while Kassidy's sentence was just beginning.

"I need to leave," she whispered, her voice barely audible.

Kassidy turned, her movements stiff, mechanical. She reached for the hidden zipper at her back, wiggling out of the costume. The shimmering fabric pooled at her feet. She picked it up and handed it to Billy without looking at him, then walked away in nothing but the nude-colored undergarments they'd given her—designed to make her look like she was wearing nothing at all.

"Get me out of here," she said, without turning around.

The parking lot felt like another world.

A wall of protesters pressed against the main entrance barricades, their voices a dull roar beneath the pounding in her ears.

Kassidy pulled her coat over her head as someone shoved a phone in her direction, the bright flash sparking panic in her chest.

She scanned the crowd. The woman—the one who had grabbed her arm earlier. The one who had tried to warn her.

Gone.

Like she had never been there at all.

In the passenger seat of the lavish SUV, Kassidy pulled on her seatbelt and hollered at Billy, "DRIVE! Get us out of here."

"Okay, okay." Billy stepped on the gas, doing as she asked. "What the hell is wrong with you, Kass? What happened in that water? You see a ghost or something?"

Kassidy didn't look at him. Her eyes were fixed on the road ahead as they drove away from Capri Son. Her voice was barely more than a whisper, hollow and distant. "Yes."

Billy glanced over, eyes narrowing slightly, like he wasn't sure what to make of her tone.

"What do you mean, yes? Kass, what did you see?"

She swallowed hard, her hands trembling in her lap. "I saw what I need to do."

Billy frowned, confused. "Which is!?"

Kassidy turned her head slightly, her eyes shadowed, as if she'd glimpsed something far beyond them both.

A future she no longer recognized. A betrayal she didn't know how to forgive. A moment in time she could never undo.

One that changed everything.

"I need a break, okay? From everything. An escape. A vacation. I don't even care where it is. I just can't be here or deal with this right now, okay?"

Kassidy knew that as soon as Capri Son dropped the ad, with her beside that orca, she'd never be able to show her face in public again.

A vibration hummed from her pocket. She pulled out her phone and didn't recognize the number. The caller ID read *Friday Harbor, Washington.*

"Hello?"

"Kassidy Karlson?"

"Yes."

"My name is Ted Moore. I'm a lawyer up here in Friday Harbor. Look, we don't have a lot of time here and I don't know the best way to say this, so I'm just going to spit it out, okay? I'm sorry to have to be the one to tell you this, Miss Karlson, but your grandfather has passed away."

Kassidy blinked, staring ahead as the yellow dotted lines of the freeway whizzed by. "I'm sorry. You must have the wrong person. My grandfather died years ago. I helped plan his funeral."

Ted Moore shuffled through papers, the sound coming through the phone.

"Kassidy Karlson? Age 29, from Des Moines, Iowa? Your mother was Karleen Karlson, your grandmother is Virginia?"

"Yes, but…like I said, my grandfather died years ago. And I don't know anyone in Friday Harbor."

"I understand, but…there's a property in your name. I'll need you to come here to sign the papers."

Kassidy's long hair clung to her back, dripping onto her bare shoulders, the shimmer from her makeup smearing against her phone screen. Her hands were still shaking—from the cold, from the wreckage of the last hour.

"Just send me the papers. I'll take a look, Mr. Moore. I'll send you my address."

A brief silence crackled over the line before Mr. Moore spoke again. "I'm afraid that's not going to work. By law, because of the size of the estate, this must be done in person. Here. In Washington. I'll be closing up for the season in two weeks, so I hate to be a bother, but I'm afraid there's no other way."

Kassidy frowned. "Washington?"

Billy raised an eyebrow, whispering, "Who is it?" She waved him off, too focused on the call.

Friday Harbor. Her grandfather. None of this made any sense.

But it did give her the perfect excuse to get away. To disappear. To figure out what the hell she was going to do after...today.

She exhaled. "Alright. I'll book a flight—"

"There's no need," Mr. Moore cut in smoothly. "Your ticket has already been arranged. It should be in your inbox."

"Wait, how did you—?"

"It was necessary to move quickly, Ms. Karlson. Time is of the essence, I'm afraid."

She blinked at how much he knew about her. How did he know her? Billy must have sensed something shift because his grin faded.

"What's going on?"

Kassidy stared down at her phone, heart hammering as she pulled up her email. Sure enough, her flight information was already there. One-way. Seattle-Tacoma International. Departure: 6 a.m.

Her pulse pounded in her ears.

Whatever this was—it was real.

"Mr. Moore," Kassidy asked, "what exactly am I signing for?"

"Well...everything."

"Everything...where?"

"Out there. On the island."

"Island?"

"More of an islet, really. I'll arrange for someone to take you out there as soon as you arrive."

# Chapter 8

The next morning, Kassidy stepped off the plane at Sea-Tac. Exhaustion etched faint lines around her eyes, the kind that didn't wash away with sleep. Not that she'd gotten any of that. Not that she'd even tried. She'd stared out the window for the entire flight, replaying the last twenty-four hours in her mind.

The cab wove through the damp city streets, the scent of rain clinging to the air as it carried her toward the ferry dock. She stepped onto a boat bound for Friday Harbor—a place she'd never been, to meet a lawyer she'd never known, to sign papers for something she still didn't understand. But for the first time in her life, the uncertainty of what lay ahead felt less daunting than the mess she was leaving behind.

Kassidy stood on the ferry's outer deck, the Pacific Northwest coastline stretching endlessly behind her—mist-veiled evergreens, charcoal cliffs, and water so dark it seemed to swallow the light. The wind tossed up loose strands of her hair, salty spray whirled in the space between her cheek and the phone.

Billy was calling. She didn't want to talk to him. She needed a break. Time to process what happened and figure out what to do next. But there were loose ends to take care of, and he was integral to her business. So she answered.

"Hello?"

"Have you made a decision about Ivy & Bramble," Billy asked.

"Which company was that and what do they want me to endorse?"

"The press-on nails," Billy droned. "And they really want you. Especially after I told them you partnered with Capri Son."

Those two words were a dull knife to the heart.

Kassidy turned her back to the sea and leaned against the metal handrail, which was tall enough to keep most passengers from falling overboard, but in boots with four-inch heels, Kass was much taller than most people. She balanced herself against the hypnotizing swell of the ferry lurching on the waves.

"No. I'm not doing it. I've made up my mind." She looked out at the water, the cold wind tangling in her hair. "And I'm taking the rest of the month off. I might even turn off my phone. Maybe. I haven't decided yet, but when I get back, you and I are going to sit down and have a long talk about what happened yesterday and the future of *my* brand, Billy."

"*Your brand* is exploding right now, by the way. I just cast a rip on your feed about your latest partnership with Capri Son, and I'm pretty sure RippleHub broke the internet. So, we can have the talk—but I'm going to show you the numbers and prove that the only thing that needs re-focusing is your brain, not your brand. Maybe this trip will be good for you. And when you get back, we can resume our great work together of beautifying the world. But if you turn off your phone, how the hell am I supposed to reach you?"

"I don't know. Smoke signals? Carrier pigeon? I'm sure you'll find a way."

"It's just...you've never turned your phone off like...in your life. So, pardon me if I'm feeling a little alarmed."

"Fine. I won't turn my phone off if you find us work that is more important than press-on nails, or boob tape, or lip gloss," she said, her voice tight. "I want to do something...meaningful."

"You're a lifestyle brand, Kass. Trying to be more than an aesthetic mood board in this current climate is professional suicide."

Kassidy could practically see Billy rolling his eyes through the phone. But he did have a point.

He continued, his voice dripping with sarcasm. "Remember when that actress—what was her name?—got into animal rights and started chaining herself to bulldozers or something? Where's she now? Oh, that's right. Gone. No one's casting her anymore." Kass let out an audible breath. "And don't even get me started on that musician, Hunter what's-his-face, who decided to get political about, well, everything, and poof—canceled faster than you can say 'let them eat cake.' These people think they're saving the planet, but all they're doing is torpedoing their careers. Nothing those celebs were fighting for even happened." He paused, a hint of smugness creeping into his tone. "It's the same story every time, Kass. Step out of your lane, and the world will make sure you regret it."

"I just don't want to talk about eyeliner anymore. It was never really my thing to begin with," she said. "It just... happened. One day. One thirty-second video and now here I am. Some days, I can't even tell you how I got here—or why I'm still doing it."

"You got here because you found something you're good at. You're still here because you make a fortune doing it. So yeah, it is your thing, Kassidy. What you work hard at is your thing. What you've built skills for is your thing. You've built an empire most people would sell their souls for. I'm not letting you throw it all away because you're having a moral crisis. If you want to do something meaningful, we'll get you a rescue dog. We'll team up with that sloth sanctuary I've been obsessing over for years. Boom. Problem solved."

"I knew you wouldn't understand. But I'm not backing down from this, Billy. Going forward, things are going to be different. I'm not going to do press-on nails and I can't even talk to you about what happened yesterday." Kassidy's grip tightened on the rail.

"I didn't know about the orca until I couldn't back out. I swear. And I'm sorry it made you so uncomfortable. But we are not the ones who should be trying to save the world, or change things, Kass. Leave that to the people who are actually in charge of the world. We're just here to make it prettier—to spread more sparkle and glitter. Stick to what you're good at. You sell beauty, not revolution."

Deep down she knew Billy was right.

Her fan base told her what they wanted. Affordable finds, fabulous new trends, everything that glitters and isn't gold. She would lose them, lose her status, lose her business if she did anything *off brand*.

Then what? The money from Capri Son was substantial, but it was already spent. Kassidy used it to pay off the note on her grandma's farm, making sure she could stay. What was left of her grandfather's savings and Ginny's Social Security checks weren't enough to hold onto the place. Without Kassidy stepping in, her grandma would have lost her home.

The home Kassidy grew up in.

The home where her grandparents raised her.

"And by the way," Billy said, "the preliminary shots Capri Son sent me of you in that pool, are, well, let's just say...wowzah. Totally on point to cause a ripple."

She paused, holding her breath. "Are they going to use the ones of me with the orca?"

"What do you think?"

"I think it was a huge mistake."

She tapped her fingers absently, feeling the vibration of the ferry beneath her.

"Don't worry about it. I've already ripped that you're teaming up with Capri Son and you've only gotten encouragement, not criticism. When the ad comes out and everyone sees your face with that orca it'll be like shaking a fruit tree—the ugly damaged ones will fall away, and the sweetest most beautiful fruits will stay with the tree."

The water under the rail churned as she watched it rush by, then the captain blew the boat's horn snapping her out of her thoughts.

"Cover for me for a few weeks. Repurpose old content, okay?"

"Of course I will, but—" his tone shifted, sharper now, like something had just clicked. "Don't turn your phone off, okay? Dammit, I knew I should've turned tracking on for that thing."

She hung up before he could ramble on.

Billy meant well. He always did. He'd been her lifeline when she had no one else. When she was an awkward teenager being raised by her grandparents. Then when she was accidentally famous, and every man on the planet slid into her DM's, not a single one of them turned out to be anything other than a trophy hunter. Billy had been there to fill the lonely void with laughter and lend his shoulder anytime she needed it.

That was worth something, no matter his mistake with Capri Son. He was caught up in the money, and glitz. She knew that. And she couldn't blame him, maybe she had been too. But not anymore. Now, she was taking her grandma's advice.

*When you take someone with you, you bring your world.*
*Go alone, that's when you find out who you really are.*

Grandma always said that. It was time she started taking her advice.

Besides, she wasn't even sure what she was doing on that boat, or who she really was anymore. Maybe that's what this trip was about— maybe it was time to unplug and figure her new self out.

She held the power button until the screen went black then slid her phone into her tote. No chimes. No dings. No vibrations from her purse—for once, the world was quiet.

And chilly.

The wind whipped across the deck, sending a shiver through the openings of her long coat. Her dark hair caught the breeze, sweeping across cheekbones sharp enough to catch the light.

Kassidy had the kind of look that made strangers glance twice— not because she was perfect, but because something about her was harder to name. Her grandmother said people stared because Kassidy reminded them that beauty comes from somewhere behind the eyes. And what was behind hers unsettled them—because it was real, and most beauty these days isn't.

Kass pulled the heavy door open and stepped inside to get warm. A news broadcast on the television caught her eye. The image was partially blurred, with a graphic warning scrolling across the screen.

A female reporter stood on a polished stone beach, rugged mountains towering in the background.

"The orca known as Marie, born in 1969 and famously studied by scientists, washed up on a beach in Prince William Sound yesterday."

The camera cut to the lifeless orca on a rocky shore, surrounded by officials. Kassidy gasped at the sight. The reporter continued.

"Marie was the last female of the AT1 pod, photographed swimming through the Exxon Valdez oil spill. The pod lost fifteen of its twenty-two members. Marie was one of the few remaining survivors. No new calves have been born into the family since the disaster. Her death marks a catastrophic loss for the pod, which now has only two remaining members—both males, and if they're still alive, they're already doomed to extinction. Orca lovers around the world are outraged by the apparent cause of death…gunfire."

A woman stepped behind Kassidy to get a better look, her words floating over her shoulder, "I'd kill the person who shot that orca and never feel bad about it," she said, her voice rising. "Gun-wielding, big-game-hunting macho assholes, that's who probably did this."

Kassidy glanced at the fisherman she'd seen on the ferry earlier. He was staring at her. Even when she turned her back, she could feel his eyes on her—a quiet intensity. He'd been on the top deck. Then at the back. And now here. Not close enough to speak, but not far enough to ignore.

Dressed in worn flannel and weathered denim, he looked every bit like he'd just been on a cold weather fishing trip—but something about the grungy fisherman gear didn't fit. His smile. His perfect posture. He carried himself like a man accustomed to being listened to, not noticed for needing a warm meal. And he looked at her the way a person watches the sunset—admiring, waiting for something he knew would happen.

Which made her very uneasy.

Kassidy was used to unwanted attention, but this man's stare was different. He wasn't even trying to hide the fact he was staring.

Kassidy knew how to deal with men like him.

Confront them head on. If she let them gawk, they kept the power. But confronting them always made them back off.

Time to teach this stalker a lesson.

She marched toward him, her boots a rhythmic click on the floor. Her coat billowed behind her, a fierce catwalk, her eyes locked on his.

This is when they look away.

Usually, they looked away.

Why isn't he looking away?

Instead—he smiled.

Why was he smiling?

# Chapter 9

The fisherman stood as Kassidy approached, squaring his body with hers. He lifted his hands slightly, as if anticipating her arrival with openness. Before she could process why he was smiling or why his arms hovered open, she stumbled.

The heel of her boot caught on the raised floor. She lurched—then the fisherman was there, catching her firm and fast, before she even realized she was falling. Their eyes met in that split second of suspended gravity—like he'd been waiting for this—just before her head hit his chest instead of the floor.

She could feel his heart beating under his worn flannel and smelled a sharp, woodsy scent that surprised her—warm and clean, like cedar and salt and air. It wasn't what she expected, not fish guts and rubber gloves at all. And for a split second, it disarmed her.

Her face flushed. His hands were already at her shoulders, gently lifting her back to her feet.

Kassidy blinked, trying to shake the feeling of being caught off guard. She straightened quickly, composing herself, then stared at him, face to face now. And realized he wasn't stalkerish at all.

Not like the others she'd confronted, with their beady eyes and unconfident drooling. This man's eyes held an unexpected calmness. His smile was confident—yet boyish—and growing wider.

"You're welcome," he said, not waiting for her gratitude, his voice a deep, casual rumble.

She scoffed, "I didn't say thank you." The words came out sharper than intended.

His grin widened even more, if that was possible, like he found her reaction entertaining.

Kass couldn't shake off the fluster. She glanced down, then pointed to the raised floor. "They should really fix that, you know. Before someone gets hurt. At least put up a sign or something."

The fisherman pointed toward a sign, eye level, tacked to a post. The large neon yellow words were in capital letters: CAUTION: WATCH YOUR STEP.

"Looks like they tried," he said, amusement flickering in his eyes.

Kassidy bit her lip, embarrassed and off her game. Then she cleared her throat, straightened her jacket, and remembered why she'd approached him in the first place.

"Do we know each other?" she asked, eyes fierce on him.

He raised an eyebrow. "I'm pretty sure I'd remember if we did. Why? Do you think you know me?" His confidence unnerved her. "Or ...maybe you...want to?" There was a teasing edge in his tone, light and deliberate, and overly confident. "People around here say I'm a pretty nice guy," he added.

She scoffed again. How brazen! "Um...no. I don't know you. I'm asking because...well, you've been stalking me around the boat. Like you think you know me or something. So, I thought I'd ask." It came out all wrong. This wasn't how it normally went. "And...well...I'd really appreciate it if you stopped."

"Me? Stalking *you*?" He tilted his head, folding his arms across his chest. She saw a twitch in his jaw, and the muscles under his shirt flex. "I most definitely was not stalking you." He paused, eyes softening. "Admiring," he cocked his head from side to side, "yes, but definitely not stalking."

Kassidy's heart raced as he spoke—he was honest and direct, something she didn't always experience in her line of work. He didn't flinch, didn't hide behind excuses. The other men she confronted would have backed down by now, ran away, offered some lame apology, or tried to weasel out of the confrontation. But this man—this fisherman—was unfazed.

Her cheeks burned with embarrassment. This wasn't how it was supposed to go. She hated feeling flustered—out of control, hated how he'd literally, caught her off guard.

He didn't fit the dirty fisherman stereotype she'd assumed either. Not up close anyway. He was rugged, sure, but the calm confidence, the ease with which he smiled and stared at her—it threw her.

Kassidy was used to having the upper hand with men. Always. But it didn't feel that way with this one. He watched her closely, his gaze unwavering, waiting. His smile never faltering. It was disarming. And damn it, she was letting herself be disarmed.

He unfolded his arms and talked with his hands. "Look, I didn't mean to make you uncomfortable," he said in a much softer tone now. "I guess I was...*looking* at you but not stalking. I'm not used to seeing tourists around here this time of year. And you're well..."

She folded her arms. "I'm...well...what?"

"This is a small place, and you stand out."

Kassidy frowned, crossing her arms defensively. "I stand out? Is that supposed to be some lame tall-girl joke?"

He shook his head, a small smile tugging at the corner of his mouth. "No, I didn't mean it like that. Although, now that you mention it. You are quite a bit taller than average. And those boots don't exactly scream 'ferry ride.' So perhaps that's why you stood out." His eyes flicked down to her boots, then back up and she could have sworn he stopped a moment on her lips. "Most people around here wear...more practical footwear."

She glanced down at his shoes and recognized them immediately. They were from that new company, Omni, who made eco-friendly clothing and pledged to give money back to environmental causes. Now that would be a company she could collaborate with.

"What if I have a job interview?" Kassidy said. "Then these boots are practical. And appropriate."

"Do you?" he asked, one brow lifting. "Have a job interview?"

She scoffed. "That's not the point." She turned slightly, searching for a better comeback—but nothing came. "I can't think when you're staring at me like that."

His smile spread slowly, then broke into something real. A laugh that didn't ask for permission or scan for approval—just rolled out, full and easy. She envied that laugh. What it meant.

It was a laugh that came with the certainty of knowing who you are. Of living effortlessly—no trimming edges to fit expectations, no weighing every word before speaking.

Just existing and laughing and living, without apology.

Did she even know what that felt like?

Embarrassed, she turned to walk away but he reached out and touched her arm. "I didn't mean to offend you. Or judge you. That wasn't my intent." She turned back toward him. "I was, like I said, admiring you."

"Are you a fan?" The question slipped out before she could stop it, part curiosity, part defense.

"Are you famous?" he shot back, his voice playful, but with an edge she didn't like—one too close to mockery.

Kassidy stared at him, unsure what to say or whether to feel insulted or intrigued. Something about how he looked at her—like he saw straight through the image she projected to the world. She didn't like feeling this vulnerable. Didn't like feeling this... seen.

"Of course not."

She shifted her weight, ready to walk away from the uncomfortable conversation when the ferry lurched, sending her stumbling again. This time, she caught herself before she could fall, but the fisherman reached out instinctively, his hand clasping her elbow. The contact was brief, but it sent a strange awakening through her.

"See... practical shoes would have kept you upright," he said, chiding her.

Kassidy pulled away, composing herself. "Practical is boring. And I am anything but boring."

"I don't doubt that," he said with a flicker of amusement.

She couldn't tell if he meant for her to hear it.

Kassidy could feel his eyes on her as she walked away, as if he was studying her, trying to figure her out. There was something about his interest in her, his intensity—quiet but focused—that made her feel noticed in a way she wasn't used to.

She was reluctant to leave, but she didn't even know why. Other than she liked the sharp exchange of jabs. It was fun. And he could keep up, in a rugged, charming, nice-smelling fisherman kind of way.

But how was she supposed to recover from their encounter? She'd been so rude—felt so... exposed.

In line to disembark, she worked hard not to turn around and look for him. And yet, curiosity overtook her. Despite the unspoken friction between them, she glanced over her shoulder, looking back at him as she stepped through the doorway.

He hadn't moved from his spot. He was still there, leaning, hands in his pockets, as if he hadn't taken his eyes off her. He was watching her with that smug grin.

Her heart tripped over itself when their eyes locked for a second longer than she intended. His gaze was magnetic, like he was daring her to come back and fall into his arms again.

She felt the undeniable pull toward him, and yet, she forced herself to break the connection and look away. Her past with men like him had proven she knew exactly what he wanted. And she was sick of being their Barbie doll—even if she'd willingly played the role too many times, she wasn't doing it again. But now she had no idea how to break free, how to reinvent herself. Or if she even could.

Kassidy felt the sudden chill of the wind biting at her skin as she stepped out onto the open deck as the ferry pulled into Friday Harbor.

The morning mist was beginning to lift, revealing the outlines of the marina. Boats of all sizes were moored in the harbor, their masts swaying gently in the breeze, white sails ghostly in the fading light.

Kassidy let herself get lost in the view, in the peacefulness of the sea. But even as she stood there, the strange encounter with the fisherman loitered in the back of her mind, as if she could still feel him watching her. A feeling that never felt welcome, until now.

She took a deep breath, centering herself. Stop it. This trip wasn't about strange men on ferries. It was about being alone. Finding herself anew. Taking time away to re-focus. This was a call to adventure—time away for her to think.

But deep down, she was there because of something she didn't want to admit—not even to herself. She was running from the campaign that would end her career. Running from the commotion, the scrutiny, and the inevitable storm of cancel culture that would follow as soon as those photos got pushed out to the world.

A large black-and-white sign with an orca was hung above a gift shop down by the harbor, and her thoughts drifted back to her encounter with the whale, Keelah, and the news broadcast.

The lifeless orca washed up on the shore, the tragedy of a dying species. Why all of a sudden was her life filled with whales? Or was this like buying a new car, then seeing that car everywhere and realizing they had been there all along, if only she had looked more closely?

The image of the dead whale on the beach, limp and bloody on the rocks, flashed in her mind again, and a wave of sadness swept over her. That whale was like Keelah—only it was still wild.

Who would do such a thing?

Her thoughts returned to Keelah still in that tank, confined. What I've done, she admitted, is part of the problem.

But she couldn't go back. She pushed the coming storm out of her mind. There was nothing she could do about it anyway.

Kassidy breathed in the salty air as they approached the pier, happy to be near the ocean. She didn't grow up near the water, didn't spend childhood summers by the shore. She grew up in the cornfields of Iowa, where the farmland stretched for miles and the horizon never changed. Maybe that was why the sea pulled at her—the way it moved, changed, and hid things beneath its surface. It was unfamiliar, untamed.

The fog lifted completely, revealing Friday Harbor in all its quaint, historic charm. The marina was at full capacity, boats moored in every available slip, their white hulls gleaming in the daylight.

Kassidy stepped off the ferry, her boots clicking on the concrete pier, the cool breeze carrying the scent of salt and pine. Seagulls wheeled overhead; their cries sharp against the dull lapping waves. The briny air mixed with the faint aroma of gourmet coffee and fresh bread drifting from a café near the waterfront.

The town looked like something out of a postcard—picturesque and inviting, yet a sense of mystery filled the air, as if the island itself held secrets waiting to be uncovered.

She pulled out a folded piece of paper—directions to the lawyer's office. With one last look at the marina, Kassidy walked through the Friday Harbor archway, done in a white and blue coastal motif, then set off down the smooth, well-worn street—polished by sea, air, and time. The town was quiet, the streets mostly empty, save for a few locals going about their business.

Kassidy didn't know what she was looking for or what forces exactly had sent her to Friday Harbor, but she couldn't shake the feeling that something—or someone—did.

Whatever waited for her, she would find it.

And maybe—she'd find herself in the process.

# Chapter 10

Kassidy followed Mr. Moore's directions and walked along the main street of the quaint town. The air smelled faintly of sea salt mingled with wisps of wood smoke from a seafood grill preparing for lunch, the promise of buttered prawns and charred lemon hanging in the air. The rich aroma of coffee from the corner café lured locals to gather, their low conversations blending with the distant hum of boats on the water.

Old character dollhouses were nestled among lush greenery, and beside them stood modern buildings with sleek lines and rooftop decks strung with modern patio lights. It was like stepping into a world caught between two eras—vintage charm beside sleek progress, as if the town hadn't yet decided which direction to commit. The city felt alive with a past so woven into the landscape she could almost feel the echoes of what once thrived there. But the modern harbor front design pointed to a future that looked to the water with quiet hope.

People bustled about—locals in comfortable sneakers and casual jackets, balancing their reusable coffee cups, and chatting as they crossed the streets.

Kassidy traveled for work but usually with a team; she was rarely alone. She was constantly surrounded by people advising her on what to wear, how to prep, and herding her along to her next move.

Being in a strange town, alone, was something else entirely. She was untethered. She had no agenda, no script to follow, no audience to please. It was the first true adventure she'd ever had. A strange and beautiful place where she'd follow clues but had no idea where it would lead, or if it was even meant for her at all.

Just being there felt freeing, and terrifying. She hadn't realized how much the noise of others drowned out her own thoughts. For the first time, she wanted to navigate life on her own terms, without anything to guide her but herself.

When Kassidy arrived at the address, she blinked in surprise. The building didn't look like a law office. It looked like someone's childhood home—a small, white cottage with a wraparound porch and ivy crawling up the walls. A swinging yard sign that read Moore Law & Estate Planning hung between two whitewashed posts.

Kassidy knocked, then turned the knob and let herself in. A set of bells jingled as the door opened, filling the small space with their soft, cheerful clanking.

"Hello? Mr. Moore?" she called out, her voice feeling oddly loud in the quiet space.

Old black-and-white photos lived on the walls—fishermen with their catch, boats anchored in the harbor, and snapshots of island life from decades past. Some showed smiling families, others captured weathered men posing proudly with giant salmon. The house was a time capsule, filled with memories she didn't share but wanted to.

The faint smell of herbs and garlic wafted through the air, and down the hallway, she spotted a cozy kitchen. This was more than an office; it was someone's life, layered into every corner.

Mr. Moore appeared from the kitchen, dabbing mustard from the corner of his mouth with a napkin in one hand and a sandwich in the other. He stopped walking and his eyes widened when he saw her.

"Oh, well aren't you a lighthouse among sea people? Tall as the corn down there in Iowa now, aren't you?"

Of all the tall person comments she'd heard over the years, his felt the least offensive, and amused her the most.

She stood even taller. "State Corn Queen three years in a row." She smiled at him. "Thank you for not asking if I play basketball."

He chuckled, a warm sound that made the space feel even cozier. "I'm Ted Moore. You must be Miss Karlson. Come on in, we have some paperwork to go over."

Kassidy followed him into the living room, which doubled as his office. Stacks of papers towered in precarious piles on every available surface, leaving only a small space cleared for a worn leather chair and a desk cluttered with file folders.

He glanced up at the cluttered room and gave a sheepish smile.

"You'll have to excuse the mess," he said, sliding a towering stack aside—it teetered but stayed upright, a delicate balance of order and disorder. "Never been much for organization."

As Kassidy absorbed the coziness of the space, the mess of papers wasn't disconcerting—it was comforting, somehow. Like proof that her inner world wasn't the only chaos around her.

"I don't mind," Kassidy said, then sat down slowly, folding her hands in her lap to keep from fidgeting. "It feels," she paused to come up with the right words as to not offend him. "Lived in."

She studied Mr. Moore as he muttered to himself, shuffling through documents, sensing that, in time, all her questions would be answered.

As he sorted through his haphazard system, he talked to himself in a barely audible tone. "Now where did I put…ah, yes, that goes over there. And this…hmm." He moved to another pile, his fingers skimming over the tops. Then, with a light clap of satisfaction, "Oh! Here it is. I have your papers right here." He tugged out a thick manila envelope.

She still couldn't believe there were papers. That any of this was real.

Mr. Moore carefully laid the envelope in front of her on the desk. His hands, spotted with age, moved with a slight tremor as he smiled at her, his cheeks lifting under his wire-rimmed glasses.

"Your grandfather's will," he said softly, pushing the envelope closer.

The word hit her like a punch. It simply couldn't be. She had only ever known one grandfather—the one that raised her. The one that she and her grandma buried.

"I'm sorry, Mr. Moore," she began, her voice trembling slightly as she pushed the envelope back toward him. "Like I said on the phone, there must be some kind of mistake. My grandfather passed away a few years ago. I was at his funeral."

Mr. Moore was unfazed. He smiled kindly, the lines around his eyes crinkling. He folded his hands in front of him and leaned back in his chair as though he had heard this before.

"I know that's what you said, Miss Karlson," his voice was calm and reassuring. "But I can assure you, there's no mistake. This property and everything on it—is going to you one way or another. Ray was very clear about this."

He opened the envelope and pulled out a stack of official-looking papers. "See? Right here." He pointed to a handwritten signature with elaborate strokes. "Raymond Hawthorne made you the beneficiary of his estate. Grandfather or not, he wanted you to have it. He even showed me a photograph of you, so I'd recognize you the moment you walked through the door."

"Raymond Hawthorne?" Kassidy said aloud. It came out in a whisper, a question. "But I've never even heard that name before."

Kassidy's mind reeled. A photograph of her? She bit her lip, her head spinning. The world felt like it was tilting beneath her.

Technically she guessed it was possible. She was adopted—at least, that's what she told anyone who asked. It was easier that way. The truth was too tangled, too exhausting to explain. And in the end, it always led to the same place—pitying looks and questions that cut like dull knives.

Questions like, why did your grandparents raise you? What happened to your mother? Followed by, I'm sorry, that's such a tragedy. What about your father? With today's DNA technology, he should be easy to find, shouldn't he?

As if she hadn't spent countless nights staring at the ceiling, wondering what would be worse—finding someone who probably had no idea she existed? Not finding him at all? Or worse, finding him and learning something she couldn't take back.

She knew the answer.

She'd made sure her DNA wasn't out there.

She didn't want to find anyone. And she didn't want to be found. Virginia and Stanley weren't just her mother and father. They were her everything. Her grandparents, her parents, her entire foundation. She didn't need more family. She didn't need a name or a stranger who might bring more questions.

They were enough. More than enough.

And she'd never hurt them by searching for someone she didn't need. Though it seems that someone was searching for her.

Mr. Moore smiled again, as if trying to quell her disbelief. "It's all in there." His fingers tapped lightly on the papers in front of her, slightly shaky but sure. "The land alone—" he whistled softly, eyes widening as though even he was still impressed by it.

"There's a tenant on the island. Land lease. They pay their rent on time, and your grandfather never had any problems with them. Should you need to remove them someday…well, let's hope it doesn't come to that, but I'd be happy to mediate if necessary."

Kassidy stared at him, dumbfounded. Her fingers curled tightly around the edge of the desk. What was she supposed to do with an island—build a moat and declare sovereignty? It felt absurd. Like one big, elaborate prank.

"Mr. Moore—"

"Twelve million dollars," he said, cutting her off, his voice tinged with awe. "I sent an appraiser out after we spoke on the phone. The island itself, without any structures, is valued at twelve million dollars. Now, it's not a terribly large piece of land—more of an islet, really. But it's pristine, untouched, except for the two homes on it."

She froze. A strange ringing filled her ears. Her grip tightened on the desk as if the solid wood might ground her. This had to be a mistake. She leaned in, her voice rising with shock.

"Twelve million dollars? An island?"

Mr. Moore chuckled softly, adjusting his glasses, his expression unreadable—like he'd expected this exact reaction. "I don't know the full details of your family history," he said, watching her carefully, "but Raymond thought very highly of you. He wanted his land to stay in the family. He could have sold it to developers, could have cashed out years ago, but that wasn't his way."

Kassidy shook her head, trying to make sense of it all. She didn't even know this Raymond.

Her voice dropped as she leaned back, her eyes searching Mr. Moore's face for some hidden answer. "What if it's a mistake? What if there's someone else? Someone who actually is his granddaughter that deserves it?"

"There's no one else," Mr. Moore said firmly but gently, his tone never wavering. He held her gaze, then leaned forward, his elbows resting on the desk. "Raymond was sure of that. This land is yours. And only yours. He made a very wise investment a long time ago. Land like this isn't for sale anymore. The only way to own it is to already have it in the family."

He paused, pushing a photograph across the desk toward her. Kassidy reached out hesitantly, her fingers brushing the edges of the glossy paper. In the photograph was a cabin nestled among towering trees. The isolation of it struck her immediately—a world apart from everything she knew.

"The cabin," Mr. Moore pointed to the picture. "Has good bones."

She stared at the photo of the cabin, quaint, almost charming. But the overwhelming sense of responsibility, the enormity of the gift, sat heavy in her chest. Could this really be hers? What was she supposed to do with it? Sell it? Move there?

Mr. Moore continued speaking, his voice like background noise as her thoughts spiraled. She was overwhelmed, her mind a storm of questions and doubts, and yet…something else. A curiosity. A pull. It was small at first, but it grew, taking root deep inside her, refusing to let go.

"There is one tiny catch," Mr. Moore said, snapping her out of her daze. He leaned back in his chair, crossing his arms, as though preparing to deliver the final blow. "You can never sell it. The island, that is. You can gift it to a *blood* relative, like it's been gifted to you, but it can't be sold. Ever. And should you become unable to care for it, the land will go into a trust for the Salish Sea Orca Conservation Center, the SSOCC."

She stared at him, her mind struggling to process everything. Whale conservation. A grandfather she never knew.

Mr. Moore smiled gently, perhaps sensing her turmoil. "I'm sure it's a lot to take in," he said, his voice soft, almost fatherly. "But I believe Raymond wanted you to have this land for a reason."

"Why me Mr. Moore?" she whispered. "And why now?"

"Take it," he said, his hand reaching out to cover hers. The skin on his hand was thin, speckled with dark spots, his touch surprisingly firm. "Take the gift. The whale conservation would do great things with it, but Ray wanted you to have it." He gave her a gentle smile. "You seem like a lovely girl. Raymond certainly thought so. Not many people get to live out their days in a place as enchanted as this. Take the gift."

Mr. Moore tapped the papers with two fingers. "What Ray has out there is truly special—especially around here. With everything going on and whatnot." He pointed toward the window, in the direction of the water. "Out there is the most unique ecosystem on the planet. Enchanting. Magical. Historic. And vanishing."

He paused, his gaze distant, as if seeing something Kassidy couldn't. Then he refocused, his tone softening. "Forgive an old man for doling out unsolicited advice, but if I were you, I'd soak up every moment of this place before it's gone. What's under the waves here changes people. Most folks visit for a weekend, maybe a week. They fall in love and never want to leave—but they have to. There's no land to buy here anymore."

He leaned back slightly, giving her space but keeping his voice firm. "What you've been given is a gift of enormous proportions. Don't ask how or why, just take it. These islands will teach you who you are— good or bad. And what lies beneath the waves out there?" He tapped the papers again, a little firmer this time. "Will bring out the best and worst in everyone. This place will show you who you are at the core. And it'll show you who everyone else is too—or at least who they're pretending to be."

"Do you know why he thought I was his granddaughter?" Kassidy asked, knowing that it was possible.

She didn't know her biological father. So maybe this Raymond really was her biological grandfather. It was certainly possible. A flicker of unease crawled up her spine. If that was true, whatever was waiting for her on that island might lead her to all of them.

Did she want that?

She'd spent years locking that door and hiding the key. She was happy with her life. But now—now, she was here. Too curious. Too committed. She'd come too far to turn back, too close to walk away.

The ferry was still at the dock. She could leave. Forget all of this. But her feet stayed rooted to the ground.

Mr. Moore leaned forward, resting his arms on the desk, his gaze fixed on Kassidy. "We all have our secrets, Miss Karlson. Maybe Ray saw something in you that reminded him of himself. Or maybe you should ask your grandmother. Perhaps she knows something you don't. Whatever the case, I think Raymond wanted you to have a fresh start."

His words settled over her, heavy and confusing. A fresh start? She didn't even know where to begin. How could he know?

Mr. Moore stood, opening the door to the porch. Sunlight spilled into the room, dust particles dancing in the air.

Kassidy stood too, feeling the moment on her shoulders like a weighted vest.

"Mr. Moore," she said, her voice quiet as she stared through the dust at the man who was in the twilight of his mortality. "What is the name of the island?"

He smiled, a knowing smile, one that seemed to hold a thousand secrets. "Ray called it Isla Virginia."

Kassidy froze, the name sending a shock through her body.

"Virginia," she whispered, feeling the ground shift beneath her feet. This wasn't a coincidence. It couldn't be.

Virginia was her grandma—her mother, the woman who raised her. Had she known? About the island? About Raymond Hawthorne? About everything Kassidy didn't?

A hundred questions flooded her mind, but one burned hotter than the rest. Was this tied to a family she'd never known? Or was it connected to the only family she'd ever had?

Either way, Virginia was sure to have answers. Answers she had kept from her only daughter.

Kassidy's grip tightened around her phone. She would get them. Whether Virginia was ready to talk or not.

"Mr. Moore, you didn't tell me, this man, Raymond, how did he…you know, pass?"

Mr. Moore closed his eyes for a long moment.

"I don't know for sure. But I suspect Raymond's demons finally caught up with him." Mr. Moore sighed. "But sometimes, death is the last gift life can offer—and with it, something new can rise."

# Chapter 11

The San Juan Islands unfurled around her in a breathtaking panorama—an archipelago scattered across the enchanting waters of the Salish Sea. The sight made her pause, her body instinctively going still in its presence.

Since the ferries only stopped on the main islands, getting to Isla Virginia required personal transportation by boat or sea plane. Mr. Moore had called for a private water taxi to take Kassidy the forty-five-minute ride out to Isla Virginia. Her new, private island.

The briny scent of the ocean mingled with the earthy aroma of pine and damp moss as they got farther out from the main ports. Each island rose like an emerald jewel from the deep blue, cloaked in dense forests and surrounded by rocky shores. The sky above was a canvas of silver clouds, pierced occasionally by golden sunlight.

Quaint cottages and elegant seaside villas dotted the landscape. Walls of windows and expansive decks offered panoramic views of the sparkling water and distant coves. Private docks stretched out into the sea, with boats and seaplanes moored around the edges.

She leaned forward, resting her hand on the boat's edge, feeling the sea spray settle on her hair. Every time they rounded the corner of an island, the weather changed, as if the sky couldn't decide on a mood.

As they got farther out, the air seemed to thicken and cool. The scent of seaweed and the faint metallic tang of a coming storm wafted over them.

She hadn't known this Raymond Hawthorne, but now she was following his ghost across the water. The thought unsettled her.

Why her? Why now?

She had spent her whole life certain of who she was, where she belonged. Yet now, here she was, gliding on the waves toward a past she'd never asked for, toward a place that someone thought was meant for her.

Was she making a mistake?

Digging up bones that were better off left buried?

She gripped the boat's edge, her fingers stiff against the damp wood. Too late for second thoughts now. Whether she wanted it or not, the island—and whatever secrets it held—was right there waiting for her.

The taxi driver cut the engine and the boat glided into place alongside a long wooden dock. The driver jumped out and held the boat steady for her.

Kassidy hesitated to step out, her pulse drumming in her ears. The dock stretched before her like a threshold to another life—one she hadn't chosen, or sure she even wanted.

The island was silent, almost eerily so. A narrow channel of water separated it from what appeared to be a much larger, equally uninhabited island across the way, with a dense wilderness and no cabins that she could see.

To her left and right, open water stretched to the horizon.

The cabin looked exactly like the photo Mr. Moore had shown her. Same autumn leaves, same rustic beauty. She let her eyes sweep over it, taking in every detail. Pine trees dominated the forest, their burnt-orange needles carpeting the ground. There was no grass to mow, no manicured lawn—just wilderness.

Two sea lions glided through the calm water, their wake forming a perfect V, pausing just long enough to touch noses in a gentle kiss before vanishing beneath the surface.

A flock of small birds suddenly burst from the trees, their frantic squawking shattering the stillness. Kassidy froze, scanning the surroundings. Were there bears here? Snakes? Other predators? She knew absolutely nothing about this place or the critters who roamed here.

"I didn't plan for a deserted island when I packed," she said to the driver, who nodded toward the cabin, his skin dark and his hair sun-bleached from years on the water.

"Mr. Moore arranged for all the essentials you'll need. The cabin should have enough basics to get you through for a few days. But take this—" He reached into his pocket and handed her a business card. "Here's my number. Call if you need a ride or supplies, and I'll make arrangements."

Careful not to let her boot heel slip through the wooden slots, she took his business card, then his offered hand and stepped out. The man glanced down at her boots. Before he could comment, Kassidy shrugged and gave a wry smile. "I know they're not practical. But I have a job interview."

He shrugged, as if he didn't care either way. "Might I suggest making friends with your neighbor on the other side? There's a sea plane over there that can fly to the main islands in case of an emergency. There's a storm coming too. Rare around these parts, so keep an eye on the sky," he said before pushing off.

Kassidy glanced up at the clouds.

"They're saying it's a big one. Thirty-five knots. High wind. I suggest lighting a fire in case the power goes out. It gets cold at night this time of year."

Kass looked again toward the sea—the clouds above were bright and transparent—not a gray rain cloud in sight. But the ones on the horizon were ominous and churning, ready to spit out whatever they'd swallowed up. She felt a nervous flutter in her stomach, the first tendrils of fear curling around her.

She was stranded.

"There should be cell service somewhere on the island, but I don't know where. I'd walk around before it gets dark and find out!" He yelled, his voice growing fainter as the boat pulled away.

The hum of the throttle dimmed until the only sound left was the gentle lap of water against the dock. Kassidy reached into her pocket, pulled out her phone, turned it on and stared at the screen.

No service.

The driver had pointed down the shore—crushed shells and a rocky shoreline scattered with driftwood.

Panic wrapped its fingers around her heart. She turned toward the boat, her pulse hammering, ready to call the driver back—to wave her arms, phone in hand, and tell him she'd changed her mind.

But it was too late.

The boat had already rounded the corner, its wake dissolving into the endless expanse of blue.

She was alone. She drew in a slow breath, pulling every ounce of bravery she had into her ribs to keep her focused. This was real now.

No turning back.

She looked down at the cedar boards beneath her feet and rolled her ankle slightly to look at her heels which would fit perfectly between the slots. She pictured herself tripping, breaking her ankle, and being stuck here alone, screaming for help that wouldn't come.

She should have packed more shoes and clothes. But all she had was her weekender bag. She'd left home too fast and didn't have time to pack anything else. Kass figured when she got where she was going, she could buy any supplies or clothes that she needed.

The boards beneath her varied in color. Some were warm, with a golden hue, as if freshly replaced, others weathered and gray, lashed by salt and time.

The quiet surrounded her. Not total silence, but the absence of noise. It was the kind of silence that can be felt in your bones—the kind that only exists in the most remote corners of the world, where seagulls and trees speak to one another when no one is listening.

But Kassidy was listening, and there was serenity in their chittering and welcomeness to the wind in the leaves, a feeling of peace and harmony she hadn't felt in a very long time. But with it also came the reality of how alone she was. Truly, completely alone. Her hand flexed around the strap of her bag and she turned to face the cabin.

*"When you take someone with you, you bring your world,"* she said aloud, repeating her grandma's words, reminding herself to be brave. Kassidy closed her eyes, inhaling deeply. *"Go alone, that's when you find out who you really are."*

A breeze blew across her skin, as if in answer. Maybe this place was exactly where she needed to be.

She felt scared and exhilarated all at once.

She ran a hand through her hair, smoothing it down against the wind.

No cell service meant no one could call.

No pings and chimes.

No notifications.

No pressure to be available, to look a certain way, to come up with content. No work, no schedules, and no deadlines for the foreseeable future.

Yet here she was, on a dock, afraid to go inside, afraid to see what lay ahead for her, or encounter the ghost of a man she never knew.

A man they called Raymond.

The wind picked up, sending leaves blowing around her and a shiver down her spine. Kassidy stepped carefully along the dock, each footstep a hollow echo.

She set her weekend tote and the plastic grocery sack down on the front porch and wrapped her fingers around the small handle on the porch screen door.

She exhaled slowly, preparing herself as she pushed the door open. Nothing creaked the way she had imagined it would. The door opened smoothly, as if someone had oiled it, as if someone or the cabin itself had been expecting her arrival.

# Chapter 12

Kassidy walked into the cabin. The scent of wood varnish and rainforest and coffee cans enveloped her. The interior was a warm, inviting palette of earth tones and plaid cotton throw blankets. The small living room and kitchen were spotless, cared for with obvious love. A home that smelled faintly of a life lived simply, yet deeply. Not extravagant or modern like the palatial homes she'd seen along the way. This place was charming and rustic in all the right ways.

The living room and kitchen were congruous, and every piece of furniture and picture frame looked handmade from materials found on the beach or in the woods. Kass ran her hand across the smooth, polished wood of an armchair, the grain shifting like liquid amber when it caught the light. She imagined it washed up on shore, driftwood given a new purpose.

Each window peeked into the forest or framed a view of the sea, as if it had been designed that way from the start. There were no shades or blinds to obstruct the wilderness, no neighbors or streetlights or traffic noise. The whole cabin blended seamlessly into the land, not disrupting it in any way—making it as natural inside as the forest that surrounded it.

Kass took off her tall boots and set them on a small clean rug by the door. Then she walked into the kitchen, the wood floor polished and cool under foot. She turned on the faucet, relieved there was running hot and cold water.

"Not totally off the grid then," she said, and smiled at the welcome surprise.

She tested the lights—they worked too, as did the heater. "Modern amenities one. Camping zero. Civilization points for the win."

Everything seemed in perfect working order. The smoke alarm blinked its small green light, the refrigerator hummed softly, its freezer kicking out a blast of cold air. Both had been scrubbed and stocked with just enough to get by—coffee, a variety pack of tea, bread, eggs, fresh produce, a few canned goods.

Thoughtful, practical.

In the fridge, front and center, sat not one but two jars of Natural Joe's organic almond butter. She huffed out a laugh. She'd done a collaboration with the company and been paid to rave about it in a video—"A pantry must-have!" she'd said. The truth was, she hated the stuff. Dry, pasty, sticks-to-the-roof-of-your-mouth kind of awful. Apparently, someone had been paying attention.

Shaking her head, she shut the fridge and exhaled. The cabin was waiting for her to settle in, to fill the empty spaces. But she wasn't sure yet if she was meant to be here—or if she was just passing through.

She wandered through the quaint space, looking for hints of who might have lived here. She opened a few cabinets, peeked into drawers—bare, emptied of personal traces, yet not abandoned just Everything had been scrubbed clean, reset, waiting.

The kitchen drawers were stocked with the basics—a small collection of old utensils, the kind built to last—sturdy, slightly worn, their heaviness unfamiliar in her hand. Not the flimsy, disposable kind. Someone had taken the time to remove the rust and leave them behind as if they always belonged.

Even the air inside carried a strange mix of emptiness and readiness. The scent of freshly cut timber lingered from the logs stacked beside a cleaned-out fireplace. It was the smell of welcoming— as if the cabin was waiting to be lived in again.

What surrounded her on the walls, though, spoke to this being a seaman's cabin, belonging to someone who devoted their life to the salty ways. And to whales—pictures and depictions of orcas were everywhere on the walls and in the stacks of books.

Her gaze drifted to the medals arranged meticulously on the wall— insignias encased in glass, untouched by dust or time. They looked important, honorable, but their meaning was lost on her. Sacrifice? Dedication? Recognition from a world she didn't understand. Carved into the metal were bold, fluid designs—whales, ravens, and patterns— symbols of a culture and history she knew nothing about.

Kassidy picked up a small, palm-sized wood carving of an orca from a nearby shelf. It was intricate, hand-etched with a precision that made her want to examine it for hours and still, there would be more to uncover.

The eyes—deep, ancient—intelligent.

This place, this world, all of this was someone's life—a life she had no idea how to untangle or step into. She didn't even know if she should.

The hall leading to the back bedroom was narrow, when she flipped on the light, she gasped.

The entire wall was a mural—and not just any mural—a carved, magnificent map. And not the kind of art that hangs on a wall. The wall was the art. Etched with the painstaking details of the Salish Sea—its islands, islets, bays, waterways, and creeks.

Kassidy stepped closer, her fingers tracing the grooves of the wood, feeling the places that were unfamiliar to her yet right outside her window.

"Haro Strait…" she said aloud, tilting her head to read the words, "Deception Pass…" she whispered.

Then, her finger stopped. Her island. Isla Virginia. A tiny blip, barely noticeable, yet there it was. A single star marked its center, as if to say: You are here. This is where everything begins.

The main bedroom in the cabin was clean, the sheets freshly laundered. New pillows lay with tags hanging on them. At the end of the bed was a small desk and bookshelf covered with papers—charts, graphs, and what looked like genealogies and ancestry charts. Kassidy leaned over, curious, maybe she'd find her own name, or her mother's, or her grandma's. But these weren't family trees for humans.

They were matrilines.

For orcas.

Photographs, notes, pages upon pages of careful observations and names of individuals—each cataloged with meticulous detail. J Pod. K Pod. L Pod. Their births, their deaths, their movements.

Every single day was filled with notes, documented for as far as she flipped back. Every hour mattered, down to the second. Their hunting behaviors. Their calls, clicks, whistles. Who interacted with who and where. How fast they traveled and where they went. Every sighting no matter how small or large, documented in meticulous detail.

Kassidy ran her fingers across the spines of old, worn books, titles barely legible from overuse. Journals, scrapbooks, maps, ledgers, more depictions of the whales in drawings and photographs.

A chill rippled across her skin as she backed away. To care that much about something was…inspiring. But why? Why did Ray care so much about these orcas? *Who* was this man?

And…how did he die? Or maybe the most pressing question of all, why did he send her there?

The unknowing felt empty. She had so many questions and no answers at all. Not even clues. Nothing about her or her family was in that cabin. She felt like a thief. An imposter. She also felt like this man had found her at the most perfect time, and even if she didn't yet know why, he'd sent her there for a reason.

"I will find out who you were," she whispered, her voice resolute. "And why you brought me here." She looked at the photos on the walls. "These whales mattered to you. And I bet you mattered to them, too, Raymond."

Down the hall from the main bedroom was another door. When Kassidy walked in, she turned in circles at what she found. It was a dark room for developing photographs. Photos in all shapes and sizes covered the walls from floor to ceiling that were devoted to the orcas of the Salish Sea. Thousands upon thousands of photographs. Each one depicted the graceful giants—some in black and white, some in full color. And in the middle of it all, a camera.

Each photo was taken by a man who so clearly lived for and loved these beautiful creatures. She picked up a picture of a mother and calf, inspected it with her fingers, turning it in her hands. Then she picked up another, and traced her thumb along the delicate edge of the whale's fluke. Hundreds, upon hundreds, maybe thousands of pictures of dorsal fins, saddle patches, and flukes. Each one, high resolution, detailed—crisp. Taken up close, nose to nose as if he were in the water right next to them.

The orcas came alive to her in those photos. Individuals with bright eyes, unique markings, and identifying scars. Each photograph depicted some fragment of an orca—sometimes just an eye, other times a scar, or a unique marking. And every photo was labeled with a date, a number and name.

L94 Calypso
J35 Tahlequah
J27 Blackberry
J31 Tsuchi

Some were marked with a status: captured, missing, or deceased. The earliest photos dated back as far as the 1970's, but then they got fewer and fewer as the years progressed, almost disappearing all together in 2020.

As Kassidy touched the photos with her fingertips she felt a tug on her heart—the pull to know more about the whales, who they were, where they were, and what their world was like. She also had a deep desire to know more about the man behind the camera.

When she walked back into the living room, Kassidy's breath caught in her chest as she realized many of the photos were taken in the narrow channel at the end of her dock. She pressed her palms against the large window overlooking the water, as if hoping to catch a glimpse of them now.

The largest photograph on the wall was framed in thick mahogany wood, she stepped up to it, her nose almost brushing the glass as she squinted. A pod of six, their black bodies near the surface, spouts of mist in the air, and six fins stood majestic out of the water.

Her gaze drifted again from the photo to the window that framed the waterway. It was taken right there; she could see the same grouping of rocks and trees. Her chest tightened at the thought of them swimming by. Killer whales. Orcas. Wild ones.

She thought of Keelah.

She imagined what it might be like to see them swimming by—close enough to touch. Everything in her body seemed to quiver at the thought. How long would she sit on that dock and wait for a chance to see an orca? And if she did see one, would she wait for them to come back? Would she wait forever?

Something inside her shifted—like a current pulling her in, deeper.

As if an invisible thread had tied her soul to everything there—to the sea, the cabin and somehow to the orcas. Standing there, among their spirits, she felt part of something larger—a connection that felt right.

The world she thought she lived in felt insignificant compared to the vast, eternal pulse of the rolling ocean in front of her and the creatures that roamed it.

She pulled out a large leather-bound journal from the bookshelf that caught her eye. The cover was heavy, worn at the edges, as if it had passed through many hands before hers. She flipped it open to the first page. The handwriting was unmistakable. It was the same elaborate strokes as Ray's signature on the papers from Mr. Moore's office.

*August 8th, 1970*

*They came for them at dawn. The whale hunters arrived in boats, armed with explosives and nets, driving the pod into the cove. Their cries—panicked, high-pitched, desperate were haunting. The mothers swam in circles, slamming their tails, calling to their calves as the nets closed in.*

*Seven.*

*They took seven.*

*The calves were hoisted from the water. Slick bodies writhing. Eyes wide with terror. The largest female fought hard, thrashing against the net, diving deep, surfacing again with the others at her side. She would not leave her babes behind. When they hoisted the youngest calf onto the flatbed truck, she pressed herself against the netting, her breath ragged, her clicks sharp with rage and grief.*

*The men cheered as the calf was lifted away.*

*The ones left behind never stop crying. Never stop searching for the family they lost.*

Kassidy's stomach twisted, a cold dread settling deep in her bones. The words were a quiet horror pressed into ink that carved a fresh wound—raw and irreversible.

She swallowed hard and turned the page, unaware that the worst was still waiting for her.

A black and white photo.

When she looked closer, her heart broke.

A small orca, a calf, tangled in a harsh web of netting, her eye—a haunting mix of sorrow and intelligence—fear and confusion. It was laying trapped, out of water, on a flatbed truck.

A tear seeped from her eye and dropped onto the photo. Kassidy quickly wiped it away, forcing herself to look closer, and as she did, a hot flush of anger took over, and then a heavy cloak of guilt punched her square in the gut.

The label read:

L25 Qilalugaq

4 years Old

Captured August 8th, 1970, Penn Cove.

Below it was a newspaper clipping with a photo of the same small orca in a tank. The caption said: Mexico City Aquarium Welcomes Their Newest Whale, Keelah.

No. It couldn't be.

Her pulse thumped.

The name, the markings. They were the same. Maybe there was more than one Keelah? But she knew the answer in her heart—cold and undeniable. There was only one. And now, against all logic, all impossible odds, Kassidy was here, in this cabin, staring into a life devoted to saving them. And Kassidy had been the one who sold her soul to keep Keelah trapped.

A sharp, twisting nausea curled in her stomach. Guilt, shame, disbelief—she wasn't sure which hit harder. But the truth stood before her, staring back at her with dark, defeated eyes. A ghost, not of the dead, but of a magnificent creature stolen and betrayed.

Kassidy felt the burden of her complicity, and it shattered her to the core. The glossy sheen of the image couldn't hide the truth behind the tragedy. And that she was part of the machine keeping Keelah in captivity made her feel sick.

She bit her lip, tears fell down her cheeks as she felt the immensity of her regret—she should have walked away. Found a way out somehow. She knew it was wrong. And she knew she had yet to pay the debt for it. And that if her actions were keeping that orca in prison, she should have to pay for her part in it.

In that moment she felt a steady resolve. Whatever happened, whatever she lost, was nothing compared to what had been stolen from Keelah and she felt a responsibility to try and make it right.

Kassidy stared at the photo and all she could see was the cruel truth. The whale had been captured and confined and was still being paraded like a showpiece for corporate campaigns. And she played right into their hands, smiling for the cameras.

Her chest tightened, a pressure building behind her ribs as the reality of what she'd done caved in on her.

Kassidy sank into the worn armchair by the window in the living room, the journal still clutched in her arms, sobbing, mind reeling. Worse, she could feel the beginnings of a truth gnawing at her from the inside. The world would see her swimming with that orca, Keelah, and in her complicity, she was endorsing captivity.

She remembered looking into the whale's eyes, as if her spirit had been emptied out, leaving a shell of what once was free.

A deep, lonely ache crept over Kassidy thinking that Keelah was still confined with no way out.

She felt shallow, all the things that her sponsors and followers thought she was— a pretty talking head driven by money and celebrity status. But she was none of those things.

Not anymore. Never again would she be pushed around by someone else's agenda.

She didn't know how, or if it was even possible.

But she was determined to undo what she'd done, and if there was a way…set Keelah free.

# Chapter 13

Of the eight decades Virginia Karlson had walked the earth, she'd never seen anything like it. The whole town—hell, the whole world had gone mad! On her way to CostMart in Abilene, Iowa, she stopped for gas. At four dollars and seventy-six cents a gallon, it cost her over fifty bucks to top off the tank. She'd wanted one of those new electric cars that sucked less resources from the earth, but there wasn't a single charging station in Abilene.

At the grocery store, she read every ingredient on every label, grumbling about high-fructose corn syrup, GMOs, and artificial sweeteners. Even sticking to the store's perimeter was getting harder. Each trip was like walking into a new battlefield, but Virginia wasn't ready to surrender the fight to keep her body and mind in working order just yet.

Virginia pulled out her crumpled list of the dirty dozen—the twelve most pesticide-laden fruits and vegetables to avoid while everyone else mindlessly tossed food into their carts. Hell if she was going to die of breast cancer from xenoestrogens.

Gone were the days when food was fresh, water was clean, and lakes weren't polluted. Now the rivers were clogged with pharmaceuticals, the lakes smothered with algae, and even the freshwater fish were gone, replaced by weeds and invasive mussels. Greed and corruption had destroyed the whole damn world, so much that Virginia couldn't even be comfortable at the grocery store.

Her long silver hair fell forward, framing her face as Virginia peered into the fish case. Her expression alone could wither even the freshest catch. Her sharp eyes cut through the glass, scrutinizing every detail. Her forehead was etched with hard-earned wisdom, her lips curved with a wit that hadn't dulled with age—rather, time had sharpened it into a blade.

"Goddamn salmon from the Pacific. Farmed crap from Chile. Not a single fresh or wild sustainably caught fish in the whole case!" She announced, not that Virginia would eat salmon anyway.

The staff behind the counter watched with trepidation, aware of her stringent standards. Her sharp words were as predictable as her weekly visits.

She looked up at the sign above the fish counter: "We sell sustainably-sourced seafood only," she said aloud making sure everyone could hear. There were pictures of happy fishermen on small mom and pop type boats. The lies the fishing industry told hit her like a slap in the face.

"Bull. Shit," she said, her voice tearing through the hum of the store. "Farmed salmon from Chile and Norway don't come from fishing boats. Who put that sign up there? It's fraud! And that farmed Pacific salmon you have in there is the most unethical of all." She pointed a knobby finger and scoffed. "Hank, why can't you stock any actually sustainable wild-caught fish? How many times do we have to discuss this?"

"Every week, Virginia," Hank droned. "That's how many times we have to discuss this—every week." He didn't look up from behind the counter. "And every week I tell you the same thing. I don't make the purchases. I just work here and take fish out of the case for lovely ladies like yourself."

"Well, you'd sell a lot more fish to lovely ladies like myself if the marketing wasn't so unethical, and the product wasn't laden with disease. Tell that to your manager." Her voice rose, a mix of sharpness and resignation.

"I'll pass along your feedback, Ginny. Again. See you next week." Hank's tone was even, but his eyes held a familiar exhaustion.

"Thanks, Hank!" Virginia said, her voice monotone. She waved a dismissive hand over her shoulder as she walked away.

In the checkout line, the noise was enough to drive her mad. Kids crying, moms scolding, bags rattling. When had the world gotten so loud that she couldn't even hear herself think?

Iowa used to be quiet. Now it was all expansion and chemicals and noise. No one ever shut up anymore—not even at church! Virginia felt like her ears were going to bleed. She pulled two small torn pieces of cotton from her coat pocket and stuffed them into her ears. Maybe Iowa had changed too much. Maybe it was time to find somewhere with cleaner produce and water that didn't start on fire.

Virginia slid her last item across the counter, "Morning Earl, how did the rest of your night go with Margaret?" she said, as the spry elderly man bagged her groceries with the same care he'd shown for years.

Earl's thin frame hunched slightly as he leaned over the paper bags, setting in her groceries—each movement unhurried.

The wrinkles around his lips deepened as they met the ones around his eyes when he smiled. "One week ago, if you had told me that after all these years, I'd get to reconnect with my high school sweetheart, Margaret Robinson, I'd have bet my last meat raffle ticket against it."

Virginia smiled, "I guess age doesn't stop the road from turning, now does it."

Earl looked up at her, his eyes soft but knowing. "And some roads never stop winding back, now do they?" he replied quietly, his voice low, almost a whisper, almost a warning.

The words enveloped her, heavy and slow, like smoke rising from a dying fire, and for a moment, the grocery store, with its fluorescent lights and noisy customers, faded. The sound of waves, the scent of the sea...those memories came flooding back.

She forced a tight smile, murmured a quick goodbye, and hurried across the parking lot like she could outrun the memories clawing at the edges of her mind. Earl was right. Some memories never drift too far— they anchor. The past she'd long buried, the decisions she'd shoved so far down they rarely surfaced—were fighting their way back.

She threw her groceries into the trunk with more force than necessary, slamming it shut like she was trying to trap something inside. Her hands shook as she gripped the door handle, and she hurried to get into the driver seat of her Lincoln and slammed the door shut behind her. Virginia pushed the button, and all four doors locked.

She let out a ragged breath, almost panting as if she'd sprinted for miles. She was still shaking, trying to regain her composure, to push it all back down when her phone rang from her purse, jolting her into the present moment.

It was the most welcome ring tone of all—the one true joy she had left in her life.

"Kassidy," Virginia answered, her voice softening as she took the call. "I'm so glad you called, sweetheart. I just picked up groceries, would you like to come over for lunch?"

"Virginia? Can you hear me?"

The line crackled, cutting in and out.

On the other end of the call, Kassidy was hiking through brush, thorns catching at the oversized rubber boots she found in the cabin closet. She'd climbed to the tallest spot on the island and held her phone high to get two bars and call her grandma.

"I can hear you just fine. I'm not deaf. It's just a bad connection, is all." Virginia turned off her car and pulled the cotton from her ears.

"You sound perturbed, Grandma what's wrong?"

"I am perturbed," she said. "I almost had to wipe my ass with a newspaper this morning because the whole town is still hoarding toilet paper." Virginia's voice was deadpan—it was just another item on her long list of grievances. "I tore out the political section. Figured I'd use that first since all those assholes caused this mess in the first place."

"Do you need me to send Billy over? He could bring you toilet paper or anything else you need."

"No! Do not send that slicked back over manicured city boy to my house. I'll get along just fine." Her voice snapped back to its usual sharpness. "Where are you, sweetheart? Working somewhere fabulous, I hope?"

"It is pretty fabulous, Grandma." Kassidy answered, the connection still scratchy, "I wonder if you've ever heard of it. I'm on a private island. In the San Juan Islands. Off the coast of Washington. Yeah, I spent the whole morning in a little city called Friday Harbor. That ring a bell, Ginny? Or should I call you, *Isla Virginia?*"

The silence between them stretched out, dense and unyielding Kassidy spoke louder into the speaker.

"Did you hear me? I said I'm—"

"Yeah, I heard you," Virginia's voice hadn't lost its edge.

"Well?" Kassidy paused, as if waiting for a reaction. But Virginia stayed silent a moment longer, keeping their lives the same for another minute before— "Since you're clearly not recalling things or you'd be spilling your guts, here let me refresh your memory."

Virginia heard the snap of a camera. A moment later, a photo appeared—Kassidy, beautiful as ever, face still untouched by time. But that smile—it was more of a smirk, her finger aimed at the cabin behind her.

The cabin.

"Does that jog your memory, Virginia?" Kassidy added. Years of dealing with her had taught Ginny exactly what that tone meant— Kassidy was digging.

"Yes, I see the cabin," she said, as though the past had caught up to her in that single image. "If it weren't for me, you'd be using an outhouse right now."

"What?" Kassidy's voice shot through the phone. "You knew?"

A sigh and eye roll traveled across the distance. "I suppose I have some explaining to do, don't I?"

"It's true then. You knew about this place? About this man, Raymond? This island?"

"Well, of course, I knew. I just didn't think you'd ever find out." Virginia's tone was unapologetic, almost defiant.

Two thousand miles and a million questions stretched out between them. "What!? How come you didn't tell me about this, whatever this is. I can't believe you kept it from me."

"I guess I just didn't think it mattered anymore." Virginia's voice had that confident tone again. The secrets she'd kept for decades, hung between them like a dark cloud.

"Tell me what you know, Grandma." Kassidy's demand was soft, but unrelenting. "Why am I here? Who is this man, Raymond, who thinks I'm his granddaughter."

Another pause. His name, spoken aloud was enough to make her feel faint. Virginia finally conceded. "I'll tell you everything. I promise. I'll be there in two weeks. I need to eat up all these groceries I just bought before I can leave town."

"Two weeks? You're coming here? How do you—oh! Of course you know where it is. You probably lived here for God's sake."

"Don't use that tone with me, little missy, and no, I never lived there." Although, what could have been flooded back to her. There was finality in Virginia's voice. "Stock up on food and, for God's sake, make sure there's enough ass wipe. I'll call before I arrive so you can meet me on the dock. I'll need help getting out of the boat. I love you."

Kassidy scoffed.

Virginia hung up.

She leaned back in her seat, phone still clutched in her hands. Her eyes fluttered closed, and her heart raced with a mixture of dread and relief. She had known this day might come—a day when everything she'd hidden might finally float back to the surface. She pressed the phone to her chest and breathed out a long, slow exhale.

Flashes of the past—Ray, the island—flickered behind her eyes. The bitter taste of regret, mingled with excitement about going back surged through her like an electric current.

Virginia thought back to her exchange with Earl.

*Some roads never stop winding back.*

A great heaviness washed over her, sitting in her chest with the weight of all the years they'd lost. Tears came suddenly, violently, as if decades of love and regret had been bottled up, waiting for this moment to shatter the surface.

Virginia gripped the steering wheel, her body shaking as sobs tore through her, raw and unrelenting. She cried until the world outside blurred, until the sound of her own weeping was drowned out by the rhythm of the rush hour traffic. And when there were no more tears left—all she felt was the hollow ache of what could never be.

# Chapter 14

The island was a lush tapestry of mossy wonder. Springy and damp underfoot, the ground felt alive. It was a vibrant green carpet, woven with layers of fallen leaves and pine needles atop rich, loamy soil.

Kassidy paused to look down at her feet, feeling an odd sense of gratitude for the man who had left behind the oversized rubber boots and thick flannel jacket. It was almost as if the island had known she was coming, leaving her exactly what she needed to be comfortable.

Kassidy climbed down from the highest point on the island, the clumsy boots making her steps unstable. She had no clear plan in her mind, only the vague hope that befriending her neighbor might help her to survive until she figured out what to do next.

Even though the island was small, it felt immense and untamed. A rugged coastline glistened in the sunlight, scattered with broken shells. Whole forests of driftwood lay on the beach. Beside them stretched a mosaic of polished stones, each one smoothed by the relentless rhythm of the ocean. The water was calm, the waves a mere whisper—a soothing sound that made her feel connected to the land and sea around her.

Kassidy picked up a thin, smooth stone, feeling its gritty texture in her fingers before sending it skimming over the glass surface. It bounced once, twice, then disappeared, leaving behind ripples that expanded in every direction. She watched as they grew, then faded, the water returning to stillness as if nothing had disturbed it at all.

She drew in a slow breath, the cool, briny air settling something deep inside her. For the first time in what felt like forever, she wasn't bracing for anything. No phone calls. No decisions. No being shuffled around from one place to the next.

Just the rhythm of the tide, the whisper of the wind, and the silence of a place that asked nothing of her.

She didn't know if such a simple existence was for her, but at least for now, she was happy to give it a try. The quietness around her was something she'd never experienced before.

There wasn't a single other human in sight. No boats. No horns. No tourists. Only the distant call of seabirds circling and the gentle flitter of the wind in the woods around her.

Kassidy found herself mesmerized by the tranquility of it—a stillness, pure and untouched, as if she had been transported to another planet, like she'd stumbled into a place time forgot. This wasn't her world—but it was growing on her, like moss over stone.

Kassidy wove her hair into a long, thick braid as she walked along the shore. It felt good to get her damp hair off her neck and face, just like it had felt good to trade her tall boots for the oversized galoshes and her tight coat for the floppy warmth of a cozy jacket. Both were clean—but worn, their fabric softened by time, their edges frayed just enough to show they'd been well-used. Yet there was no mud caked on the soles, no lingering scent of someone she didn't know. The jacket smelled of freshly laundered soap, like someone had taken care to wash it before leaving it behind.

Where the beach ended abruptly with a large outcropping of rocks, climbing was her only option unless she dared a swim in the frigid water, which she most certainly did not. At the top of the boulders, a narrow, lightly worn trail snaked through the trees.

Kass followed it deeper into the woods where the trees towered above, creating a thick canopy that protected the island's surface. Their roots, tangled deep beneath the earth, held the foundation together and protected its secrets.

The lightly worn trail spit her out into the backyard of a palatial coastal home. The sight of it was jarring—unexpected, almost out of place. A modern luxury retreat with sleek, black-framed windows, pale yellow siding, and towering glass walls so high they competed with the surrounding trees.

Who lived here? The house was too pristine to be abandoned, too lived-in to be just a vacation home. A single chair sat on the deck, angled toward the sea, as if someone had just been there, watching the sunrise.

Kass wondered if she could see all the way to Friday Harbor from the sprawling balcony deck—maybe even beyond—to a world that felt distant, and one she was happy to keep at arm's length for now.

The entire property stood in stark contrast to the rugged beauty of the island, a jarring departure from the cabin she'd left behind. Her cabin was free of contemporary edges and modern frills—a simplicity Kassidy hadn't expected to embrace. She was familiar with modern comforts; they were the world she came from, the world she once gravitated toward. Yet now, somehow, the quaint, den-like safety of her cabin felt like…home.

Next to what was more of a pier than a dock, and moored to one side, was a white sailboat with a towering mast. On the other side, a man was securing a floatplane, its buttery yellow paint matching the color of the house. He was tying lines with the confident efficiency of a man who knew his surroundings.

Kassidy squinted, feeling a flicker of familiarity.

She raised her arm and called out, "Hello!" The wind carried her voice away. "Hello?" she called again, louder this time, cupping her hands around her mouth as she got closer. Still, he didn't hear her.

She was halfway down the dock when he finally noticed. The man with broad reflective sunglasses straightened, took off his gloves and tucked them into his back pocket.

He walked toward her, and when he removed his dark glasses, Kassidy's stomach twisted into a knot. It was him—the fisherman—from the ferry. Except now, clean-shaven and dressed in casual, well-fitted clothes, he looked like a completely different person. A completely attractive, boy-next-door-all-glowed-up-to-be-a-hottie, different person.

"Well, well…" he said with casual arrogance, and she narrowed her eyes, knowing what was coming. "Now who's stalking who?" he added with a smirk, his voice low and teasing. It was that same smugness she remembered from before—the kind that made her want to both walk away and step closer, just to engage him in a rowdy fight.

"I'm not stalking you," she shot back, crossing her arms, her defenses snapping into place. "Why would I stalk you?"

They stood eye to eye—he was tall, taller than she'd remembered. Up close, his bluish gray reflective eyes hid all traces of vulnerability.

"Well, let's see…" he said, an amused glint in his eye and eyebrows, sharp and expressive, arched as if daring her to deny the obvious. "You're standing on my dock, on a very remote island that few people ever visit, so… by my estimation, either you got a water taxi driver who's lost all sense of direction, or"—he rubbed his chin—"you're stalking me."

Kassidy swallowed hard, her skin tingling under his gaze.

His confidence was irritating, yet… so damn alluring. Like he was the kind of man who could stand up to her. But also… bow down. She hated the way it made her feel—and loved it in equal measure. It was that kind of rare intensity that makes a person feel alive, only this time, it was dialed up even higher.

"I'll have you know that *your estimation*," she exaggerated the words, "is entirely inaccurate. It seems that you, are my new tenant, since this is my island now," she retorted, planting her hands on her hips. Her words came out more defensive than she intended, but his cocky attitude pushed her buttons.

He didn't flinch, just tilted his head slightly. "Really? Your island."

"Yes. Really. My island," She repeated, trying to regain some control over the conversation.

His faint smile deepened. "Is that so."

Something in his tone was unsettling. Why did he have to be so aggravatingly calm, so sure of himself?

"Yes. That's so. Are you the only resident here?" she asked, struggling to maintain her composure. "Or is there—"

"A Mrs. Or a Mr.?" he finished her question with his eyebrow raised and a sly smirk on his face. "Nope. Just me. Just us." She felt a hot flush rush over her. "What about you? Is there—"

"A Mr. Or a Mrs.?" she finished his sentence. "No. Just me. Just us. Where's your family?" Kassidy asked.

"My family?" He lowered his chin but raised his brow. "Unless you consider the black bear, red squirrels, and occasional cougar that walks through here to be my family, aside from them, my family lives on the mainland." He made her fidget, and she rarely fidgeted.

"Bears? Cougars?" She couldn't stop herself from scanning her surroundings, her eyes darting in every direction.

He laughed softly, the sound sending a warning down her spine. "Welcome to the edge of nowhere. This is where the wild things like to hang out." His eyes sparkled as he added, "But don't worry. You're more likely to get crushed by one of these old trees falling in a storm than be eaten by a cougar. Or a bear."

Kassidy looked up, her gaze following his. She could feel the presence of the ancient trees looming around them. As if the whole island was waiting for something.

She wasn't sure if that felt comforting or terrifying.

"Oh, I was told a family lived here."

He furrowed his brow. "Like I said, it's just me. Well, just us, now, since you...how did you say you came to acquire this place?"

"My...um...relative," she said, not exactly sure how to explain it, "used to live here, but he's...gone..." she trailed off, unsure what to even say. "I'm sure you knew him, or maybe not. He might have been a recluse."

"So this is your inheritance?" he asked with an irritating smirk, as if he was in on some joke she wasn't privy to.

Her skin stood at attention. She didn't like how he always seemed one step ahead, like he was playing a game she didn't know the rules to.

"Did you know him? Raymond?" she asked, hoping to turn the conversation back in her favor.

"Of course. Ray and I were the only ones on this island for the last nine years. I knew him well."

Kassidy bit her lip, feeling her pulse quicken. "Were you...aware that he...passed?"

Something flickered in his eyes—a momentary crack in his armor, but it was gone almost as soon as it appeared.

"I wasn't." He looked down. "Did someone find him?"

She shrugged, her voice softer now. "I don't know anything about that. I just got a phone call to come out here and sign the papers for this place."

"You mean, sign papers to inherit an island from a man you didn't even know?"

The words stung more than she expected. Kassidy looked away, biting back her retort. He was right. She didn't know what the hell she was doing here. Frustrated, she stabbed back, "What makes you think I didn't know him?"

"Well, because Ray never mentioned, a relative. Not one like you. I'd have remembered."

"What's that supposed to mean? Look, if you think I'm here for money," her voice was a touch too sharp. "If that's what you're implying. I don't even want this place or know why he thought I was his granddaughter." Her words hung in the air alongside a truth she wasn't ready to admit. She shifted her weight, averting her eyes from his knowing gaze. "Honestly, I don't know why I'm here. But it's not for money."

She felt defeated, vulnerable under his gaze, like he could see right through her.

He studied her, his expression changing. "Well, I don't know what your history with Raymond was, he never mentioned having a granddaughter. But, if Ray wanted you to have this place, then I know he wouldn't want you to feel lost here. He'd want you to feel at home."

Kassidy looked at him, really looked at him this time. He wasn't as smug now, not as guarded.

"How do you know that's what he'd want?"

"Because he practically raised me. I consider myself like his son, or his grandson, I guess would be more accurate."

"I thought you said you'd been here nine years."

"I said I'd been alone here with Ray, on this island, for nine years. Before that, my family lived here. I grew up here. When everyone else wanted to move away, I bought the place, tore down the old house and put up my own."

Kassidy glanced back at his house. It was almost as magnificent as the male specimen that lived in it—the man that this…Raymond, had practically raised. The only thing about any of this that made sense was that her grandma must have been hiding a very big secret.

"Well, maybe you can tell me more about Raymond sometime. And…I'm sorry. For your loss."

He smiled, this time genuinely. "Thank you. And, I'd like that."

He offered his hand. "Shephard Maddox. Call me Shep."

The warmth of his palm against hers felt electric, and they were close enough she could smell him again—airy and woodsy.

"Kassidy Karlson." She introduced herself, and the current that passed between their hands heated up. Neither spoke another word but just stood there staring, as if they both knew something had brought them together in that place.

Kassidy pulled her hand away first, not wanting to linger in the tension that had begun to boil over.

"I'd better get back before I get mauled by that bear, or cougar, or red squirrel of yours," she said, forcing a smile but genuinely scared of being caught there after dark. Though she did wonder if she got lost, would he come looking for her? Or invite her over?

She shook off the thought. That's not why she was there and getting involved with a tenant was never a good idea. It was like dating your boss or your next-door neighbor—everyone knows that never ends well.

Shephard nodded toward the trail. "Well, if you need anything, just give a shout. You're not stranded unless you want to be."

His words felt comforting. Exactly what she needed to hear. Kassidy started walking back toward the trail she'd come from, her heart still racing, unsure if it was from the exercise or the steamy man she'd met and was trapped on that island with.

"It's nice to see a new face around here," Shephard called after her, a teasing edge to his voice. "Raymond wasn't nearly as pretty to look at."

She stopped and turned, unable to stop herself from smiling, despite her better judgment.

"Is that why you were stalking me on the ferry?"

He grinned. "That's exactly why I was stalking you on the ferry."

# Chapter 15

By the time she was back at her cabin, a wet mist clung to Kassidy's hair, and soaked through her clothes as she trudged through the dense forest. The dampness that kept the island lush and green also sent shivers deep into her bones.

The only warm thing she had to wear was her memory—the intensity of Shep's gaze, the alluring way he smiled, and the heat that sizzled between them. Better still, by the looks of it, he didn't need a trophy, he already had money and was handsome enough to get any woman he wanted, so his flirting must have been genuine.

The connection she felt to him was puzzling. It was a strange magnetism that caught her completely off guard and defied explanation. If he were there, she'd want nothing more than to be closer to him. And it wasn't just attraction; it was something…more. It was a spark that came out of the darkness that she couldn't quite explain.

Inside, she peeled off her wet clothes, stripped down to her bra and underwear, and draped her sopping garments over the kitchen chair. A chill brushed against her exposed skin. She pulled a red plaid throw from the back of the couch and wrapped it around herself.

Kassidy crouched in front of the fireplace, eyeing the neatly stacked logs. She'd seen people do this before—kindling, logs, fire—but standing in a circle around a bonfire in the middle of a farm field was not the same as starting one from scratch in a damp ocean environment. She grabbed a log, set it in the hearth like she knew what she was doing, then stuffed some crumpled paper underneath.

With a flick of the lighter, a tiny flame lit the edges, curling the paper into fragile black ribbons. Encouraged, she blew on it gently— only to snuff it out completely.

She groaned, tossed in more paper, and tried again, this time with more gusto. A flicker, a hopeful crackle—then nothing but the faint scent of burning ink.

For ten more minutes, she fed it more paper, adjusted the logs, and muttered curses under her breath. But the fire refused to cooperate, and the wood sat there smug, daring her to keep trying.

She sat back on her heels, arms crossed.

"Screw it," she muttered, pushing herself to her feet.

The fire could win.

After turning up the thermostat, she sank into the cushions, knees tucked tightly to her chest.

The storm outside was growing louder. The wind howled through the trees as though the forest itself had come to life. Her stomach cramped with hunger, but exhaustion forced her to lay down and close her eyes. She couldn't think about the man on the other side of the island—*her island*. She couldn't think about any of it now that her body ached with exhaustion, and her mind needed a break.

When the shivers subsided, she drifted into an unplanned, deep sleep. The last thing she saw before closing her eyes were the photos of orcas adorning the walls around her.

A sharp clap of thunder jolted her awake. Disoriented, and unsure of how long she'd been asleep, she sat straight up. Silver flashes of lightning revealed the churning sea and white cresting waves crashing over the dock.

The cabin was pitch black, the power had gone out, and the heat no longer blew from the black rustic stove in the corner. The storm outside was roaring even louder than it had when she fell asleep.

The scratch of branches on the outside walls sounded like the claws of an angry beast, and the thunder rattled the windows as if it were trying to break inside. Every shadow was sharper in the sudden dark, each sound more ominous and unfamiliar.

Kass hugged her knees and wrapped the blanket tighter around herself. She didn't want to stand up and risk losing what little heat she had. The night outside the picture window was the blackest black. It was the kind of darkness found only in the heart of a forest or in the middle of the sea—an impenetrable wall of darkness that made her wish the adventure was over.

Kassidy nearly jumped out of her skin, letting out a loud gasp when she heard a knock.

*Bang. Bang. Bang.*

"It's me, Shephard!" His voice was muffled by the storm. "You okay in there?"

Relief flooded in but was quickly followed by a self-conscious jolt. She was half-naked beneath the blanket. She rushed to the door, holding the soft threads tightly against her chest as the wind thrashed through the trees outside.

When she opened the door, Shephard stood there, soaked all the way through, his wet hair in wild tangles, rain dripping off the stubble along his chin. The storm illuminated him in flashes, his rugged features caught in the flickering light.

It was hard to ignore how his water-soaked shirt clung to every muscle in his torso, and the casual confident way he carried himself despite the storm, as if he didn't even need, or bother to put on a jacket, he just came rushing over.

His eyes roamed briefly over the blanket she clutched. "Power's out. I'm not sure what Ray has over here for a generator, so I thought I'd check on you. I figured you might need a flashlight." He looked around her to the blackness of the cabin. "Or heat. How come you didn't light a fire?"

She scowled, then shivered and as if on cue, her stomach growled. "Hungry?" he added, with a grin. "I've got plenty of food back at my place. You're welcome to come over and ride out the storm with me."

"How long until the power comes back on?" Kassidy asked, teeth chattering. She knew full well she was going with him and thank God he came to get her, but she needed to play a little hard to get.

A chill crept in from below as she repositioned her blanket and stepped aside making room for him to come in.

Shephard was dripping water from his arms as he closed the door behind him, trapping them in the intimate darkness of the small foyer. She could feel the heat coming off his body. The way he carried himself with such confidence made her acutely aware of her own vulnerability. She had never been the type to rely on someone else, especially not a man she barely knew. But under the circumstances…

"Could be a few hours…or days," he said, and she'd almost forgotten the question. His eyes locked onto hers. Intention hovering beneath the surface. "I could make dinner while you use the steam shower. And I have plenty of bedrooms. I promise to be a gentleman."

*Now why'd he have to go and ruin the fantasy.*

"That sounds…" Her teeth chattered and the wind rattled the screen door again, as if playing his wingman.

Then her better sense kicked in, telling her to keep her distance. She was trapped on this island with a stranger she barely knew. She should be careful. Only…there was something about Shep. He made her feel safer than she should.

She swallowed. "A steam shower?" The thought alone was enough to make her toes ache with longing.

She shivered, more from exhaustion than anything else, and glanced toward the cold dead fireplace.

This wasn't about him.

It wasn't about the way he nodded, or how his slow, easy grin sent a flicker of heat through her chilled body. This was about practicality. Warm water, real heat, a chance to actually thaw out.

She exhaled, tucking away whatever part of her that had hesitated. "Count me in," she said. "I'll get dressed."

She turned away, heading toward the pile of clothes she had discarded earlier. Her mind reeled. There was no denying the attraction she felt whenever Shephard was around. There was also no denying that nagging feeling that nothing about him, or how she got there, was as straight forward as it seemed.

She slipped into her damp jeans, the fabric clinging to her legs, acutely aware of Shep's presence in the room. His voice broke through the silence as she struggled to pull her damp shirt over her head.

"Need help?"

Kass raised an eyebrow and gave him a look before yanking it all the way down. She slid her feet into oversized rain boots without responding. "I was just trying to be helpful," Shep said with a chuckle, hands raised in mock surrender. But his eyes followed her as she moved, making her heart beat faster than she cared to admit.

Shephard held open a rain slicker from Ray's closet. It smelled faintly of wood smoke when she slipped it on. Their hands brushed for the briefest moment on her shoulders, making her pause.

"Stay close," he said, as they stepped onto the porch.

And she did. Too close.

As they moved through the trees, Kassidy practically glued herself to him as the storm raged around them. When a flash of lightning cracked above, she instinctively grabbed the back of his shirt, clutching it tight. He stopped and without a word, reached back to take her hand in his. His palm was warm despite the rain, his grip strong and reassuring and he didn't let go.

They moved together along the narrow trail. He guided her over fallen branches and around slick patches of mud, as if he were leading her in a dance. Every time thunder boomed, she squeezed his hand a little tighter from the sudden quake, and he pulled her a little closer. It was a dance in which both partners instinctively knew the moves.

Being led by capable hands was a rare and comforting feeling, and she couldn't get enough. Shephard's hands were the kind you'd reach for in the dark—when your world was ending.

When they reached the edge of the forest, Shep's house was glowing from the inside, its lights a beacon of safety. Everything about him felt solid and unwavering—like he could hold back the storm.

When they stepped inside, the world went quiet, the frenzy of the storm fading into a soft hum beyond the watertight walls. Shephard sealed the door behind them, locking out the rain and wind. His home seemed to envelop her, the same way his arms had when he caught her on the ferry. Ever since she'd arrived in that strange new place, she felt like her world had been turned upside down. But with him, now, she felt both at ease and alive.

"I see you like to live modestly," her voice was low, teasing as she appraised the spacious home. The place was immaculate and breathtaking all at once. The sounds of the wind and rain and tempest sea gave way to a comforting silence, and a soothing wave of warmth that reverberated through the house.

"If I couldn't see the storm, I wouldn't know there was one at all. How do you build a house of glass that doesn't let in any sound?" she asked, spinning around.

Shephard gave her a subtle, teasing smile. "Tempered glass. Keeps me sheltered I guess."

She watched him pull off his soaked shirt, the fabric clinging stubbornly to his muscled frame. It was impossible not to notice how sculpted he was, like the rugged landscape around them had chiseled him into shape. She quickly averted her eyes from his ruffled hair and bare torso, but her mind clung to the image.

"Sheltered from what," Kassidy laughed. "Armageddon?"

His eyes held hers. "It wouldn't be the end of the world to be trapped out here. At least not now."

Kassidy didn't look away, though something warm rose up inside of her. Shep moved past her, his arm grazing hers, sending a jolt through her. Kassidy's pulse quickened, but she refused to let him see how easily he unraveled her composure.

"Come on, I'll show you the steam shower," he said, nodding toward the open stairs with a smirk that left her wondering if he already knew how much he unraveled her.

He was definitely not the stinky homeless fisherman she thought he was. This man was more like an adventure athlete who lived in an isolated luxury wilderness.

Kassidy followed him as they climbed the stairs, her eyes drawn to the way his jeans hugged his narrow waist—his every step a reminder of how effortlessly fit he was.

"Guest room's yours." He nodded toward an open bedroom door. "But feel free to grab whatever you need from my bedroom closet. It's next to the steam shower. This way."

Shephard led her through his spacious bedroom to the master bath and turned on the lights. It was a sanctuary of sleek elegance, with floor-to-ceiling charcoal tiles that gleamed under the soft lighting, each surface as smooth as polished stone. The steam shower itself was like something out of a dream—spacious, with tiers of stadium-style seating built into the walls. A waterfall showerhead hung in the center, suspended like a raincloud, releasing a cascade of water so soft it looked like liquid silk when he turned it on.

Shephard flicked a switch, and the hiss of steam began to fill the air. The scent of eucalyptus mingled with the warmth, turning the space into a sultry private oasis.

Kass closed her eyes, inhaling the subtle sweetness of mint and cedar, and the faintest hint of…him. When she opened them, she glanced over her shoulder—and there he was. Hair damp, chest bare, his gaze unwavering and unapologetic as it locked onto hers.

She should have felt hesitation—this was a strange man, after all, and she was about to strip down in his shower. But she didn't feel any trepidation. Instead, the thought sent a thrill through her. Whether she got in that steam shower with or without him, she wasn't sure which option she wanted more.

He stepped back, giving her space, but the curve of his grin lingered. His eyes glanced to the shower controls.

"If you like it extra hot"—he murmured, his voice low and intimate—"adjust the temperature here."

She nodded, but his words barely registered as the steam began to rise, curling between them like a living thing.

"And if you need a cold shower"—his hand moved to another control, his fingers brushing over the knobs with practiced ease—"that's here."

Water trickled down his arm as he demonstrated, the droplets carving paths over his torso. Her gaze followed their descent, unwilling, or perhaps unable, to look away. The air grew heavier, thick with steam and the sharp, clean scent of cedar.

Heat enveloped her, but she couldn't tell if it was from the water or his proximity. He stood so close that his presence was as tangible as the water swirling in the air around them.

"There, you're all set," he said and stepped aside, yet she wished he hadn't. She felt a pulsing between them in all the right places. "Take all the time you need. I'll get started on some dinner."

Kassidy held his gaze, refusing to be the one to look away.

"Thank you," she said softly. "I'd be freezing my ass off right now if you hadn't come."

"My pleasure," he nodded, as though acknowledging some unspoken truth. "Wouldn't have been very hospitable of me to leave you over there alone, in the cold and dark. I don't get many visitors out here. It's isolating sometimes. So, yeah, it's my pleasure to make sure you're comfortable and have the necessary accommodations."

"Steam shower? Float plane?" she asked, arching a brow. "Those are your necessary accommodations?"

"I don't have many…pleasures. So yes, in my world, those things are necessary," his voice dipped, carrying a weight that lingered in the space between them.

Was he saying what she thought he was saying? She couldn't be sure. He was very mysterious and secretive.

Then, with a final glance, he stepped out, turned the lock from the inside, and pulled the door shut, effectively locking himself out.

She slouched against the wall, exhaling disappointment. Yet she knew putting some space, and a locked door, between them was for the best. She hadn't even stepped into the shower yet, and already she was starting to think that cold water feature might be necessary.

Kass slipped out of her damp clothes and stepped into the steam shower, letting the heat pour over her like a sultry, fragrant embrace. It was pure, indulgent heaven—except for the fact the intoxicating man downstairs wasn't in it with her.

How, on this planet of infinite possibilities, had she ended up in this secluded paradise with the most breathtaking specimen of a man she'd ever laid eyes on? The whole situation felt too perfectly orchestrated to be mere coincidence. Something deeper was at play, she was sure of it—some unseen force in the universe pulling strings.

# Chapter 16

Kassidy walked down the stairs wrapped in Shephard's world. His oversized sweatshirt swallowed her frame, stopping above her knees, and a pair of his shorts hung loose over her thighs. The soft fabric hugged her like a second skin and carried the faintest trace of his scent. She was glad they'd left in such a haste that she didn't have time to grab her overnight bag.

She'd come from his closet, his shower, his bedroom—all of it should have felt foreign. Instead, she felt like she'd stepped into a cocoon where she belonged, every part of his home an unspoken invitation to stay.

As she reached the bottom step, her eyes swept across the open design that seemed to invite the wilderness in through floor-to-ceiling windows. Earthy tones, indoor plants, and art pieces that were a distinctive style she recognized but couldn't name—bold red, black and white tribal depictions of animals from the land and sea adorned his living space.

The whole place was welcoming and masculine—the reflection of a man's quiet strength, of his deep connection to the land.

"I hope you're hungry?" Shep's voice carried from the kitchen. She turned to see him rummaging through the fridge, his movements unhurried and self-assured.

"Starving," she admitted, taking a seat at the counter, and watching him hustle about.

Her gaze lingered on him, making her stomach flutter in ways that had nothing to do with hunger.

"I hope you like grilled cheese," he teased, holding up a loaf of bread and flashing a grin that could melt a steel heart. His eyes flicked down to her legs, where his shirt skimmed just above her knees. "My shirt looks good on you, by the way."

Her cheeks warmed, but she folded her arms across her chest. "Flattery and grilled cheese? Are you always this prepared?"

He chuckled. The sound was low and warm as he set a pan on the stove. "Had I known I was having company, I would've prepared better food and flattery. Here's to hoping the steam shower and full wine cellar make up for my lack of dinner choices and anywhere else I'm lacking."

"Works for me," she said, popping a grape into her mouth from the tray he'd set out. "I'm a red gal. How about you?"

He reached for the bottle of red.

"I'm a red guy."

He held it up in a playful presentation before uncorking it with an easy twist of his wrist. As he poured two glasses, the faint aroma of chocolate and melted butter filled her nose.

"To new adventures," he said, holding his glass up for a toast.

"And new friends," she added, then sipped her wine as his eyes lingered on hers much longer than necessary.

"So," Shep said, flipping the sandwiches. "Do you really believe you're Ray's granddaughter? It's not that I doubt you—it's just surprising. He never mentioned family."

Kassidy hesitated. The question was on her mind too. "Honestly? I don't know. I don't even know who Raymond is. Or was. Other than he clearly likes whales."

"Orcas," he corrected. "Technically, they're dolphins. Not whales at all."

Kassidy smiled, remembering when she'd told Billy the same thing. She set her glass down and leaned her elbows on the counter.

"This whole thing has been the strangest experience of my life. One day I was working, then I got a phone call, and the next thing I know, I'm on a boat heading to this island. And now I'm here…with you. I don't know what to think."

"Maybe it's *Maq*?" he offered, lips curving into a smile that made her pulse quicken. She furrowed, not understanding. His intense eyes met hers and he explained. "*Maq* or *Maqluna* means fate. To the Coast KaWaltish people anyway."

"Is that what this style of artwork is?" She glanced over her shoulder, recognizing the name now. "On your walls. KaWaltish."

"It is." He smiled. "It's everywhere in the islands. So, do you believe in *Maq*?"

"Maybe." She picked up a cracker from the tray. "Or maybe all this is just a mistake. A case of mistaken identity. Maybe I'm not who he thinks I am, and somehow, I've stumbled into the biggest misunderstanding of my life."

Shep turned to face her, pressing his palms against the counter. The movement was casual, but his immense presence felt intentional.

"Ray didn't make mistakes," he said, his tone resolute. "He was meticulous like that. Detailed. Which is why I find it strange that he never mentioned you. I didn't even know he had a child, let alone a grandchild."

Kassidy swallowed. "He doesn't—at least not anymore. My mother died. And I never knew who my father was. My grandparents raised me. So, if Ray is my biological grandfather, I don't even know which side that would be on. But I have a stinking suspicion my grandma Virginia, does."

"Virginia?"

Kassidy pressed her lips together, her eyes narrowing as she gave a small nod, confirming.

"That does seem awfully coincidental. And I'm sorry," he said quietly. "About your mother."

"Thank you, but it's okay. I never knew her. And my grandparents were great parents, except for the whole *family-I-never-told-you-about* thing. That is, if this Ray is my family. I'll know soon enough. My grandma will be here in two weeks, and I intend to get the truth out of her even if I have to tie her up with her neck scarf."

"She'll be here in two weeks?" he asked, a note of something unreadable creeping into his tone. "You're sticking around? What are you going to do on this mostly deserted island for two weeks?"

She didn't know if there was anything more in his question, but she sure wasn't going to tell him what crossed her mind. At least, not yet.

"Stare at the water. Read through Ray's journals about the dolphin whales. I don't know. I've never had two weeks off to do nothing before. And considering the location, I don't exactly have a way of getting around. What do you suggest I do?"

The air between them crackled with an unspoken current as if one wrong move would set everything ablaze. She wondered if she was imagining the pull between them—or if he was feeling it too. She swore she could almost hear his heart beating. The way his eyes locked onto hers, the way his body hovered a little too close—no, he was definitely feeling it too.

"I know someone who has multiple modes of transportation and he'd be happy to show you around for two weeks."

"Oh, really? And who is this intermodal chauffeur? Anyone I can trust?" she teased, though her voice caught slightly when he moved around the counter, closing the space between them.

Now standing in front of her, his proximity caught her off guard. Words caught in her throat. She wasn't used to someone being so confident with her. Not like this.

"After you fell into my arms on the ferry," his voice dropped to a near whisper. "I couldn't stop thinking about you. And then, you showed up here. On this lonely island. That *almost* no one even knows about. If that's not *Maq*. I don't know what is. So, if you'd have me. It would be my pleasure to chauffeur you around these islands for the next two weeks. Or however long you'd like to stay."

Her lips parted, a smile teasing at the corners. "So *you* believe in fate? In destiny?" she asked him.

Shephard's gaze lingered on her as he swirled his glass. "Yes. I do," he said, his voice self-assured. "But I also believe that it takes courage—real courage—to reach out, seize it, and make it yours." Clearly this man had courage. But...did she? She wasn't so sure.

"I take it you don't believe that we're guided in the direction we're meant to be?"

"I don't know." She shrugged.

"What would it take to convince you?" He inched closer, eyes lingering on her in a way that made her start to sweat.

"I don't know that either. I guess I'll just...know when I feel it."

His gaze dropped to her lips, the tension between them reaching a breaking point. "I believe that something guided you here. To me."

His bold, brazen words made her heart hammer in her chest. He was so forward. It made her nervous. Yet she couldn't help but love every second of it.

"You're really…" she began, an attempt to stall, and play hard to get. But before she could finish, he leaned in, closing the space between them. Then he paused, giving her time to pull away.

She didn't. The faint smell of wine lingered between them. The magnetism between them was intense. It was something she'd never felt, not even close.

The smell of burning grilled cheese tore his attention before their lips could move any closer. While he dealt with the charred dinner, she took the moment to catch her breath, straighten her face, and take a quick sip of courage. She was a mess. He made her a mess. A total smitten, gushing mess.

Shep held up the burned bread, smoke billowing from the pan and they laughed together. About the food. About their almost kiss. About the fate of it all.

Then the fire alarm went off and they laughed even harder.

After silencing the sharp beeping and rummaging through the pantry for not burnt food, Shephard returned with a tray of snacks piled high. They settled together on the sofa beneath a shared blanket, their fingers touching as they reached for food and sipped another glass of wine. The easy conversation, the quiet hum of contentment between them—it felt effortless. It was after midnight, but she felt like she'd just arrived. And like she never wanted to leave.

"Are you tired? Do you want to go to sleep soon? I promise that I'll try not to stalk you while you're sleeping."

She moved their snack tray aside, kicked her bare legs across his, and sighed dramatically as she reclined on the sofa. "Well, now I definitely won't be able to fall asleep." She narrowed her eyes at him, but her smirk gave her away. "If I catch you standing over me with a flashlight, we're done."

"Same," he said. He smirked, then rubbed his hand across her leg, lighting her skin on fire. "I'm starting to wonder if Ray sent you out here for a reason," Shephard said. "And that maybe he knew what he was doing after all."

"Why do you say that?"

"Well, he was always trying to play matchmaker and find someone suitable for me." The mature wrinkles around the edges of his mouth curved upward. "He just wanted to see me happy, so I tried to go along with it. But he really didn't know many people, so his matches were...*off.* He was a bit of a recluse. But not to me. To me, he was family." There was sadness in his voice.

"Did anyone ever come to visit him out here?" Kass was fishing. There was no way this island was named Virginia by coincidence, and Kass was going to be ready if her grandma tried to hide anything.

"None that I ever saw. But my father did once. Said he saw a woman stay with Ray for a week. One time. After she left, no one ever saw her come back. I figured Ray's love life was never my business, and if he wanted me to know about someone, he'd have told me. He seemed happy enough, mostly. Ray was private—he spent all his time on the island or in his boat. And you've seen his obsession."

"How could I miss it. It's sweet. Endearing."

"It isn't just him. It's a national pastime around here. The whales are all anyone talks about."

"Orcas, you mean. They're dolphins really, but who's counting." She mock teased him, and he tightened all his fingers around her thigh in a playful squeeze.

"Ever since I was a kid, people have been going to battle over the orcas. Some places fight over borders or politics, but around here, it's the killer whales. My biological grandfather called them the Orcatics."

"And that was Ray? An Orcatic?"

"No, Ray wasn't crazy. He knew you couldn't save something by enslaving it or putting it on display. He revered them, wanted to protect them. He understood that the best way to help them wasn't through control, but through respect—by leaving them wild and protecting their habitat. Ray believed in policy and science to save them. He spent thousands of volunteer hours documenting them, tracking them, submitting his data to try to persuade officials to expand their protections. He thought—maybe even believed—it would be enough to make a difference, to pass real laws that protected their water and food supply."

"You make it sound hopeless."

"The work he did was critical. But, documenting them won't bring them back. Or save the few that are left if real laws can't be passed."

"Sounds complicated."

Something in him changed when she said it—like it was the truest thing anyone had ever said.

"Yeah, the kind of complicated that ruins lives, wrecks families, and leaves nothing but fallout. A journalist came out here once, did a story on what Ray was doing and said there was no one on the planet with more extensive notes on those whales than him. If anyone could find a way to save them, it was him. But he couldn't. Even after their numbers recovered for a while. It was like he knew what was going to happen before anyone else did. And he was right."

"What happened?"

Shephard sat up, his voice dropping down. "They're going extinct. Only a few individuals are left. And no one has seen them in quite some time. They might already be gone."

Kassidy swallowed hard, trying to wrap her head around the issues and the new information about Ray.

About what he loved and tried to save.

She couldn't shake the feeling that the island held more secrets than she'd ever have time to uncover. And Shep? The way he spoke about Ray and the orcas, it was like they were in a secret club and knew things others couldn't understand.

"If you stay in the islands long enough, you'll catch it too, you know," he said.

"Catch what?"

"Orca fever. Everyone who spends enough time here comes down with it and lands on one side or the other. Whale politics is a religion out here."

"You sound annoyed by it." He was too polished—almost—rehearsed.

"No, I'm just used to it. You will be too. And if people aren't talking about the whales, they're talking about the salmon."

Kassidy furrowed her brow. Whales? Salmon? She knew nothing about any of it.

Shephard exhaled, his voice taking on a different tone, like saying it out loud was its own kind of release. "Ray knew everything about the salmon, too. Where they were. Where they weren't. He knew every inch of these waters and river systems. Sometimes he'd sleep on his boat all night. Spend all weekend on the water."

He paused, staring past her, like he could still see Ray out there. "There is so much coastline in the islands. More than one person could explore in their lifetime." He shook his head and laughed. "Except for Ray. I believe he walked every beach. Explored every cove. There was something profound in his connection to the land and water. He knew every inch of every island in this sea."

"That explains the map."

"You saw the map?"

"How could I miss it? And it's not just a map. It's the most incredible hand carved mural on the planet."

"He was talented. And he had a lot of time to perfect his craft, seeing how I was his only family."

Kassidy hesitated. She hadn't fully grasped it until now—Shephard had lost someone close. A grandfather. Family. She knew what that felt like. The quiet, hollow space grief left behind. She had lost a father and a grandfather, too. No matter how complicated the relationships had been, that kind of absence settled into a person, shaping them in ways they didn't always see.

"I'm sorry he's gone."

Shephard's jaw tightened for half a second—barely noticeable, but enough. "Yeah…gone."

The storm outside softened into a gentle lull, but a charged atmosphere lingered between them, pulsing quietly beneath the surface. Kassidy could feel his attention on her, the quiet magnetism that drew her to him. Shep's hand rested lightly on hers, his thumb tracing slow, circles against her skin.

The touch sent a spark coursing through her. She loved everything about how he was touching her—so deliberate, so tender. His confidence and maturity made every gesture feel meaningful, every glance thoughtful—as though she were the only thing in the world that mattered. Every moment with him left her craving more.

Kassidy froze. She held her breath as she noticed something peeking out from the built-in cabinet on the wall.

"What is that?" she asked, pointing toward what looked suspiciously like a woman's head mounted on a stick.

Shep followed her gaze then laughed a hearty laugh. "It's a braiding doll. My niece comes out here sometimes. She loves braiding hair, and since there's not much else to do, she'll spend hours on it—watching videos, learning all these crazy intricate braids. She even sends me videos of her progress and asks me to practice."

Kassidy raised an eyebrow, amused as he continued.

"There was one video she sent me a while back," he said, his grin turning sly. "This gorgeous woman was doing a fishtail braid tutorial—looked just like you, now that I think about it." He rubbed his chin and narrowed his eyes. "She had these amazing pouty lips, sultry eyes, and a smile that could get a man like me in a lot of trouble."

Kassidy's heart skipped, and she scoffed, her cheeks flushing. She slapped him on the shoulder.

"You knew!?" she accused, her tone part disbelief, part laughter.

He smiled like a man holding all the cards. "Of course, I knew. It took me a while, but yeah. That's why I kept staring at you on the ferry. I couldn't figure out why you seemed so familiar, and then it hit me. After that, I *had* to meet the woman who weaved such an amazing fishtail braid. I was going to ask if I could take my photo with you. You know, for my niece, but then, well, you didn't seem very interested."

Kassidy laughed, shaking her head. "I should have known."

"Yes, you should have—seeing as you're famous and all."

Still smiling, Shep stood and walked to the cabinet, retrieving the doll head.

He clutched it to his chest like a football as he returned to her.

"Kassidy, meet Ginger," he said, presenting the head with a dramatic flourish. The doll's face was smudged with what looked like Sharpie residue, the front of its hair sporting a horrendous bang trim that told the story of a child's early experiments with scissors.

He set the doll down on the coffee table, then lowered himself to sit on the floor in front of it, patting the seat next to him.

"My niece, Sophie, is *obsessed* with your videos. She'd absolutely kill me if she knew you were here, and I didn't ask you to teach me how to do that killer fishtail braid. Though," he added with a teasing smirk, "she's probably a little young for the boob tape tutorials."

Kassidy's cheeks warmed with a mixture of embarrassment and laughter. "Hey, boob tape pays the bills."

Shep raised a hand in mock surrender. "No judgment here. Clearly, you've done well for yourself."

The mention of her work brought a fleeting pang of guilt and regret, but she pushed it aside. She was having too much fun with Shep to let her pain ruin the moment.

"Think you could give me a private lesson?" Shep asked, combing through the doll's red plastic hair with his thick fingers.

Kassidy slid off the couch to sit beside him on the floor, the whole right side of her body brushing against his. They both stared at the doll's lopsided bangs.

"I don't know. Can you afford my hourly?"

"Probably not," he replied, his smirk widening. "What do you say we trade? Hour for hour?"

"Depends," she said, arching a brow. "What do you have to trade me?"

"Well…" He cleared his throat. "I have plenty of skills I think you'd find useful." She had no doubt he meant it. "First. Have you ever been in a floatplane?"

Kassidy shook her head, a spark of curiosity slipping past her defenses. "Is it safe?"

"With me, it is," Shephard said, his tone intentional. Her heart skipped a beat as he leaned a fraction closer. "I could be your personal tour guide," he continued, his sly grin softening into something more sincere. "Among other things. We can work out those details later. But you'll have to trade me, hour for hour. You teach me how to braid, and I'll take you up, out on the water, and anywhere else you want to go."

It wasn't just about the plane ride, and they both knew it. Kassidy felt the pull in his words—the unspoken invitation to something deeper, something she wanted to embrace. This man, this place, this island—*her* island—it all felt too surreal, too good to be true. Yet, here he was, tempting her and she was beginning to wonder why, or if, she could resist.

Her gaze lifted to his, their faces inches apart. The world seemed to shrink, leaving only the warmth of his breath, the intensity of his eyes, and the charged space between them.

Shephard reached out, cradling her face in his hand, his thumb brushing softly against her cheek. Her pulse quickened, her breath catching as he leaned in.

But instead of kissing her, his lips grazed her cheek, lingering long enough to leave her breathless and aching for more.

Then, as if nothing had happened, he turned his attention back to the doll, his fingers awkwardly separating its hair. "I'm a pretty slow learner when it comes to this stuff."

"Give me that." Kassidy grabbed Ginger, setting the doll in front of her with mock exasperation.

Her fingers moved deftly through the plastic strands, twisting and weaving as she explained each step. Shep watched her—not her hands, but her face—her eyes—and he stared at her lips. The air between them was electric, unspoken tension weaving through the occasional brush of their hands, and playful bump of their shoulders.

When Shep finished his first attempt at the braid, they both stared at it in silence before bursting into laughter.

"It's not that bad," he defended.

"Yes, it is. It's terrible," she said with a grin. "Good thing I've got some time off. You're going to need serious tutoring."

An accidental yawn overtook her, reminding her how late it was and how this had been the longest, and most adventurous day of her life. "I think I need to get some sleep. Walk me to my room?"

He nodded, though the warmth of his earlier touch still lingered on her skin, the pulse between them unbroken, only deepened.

Outside the guest bedroom door, Shep paused, his hand resting on the doorframe above her head as he leaned in.

"Can I kiss you goodnight?"

Then he waited.

Kassidy nodded, holding her breath.

He closed the space between them, giving her every chance to change her mind. No way was she going to change her mind. His fingertips skimmed along her jaw, a light, lingering touch that sent a shiver down her spine. When his lips met hers, it wasn't rushed. It wasn't demanding. It was a slow unraveling, a quiet exploration, the kind of kiss that asked as much as it gave.

His breath was warm, steady, as he tilted his head slightly, deepening the kiss just enough to send a slow ache into her chest. Her fingers curled against his shirt, not quite holding him there, but not letting him go either.

When he finally drew back, his lips lingered a moment longer, as if reluctant to leave.

"Goodnight, Kassidy Karlson," he murmured, his mouth curving into a smile that promised so much more. "I can't wait to take you places."

Kassidy forced herself to turn away but everything in her was screaming to clutch on to this man and never let go. She couldn't wait to go with him, to see where this might lead. Two whole weeks of adventures with Shephard. She'd need that cold shower function if things kept up like this.

A shadow lingered in the back of her mind as she closed her eyes that night—she couldn't shake the feeling that Shephard, this island, and everything she'd stumbled into were just the surface of a tangle of secrets. Secrets she was drawn there to uncover.

# Chapter 17

That night, she dreamed of orcas—wild ones swimming free. And she dreamed of the caged one too, her dark eyes searching for answers Kassidy didn't have.

And she dreamed of the man with sea-water-colored eyes. The one who had kissed her last night. She felt the phantom press of his lips even now, lingering like salt on her skin.

Kassidy slid out of the oversized bed and wrapped herself in a plush, sage green blanket that lay on the foot of the bed. She walked to the sliding glass doors overlooking the calm sea and stepped outside. It was hard to believe there had been a raging storm the night before. From the guest room balcony, she saw Shephard in the front yard, gathering the large branches that had broken off of the trees. The earth was waterlogged, puddles reflecting the pale morning light, struggling to absorb the remnants of the storm.

The early morning air, damp with the scent of fresh rain and wet earth, mingled with the mist off the Salish Sea. Everything was alive, as though the storm had left the plants greener, the ocean fuller, and the air cleaner. And what she felt about the man outside hadn't faded in the early morning hours. It was deepening—steady and certain—cutting through logic and doubt. It was reshaping everything she thought she knew about falling for someone you've just met. About how sometimes, you don't need time to be sure. You just are.

His courage and quiet strength seemed to seep into her, simply from being near him. He embraced this isolated life—completely unplugged, away from the noise of the world—made it feel not just bearable, but freeing.

For the first time in her life, she found herself excited about time off, about disappearing into the wild beauty of the islands. No phone, no followers, no Billy—just her and the man who looked at her like she was the most captivating thing he'd ever seen.

The man who offered to share his world, and all of his skills, with her, and oh how she longed for it.

Kass watched Shephard move across the rain-soaked lawn, his shirt clinging to his muscled frame. Everything about him was effortless—like he belonged there, and was an integral part of the island itself. Shep's expression turned upward when he saw Kassidy.

He gave her a warm smile. "Morning" he called up, pausing to wipe his hands on his jeans. "How did you sleep?"

Kass leaned on the railing and hollered down. "Like I was trapped on an island without my cell phone."

He raised his eyebrows, grinning. "Sounds like my kind of place."

The pull of the digital world felt distant—almost unnecessary. There was only one place she wanted to be. Near the man who kissed her last night—whose lips seemed as drawn to hers as she was to him.

"I checked on your place this morning," Shephard said from below her balcony, then tossed another branch onto the pile. "It's still standing. But the power is still out. I hope it's okay, but I took it upon myself to grab your bag. Figured there might be something in there you'd want this morning and save you the walk back." He nodded to her oversized tote sitting on his front step.

"Think I'll head into town this morning for supplies and groceries, unless stale crackers and burnt grilled cheese sounds good again. You're welcome to come with. And"—his eyes flickered to the floatplane—"it's a perfect morning for a flight. I thought we could do some sightseeing."

Kassidy followed his gaze to the floatplane; it's shimmering yellow a beautiful contrast against the glassy blue surface of the sea. The whole place, and the man that came with it, looked like it belonged in an outdoor adventure magazine.

"Are you sure it's safe?" she asked, eyeing the plane. "It seems kind of risky."

Shep's grin widened, his confidence as easy as the morning breeze. "The best things sometimes are, don't you think?" His voice dropped slightly, warm and low. "You'll just have to trust the one holding the controls. Can you do that?"

"Only if I can use your steam shower again before we go."

A broad smile spread across his face.

The steam clung to Kassidy's skin as she stepped out of the shower, a towel wrapped tightly around her body, another twisted in her damp hair. She padded onto the plush carpet in Shephard's bedroom, her senses heightened in the quiet. Everything here felt softer, more intentional—life beat to a slower rhythm that was unfamiliar to her.

The door to his bedroom closet was ajar, and as she moved toward it, she froze. Shephard was there. His back partially to her, a towel slung low on his hips, and drops of water slid down the hard lines of his body. He didn't look surprised when he turned and caught her watching, though his body stilled. His brows furrowed slightly, his lips curving into an intimate smile that was almost too bold—almost.

Kassidy didn't move. She couldn't. She was vulnerable yet felt completely safe. He wasn't just gorgeous. He was utterly magnetic, and every part of her felt like it was screaming to close the distance between them. The silence stretched out with an unspoken invitation.

Shephard stepped closer. Not fast. Not hesitant. Every step was intentional and gave her all the time in the world to stop him, or back away. Her pulse quickened as he got closer. He stopped in front of her, his eyes never leaving hers. She could feel the heat radiating from him, as his presence overwhelmed her in the best possible way.

"You're dripping," she said softly, her gaze following the water trailing down his chest, his arms and onto the carpet.

"You're not," he added, his voice low and teasing, his lips curving as he reached out, his fingers brushing her neck. His touch was barely there, but it lit something inside her—a fire she couldn't hold back—and didn't want to. "I could offer my services, you know, for our trade."

Her voice came out in a whimper. "Yes."

She didn't know if she moved first or if he did, but suddenly the space between them was gone. His hands were on her, the heat from his body seeping into her, and her towel felt like the only flimsy barrier between them, and she wanted it gone—wanted him.

Shephard led her toward the bed—unmade but clean, crisp sheets waiting for them. He moved slowly, his actions intentional, giving her every chance to stop, to change her mind. Was this too fast? Too sudden? Maybe. But who cared? This is what she wanted—needed.

Kassidy didn't want to think. Not about Ray's will, not about her grandma's secrets, not about Billy or the ad campaign looming. She was tired of the stress, of the obligations that consumed her and sucked the fun out of her days.

Right now, she didn't want to analyze or second-guess. She just wanted to feel—something real and alive—with Shephard. She wanted to get lost in this, in him, in the way he looked at her like she was the only thing that mattered.

When his fingers brushed the edge of her towel, she knew what was coming—and wanted it. He paused, his gaze searching hers, waiting for her to take the lead or stop him. She let her towel fall to the floor, and the look on his face was more priceless than anything she could have imagined—raw, unguarded, a mixture of awe and desire that sent a thrill racing through her. It wasn't just lust; it was something that made her feel powerful and vulnerable all at once, as if she'd handed him the key to unlock her completely.

Shephard guided her back on the bed, hovering over her. Then he kissed her—soft at first, then with more intensity. His lips found more than just hers as they made a trail to her neck, then to her breasts, every caress leaving her breathless. His hands roamed, slow but purposeful, igniting her skin with desire and longing to release.

"I don't want to rush this," he murmured against her skin, his voice rough and raw. "But you make it hard to be patient."

Her pulse thundered in her ears, drowning out everything but him. She reached for him, her fingers tangling in his damp hair as she tilted his face toward hers.

"I don't want you to be patient," she said, her voice firm despite the tremor of need running through it.

That was all he needed before his lips pressed against hers, and suddenly, nothing else in the world existed—nothing but the heat between them, the slow unraveling of restraint.

His focus was entirely on her, on every shiver, every sharp intake of her breath. He didn't rush, didn't take. He learned her, traced the places that made her sigh, and the ones that made her pulse quicken.

Every move was a gift, every touch a silent promise wrapped in heat. The way he held her, the way his breath tangled with hers—it wasn't just desire, it was something deeper, something that made her feel like she was stepping into the unknown and somehow, finally, home.

She wasn't sure how long they'd been tangled, exploring each other in every way two people could. But time ceased to matter. When they finally slowed, they were both breathless. Shephard lay beside her on the tangled sheets, his gaze fixed on hers, his chest rising and falling in a rhythm that matched her own. The mattress was soft beneath her, still warm from their bodies, the faint scent of him—salt and cedar— mingled with the lingering heat in the air.

"I don't usually move this fast," he murmured, his voice rough with emotion.

"You think we went too fast?" she laughed.

She'd never given in to desire so quickly before either. But staring at him, his soft smile, the way he brushed her hair away from her face, all she wanted was more. The morning light cut through the slats in the blinds, striping his bare chest in pale white streaks, and making it impossible to look away.

Her lips curved, slow and wanton. "How about we try again then?" she said, her voice a purr of challenge. "You know, just to make sure we go slower?"

His smile widened. He pushed his tongue into his cheek. Then, without another word, he flipped the sheet over his head and disappeared beneath the covers.

Another shower and cup of black coffee later, Kass stood on the dock next to his float plane, her hair still damp and braided loosely down her back. Her body sizzled with endorphins from their very steamy morning.

Shephard walked up behind her, wrapped his arms around her waist and whistled softly. "You've got the fish braid down. I think I might be hopeless."

She turned, smirking and he kissed her lips again. "How about I give you another lesson tonight. Maybe you can try on my hair instead of Ginger's."

"Sophie would be so jealous if she knew."

"Well, maybe I can meet her sometime."

"Maybe," Shephard said, and for the first time since they'd met, Kassidy felt it—something was off. It wasn't in what he said, but rather, in *how* he said it. The word lingered in the air, with the weight of the unspoken.

Everything until this moment had been perfect. She'd given herself to him completely—and loved every second of it. But now, a quiet unease crept in, uninvited, threatening to unravel the bliss she'd just experienced.

*Stop it, Kassidy. Don't overanalyze this.*

She forced herself to let it go, to focus instead on the feel of his hands as they caressed her in a sweet embrace. The man was dangerously charming. Too good to be true, perhaps. And if life had taught her anything, it was that perfection came with a price.

Kassidy stood next to the yellow floatplane tied to the dock, its glossy wings catching the afternoon sun, casting golden ripples onto the water below.

"Why yellow?" she asked as Shephard helped her into the custom daffodil-colored plane with daffodil-colored seats. The soft leather was warm against her skin and smelled faintly of the sunshine it portrayed mixed with engine oil.

"Winters are long and gray out here on the edge of nowhere," he said, leaning in to help her buckle, his arms and torso pressed against her. "I figured a little brightness in the rainy months is always a welcome sight."

Kassidy glanced out at the water. "I don't know how you do it," she said, as Shephard tightened the straps across her chest. His hands were so close, his fingers brushing past her skin. "Living out here, isolated. Alone. Do you ever get lonely?"

Shep's movements slowed, his fingers lingering on the strap longer than necessary. His breath warmed the space between them as he leaned in, close enough that she could feel the heat of him. Every second their lips were apart was a second too long.

"I didn't before. But now that I know what it's like to have you next to me…I might turn into that stalker you thought I was."

Shep gave her another quick kiss on the lips before shutting her door and walking around to the pilot's seat. She watched him move—sure, confident—his hands easily finding the controls as he adjusted switches and checked gauges. Then, with a flick of his wrist, he fired up the engine.

The propeller roared to life, slicing through the stillness, and sending gusts of wind rippling over the water. The vibrations hummed through the seat, through her bones, and she felt the exhilarating shift from stillness to movement as the plane prepared to launch.

"You ready?"

"Where are we going?"

"Like I said, I'm going to take you places."

Kassidy glanced at him, a smile playing at her lips. "Yeah, but *what* places?"

He gave her a look, his eyes flicking briefly to hers, full of meaning. "All of them."

She raised an eyebrow, intrigued. "Is that a promise?"

Shep's smile was slow, confident. "Yes. And I never break a promise—I aim to overdeliver."

She wasn't sure what made her feel more alive—the rumble of the engine, the whir of the engines propeller, or the way Shephard made her feel.

The takeoff was exhilarating. Rumbling filled her ears as they sped across the water. The plane skimmed over the smooth surface before lifting into the air. Kassidy's heart raced, not just from the thrill, but from the man beside her, his occasional brush of a hand against hers. He glanced at her and smiled. Checked in on her and made her feel safe.

Her eyes widened as the plane soared and the island and inlets grew smaller beneath. Deep, shimmering blue water stretched to the horizon in every direction. The panoramic view made her feel both small and limitless at the same time.

Shephard glanced sideways, his gaze lingering on her, as if he were experiencing it for the first time through her eyes.

"Wait till you see it from the inside."

Kassidy blinked. "What inside?"

He said it like he was letting her in on a secret or daring her to see more than just the world below them.

"You'll have to stick around long enough to find out," he said, everything about him and his world layered in mystery.

As the islands and ocean sprawled out beneath her, Kassidy's thoughts drifted back to all the other mysteries in her life. The strange call from Mr. Moore, Isla Virginia, Raymond, now Shephard—perfect, wonderful, Shephard. This new story that had become her life was unfolding faster than she could keep up.

The scattered island landscape was dotted with cabins nestled among trees and the shoreline, where modern mansions flaunted massive white boats and floatplanes tied to every dock. The seascape was a beautiful maze of channels and bays offering protection from the open ocean.

"That's Whidbey Island," Shephard said, pointing down toward the trees below. "And there's Fidalgo. See that bridge?" His finger traced the horizon. "That's Deception Pass."

Kassidy pulled her brows together. "Sounds ominous."

The floatplane hummed steadily as it veered toward the Deception Pass Bridge. Shephard guided them over the swirling currents beneath, passed the rugged cliffs towering above that guarded the narrow strait and churning waters. Kassidy watched the currents as they fought and swirled in all directions, the depth of the blue mesmerizing.

"Why is it called Deception Pass?"

Shephard smiled, his hands steady on the controls. Then he angled the plane slightly, giving her a better view of the channel below. Shadows from the cliffs stretched across the turbulent waves.

"It's a Samish legend. About a woman who used to walk these shores, long before the settlers arrived." Kassidy shifted, her attention fully on Shephard as she listened.

"Then one day, an ancient sea sprite saw her and had to have her." The plane drifted slightly, the waters below rippling in the early light. "The sprite came up from the deep and was so mesmerized by her that he asked for her hand in marriage the moment they met.

"The sprite promised her family that if she went back into the sea with him, the sea would always provide. Salmon, clams—everything they wanted. But if she refused…" his voice trailed off, leaving the unspoken threat hanging in the air like the mist.

Kassidy felt a chill that had nothing to do with the altitude.

"Well, what did she do?" Kass insisted, her gaze drifting from the water back to Shep, catching the way his fingers tightened on the controls.

"She said no." Shephard glanced at her, his eyes catching the light. "She said she wanted to marry for love, she didn't want to marry him to appease her people. But the sea sprite didn't forget his threat. He was evil and true to his word. Soon, all the salmon started to disappear. The water became unpredictable, and they knew it was him. The maiden's family begged her to save them all. To sacrifice herself to save all of them. She finally agreed."

The plane banked gently and Shep's voice dropped even lower, almost reverent. "She married the sea sprite and he took her beneath the waves. At first, she came back to visit her people. To make sure he kept his word and returned their bounties. She walked the shores of Deception Pass like she had before she was taken into the sea. Every time she returned though she was different—her hair turned to seaweed, her skin had become rippled and blue like the ocean's surface. Until one day, she stopped coming back. Her people said the sea had claimed her. She was their sacrifice. The maiden of Deception Pass."

Kassidy swallowed, as if she could feel the pull of the waters below, the calling of the woman's duty to save her family despite her life and her own wishes. "So did she save all her people at least?"

"The sea sprite kept his promise. The salmon came back, so did the orcas. And the Samish never went hungry again."

"She sacrificed her life to save her people."

"And the whales. Who also depend on the salmon. Yes, she saved all of them."

"At the cost of her life," she added.

Shep looked at her, his eyes solemn. "Sometimes we have to sacrifice what we love, in order to save what we can never get back."

She stared at Shep, wondering how much he was still talking about the legend.

# Chapter 18

As the plane glided over the waterways of the Salish Sea, Shephard pointed out landmarks, and named the islands while Kassidy kept her eyes on the waves below. But her mind traveled to much deeper currents than those on the surface.

Shep's knowledge of the area was impressive—he wasn't just some rugged islander. He was a man connected to that place in ways she didn't yet understand. He steered the plane toward a wide stretch of open water, eventually landing on its smooth surface before taxiing toward an enormous house on the shoreline.

"That's where we're docking?" Kassidy asked, raising an eyebrow. "Whose place is this?"

Shephard smiled, a little less comfortably this time. "My grandfather's. He likes luxury."

"I'd say. Is that a cruise ship or a yacht?"

Shep nodded, an air of disapproval. "He had to have a channel drudged just to be able to keep it here."

"I don't know what that means but it doesn't sound cheap. Have you been on it?"

"Once. In Alaska. That's where I was coming back from when we met."

"What does your grandfather do, traffic in kidneys?" her voice was teasing but edged with curiosity.

"No, nothing like that. Kidneys couldn't afford what my grandfather has. He deals in water. And around here, whoever controls the water, has all the power." Kassidy caught the brief flicker of discord in his face.

"I have no idea what you're talking about. How does water equal power?"

Shephard was more cryptic than anyone she'd ever known. Legends. Secrets. Islands in the mist. Then he adjusted the plane to lift off the water again.

"I'll show you," he said and pushed the controls forward.

The plane veered inland now, toward the winding rivers and dense forests. As they left the coastline behind, the trees thickened beneath them, and streams crisscrossed the landscape like veins.

The rivers below were swollen with rain, waterfalls spilling over cliffs and rocks, hidden from the world at eye level, but visible from their height.

"This is breathtaking," Kassidy said, awe dancing in her eyes. "There are so many waterfalls out here."

"You can't see them from the ground or get to them unless you want to take a long, slippery hike."

"I'll stick with the view from up here," she said, shimmying in her seat. "I could totally get used to this."

"Good," he said, reaching to put his hand on her knee. She couldn't help but feel giddy about it—about him—about everything they'd done.

As they flew farther inland, the lush wilderness gave way to a jarring contrast—a massive concrete structure stretched across the river, slicing through the landscape like a scar. The dam rose out of the earth, imposing and cold, its massive wall swallowing the natural beauty around it.

"This is my grandfather's," Shephard said, his eyes fixed on the dam below. But it wasn't pride in his voice, it was something else. Something she couldn't read. Kassidy took in the scale of the massive operation stretching across the river.

"The US Army Corps of Engineers built it. This one, and three others. But my grandfather—Gunter—bought this one for Deville Power. See, no human kidneys involved. Just water and a grid to channel its power." His grip on the controls tightened.

Kassidy's gaze remained on the dam as they flew over it.

"He owns a power company?"

"Yes. Deville Power. Where I work as an engineer."

Her eyes narrowed as she watched the river below, the water barely moving as it pushed against the concrete wall.

"There's hardly any water flowing. I don't see how it can produce power."

Shep's laugh was short, almost bitter. "Good observation. The truth is that this system is mostly outdated—the little power it does generate only goes to a handful of places. The rest is…" he trailed off, as if reconsidering his words. "Well…let's just say it's not efficient."

Shephard kept his gaze on the dam below, his easygoing mask slipping just enough for her to catch the tension beneath—the strain in his jaw more pronounced, as if he were holding something back.

Whatever was behind his words lingered between them long enough that she saw the faintest crack in his easygoing facade, a glimpse of something sharper and unresolved lurking beneath.

It was in the quiet command of his posture, the effortless way he kept control without needing to flaunt it—where she saw the businessman, the engineer, the man who had been shaped by people and places she knew nothing about.

There was something more to him than she understood. Something formidable. He was a man built on legacy and expectation. Then, just as quickly as he'd slipped into a polished and impenetrable mogul, the hard facade disappeared, the crack sealed, and that easy charm was back.

"Why not update it if it's outdated?"

"My grandfather," he hesitated, his voice careful, "is a complicated man." Shep glanced at her briefly, his smile half-hearted. "Set in his ways you could say. I'm the only one in the family who still puts up with his eccentricities. Him and my father haven't talked for twenty years."

Kassidy was quiet for a moment. "Twenty years? That's some falling out. What happened?"

Shephard adjusted the plane's altitude slightly, flying closer over the water now. "Let's just say he keeps a lot of secrets," he said, his voice tighter now.

Kassidy huffed, though it didn't hold much humor.

"If there were a competition for keeping secrets, I'm pretty sure my family would take home the gold. After what I've learned this week, that is." She turned to Shephard. "I'm done with secrets," her voice soft but pointed. "So, if you've got any big ones, now would be a good time to spill it. Multiple wives? Hidden babies? Obsession with dolls? Whatever it is, tell me now."

Shephard gave her a polite smile, but when their eyes finally met, his expression turned serious. "I can't promise you'll like everything you find out. But I can promise that, in the end, there won't be anything you don't know. Fair enough?"

Kassidy sensed his reluctance. "That is an awfully roundabout way of avoiding an answer."

"I'll tell you what you need to know. *That* I can promise. The rest—you don't want to know."

Kass swallowed hard, sensing that whatever he wasn't telling her was much bigger than a family feud or secret baby.

She shifted in her seat, staring back at the dam that was crumbling at the sides. The water behind it barely moved creating a stale algae sheen on the surface.

"It's a marvel though, isn't it? That something as powerful as an ocean of water, can be held back by human design."

"Spoken like a true engineer."

Shep turned his head to look at her. "If I've learned anything from my training, it's that something that big, at some point, is bound to break." Then his tone changed. He was back to all-business. "It takes a lot of upkeep to keep it from crumbling. We have crews out here constantly monitoring and fixing things."

She stared out at the dam again, seeing it in a new light. The cracked and weathered structure was a reminder of how even the strongest things eroded over time. She didn't press him further, sensing the invisible line he wasn't ready to cross.

The drone of the plane's engine filled the silence between them as Shephard adjusted the controls and headed back toward the sea. Below them, the dense green of the mainland gave way to the coastline stretching like a jagged seam between land and water.

Shephard eased the plane onto the calm surface, slowing to a stop in front of the massive estate.

"This is it," he said, cutting the engine. His polite smile returned, but the tension in his shoulders betrayed the calm he tried to project. "No one is home, except for the staff. But we won't go in. I keep a car in the garage. We can take that into town."

Kassidy gawked at the palatial mansion sprawled before her, its grandeur almost blinding in its excess. It looked less like a home and more like the set of a film about old-money dynasties. Ornate stonework and towering glass windows, and then——a polar bear, its massive frame frozen mid-swipe, and behind it, an elephant, tusks gleaming under dramatic overhead lighting.

Her mouth fell open in shock and horror. "Is that an elephant? And a polar bear?"

Shephard exhaled sharply as his eyes flicked toward the massive glass-enclosed room, its contents showcased like an exhibit for anyone passing by. "Yep. That's his trophy room. Like I said, my grandfather is an eccentric man."

She studied him as he said it, trying to decipher if he was in support of this or simply tolerated it. There were no animal heads in his island home. Just artwork. Depictions of nature and its creatures in a different way—preserved but not conquered.

"Are you a hunter, too?"

"No."

His answer was clipped, his tone sharp. Her question had struck a nerve. It wasn't just irritation—it seemed more guarded, making her wonder if he was telling the truth, or if the truth was more complex.

She knew all too well that the truth was always more complicated than a single word.

As they walked past the massive house, the unease in her chest deepened. Her attention returned to the towering room visible through the floor-to-ceiling windows. Inside resembled a vast museum-like exhibit. It wasn't something one would expect find in a private collection. Mounted heads, snarling predators, and creatures from every corner of the globe crowded the space, their glassy eyes fixed in eternal stares. The sheer scale of it was haunting.

Kassidy's chest tightened. She hated the thought of killing those animals just to have a trophy. The very idea made her stomach turn—to be reduced to something lifeless, a symbol of conquest rather than a unique and precious life to be valued.

She knew that feeling too well. She'd been admired, displayed like something rare, but in the end, every man she let in had made it clear—that was all she was. A trophy.

With Shep, it felt different. There was no sense of possession, no quiet claim. If anything, he was the one holding back. He had a depth she hadn't encountered before, a man who kept his cards close to his chest, revealing only what he wanted her to see.

Then another thought crossed her mind, if someone photographed her next to that trophy room, she wouldn't be canceled—she'd be crucified. She wanted nothing to do with that house or whoever owned it. Whoever his grandfather was, he was nothing like her.

It was the first time since meeting Shephard that she felt a flicker of doubt. Everything about him had been kind, sweet, and controlled, like the calm rhythms of the sea. But this place? It screamed of power, excess, and danger.

To be aligned with a family like this—a family with literal power coursing through the grid and an obscene fortune behind it—was one thing. But to use that privilege for killing? For trophies? Was archaic. A relic from another era, maybe acceptable decades ago, but now, no one did this type of killing anymore. Did they?

Now, there were laws. Purpose-built sanctuaries protected what was left after hunters had driven the world's mammals to near extinction. Displaying them wasn't just out of touch—it was a deliberate act of defiance against progress. A refusal to move forward, and to join the global effort to save endangered animals after eras of pillaging.

Her unease deepened as her thoughts churned. A man with this kind of house—this kind of collection—didn't just have money. He had influence. The kind of influence that could bend the world to his will. And Shephard, for all his charm and quiet strength, was tied to it. How deep? She didn't know.

She only knew she didn't want to be tied to it. Big-game controversies, anything reeking of exploitation—it was everything she wanted to avoid. Especially now. She could already see the headlines: *Trophy Hunter's Heir Hooks Social Media Star = Exploitation x2.*

The mere thought sent a sour twist through her stomach, a bitter cocktail of shame and inevitability she couldn't shake.

She glanced at Shephard again as they hurried toward the garage. But his expression was hard to pin down. She reminded herself that they'd only just met. That she didn't really know him at all. Did she? He wasn't calm anymore either. His usual relaxed stride was gone, replaced with a hurried pace as he led her into the sprawling garage with every type of car and SUV imaginable.

"Does he own a car company too?"

"No. He's just a collector."

"Shephard," she said, her voice tighter than she intended, "What else does he collect? What exactly are we walking into here?"

He paused for a beat but didn't turn to face her. "Like I said, it's complicated," he admitted.

That word—complicated—did nothing to ease her mind. If anything, it made her pulse quicken.

He opened the car door of a modest black sedan and helped her in. She looked around the car, which felt, normal. Not like the others beside it. It was nice, but not obscene.

Everything about where they were felt off, like the whole place carried secrets she'd never be told. Nor did she want to know. For the first time, she wondered if Shephard's calm demeanor was more of a shield than a truth. He hurried them through, as if protecting her. And what exactly was he trying to protect her from?

At the gates, Shep's gaze flicked to the left, where a sleek town car with dark-tinted windows approached.

A muscle ticked in his jaw. "Shit, he's not supposed to be here."

Without hesitation, he turned sharply to the right, the tires biting into the pavement with a squeal, loose gravel spitting up in their wake.

The sudden burst of speed sent a jolt through Kassidy, kicking up her pulse to match the sharp turn. But it wasn't just the sudden motion that caught her off guard—it was the look on Shep's face. Her heart might have sped up, but his didn't. He was controlled, calculating—a man used to being a step ahead, even when caught off guard.

"So, let me get this straight," Kassidy began, her tone dripping with mock incredulity. "You work for your grandfather's company—a power company that collects outdated energy. Owned by a man who also collects outdated things.

"In a family that, for reasons unknown to me, won't speak to him. Except for you, who, might I add, seems to be the least ruthless business-tycoon type I've ever met. And yet, you're the only one who tolerates him.

"Oh, and let's not forget—clearly, you don't want me to meet him, or we wouldn't have, you know, sprinted across the lawn.

"Did I miss anything?"

"No, that pretty much sums it up." His lips curved into that polite, disarming smile he always seemed to use when cornered. "Like I said, it's…complicated."

"But I'm not wrong," Kassidy pressed, raising an eyebrow.

His lips twitched in that maddeningly polite almost-smile. "Let's just say nothing about this is easy. And no, you're not wrong, but it does sound a little dramatic."

Kassidy shot him a look. "Dramatic? Shephard, dramatic is me crying over a rom-com. This is a multi-season Netflix series."

He exhaled a laugh, the tension in his shoulders easing slightly.

"You've got the gist of it; I'll give you that. But maybe leave out the part about the sprinting and squealing tires. It makes me sound uncomposed."

"Please," she scoffed, rolling her eyes. "You've got enough composure to spare."

Shephard glanced at her sideways, the corner of his mouth turning up. "Well, at least I'm not boring."

Kassidy sighed, leaning back in her seat. "No, you're not that. But I think I'd like a little less drama and a bit more transparency, if it's all the same to you."

He nodded once, his grip on the wheel loosening a bit. "Fair enough," he murmured, his tone softer. "My family has…a lot of history," he added quietly.

Kassidy tilted her head, narrowing her eyes. "History? What kind of history?"

He glanced at her, the polite facade slipping ever so slightly. "Would you be satisfied if I told you that it's better if it stays buried, for now? I'm trying to impress a beautiful woman here. Not scare her away with family drama."

She stared at him, her chest tightening. Whatever lay beneath his polished demeanor was bigger—and darker—than he was letting on. And yet, despite every alarm bell going off in her head, she found herself leaning closer, drawn to the cracks in his stunning armor.

# Chapter 19

The grocery store was busy with people restocking after the storm. Kassidy filled her cart with essentials: produce, snacks, and toiletries.

Everything about being there with Shephard—holding his hand, him carrying her groceries—felt too normal, too easy, but she was aware that there was a whole world about him she didn't yet know.

As they walked back out to the parking lot, soft chatter coming from around the corner made them look up. Her heart sank as the sound grew louder and she could make out the words—the chanting.

"Free. The. Swift!"

The crowd rounded the corner, signs raised high.

"Free. The. Swift!"

Shephard stiffened beside her, reaching for his aviators and sliding them on. "They've been ramping up for weeks," he said, quickly putting their groceries in the trunk.

"What's the Swift?" Kassidy asked, turning her head from the crowd, terrified of the answer. She'd heard the chant at Capri Son.

Which meant…

The same guilt that had been gnawing at her, the nagging feeling of dread she'd pushed aside in Shephard's wake, bubbled up and twisted her stomach into a tighter knot.

"The Swift is a river. Swiftcreek river. They want the dam removed from it."

"Why?"

"To save the salmon," he didn't hesitate.

"As in, your grandfather's dam? The one we just saw? The one where you work?"

"I'm not racking up positive impression points today, am I? Maybe we should stay at my place and skip the supply run into town next time."

He shut the trunk filled with groceries.

Kassidy turned to watch as a Native American woman stepped onto the stage in the town square. She stood behind a podium in front of the town's historical landmark, the majestic statue of an orca, rendered in the intricate KaWaltish style.

Its bold black and red lines, coupled with the flowing form and detailed carvings, celebrated the cultural heritage of the KaWaltish people while symbolizing the deep connection between land, sea, and spirit. The orca's iconic form was immortalized within the breathtaking sculpture.

"Who is that?" Kassidy couldn't help but stare. The woman had a presence about her that hushed the crowd.

"That—is a Seawalker," Shep said, his voice measured, calm—almost too calm—as if weighing each word.

He didn't seem annoyed, but every line of him looked strung tight. A man balancing on a wire. Not nervous, but careful. Very careful.

If she hadn't been watching him so closely, Kassidy might not have noticed the way his eyes watched the woman on the stage, the crowd, and the whole area. It was as if he were secret service agent looking for all the possible threats.

The woman looked to be Kassidy's age. She didn't introduce herself, it seemed that everyone already knew her by name. She was adorned in traditional KaWaltish regalia that seemed to embody the essence of the sea—her flowing garments reminiscent of ocean waves. Each intricate detail, from the shimmering blue hues to the delicate shell and pearl embellishments, mirrored the fluidity and beauty of the underwater world.

She stood in a full headdress, black and white, an orca motif—a living embodiment of the connection between her and the orcas and the sea.

"If we don't do something today, *all* of our orcas will be gone tomorrow, and there will be no chance of bringing them back!" Her voice amplified and reverberated through the speakers. "All the easy things have been done," the woman called out with immense passion. "It's time to be brave! Do the hard things!"

She raised her arm in the air, fingers spread wide and moved it slowly from side to side. The crowd cheered, throwing their arms in the air too, moving as one, fingers spread wide, their hands swaying in a side-to-side motion.

The wave-like gesture swept through the gathering, a powerful and unified tribute to what they had come together to protect.

"What are they doing?" Kassidy asked, standing beside Shephard as they stopped to take it all in from afar. She could sense how different he'd become; how uneasy he was with being there.

"It's a thing. I think it's supposed to mimic the ocean or the orcas. Or something."

Someone chanted, "Free the Swift!"

"You sound annoyed," Kassidy pointed out, looking at his tight face, his expression not nearly as easy as it had been.

Though it softened when their eyes met. "They protest every month. Sometimes every week."

The woman spoke again into the microphone.

"The only way to bring back the salmon is to breech the dam! There is no other way!" she shouted, and her fellow protesters cheered and chanted, arms in the air, fingers splayed, swishing from side to side.

She spoke with such passionate conviction it was hard for Kassidy to look away.

"I am WeNala Seawalker of the Coast KaWaltish people, and the orcas that live in the Salish Sea are my ancestors. They are not blackfish. Each one of them is a Kwal, a mother, a grandfather, a brother—an ancestor. The orcas that live here are our family, our KwalOhMechen—the people under the sea." The crowd erupted again. "Every whale carries the soul of an ancestor. Qilalugaq is Kwal. She was born of the Coast KaWaltish people. And she belongs in the Salish Sea! This is her home and when she is returned, her family will come back. When they do, we will be ready to feed them the salmon from the Swift. Set Qilalugaq free!"

The realization of what was happening hit Kassidy like a rogue wave, pulling her under.

Qilalugaq.

Kee-lah-loo-gahk.

Keelah.

Shephard.

The swift.

The dam.

They weren't just names or places or people. They were battle cries, etched onto signs, shouted into the air. Her chest tightened as she scanned the crowd, the faces, the fury—it was all for Keelah.

Shepherd was their enemy.

And so was she.

Even if they didn't know it yet.

She looked at him, information flooding to her now. And somehow, impossibly, she was here, at the epicenter of the controversy she tried to escape. It was as if the islands had summoned her, forcing her to face the very thing she had been running from.

She remembered the woman's warning: *Return her or everyone who has kept her hostage will be cursed.*

This was Kassidy's curse.

"Are you okay?" Shep asked. She could feel her face turn white and her stomach begin to churn.

"We should go. I'm not feeling well," she said, and turned to the passenger side door.

Before she got in the car, a young man with a clipboard and long black hair approached Kassidy. He wore a patch on the shoulder of his jacket. It read "*SSOCC*" in bold black, with red and white letters, matching the art style of the piece that Shephard had in his cabin. In the center, an orca was arched over in an unnatural position, almost as if it were dying.

"We're collecting signatures to bring Qilalugaq home," he said. "Will you sign?"

"Shep," she whispered leaning into him. She felt like her knees might give out. He wrapped his arm around her back and helped her into the car.

The young man kept talking. "They took her from Whidby Island when she was four. She's been in captivity for fifty-three years. Her family is still out there. She can come home. Help us before it's too late. Don't let her die in that tank. She belongs to the Salish Sea."

Each of his words hit Kassidy like a punch to the gut.

Shep helped her into the car, shut her door and explained to the young man that she wasn't feeling well.

The Capri Son campaign hadn't even launched, yet there was no way Jonah was letting that whale go free. They were using her not only to re-open the orca entertainment industry, but to re-create it into something new that the laws and regulations couldn't touch.

And once they did, these protests would ignite—burn hotter than they already were. And she was there. This was her karma. Her fate for not standing up for what she knew was right.

She could have walked away.

Should have walked away.

Found a way.

"Kassidy?" Shephard slid into the driver's seat, his voice gentle. "You want to tell me what's going on?"

The chants from the protesters grew louder, filling the air with urgency and anger.

Shep's hand moved to her thigh, cupping her knee. He leaned in, eyes still hidden behind those dark aviators. She could feel that he was holding back, keeping something from her. The whole plane ride that morning felt cryptic.

But she was keeping something from him too—a secret that felt darker than any secret he might carry. One that would eventually be out in the light for all to see.

She couldn't bring herself to speak about what she'd done. She was hiding, using him as a distraction, and was too much of a coward to admit what was coming.

"Will you take me home? Please?"

Shephard nodded. That was all he needed, and they were gone.

Kassidy didn't say a word on the way back to Shep's grandfather's house, other than to reiterate that she wasn't feeling well and needed to be alone.

The truth was that her heart was breaking—fraying around the edges, from guilt and confusion over what to do next. Or, if there even was anything she could do next. How do you stop a freight train that is coming straight for you at a hundred miles an hour?

Shep carried her groceries inside as Kassidy retreated deep into herself, to a place where guilt and fear clouded her thoughts and pulled her under. She wrapped herself in a blanket and sank into the couch. The whole situation clawed at her chest. The guilt she'd been trying to smother with the distraction of Shephard—everything exciting and new—crept in, threatening to overwhelm her.

Knowing her image would be plastered across a campaign to re-invigorate a dead industry and celebrate captivity—how could she face that truth? She'd inadvertently aligned herself with everything these people were fighting against. She knew they were right to fight, and she was the coward who stood for nothing. Every post, every smile, every empty word she'd ever said or sponsored—was just noise, feeding a machine that would never stop. A machine that didn't heal or fix or bring peace, spreading only isolation and emptiness.

And she was one of the cogs that kept it turning.

*"You're either the one fixing the leak, or you're the one letting the water in."* Her grandma's words echoed in her every thought. How could Virginia be proud of her now?

She heard Shephard shift in the doorway, felt his lingering presence even as she kept her eyes closed, her pain locked away.

"You don't have to tell me what's wrong," he said, his voice reassuring. "You also don't have to go through whatever this is alone."

Her fingers tightened around the edge of the blanket. She didn't look at him, didn't trust herself to speak. A moment passed. Then another. A deafening silence hung between them.

"All right," he said finally, more to himself than to her. "I'll be on the island if you need me. I won't leave."

But then he was gone, the cabin door clicking shut behind him.

Kassidy exhaled, sinking deeper into the couch.

She told herself she wanted to be alone. Needed to be alone.

She knew she'd pushed him away.

So why did his absence make her world feel that much emptier?

# Chapter 20

Kassidy didn't sleep.

She tried—first on the couch, twisting the blanket around her as if it might offer some protection. Then she moved to the bedroom—flipping the new pillow to the cool side, willing her mind to be still—but nothing worked. The guilt was too loud. It was the kind of guilt that made the silence unbearable.

She lay in the dark, eyes closed, mind wide awake with her thoughts circling the same truth she'd been trying to ignore: she could hide for a little while, but soon, her face would be out there—next to that whale. She'd become the very symbol of everything those people despised—everything she despised.

How could she not stand up for herself? Say no? Find a way out?

Regret nagged at her, refusing to let her sleep. Then the answer to all of her questions became clear—it occurred to her all at once. This had happened because she wasn't in control of her own life.

But how had she let it come to this?

Kassidy rolled onto her side, curling her knees toward her chest. She should have seen this coming. Billy kept pushing, and she let herself be pushed—took every sponsor who dangled a check, aligned herself with everything new and shiny. It had been going on for years.

It should have been easy choosing the right side, saying no, and standing for something instead of feeding the machine that chewed people up and spat them out shinier, emptier. Now it was her that felt empty. Alone. And lost more than ever before.

Her fingers clenched the blanket.

Yet she didn't have to be alone. She could run to him. Tell him. No. She couldn't tell him. Not yet. She didn't want to think about that. There was still time. Two weeks until her grandma arrived. She'd tell him then. Both of them. The campaign wouldn't launch until then. She could wait—live in blissful ignorance until then.

Part of her knew it was wrong. Another part of her thought, why not? The freight train was coming. It was going to hit no matter what. She'd die when it did, so she might as well live it up until then.

Another part of her whispered that it was okay, because Shephard was hiding something, too. She didn't need to know his secrets, if she could keep hers to herself.

At some point, exhaustion pulled her under. When she opened her eyes, the little back room was washed in pale morning light, a faint orange glow slipping through the curtains.

She sat up, pulse hammering, her body strung tight from too little sleep and too many thoughts.

She needed out of that bed. Out of that cabin.

She needed air.

She needed him.

Kassidy shoved back the blanket, brushed her teeth, tied up her hair, and grabbed the oversized boots. Stepping into the crisp morning air, she found the sky tinged with soft pink at the edges, the world and water impossibly still. The only sound was the crunch of rocks beneath her feet as she walked the path to Shephard's house.

She didn't plan what she was going to say.

All she knew was that he was the only thing that made sense.

Her palms were clammy as she lifted a hand to knock. Before her knuckles could touch the door, it swung open. Shephard stood there in nothing but a pair of faded jeans, looking like he'd been expecting her.

His hair was tousled, his face unshaven, and the sight of him—so undone, so sexy—made it hard to breathe. She didn't know about any of the other decisions in her life except for this one. Being with Shephard was the only thing that felt right. And felt like … fate.

He opened his arms, and she fell into him. He pulled her into a tight embrace that felt like everything she needed and wanted, with the unspoken understanding that he wasn't asking for anything in return.

His warmth surrounded her completely, his heartbeat steady beneath her cheek. He grounded her in a way nothing else had.

She let herself melt into him, let the worries that kept her up all night melt away as she pressed her face against him, rising and falling in sync with his breath.

The world paused to let her have that moment. As though nature itself had conspired to give her that little gift—this perfect, fleeting moment with this man, where everything painful seemed to fall away.

Shephard's hands began to move, his fingers tracing slow patterns along the curve of her back, igniting sparks that spread like wildfire.

Her eyes met his, unwavering and intense, as though he could see straight through her into the quietest parts of her heart. For the first time in weeks—no, years—Kassidy felt a clarity she couldn't explain. It wasn't about logic or timing or what the world might think. With him, maybe she could face what was coming.

There are those people that, when you meet them, they make you want to be the best version of yourself. He felt like that for her.

She looked up at the rough stubble on his face and into his eyes. "I don't know about anything else in my life right now, and this has all been so crazy," she whispered, her voice trembled. "But I know that being here, with you—feels right."

The corners of his mouth lifted in a smile that was equal parts relief and triumph. He brought one hand to her cheek, thumb brushing her skin as if committing the moment to memory.

"It feels right for me too."

"Shephard, there are things I need to tell you. About me. About something I've done. But this—us—without any complications or the outside world interrupting, is what I need right now."

Shephard exhaled, his hand settling at the nape of her neck as he rested his forehead against hers for a brief second before pulling back just enough to meet her eyes.

"Whatever's going on can wait. You've had a lot of eyes on you in your lifetime. Not on the same scale, but I know what that feels like. I know that every problem isn't black and white."

His voice was low, measured. "Why do you think I live out here? No one to stare, no one to judge. Sometimes, we need a place to escape—to strip it all back and remember who we really are. What we're fighting for."

He held her gaze. "If that's what you need right now—an escape—and if this place can be that for you, then count me in."

He pulled back just enough to look at her straight on.

"Whatever it is, you can tell me when you're ready. We'll figure it out together. But if you're not ready to talk about it, I understand that, too. Right now can just be about us."

With him, the noise of the outside world, even the looming chaos of what was to come, melted away. Kassidy wasn't sure how long this would last, or what their future might look like, but right now, she didn't care. She didn't need answers or guarantees. She just needed him—the ultimate escape.

She had two weeks before her grandma arrived, before Kassidy's face would be plastered across the globe in a campaign that could tear apart everything she'd built and crumble her career.

But for now, none of that mattered. What mattered was the way Shephard made her feel, as if she could live entirely in this moment, in the warmth of his embrace.

His lips brushed against hers. "Stay here, with me. I can't sleep with you on the other side of the island," he murmured, his lips grazing the top of her head.

"You can't sleep with me in your house either."

"That's true. But I'd rather have it that way. Wouldn't you?"

She nodded. "I don't want to spend the next two weeks trying to untangle everything in both of our lives that's complicated. When my grandma gets here, I have a feeling she's going to upend my world. So, until then…let's just have this. No expectations. Just you and me. And everything that feels good, and nothing that doesn't." Then she added, "We can be each other's escape."

Shephard brushed a strand of hair from her cheek, his thumb lingering for just a second too long. "So…your secrets stay yours, and mine stay mine? Is that what you're saying?"

"For now. Yes."

Each word carved out space for them, as if he needed the distance from something just as badly as she did.

Shephard's fingers curled against her waist. "Two weeks? No expectations. No past, no future—just us?" His fingers traced a slow line along the curve of her back. "And when the two weeks are up? What then?" he asked.

Kassidy swallowed, her throat tight.

When the two weeks are up, everything falls apart.

But she didn't say that.

"Then we find out if this is real or just a really good dream."

He held her gaze for a long moment before nodding. "Alright. Two weeks."

A silent contract.

A shared secret.

A line drawn between them that neither would share their secrets—not yet.

"But if we're not going to talk for two weeks, what are we going to do?" she asked.

He replied with his lips on hers, soft at first, then deeper, more insistent. Every thought dissolved as he pulled her through the door, closing it behind them with a finality that locked out the world. His hands gripped her waist, drawing her close. Their bodies fit together like they were made to be this way.

"You didn't say we couldn't talk," he managed between kisses. "We'll just…keep it light."

"You mean, wake up every day and do what we did yesterday?"

"I could only be so lucky. You know, you're making it way too easy to fall for you."

She didn't protest when he led her upstairs, his hands never leaving her body.

For the next two days, the rest of the world didn't exist. They moved between the steam shower and his bedroom, the balcony and the kitchen, a slow rhythm of connection and heat.

Wrapped in Shephard's arms, Kassidy let herself live entirely in the moment knowing she would never forget the warmth, the quiet, and the way he made her feel. Like she was enough without needing anything more.

He worked in a small den on the second floor between their lovemaking sessions, while Kassidy napped or curled up under a warm blanket, gazing at the ocean through a pair of binoculars. And more often than not, she got lost in a worn paperback his niece had left behind—*Island of the Blue Dolphins*.

Kassidy didn't check her phone. Didn't look at the news. Didn't let herself think past the four walls of Shephard's house, past the heat of his skin against hers, past the indulgence of slow mornings tangled in his sheets and afternoons spent on the balcony with their feet propped up, watching the sea stretch endless before them.

One night, curled up beside him, their bodies slick with heat and exhaustion, she whispered, "What if we never leave this house?"

Shephard chuckled, his breath warm against her temple. "We'd starve."

"We could try to live off the land. Off the grid," she teased, but there was something else beneath her voice—something dangerously close to the truth.

"Aren't we? No phones. No plans. Just you, me, and whatever comes next."

She let him pull her closer, let herself believe—for just a little longer—that this could be enough.

But even in the stillness, a thought lingered at the edges of her mind, refusing to disappear.

Two weeks.

That's all they would have.

And then?

She refused to let herself finish the thought.

# Chapter 21

After being sequestered for days, Shephard took Kassidy on an outing, insisting she wear a blindfold. The evening air was crisp, scented with pine and mist. He guided her down a secluded, winding trail on the farthest side of the island—a place she'd never been. Bundled in extra layers, hats, and gloves, she clutched his arm, her breath hanging in the cold air while the blindfold pressed softly against her skin.

Without sight, her senses sharpened—every uneven step, every rustling leaf, every shift in the breeze felt amplified. The distant trickle of water grew louder, as it mingled with the rhythm of their footsteps, and with each step, the tension between them buzzed like a live wire with anticipation and curiosity.

Kassidy's interest climbed, but so did the awareness that she was placing her trust in a man she knew was keeping secrets. She didn't know what they were, or if they would shatter everything when their time was up. For now, she let herself believe that none of it mattered.

When Shephard slowed them to a stop, his hands came up to untie the blindfold, his fingers brushing her hair, then her cheek, lingering in a way that made her skin tingle. He was stealing moments, touches that said more than words ever could.

"Ready?" he asked, his breath warm against her cheek. He slid the cloth away, his fingers trailing down to her shoulder. "Open your eyes."

Kassidy blinked against the sudden light, her breath catching as the world around her came into focus.

Before her was a hidden paradise carved into the cliffside—a lush garden that seemed to defy logic. Wildflowers bloomed in a riot of colors, spilling over cascading vines that clung to the jagged rock walls. A shimmering pool reflected the sunlight filtering through the canopy above, steam curling off its surface like a whisper of warmth. In the center, a crystal-clear waterfall tumbled into a shallow pool. Sunbeams danced off the water, casting rainbows across the lush greenery.

"What is this?" she breathed, her voice catching. "Is it even real?"

"It's real. It's been a labor of love."

His eyes locked on her, dark and intense. A quiet satisfaction gleamed in his eyes.

"At first, it was just going to be a hot tub. Then I realized I wanted something that felt more like me. So I designed this. Built it. I spent a few years getting it right. Everything is self-sufficient now. The plants grow wild without any need for maintenance. The water's heated from below by geothermal energy. The flowers bloom all year because of the heat."

Kassidy took a step forward, her hand covering her mouth. "Shephard," she whispered, "this place is incredible—magical."

"The perfect escape?"

"Yes. Perfect."

He stood behind her, arms crossed over her chest, a small smile playing on his lips. "Put my education to use on this one."

She turned to face him, her eyes wide. "You are a wonder of nature, Shephard. This place feels like we've just stepped into a dream."

"Whenever I need to get away, to think, or just…be, I come here. I've never shared it with anyone else. Until you. Until now."

Her chest tightened at the honesty in his voice, but she masked it with a teasing smile. "You mean to tell me you've never brought a girl to your magical moss garden oasis? I don't buy it. This would be an easy home run."

He pulled her closer, hands sliding to her low back, his smile turning wicked. "Home run, huh?"

She bit her lip and nodded.

"Does that mean you'll take off all your clothes and join me?" he murmured, his gaze dropping to her lips.

"No," she said with a slow shake of her head, a smile teasing her mouth. "It means I want you to take off all my clothes. Then—I will join you."

His wicked grin turned even more devious. Shephard moved deliberately, sliding her clothing down piece by piece until she stood bare and vulnerable, the greenery a magical backdrop. The water was impossibly clear, reflecting the wildflowers, vines, and the curve of her body in the fading light.

Shephard pulled his sweater over his head and tossed it onto a nearby rock. The muscles of his torso caught the light, the lines of old scars telling stories she hadn't yet heard.

He was all raw strength and effortless grace, his body a masculine work of art. Kassidy's heart beat fast with anticipation as she watched him strip down, his movements confident and unhurried.

Then he took her hand, grounding her and setting her on fire all at once, as he helped her into the steaming water. Heat climbed up her body, soothing every muscle, but it wasn't the water that made her feel alive. Shephard wrapped her in an embrace that was equal parts supportive and possessive, his hands finding her waist and pulling their bare skin together.

He was everything she wanted—warm and inviting, kind, and steady—not to mention the flutter that filled her every time he came near.

But the complications loomed. Her career. The storm waiting for her. And his secrets. The ones she could feel just under the surface. It was all too fast, and she knew it. Yet, it didn't feel wrong.

Every thought dissolved as her arms wrapped around his neck, the world shrinking to nothing but the feel of him.

All that existed was this moment, this man, and the undeniable chemistry growing between them.

Two weeks unraveled in a blur of salt-kissed mornings and moonlit evenings, each moment slipping through Kassidy's fingers like sand. She stopped trying to keep track of time—stopped wanting to— because every second with Shephard felt like something borrowed, too perfect to belong to the real world.

He made the ordinary feel extraordinary. One morning, he flew her to a remote island where driftwood lay tangled on the shore like forgotten sculptures, tide pools glimmered with trapped bits of sky, and tiny crabs skittered over the rocks.

They waded into the cold water, their hands locked together, shrieking when a wave caught them off guard. He chased her across the sand, tackled her in the surf, both of them left breathless from laughter.

That night, he cooked for her—nothing elaborate. Just seared fish, roasted potatoes, and vegetables kissed with lemon—but it tasted like something out of another life. A life that wasn't about image, contracts, or expectations. A life that belonged to her if she wanted it.

Their days stretched long and golden, filled with hikes through mist-laden forest. To their private grotto where cedar and moss swallowed sound, and the only witnesses to their stolen moments were a scattering of little animals and the lazy glide of a hawk overhead.

Afternoons melted into the sound of waves lapping against Shephard's dock as they lounged on his balcony, her head resting on his chest, his fingers tracing idle patterns along the bare skin of her back.

But it wasn't just the romance or the adventure that made their time together like a fairytale. It was the quiet moments, the ones that snuck up on her when she least expected it. Like the way Shephard's face aged in reverse when he talked about his mother, or how he ran his hand through his hair when he thought she wasn't looking. Or the time they stayed up late lying on the beach, talking about everything and nothing, the fire crackling softly beside them.

Kassidy had let herself open up to him in ways she never had with anyone else—except for the one career-killing, soul-crushing, morally-corrupt mistake she was still keeping to herself. The one that was about to be unleashed on the world. She told him everything about her.

Except that.

Kassidy stretched her legs out on the blanket, pulling her hoodie tighter around her as the fire flickered beside them. The ocean stretched out beyond Shephard's deck, so dark and endless she could barely see it.

"You asked me about my mother. My grandparents used to try to keep their grief from me," she said, staring at the dancing flames. "But I felt it anyway. I always knew there was something missing."

Shephard didn't push, didn't fill the silence. He just sat with her.

She hesitated, then admitted, "I used to dream about her— sometimes I still do. I only know her from pictures and the stories my grandparents told me, but I used to imagine she was out there somewhere, looking for me too. As a little kid, I didn't understand that she was never coming home."

His fingers brushed over hers, a quiet reassurance.

"I know we agreed to be each other's escape and hold onto our own secrets, but I can't help but think about Ray. If you don't want to talk about him, I understand. But maybe it would help."

Shephard exhaled, running a hand through his hair, his gaze was distant, as if he was sorting through his own past. She wondered if she'd crossed the line they said they wouldn't cross. Gotten too deep. Ruined their magical fantasy two weeks.

"Growing up out here wasn't easy," he admitted. "My parents had to make a deal with Ray for us to even stay. We didn't have electricity or running water at first. And I had no friends, at least not kids to play with." He huffed out a quiet laugh.

Kassidy smiled, picturing it. "But you still loved it?"

He glanced at her, something almost wistful in his expression. "Yeah. I did. Still do."

He leaned back on his elbows, staring up at the sky. "Not everyone thought Ray was a good man. But to me, he was the best. He used to tell me that if I wanted something, I had to go after it, no hesitation. That's how he built what he did out here. He just did it. Didn't think too far ahead." Shephard shook his head. "He wasn't my real grandfather, you know that, but from the first time I can remember, he was the one I wanted to call Grandpa."

Kassidy could see it now—the attachment, the loyalty. She didn't push because she knew she had no right to, but she wanted to ask about other things. About the phone calls he made. The moments when his expression hardened. The things he wasn't telling her.

They didn't talk about how Ray died or Shephard's grief, or whatever he was carrying that seemed too heavy to even lift to the surface. It was his to share when he was ready, and she wanted to be there for him. Maybe she'd give up everything to stay there forever.

Except that was an empty dream too. There was no getting around dealing with the fall out that was about to come.

The night before her grandma's arrival, Kassidy found herself sitting on the dock, her legs dangling above the water's surface, as it glowed faintly beneath her.

Shephard was beside her, his arm draped loosely around her shoulders, and for a moment, everything felt perfect.

But the thought of tomorrow hung heavy in the air, an unspoken tension neither of them wanted to address.

"You don't think that we're related somehow, do you?" Kassidy asked and Shephard's eyes shot open wide.

"Um…I hope not. But no, I don't think that." A faint smile ghosted over his lips. "However, worse case, let's say we are related. We couldn't be closer than what, cousins? I'd be okay with that."

She slapped him lightly on the chest and they laughed together. "Even though I consider him like a grandfather, and you might very well be his real granddaughter. No, I don't think we're related."

"I can't help but feel like whatever my grandma has to tell me, is going to change everything," Kassidy said, throat tightening.

"Nothing has to change between us," Shephard reassured her, but she knew in her heart, there was no way it could stay the same.

What they were doing wasn't real. They weren't living in the real world, with real problems. They were hiding—from all of it. And from each other, keeping their secrets buried beneath the illusion. And illusions didn't. What they had would have to change.

Silence stretched between them, and Shephard pulled her into his arms. He kissed her with the same intensity he had the first time, as if he was trying to memorize her. And Kassidy kissed him back, pouring everything she couldn't say into that moment.

That night belonged to them in a way that made her ache. Shephard touched her like she was something rare, something worth memorizing. He knew exactly when to make her laugh, when to pull her out of her head, and when to look at her like she was the only thing that had ever made sense.

And that, terrified her.

Because when it ended—when the world came calling, when the truth caught up to her—what would be left of them?

She didn't know what truths tomorrow would reveal when Virginia arrived, or if Shephard was ready to reveal whatever secrets he was hiding, but she knew one thing for certain: these past two weeks with that man had been the best of her life.

Whatever had brought her to this place—whatever twists of fate had led her here—she would always be thankful because they had brought her to him.

# Chapter 22

The next morning, the water taxi driver who brought Kassidy to the island returned to drop off her grandma, Virginia. When he tried to help her out of the boat, Virginia swatted him away with her purse.

"Do I look like I need help? I've been stepping out of boats since before you learned to tie a knot," Virginia barked, rattling off a few more disgruntled sentences.

Her tone was sharp, and her movements quick, the kind that came from a woman who was used to fending for herself.

"Grandma!" Kassidy called, letting the screen door slam behind her as she rushed out of the cottage in her red-checked flannel and oversized galoshes.

Her heavy boots thudded awkwardly on the dock, but she didn't care—they were growing on her in ways she hadn't expected. Like everyone and everything about the island.

"Let him help you, Grandma. It's his job. He's not doing it because you're old."

"Of course, he's not doing it because I'm old. I'm not old!" Virginia snapped, flicking her wrist dismissively as if she could swat away the very notion of age itself. "And I don't need help."

"Grandma, seriously," Kassidy sighed, "he's lending you a hand, not a cane."

"Well, I don't need either," Virginia said, her voice a mix of defiance and pride. She turned to the driver, pressing a crisp five-dollar bill into his hand before giving him a polite yet curt nod. "Thank you for the ride. It was lovely." Then, without missing a beat, she straightened her flowing skirt, re-tucked her blouse, and smoothed the soft silver waves of her hair that framed an elegant and timeless face.

Kassidy couldn't help but smile. "You look beautiful, Grandma—like you haven't aged a day past eighty-five," she teased.

Virginia's chin lifted, her blue eyes holding a familiar sharpness.

"If there weren't any mirrors in this ugly world, I'd still be as young as you, darling."

Kassidy reached for the woman who raised her, the only mother she'd ever known, hugging her tightly.

Though Virginia had once stood as tall as Kassidy, time had worn her down, literally, but her presence alone remained commanding.

Virginia stepped back and took Kassidy's face between her palms, the pads of her thumbs brushing lightly across her granddaughter's cheeks.

"Look at you," she murmured, a softness entering her voice. "You look beautiful without all that makeup. Guess you've finally taken my advice and let your face be free."

"Grandma, get your hands off my face before you give me acne. Don't you know you're not supposed to touch your face, especially after traveling." Kassidy wiped the backs of her knuckles across her cheeks as if brushing away germs.

"Oh for God's sake—this again?"

The words cut sharper than usual, and Kassidy flinched before she could stop herself.

Virginia's voice, when it returned, was quieter. Rougher.

"I shouldn't have said that. I'm sorry, sweetheart."

Kassidy froze mid-movement, a mischievous smile lighting her face. "Did you just …apologize for being short-tempered? Grandma! Are you getting soft? Come here, let me feel you." Kass reached to squeeze Virginia's arms, but the woman pulled away, "You don't see a white light, do you?" She leaned in, peering closely into Virginia's eyes, her tone conspiratorial. "A tunnel? Is Grandpa Stan waving you over?"

Virginia swatted at her, a small laugh escaped through her lips.

"I'm not getting soft—quite the opposite is happening actually. The skin on my feet is getting tougher by the day, and I'm sure my arteries are rock solid by now."

"Don't forget your heart," Kassidy added with a wink.

Virginia's face relaxed. "I believe my heart turned black the summer of 1970, dear. It's been the same useless organ ever since."

Kassidy's teasing grin faded into something gentler. "Well, I still love every cold, dark inch of it."

For the briefest moment, Virginia's sharp exterior cracked. Her lips quirked into a reluctant smile before a laugh bubbled up, a deep, cathartic sound that only Kassidy could coax out of her.

The women laughed together in a way only they could when they were together—a shared bond over quick-witted banter.

"You're a genetically gifted brat, you know that?" Virginia said, her laughter mingling with Kassidy's.

But beneath their playful chiding, something lingered—the conversation they hadn't had yet—a storm hovering over the water, waiting to hammer the shore.

Kassidy linked her arm with Virginia's, tugging her along the dock, "Now, are you going to tell me why I'm here?" Her eyes narrowed in mock suspicion. "*Isla Virginia?* Or are we just going to stand here all day and exchange quips?"

A burst of air shot passed Virginia's lips. "Honey, you're out of your league if you think you can outdo me. You'd lose before I even broke a sweat."

Kassidy stopped and turned to Virginia. "Grandma...dish it! Tell me why we're here. Now. Is this island named after you? Did you have some sizzling summer fling you never told me about?"

Virginia's smile faltered slightly. "Yes."

Kassidy scoffed, stamping her booted foot on the wooden dock. "Grandma! I thought we told each other everything! That was your rule!"

Virginia waved her off, her gaze drifting toward the sea. "I just told you that so you'd tell me everything about you. Not the other way around. I needed some way to keep a handle on you. Have you seen you? As beautiful as your mother was."

"You big fat liar," Kassidy muttered, folding her arms across her chest. "What else have you lied about, and what do you have to say for yourself?"

"The whole world is built on the lies we choose to believe, dear," Virginia said, in that same monotone raspy tone she had when she didn't care what the world thought about her.

Kassidy's smile faded as she studied her grandma. "What happened here, Grandma, tell me now."

Virginia's eyes flickered with a momentary sadness that Kassidy caught but didn't understand.

"Oh, just a midsummer night's dream that turned into a nightmare, is all. That's how dreams go sometimes—starts with stardust, ends with a mess you can't sweep up."

Kassidy's stomach twisted. The way Virginia said it—so offhand, so certain, it made it feel like more than just a passing comment. Like a warning.

She thought of Shephard, of their days wrapped in sunlight and their nights tangled in heat. Of how easy it had been to believe in the illusion of them keeping secrets.

The wind picked up, tugging at Virginia's skirt as she glanced down at the new boards on the dock, stepping on them to test their sturdiness. Virginia's eyes swept up toward the cabin, and Kassidy saw something she'd rarely seen—tears welling in the hardened woman's eyes. It was a startling sight.

Virginia Karlson, the steely matriarch who never shed tears, only at Grandpa Stan's funeral, stood on the dock with her shoulders heavy, her sharp blue eyes softened by a watery emotion she couldn't hide.

Kassidy saw a thick book of secrets hiding in those eyes—a deep trove of memories she had no idea Virginia had successfully hidden.

"Grandma," Kassidy's voice was a whisper, her heart aching for the woman in front of her, who seemed to be haunted by memories that were too painful to admit. "Who is Raymond? Why does he think I'm his granddaughter? And why would he leave me an island?"

At the mention of his name, Virginia blinked, as if coming out of a nostalgic haze.

She looked at Kassidy, her eyes clear now, sharp, and truthful in a way that made Kassidy's stomach flutter with anticipation.

"I wanted to tell you," Virginia said softly. "I really did. But I needed every bit of solid ground I could stand on in my life after your mother died and telling you about Raymond, about this world, would have shaken our foundation.

"Yes, I kept secrets from you. But not to hurt you. It wasn't to protect you either. As selfish as it may sound, I kept those secrets to protect myself. I didn't want to relive the heartache. What I wanted was to focus on being the best mother and grandma and wife I could be. What happened here, in these islands, well, I just couldn't relive it. My only choice was to keep it in the past. Where it belonged."

Kassidy's heart raced as she stared at her grandma, waiting for more answers. Virginia continued, her voice calm.

"Raymond is your mother's biological father." Kassidy's hands flew to her mouth, a gasp escaping her lips. "Your grandfather."

Kassidy's head spun, the dizzying revelation turning over in her mind. "Did Grandpa Stan know?"

Virginia's lips pressed into a thin line as she nodded.

"Of course, he knew. I would never hide something like that from him. Stanley was the love I chose, but Raymond…Ray was the other half of my soul."

Kassidy's breath caught in her throat as she linked arms with her grandma again, pulling her closer. Virginia turned toward the cabin.

"I'll tell you everything you want to know," she said, her voice burdened by the pain of the past. "But I need to warn you, Kassidy. What happened here is well, wonderful. Horrible. Tragic. Magical. This island, the summer I spent with Ray changed me," Her voice wavered, "it shaped who I was, and who I became."

The wind whispered through the trees as the two women stood on the dock, their pasts and futures tangled together like the roots beneath the island.

And though Kassidy didn't yet understand the depth of what her grandma had revealed, she could feel the immensity of it—the secrets, the pain, and the love.

Virginia's eyes glistened with unshed tears as they walked the rest of the length of the dock. At the threshold of the door, she stopped and turned to Kassidy.

"The last time I was here, I told Raymond that our daughter, your mother, had died. And then I told him how she left me you."

Tears flooded Kassidy's eyes and spilled silently down her cheeks. Her throat tightened, but she said nothing.

Kassidy reached for her grandma's hands, squeezing them tight. "You've been the best mother and grandma a girl could ask for, so if you kept something from me, I'm sure it was for a good reason. I know your heart, grandma. It's not cold, or black—it's fierce, and protective and strong, and it's kept me safe my whole life."

"Thank you for saying that, dear. It's also carried the pain of what happened here my whole life. Hidden, tucked away. I haven't told anyone. Not even Stanley. Not all of it, anyway. Only what he needed and wanted to know," her voice trembled, another crack in her steel facade. "When your mother died, I told Ray that when he wanted to be part of your life, that I'd tell you everything, and let the two of you meet. I guess that time has come. So, where is the old coot, anyway? Hiding around the corner? Ready to jump out and scare me to death, I suppose?"

Kassidy jerked her head back in shock.

She stared at her grandma, whose sharp blue eyes seemed to darken and turn gray.

She understood the truth before Kassidy could tell her. Of course Virginia didn't know—how could she? But she sensed it anyway.

"I was afraid of that," Virginia said. She inhaled deeply, her chest rising as tears welled in her eyes.

"I'm sorry," Kassidy said, not knowing what else to say.

"I didn't know what I was getting into—not that I could stop it anyway," Virginia said, and Kassidy's eyes narrowed, not fully understanding. "Great love comes with a painful price."

When Kassidy opened the door and Virginia stepped inside, she turned in a slow circle, eyes sweeping over the photos on the walls, the stacks of journals, and the carved mural. She marveled at it in the same way that Kassidy had done when she arrived.

Virginia clutched her chest, gasping as though the air had been knocked out of her, and Kass felt her grandma falter as if her knees nearly gave way.

"Oh my God," she said. "He tried so hard to make things right. He never forgave himself."

Kassidy's heart swelled with emotion. She felt as though she was witnessing a piece of the past she didn't fully understand. The two women stood in the living room, surrounded by a history so rich and deep it thrummed in the air.

Neither of them realized they were standing amid something that might save the future.

"How did Ray die?" Virginia asked quietly.

Kassidy shook her head and shrugged. "I've met a couple of people who knew him. Neither knew what happened." Virginia's gaze dropped to the floor, a shadow crossing her face. When she looked back up, her eyes held a deep sadness. "Grandma, do *you* know how he died?"

"I imagine he went out exactly the way he always said he would." She walked to the wall and touched a black-and-white photo of a single whale's fluke. "Ray believed that when it was his time, they'd come for him."

Kassidy blinked. "Who would come for him? Was he a criminal?"

"No. Raymond wasn't a criminal. It was me who did the worst of it," Virginia replied, her eyes locked on the photo as though it was pulling her back in time.

A chill crawled up Kassidy's spine, every hair on her neck standing on end.

"Grandma, you're scaring me. Who came for him?" Virginia pressed her palm to the photo and then looked out the window. Kassidy followed her gaze. "Who came for him, Grandma?" Kassidy repeated, her voice trembled, the question hanging in the air like a ripple disturbing the calm.

Virginia stared out at the waves for a long moment before slowly lifting her eyes to Kassidy's, locking onto her with an intensity that sent another chill down Kassidy's spine.

"The people under the sea."

# Chapter 23

Kassidy pointed to the man she assumed was Raymond.

It was a dusty black-and-white photo of two fishermen, standing proud between their biggest catch. The man on the left looked to be in his twenties, clean-shaven, with military-issued hair, and a baby face brimming with youthful innocence.

"Is that Raymond?"

"Oh, lord no!" Virginia huffed. Then she gently lifted Kassidy's finger, moving it to point at the other man. "That was my Ray."

Kassidy's eyes widened, her mouth agape. "Grandma! You hussy!"

She spun toward Virginia, who pushed her tongue deep into her cheek to suppress a smile.

Kassidy gasped out the words, "I knew it! I knew you were wild."

A mischievous glint sparkled in Virginia's eyes, a sly smile tugging at her lips.

Kassidy nudged her shoulder, causing her to release a bigger, blushing grin. "You sly dog, you. He was a catch."

Virginia's wrinkles deepened with amusement, and a soft chuckle escaped from her lips. "He was a catch," she admitted, her words carried on a breeze of pride and nostalgia. "The most prized catch around. Every girl from here to Snohomish wanted to be with Ray. But he only had eyes for one woman. Me."

Ray looked nothing like the starched, straight-edged man beside him. He had a visible confidence—rugged, with a tattoo snaking across one muscular arm, visible beneath the rolled sleeve of his worn t-shirt.

Virginia's voice lowered as her gaze lingered on the photograph, a wistful smile playing on her lips.

"Ray was the kind of boy my mother warned me about. Tousled hair, hard-edges, and that rebellious, untamed charm. Everything about him whispered danger, and every girl on the island couldn't resist him. We all knew he'd break our hearts."

She paused, her fingers lightly tracing the edge of the picture. "But lucky for me," she continued, her tone growing quieter, "Ray wasn't who people judged him to be. He had layers no one cared to see. And yes, that man right there," her voice wavered slightly, "is your mother's father. And my first love. The one I let slip away."

Virginia's eyes glistened as she drew in a shaky breath. "I let him go for reasons so tangled with pride and ignorance, I can hardly stand myself when I think about it."

Kassidy's mouth parted slightly as she studied the photo with fresh eyes. "Seems to me that he let you get away," Kassidy said, as she pulled her grandma to the couch. "Now, tell me everything. Except the gross parts," she added with a playful grin. She looped her arm through her grandma's and sat her down. "I'll take another week off work if we have to. Now spill it."

"Speaking of which," Virginia said, raising an eyebrow, "what on earth have you been doing on this island for the past two weeks? I mean, limited service, bare-bones supplies—this is not exactly your comfort zone, honey.

"No offense, but let's just say the 'low-maintenance' stick didn't exactly whack you on the way down."

"I'm offended," Kassidy shot back with mock indignation. "I can be low maintenance. Look at me—I haven't worn makeup all week."

Virginia narrowed her eyes, leaning in with a suspicious smirk. "Uh-huh. You're up to something. I can smell it."

Kassidy's face flushed, but she quickly plastered on a grin. "Stop it now, enough about me," she said, deflecting. "Spill it, Isla Virginia!"

"Alright…alright." Virginia's face grew serious. "I had a love affair with a man so wild and complex it's hard to imagine he ever existed. But first, I need you to understand something. I met Ray before I met Stanley. I loved Stanley very much, and you know he loved you too. You were our daughter—his daughter, no matter what.

"When your mother died, we raised you as if you were our own. Stanley never thought of you as anything less. Nothing can change that. And I wouldn't trade a single day of my life with Stan. Not one day.

"Our life was good. Easy. Not complicated like my time with Ray. And Stan was there for me when I wasn't sure if I could go on anymore, you know, after your mother."

Kassidy studied her grandma's face as Virginia's gaze drifted back to the photograph, her eyes glistening. "Ray and I—our time burned too hot to last forever."

Virginia stood and walked over to the map carved into the wall. Her fingers lightly traced the delicate edges, then she followed the inlets, double-backing along the rugged coastline as though reading a language only she understood—one written just for her.

"I never hated anyone the way I hated Ray. I wanted to kill him."

Her voice cracked, and she clenched her fist as if grasping an invisible wound. Her hand hovered over the carved inlet near False Bay. She closed her eyes, letting her fingers linger over the mural.

Kassidy stood still, watching as her iron grandma pressed both palms to the wall and bowed her head between them.

A quiet sob slipped from her lips.

She stayed like that—unmoving.

Kassidy half-believed the moment might tear a hole through time and pull Virginia back.

Virginia lifted her face, her eyes clouded with shadows from the past. She stared at a spot on the map, a word carved into the water, then whispered it out loud.

"Penn Cove."

The words slipped from her lips with a tremble.

Kassidy shivered.

Virginia's fingers skimmed the edge of the map. "When I left this island, I never thought I could forgive him for the things he'd done here. And when I came back years later, and he told me the truth about that night…" Her voice thinned, as if it were stretching across time. "I never thought I could forgive myself for what I'd done." She exhaled, something raw flickering in her expression. "In many ways, I still haven't."

A chill traced Kassidy's spine. "What happened?"

Virginia looked at her, long and hard, as if deciding whether she was ready to hear the answer.

"The story I'm going to tell you will come with consequences. I'm going to need you to listen all the way through to the end before you judge, can you do that, Kassidy?"

"Grandma, you're scaring me. What kind of consequences?"

Her grandma turned, and walked back into the living room, settling into the chair by the picture window.

The afternoon light slanted across her face, casting half of it in shadow. She stared at the narrow inlet between their island and the one across the water, her jaw tight.

Kassidy curled up on the couch opposite her grandma, grabbing a pillow and pressing it against her knees like she used to as a little girl.

"Moral ones," Virginia exhaled. "Because you're either the one fixing the leak, or you're the one letting the water in. And each of us must decide where we stand—then be ready to live with that choice."

# Chapter 24

My darling Kassidy wrapped the blanket tighter around herself. She didn't say a word, just watched me with trusting eyes, waiting for answers. I'd always known this day would come—that somehow, someway, I'd have to tell her everything. Not just the parts I wanted to share, but the ones I never wanted to admit. Not to her. Not to anyone. Not even to myself.

Because I couldn't give her half a story and what happened was a tangle of wonder and tragedy, but neither existed without the other.

I cleared my throat, closed my eyes, and let the past pull me under.

The first time I laid eyes on Raymond Hawthorne I knew instantly that he was filled with a fire no one could contain.

The year was 1970.

It was the summer of love.

I was twenty years old and a delicious peach if I do say so myself. My hair had a soft middle part, my skin was still porcelain, like yours is right now, dear. And the bell-bottoms I had on clung to my curves like they were painted on.

My momma and daddy, your great grandparents, who left this earth before you were born, couldn't agree on anything. And I couldn't wait to get out of those corn fields and go on an adventure.

When you take someone with you, you bring your world—go alone, and you find out who you really are. Now, I know I've told you that dozens of times, Kassidy, but what I never told you was that it was my mother who gave me that advice.

At least that's what she said that day standing at the door, hands tucked into her apron. She wanted me to get out and see the world like she never could.

My father leaned against the porch rail, arms crossed, face half-hidden beneath the brim of his hat, not wanting me to go anywhere. Also knowing there was nothing he could do to stop me. I was leaving for the summer and that was that.

He was stubborn.

But I was hardheaded in a way no one could control.

I remember how the suitcase felt in my hand that day—lighter than it should have, as if maybe I was leaving too much behind. But I think that's how it had to be. I had to get out there and find my own way. Even if that way led me right back to where I came from.

I wouldn't have admitted it then, but I was scared when I climbed onto the bus that day, and even more terrified when I got to the ferry station. But my dreams were bigger than my fears.

I imagined the small tourist town on the water, the salty air, and the ferry cutting across the waves like something out of a postcard. I had a job waiting, but more than that, I had a wide-open world ahead of me. If ambition could swim, I'd have beaten the ferry to Friday Harbor and left it trailing in my wake.

When I stepped off the dock, it was the first time I'd ever been to an island. My stomach was in knots, but I was free, and not even the pandemonium of the world could reach me.

The U.S. was still at war with Vietnam, Richard Nixon was still an honest man, and everybody was fighting for something. Some wanted war, others demanded peace, and it seemed like no one could accomplish a damn thing either way.

It was a time of racists, and bigamists and speciesists, even if we didn't know what that meant yet.

Evil existed, Kassidy.

But so did love.

Back then, we were free to love whoever we wanted—no one cared if you slept with men or women or both at the same time. Then my generation grew up. Nixon waged his war on drugs, everyone stopped smoking pot and tripping on LSD and moved into corporate America—as if that went better for anyone.

I didn't know who I was back then, or what I wanted to become, but I was desperate to find out. Something about these islands called to me—they were a far-off enchanted place where I could find answers about myself and the nature of my soul, and just maybe, find someone to spend my life with.

I'd only been on the island a week when I met Ray. I was a waitress at the Warf Inn—this majestic place along the waterfront in the harbor. I believe it's still there today—a polished relic from a bygone era I suppose.

Ray was standing in the bed of his truck, shoveling ice over a giant silver fish. Each day he'd bring in the day's *"Freshest Catch"* for the chef to put on the menu.

If you would have told me right then that I'd spend the most unforgettable summer of my life with that man—I would have said that *I believe you.*

Ray had a magnetism that drew in every woman for a hundred miles, and it wasn't just because he was handsome; it was because he had passion—for everything he did. He knew who he was and what he wanted, and his confidence was contagious.

The first time our eyes met, Ray looked at me like he recognized me from another life. As if there was no question that the universe had brought us together. He jumped down from that truck, and walked right up to me as if he'd been waiting for me since birth.

"You're new," he said, eyes twinkling, "I'm Ray."

"Who said I was asking? And how do you know I'm new?" I lifted my chin.

He smiled a crooked grin. "Because you don't look like you're from around here."

"What's that supposed to mean? Just where do I look like I'm from then?"

His gaze intensified. "My dreams."

I could've melted right there.

Now I know what you're going to say, Kassidy, how could I fall for that line? But honey, my head was already under water the moment we locked eyes.

I should've been more guarded, played at least a little harder to get, but something about him made sense. Or made me lose all my sense, you could say.

"You want to help me haul in this fish. Or are you just going to stand there looking all beautiful in those threads?" Ray asked.

"Stand here," I said, raising an eyebrow and planting my hands on my hips.

My answer came out in a southern drawl even though I'd never stepped a foot south of Bettendorf.

Ray just grinned. "Right on. I was hoping you'd say that." His smile an invitation to more than just a summer fling.

And that's how it started—a spark—small, but enough to set my world on fire. And if you don't believe in love at first sight, Kassidy, well then, it's because it hasn't happened to you yet.

But for those of us lucky enough to feel it, it's as real as the moon pulling the tides. The moment Ray looked at me, I knew in my heart that we were meant to share the same breath for all eternity.

Ray picked up the enormous cooler filled with ice and fish like it was nothing, his muscles flexing under his shirt. The man looked like he was carved out of the sea itself, born of salt and wind. And when his shirt lifted just enough to reveal tattoos—nautical designs, coordinates, a compass rose—I couldn't help but stare.

No one I knew had tattoos back then, not like now, where you kids plaster your skin like it's wallpaper. Ink meant something different, and I couldn't tear my eyes away from him, wondering what was so important to this man that he etched it onto his skin.

"What time are you closing up?" Ray asked, his tone as smooth as silk, as I followed him into the restaurant.

"After the dinner rush and whenever the kitchen's cleaned up I suppose. Why?" I smirked, refusing to be outdone. "You planning on taking me out?"

"Yes. I am. Anything you want to do first?" His smile spread wide, like I'd passed some secret test.

I bit my lip, thinking of the million things I wanted to see and experience—with him. "Oh nothing much. Just everything."

"Could take a lifetime for us to do that. But I can dig that. If you can."

I shrugged, feeling bolder than I'd ever been. "I don't have a lifetime. I only have one summer."

Ray winked, like he knew something I didn't. "That'll be a good enough start then, I guess."

My smile must have stretched a mile wide. "You're trouble," I teased, feeling the heat rise in my cheeks.

He grinned. "Not any more than you."

From that very first conversation, I knew exactly what he wanted—me. There was no guessing, no playing coy. Ray made me feel like the only person in the world who mattered, and there's no greater feeling. It was like being swept up in a wave you can't fight, and for once, I let it carry me.

"Don't go falling in love with anyone before I get back now," he said, his voice low, but playful.

"Why, so I can fall in love with you?"

His smile softened, a hint of sincerity creeping into his tone.

"Right on."

I blushed so hard I thought my face would catch fire, and from that moment on, I didn't stop blushing for the rest of the summer.

# Chapter 25

I lost count of how many dinner orders I messed up that night thinking about Ray, but it was enough to get me grounded to breakfast and lunch shifts for the rest of the summer. Which was fine by me because it left my evenings open to be with Ray.

By eight o'clock my apron was stuffed with tips I didn't deserve, my mind was filled with tantalizing thoughts, and my heart raced from anticipation. He was right there when I walked out the back door, eyes locking onto mine with a fiery intensity that mirrored my own. And Kassidy, it was pure, passionate lust is what it was—and lust is the spark that sets love on fire.

Ray leaned against the hood of his '69 Chevy pickup, legs crossed, arms folded, and with that same confident smirk. I was smitten with that man before I even knew his last name. Next thing I knew, he was running right toward me.

I gasped as he scooped me into his arms and carried me off like he was already carrying me down the aisle. Every nerve in my body lit up, sparking like a fuse heading straight for dynamite.

"What are you doing?"

"We'd better hurry," he said, his tone teasing but urgent.

"Exactly where are we going?"

He opened the passenger side door, setting me down gently.

"We're going where you asked…everywhere. And if we only have one summer we better get started. Right now. Starting with my favorite place."

"And why were you carrying me?" I raised an eyebrow.

He grinned. "I couldn't help myself."

"And you think I'm just going to go with you without even knowing where we're going?" I tried to sound casual, but I wasn't fooling anyone.

He leaned in and set his elbows on the window frame. His sun-bleached hair was backlit by the dimming light, and his face was lit up with the rebellious charm of a movie star.

"I'll tell you if you want to know. But it'll be more fun if I keep it a surprise."

I smirked, then shifted my gaze forward, anticipation buzzing in my chest. "Fine. I'll be surprised."

I tried to hide the excitement in my voice, but my heart was beating so hard it made my words flutter and I thought it might give me away.

Once we were sealed inside his truck, I could smell the sea on him—salt and sun. Another scent wafted from him too—freedom. His freedom, my freedom—it was right there in the air all around us as we drove across the island, and it was intoxicating—the kind of freedom I didn't even know I was missing.

Ray took me to where his fishing boat was tied in the harbor, then helped me step in. Aside from the ferry I took from Anacortes to Friday Harbor, I'd never been on the sea. Being in a smaller boat, floating lower in the water, connected me in a way I never expected— as if I was a part of it all rather than just a traveler on the waves.

The sun was nearly set when he unwrapped the mooring lines, and we shoved off. I know I should have had better sense than to trust him so fast, but I'd never felt more alive, and I knew he wouldn't hurt me.

There was nothing but blackness across the water as we got out near the open sea. The summer air was cool, and the haze made it feel like we were slipping through clouds. When I began to shiver, Ray unlocked a door in the floor that I hadn't noticed, pulled out a warm jacket, and wrapped me in it.

"Stand here. In front of me. I'll keep you warm." He made space for me to stand in front of the wheel, shielding me from the wind on all sides. One of his hands rested lightly on my waist, and the simple touch ignited a spark of electricity.

I wasn't what you'd consider…experienced, but I wasn't new to the game either. I felt all the nervous jitters a woman feels when she knows a man is attracted to her. Ray sheltered me while we skimmed across the surface, his hand stayed at my waist, and I could feel his face in my hair as it blew around him.

His warm breath grazed my neck, and I knew he was breathing me in. I didn't mind. The chemistry between us was electrifying—more intense than anything I'd ever known. Before, or since.

We were so far out on the water that the soft yellow lights from the houses scattered across the islands had dimmed to pale dots. Once we stopped moving, the weather was non-existent. There was no wind or moonlight. There was just the gentle lapping of waves against the hull and the vast, inky darkness stretching out in every direction. Ray cut the engine and turned off all the boat lights.

Now, if you think he was taking me out for a romantic moonlight stroll, Kassidy, boy are you wrong. Ray wouldn't have done anything usual or normal—he was much more of a…rugged romantic, I guess you could say.

He introduced me to his world in the most authentic way he could—by pulling me into the current, knowing I'd either swim beside him or be swept away.

I asked him, "Isn't it dangerous to be on the water without lights? What if another boat comes out and doesn't see us?"

He nodded toward the endless darkness. "There is another boat out there." I looked but couldn't make anything out. "And they don't see us. Not yet anyway. But they will."

Ray set one of his palms on my lower back and stood shoulder to shoulder with me. He pointed into the opaque wall of blackness in front of us, and it took a moment for my eyes to adjust, then slowly I saw the shape of a fishing boat come to life—one much bigger than ours—it too didn't have any lights.

Ray pulled out a large army green duffel bag from the secret compartment in the floor and took out a pair of portable roof lights—the old-school kind like you'd see on top of an unmarked police car.

My stomach dropped when he stuck them to the roof of his boat. "You can't do that. You'll go to jail," I stammered. "I'll go to jail."

He looked at me and smiled as he hooked them up to a portable battery. I took a step back when he took out a black jacket and ball cap—both had a patch sewn on with embroidered letters: WDFW, Washington State Department of Fish and Wildlife. He slid on the jacket and cap, then pulled out a megaphone and turned on the portable lights.

The flashing lights blazed through the darkness and lit the night with streaks of red and blue that reflected off the water.

I almost fell overboard at the sight.

"You're impersonating an officer. You'll get arrested for this."

"I'm okay with that. Aren't you?"

"Why would I be okay with that?"

"Because it's for a good cause."

At the time, I had no idea what he was talking about.

"I am not going to jail tonight."

"I sure hope not," he said, then pressed his lips to the megaphone and pulled the trigger to amplify his voice.

"This is the Washington State Fish and Wildlife Department. Release your catch immediately, or I will be forced to board your vessel." My heart pounded, and my stomach twisted. What had I gotten myself into? But Ray just went on like he'd done it a thousand times.

Turns out…he had.

"Under Code 14 of statute 179 article B, night fishing for king salmon is illegal and punishable by a ten thousand dollar fine and thirty days in jail," he went on, his commanding tone soaring across the still water. The mechanical distortion made each word resonate with authority and urgency. "This is your final warning! Release your catch now and exit this area or I will board your vessel."

He put the megaphone down at his side, and I stepped close to him, tugging on his shirt sleeve with both of my hands.

"Why are you doing this?" I whispered, understanding that I was an accomplice in his scheme and not wanting to get caught. My heart was pounding, and yet I didn't want to blow his cover.

"Those are salmon poachers with an illegal catch. I'm helping the wildlife service. They don't have enough boats to patrol this area at night, and poaching is a huge problem."

"So the wildlife people, they know you do this? That you're helping them—and they're okay with it?"

He waffled his head from side to side. A mischievous grin crept across his face. "Not exactly. But I'm not doing anything wrong," he said, matter-of-factly, in the calmest voice you'd ever heard.

"And what if those poachers find out we're not actually the cops? What if they have guns?"

"That could be bad. Better keep your voice down so they don't suspect us." Ray dug out a gigantic spotlight, held it in one hand and the megaphone in the other, his shoulders bulging under the weight. "You should probably sit down so they don't see you. Unless you want to put on one of these jackets. I have two." He nodded toward his duffel bag.

I threw my hands up and let them fall back down with a slap.

"Unbelievable," I said, then sat down out of sight.

Despite my nerves, when he wasn't looking, I couldn't help but smile. It was madness, but it was exhilarating. Ray was like nothing I'd ever known, and that terrified and thrilled me. I wanted to be furious with him for putting me in that predicament, but I wasn't. I couldn't be, I was alive in a way I hadn't felt before.

I could barely make out the boat in the distance or see if they were complying with his request, until he flipped on a sharp white beam from a spotlight. It cut across the surface of the water, straight to the poachers' boat.

It was a large fishing vessel with three men, clearly not complying with Ray's orders. They were hurrying to pull in their nets and stuff the fish in the livewell.

"Those bastards," I muttered. As much as I didn't want to be his accomplice, it irked me that they weren't listening to him, that they were doing something illegal. Something Ray clearly cared about. And if he cared about it, I knew it was worth caring about too.

"They're still pulling in fish," I burst out. "You're not going to let them get away with this, are you?"

Ray jerked his head toward me, and simultaneously, a smile grew on both our faces.

"We are definitely not going to let them get away with it. You should put on that life vest," he said, and I did what he asked, pulling the ugliest orange life vest you've ever seen over my head. Then he put his lips back to the megaphone. "This is your final warning. Release your catch immediately or I will be forced to board your vessel and place you under arr—"

A light flickered in the distance.

Another boat. Approaching quickly.

"Shit…" Ray said, then yanked the lights off his roof, stuffed them back into his bag along with his jacket and gear, and tossed them in his hidden compartment where they'd come from.

"Who is that? What's going on? Ray?"

My heart raced. The adrenaline of the moment had me in its grip, every nerve in my body tingling.

He looked up at me while pulling a rug over the trap door. "The real fish and wildlife."

"Oh shit. Yes kids, it's true your father did get both of us arrested on our first date," I said, exasperated but half-smiling.

Ray looked at me with a free-spirited, elated grin.

"Were you just speaking to our future children?"

I shrugged. "I was. And I was just about to tell them what a show-off, hotshot their father thought he was on our first date when he got us arrested."

"Have you ever been arrested?"

"N—no," I said, the word catching in my throat. "Oh God, is this really happening? Are we really going to— have you been arrested?"

"Maybe." He smirked. "But only for a good cause. You're up for that, right?"

There it was—Ray, daring me to cross the line with him. I was up for it, too, and though I would never admit it to him, his vigilante side drew me to him even more.

Ray fired up the engine. His modest fishing boat rumbled to life, and we throttled forward toward the real wildlife cops, who had much larger spotlights. One on us, and one on the poachers.

The men on the poacher boat were now hurriedly unloading their catch back into the water—dozens of giant silver fish slipping back into the black sea and out of sight.

I could see the anger and relief on Ray's face as we watched. Ray pulled alongside the officers, who shined their light in our faces.

"Gentlemen, you need any assistance?" Ray asked, as if they were family.

"No, Ray," one of them drawled. "How many times do I have to tell you? We got this. Go home."

I cocked my head and narrowed my eyes until the officer shined a flashlight straight at me. Ray stepped in front of me to block the light.

"Yes, sir, we were just heading back from a beautiful evening cruise. Glad you guys got here in time, or they would have taken off with a whole season of fish and put me out of business. Bet they've got a stash back at their cabin too." Ray pointed to the poachers. "I've seen that boat lurking around Shaw all week."

"We'll check it out. Thanks, Ray." The officer turned off the spotlight, and I could almost feel my pupils get as large as planets trying to adjust to the night sky. "Say, Ray—we got another call tonight about flashing lights out here. A woman wondering what was going on. She thought it was us. You know anything about that?"

"Uh, no sir, I didn't see anything like that tonight," he said, turning toward me. He put his hand around my waist and pulled me to him, hip to hip. "You see anything, baby?"

I shook my head, unsure whether I should be furious or if I'd just had a lawless night with an even more lawless man I'd never forget.

My head was swimming. This wasn't just some fun night out—this was a glimpse into Ray's world. A world that was exhilarating, chaotic, and I didn't know how dangerous at the time, it was so far removed from anything I'd ever known.

When we were far enough away for no one to hear I said to him, "Vigilante justice undermines the rule of law, you know."

"I'm not undermining anyone," Ray said, hand over hand on the big wheel. The boat lurched into a tight turn, narrowly avoiding a jagged rocky shoreline. "I'm free labor for them. There are too many poachers and not enough help to enforce the laws."

"What would you have done if those men refused to throw their fish back? What if it turned violent? You put my life in danger, you know? Not too smart for a date," I said, my voice light, but my heart still thudding from the night's events.

The wind blew through his shaggy hair as he turned and looked at me, his eyes gleaming in the moonlight.

"Do you feel like you're in danger? You don't look like you're in danger. You look...off the hook. And entertained. And beautiful, by the way. Out of sight beautiful."

Those words sent a rush of warmth through me. His eyes held mine. His voice softened for me. Air escaped past my lips, and I shook off the haze he had cast over me, trying to keep my head on straight.

"You didn't answer my question. What would you have done if they hadn't thrown the fish back or the officers hadn't come?"

"What I always do. Harass them until they decide to do the right thing. You should see what else I keep in that duffel bag."

I laughed, trying to fight the pull I felt toward him, but it was useless. I couldn't stay angry at him. I couldn't stay anything except wanting more of him.

"You're far out, you know that? Why do you care so much about fish, anyway?"

Ray pulled up next to the dock where we'd launched from and began tying up the boat with the ropes. His movements were deliberate, practiced, but his shoulders looked tense.

"Because if those men were allowed to take those fish, between them and the wolves of the sea, there wouldn't be any salmon for fishermen like me who play by the rules. I count on those fish to survive."

His words hit deeper than I expected.

"Well, aren't you just a stellar picture of law and order?"

Ray turned and grabbed the jacket around my shoulders, pulling me close to him. His arms wrapped around me, sheltering me from the cool night. Everything about him felt natural, good, and right. And that was the danger.

"It's those same salmon that are going to pay for our island."

"What are you talking about, our island?" I blurted, surprised, my mind spinning with the thought.

Could he really see that future for us? Could I?

It was all happening so fast. Whatever this was…it was just a summer fling. I couldn't stay. I had a life waiting for me back in Iowa—college, a future my father had carefully carved out for me.

My father pulled strings to get me into one of the top STEM programs in the country, with a scholarship that came with conditions. No girls got into STEM back then and it wasn't even called that. So if I didn't go back, my family would be on the hook for more money than we could ever afford.

"Ray—" I started, but he hushed me with a look, his forehead resting against mine.

It was as if he could hear the thoughts in my head before I could say them out loud. He seemed to understand, too, that we could pretend all we wanted, but at the end of the summer...

"Don't say it..." he said. "Not yet."

I looked up at him, and before I could say another word, his lips were on mine. It wasn't just a kiss—it was more like a promise, a plea. His hands slid up my back, and I felt the desperation in his touch. His need to make me understand how much finding each other meant.

I melted into him, unable to resist the pull between us, and the world blurred away until it was just Ray and me. His hands and lips stayed pressed against mine and I felt like he was never going to let go, like he was trying to keep me there, like holding me close could stop time itself.

I've thought about that night, that kiss countless times, and sometimes I wonder what would have happened if time could have stopped right then. If that had been our kiss goodbye instead of the tragedy that came at the end of that summer.

# Chapter 26

Before I knew it, Ray was everywhere. On the docks. On the water. Outside the restaurant, waiting for me each afternoon as my shift ended. We'd take out his boat and weave in and out of the islands at dusk, watching the sky turn pink over the sea, the breeze sultry on our already heated skin.

He'd talk about king salmon and how he was supposed to take over his father's fishmonger business. But even then, I could tell, Ray's love for the ocean ran deeper than just the pink-fleshed fish. He loved everything about the ocean, these islands, and every creature in them. Except for one that is the fisherman's nemesis—the wolves of the sea. At least that's what they called them back then.

After one week with Raymond, I was already too far gone to turn back. When you're young, Kassidy, love consumes you faster than a riptide can pull you out to sea. It had only been a short while, but it felt like Ray had always been a part of my life, as if coming here and meeting him wasn't just chance—it was meant to be.

One night, we were on the water in False Bay. The moonlight shimmered on the surface, casting silver shadows all around us, and Ray wrapped his arms around me and whispered something that, even now, all these years later, I hear in my sleep.

"I'm going to build us a home here, a life. Buy us some land," he said, his voice low and determined, "I've been saving all my money so I can move out of my parents' place, and I found exactly which piece of land I want for us. I'll take you there tomorrow when it's daylight. It's not really an island. It's more of an islet. But it's private Ginny. And more than enough land for a house, or two. And it'll be just ours." His words were filled with that same wild energy that made him irresistible.

"We can live by the water. Just us. No one else. No rules. Only you. Only me."

The idea of a life that was only ours, away from everything—no expectations, just us and the ocean—was as fantastical as it sounds, and with anyone else, I wouldn't have believed it could be real. But with Ray, I believed anything was possible.

In that moment, we acted like time didn't exist, like we had all the time in the world to be together. We acted the way young people do before they become aware of time and how fleeting each moment is.

Ray didn't talk about me leaving, and neither did I. It was like we didn't dare break the spell.

That summer, people from all over the world started buying land in the San Juan Islands. They built fancy vacation homes and paved roads like crazy. Back then, I could bike almost anywhere on the island. Ray and I would take his boat out to explore everywhere else—five hundred miles of untouched shoreline.

Now, I know you said nothing gross, Kassidy, but you also said you wanted to know the truth so here it is.

Ray told me he wanted to kiss me on every beach that covered those five hundred miles, and by golly by the end of that summer I think we almost did it.

Now, where was I? Oh, yes. I was about to tell you about the lighthouse. Be patient, dear, stop raising your hand and fidgeting so much, it looks like you're about to strangle that pillow. As promised, Kassidy, it'll all make sense real soon.

Every morning, before my shift, before my day was consumed with waitressing then Ray, I'd bike out to the lighthouse where I fell in love in a whole different way.

Perched on the rugged cliffs of San Juan Island, the lighthouse stood watch over the land and sea. Its brick-red roof and whitewashed walls glowed in the early light. The windswept cliffs below were lined with fragrant pine and kelp, the salty air wrapped around me like a warm embrace.

My mornings spent there, sitting on those rocks and looking out over the water, were enchanting. Black-and-white behemoths patrolled the waters below, and it was them—and Ray—who held my heart captive. I'd sit on the cliffs, waiting for a glimpse of the whales. Some days they swam by and played in the kelp; other days they didn't.

I'd wait patiently for the mist to lift, hoping to catch just one glimpse. I could have sat there for days and watched for them. I'll never forget the first time I saw them—wild orcas gliding through the waves, slapping their tails, and rolling through the kelp. I was completely mesmerized. Transfixed.

My heart raced at the sight of them breaching, their tall dorsal fins cutting through the water. It was like seeing something from another world, something powerful and woven into everything above and below the surface. I was hooked. As if a part of me had latched onto them, and no matter how hard I tried, I couldn't pull myself free.

The resident orcas weren't famous like they are today. They were feared. No one knew about their fourth lobe, or their tight-knit families. Back then, no one gathered at the lighthouse to watch for the whales either.

It wasn't like today, or least not like it was twenty years ago, with boats full of tourists chasing them across the water. In the summer of seventy, if you wanted to see them, all you had to do was sit on those cliffs and wait.

Some days, I'd go alone, watching in silence as they foraged in Deadman Bay. Other days, another woman joined me, and she was as bewitched by them as I was, but connected to them in a much deeper way. SaLita Seawalker was her name—a true ambassador for those magnificent creatures. I haven't seen her since that summer. But I'll never forget her. Or what we did.

SaLita glided into my life like something conjured up from the sea gods themselves. But she didn't sit on the rocks next to me, she had a canoe. SaLita would paddle out through the silvery waters, her raven-black hair adorned with a single feather, her cloak of vibrant colors draped over her shoulders. She was a vision of strength and tradition and quiet power unlike anything I'd ever known.

When she reached her spot, she'd pull out a small drum then play and sing. Her song was haunting and to this day, I'll never forget it.

The words floated on the air, ancient and powerful. I can still hear them in my mind.

*Tara'lokoni, Shaya'ka,*
*Itara'ni kwesh.*
*Nokati shal, kwetala shaya.*
*Eski lanawit, watash kini ala.*

The language was so strange to me, but it resonated somewhere deep. My curiosity grew too strong to ignore, so one morning, I finally found the courage to ask her what she was singing.

"A Coast KaWaltish prayer," she said, her eyes resolute as they met mine. "My people have lived here for twelve thousand years. The orcas are my ancestors."

"What does your song mean?"

She didn't hesitate, her voice shifting into an ancient rhythm.

"I call to the great spirits of the deep, guardians of the sea," she said softly. "I honor their presence and feel their hunger." She placed a hand over her stomach, her expression solemn. "May their bellies stay full, and their spirits remain free, until we meet again in the city of the deep."

Her words stirred something in me, like she was speaking to a part of my soul I hadn't known was there until that moment.

You wouldn't know it by looking around this cabin, but back then, Ray, and everyone else who fished these waters hated those whales.

Blackfish, they called them. The vermin of the sea. Wolves.

Back then, people didn't know any better. Women and children feared the great killer whales, and no one dared enter the water. Can you imagine, a whole island community with hordes of people who were too scared to step foot in the water because of the orcas.

You can blame the fisherman and their tall tales of orcas capsizing their boats and eating anyone who fell into the water for that. Oh, how the fishermen reviled them. Shooting at them. Spearing them on sight. Worse still, no one even questioned if it was right or wrong.

Some say the capture era changed that, turning the 'killer whale' into the 'beloved orca' we know today. But that's another lie, Kassidy. A lie those industries spun to justify their murders and kidnappings. What isn't a lie, is that no one ever saved anything by torturing and enslaving it.

Ray knew I went out to the lighthouse in the mornings before work, but he didn't like it. He was a fisherman through and through.

So I was forced to keep my growing love affair with the orcas separate from my love affair with Ray.

# Chapter 27

With Ray, life had no brakes. It was all speed, heat, and a rebellious rush I couldn't slow down—nor did I want to.

When Ray showed up at the restaurant, I felt his presence in the room before turning around and confirming he was there. He'd stroll in all sun-kissed and wind-tousled, with a fresh catch in his cooler. The chef would come out, grumbling, and inspecting. They'd haggle over the price all the while I'd try to act as if Ray wasn't irresistible, but I couldn't keep my eyes off him.

I'd help him haul the fish into the walk-in cooler so we could steal a moment. The cold air would hit my skin and cause full body shivers, but they were nothing compared to the sensation I felt when Ray touched my skin.

His hands were hot as they gilded over me, the heat between us immediate and overwhelming. His lips would find mine, urgent and insistent—our breaths white puffs as he pinned me against the icy wall.

Reality always crept back in. Someone would knock or swing open the door. We'd straighten ourselves up, my face flushed from something other than the cold. Then my shift would end, and he'd be there again, leaning against his truck, eyes glinting with that mischief that made me forget everything but him.

He'd sweep me off my feet, literally, first carrying me into his Chevy, then into his boat. We explored the world and one another like no one else existed.

We spent nights and weekends on his boat, plunging into icy waters that stole our breath, only to find heat again in each other's arms. We explored beaches so isolated we might have been the only two people left in the world. Built bonfires with flames as high and hot as the passion that burned between us, and when we kissed, it was so utterly consuming that time seemed to stop until the stars came out.

Even then, we couldn't pull our lips apart.

Ours was a reckless kind of love—a chemistry too strong to resist.

One evening as the sun was low in the sky and the water turned to gold, Ray let his hand drift onto my thigh as I stood in front of him at the wheel of his boat.

He pulled me close, whispering against my skin, "There's somewhere I want to show you."

I turned, catching a familiar glint in his eyes, the one that never failed to make my heart skip a beat.

"And you think I'm just going to go with you without even knowing where we're going?" I said, echoing the same teasing tone I had used the first night we met.

Ray's grin widened and he played along, his fingers trailed lightly over my shoulder, sending a warm tingle down my spine.

"I'll tell you if you want to know," he said, his voice tempting me. "But it'll be more fun if I keep it a surprise."

His breath was so close I could feel the heat of it against my cheek, and I had to remind myself to breathe.

I turned back to the wheel, trying to focus on steering, but his presence made it impossible to concentrate.

"Fine," I said, my voice softening. But my heart raced for him. "I'll be surprised."

The boat sliced through the water; the engine roaring as we sped past the familiar islands. Ray's grip on the throttle was tighter than normal, and I could feel the excitement radiating off him.

The islands blurred into a green-and-blue haze until suddenly, the landscape changed, and a new shoreline came into view.

This one wasn't like the others. No docks, no houses, no boats—just jagged rocks and a pristine stretch of untouched beach.

"Ray," I started, my voice catching. "Are we supposed to be here? We're so far out, what if—"

"Trust me," he cut in, his voice barely audible over the roar of the engine. "This is exactly where we're supposed to be."

My heart pounded as he steered us straight toward the shore, not slowing down. "Ray, slow down! What are you doing?"

He grinned the kind of grin that told me he was up to something. "Hold the wheel tight. Keep it straight."

Before I could protest, he was at the back of the boat, cutting the engine and yanking the motor up just in time as we slid onto the sand with a soft thud.

My pulse raced as we skidded to a stop, the boat settling like it had always belonged there. My heart continued to beat wildly as I looked around at the rocky landscape and the untouched beach, the uninhabited island.

"Some landing," I said, laughing.

Ray leapt from the boat and extended his hand, pulling me into the shallows, the cold-water biting at my ankles. "Come on, I want to show you...our island."

"What do you mean *our* island? Is this like, instead of us having a secret song, we have a secret island?" I asked, jokingly.

"Exactly. This is our future, Ginny. This is our island." He pulled me along the beach, our bare feet sinking into the sand as we made our way toward a rocky outcrop.

Surely he was being metaphorical about *our island*. When he mentioned it before, I thought he was just joking—a dreamer with his head where it could never be.

But I could feel something different in him—excitement vibrating through him, almost electric. I couldn't believe it. If I told you that Prince Charming swept me away one summer and made plans for us to live on this island forever, I bet you wouldn't believe me.

But Kassidy, let me tell you—Ray was as serious as a heart attack.

When we pulled up to this place, I stared at that rocky shore right out that window there. At the time, this whole place was completely untouched. It was beautiful, yes, but it looked like nothing more than an uninhabitable rock.

No houses, no power, no water.

"I'm going to buy this island, Ginny," he said, his voice full of certainty. He wasn't joking, not even a little. His eyes were fixed on mine, unwavering.

"Ray," I laughed, "what are you talking about? There's not even a dock, or an outhouse," I said, shaking my head in disbelief. "Not to mention, how are you going to pay for an island? You don't just...buy an island."

"Watch me." He rocked onto his heels, hands in his pockets like it was no big deal. "I'll build a dock, and a house, and a regular bathroom and shower too."

"Ray—" I said, about to protest but he cut me off like his dreams were too big and real for my gripes.

"I know the guy who is selling this land. He thinks it's a useless rock too far out to do anything with." He turned to me, that glint back in his eyes.

I stared at the shoreline, the waves lapping at the rocks. It was stunning, rugged, and unrestrained.

"But Ray, what about water? Electricity? This is crazy—"

"I'll figure it out," he said, stepping closer, his voice unwavering. "It's not all here yet, but it will be. I can make it happen. I've got connections—friends who know how to set up a well, a generator. I've got a plan for us, Ginny." His hands rested gently on my waist, pulling me closer until our foreheads touched. "I'm serious about this, and I want you here with me. I want us to build a life here, together, forever. And when I buy this place for us, I'm going to name it Isla Virginia."

I laughed, wrapping my arms around his neck. "Oh really? You're going to name an island after me? That's bold, Ray—even for you."

"Yep, and the rules are, if you have an island named after you, you have to live on it."

I threw my head back, still laughing. "You're insane! Absolutely out of your mind!"

He grinned, eyes flashing with that wild, reckless certainty. I leaned into him, breathing in the salt and warmth of the moment, feeling freer than I'd ever felt in my life.

I wanted nothing more than to be swept up in Ray's dreams for us and stay there forever and forget the real world back home. I wasn't sure that was even possible, but Ray had a way of making the impossible things feel real, so I let myself believe the dream.

But if I've learned anything, Kassidy, it's that no matter how far we run from home or how long we try to hide, the truth is a living, breathing thing—like the seasons.

And summer always ends.

"I've got a big job lined up," Ray said. "Once it's finished, I'll have enough for a down payment. And when I do, I want you to live here, with me." He pulled me close, his hands resting at the small of my back. "It won't be fancy, but it'll be ours.

"You don't have to go back to Iowa, Ginny, you can go to college here, there's a community college—"

"Ray—" I looked up at him, searching his face for some hint of hesitation, but there was none. "I can't back out of going to college back home. It's a done deal. The papers are signed. If I don't show up, I'll never get another spot.

"My parents will have to pay back the money they put up, plus more as a penalty. It's more than they own, Ray. Even if I wanted to, how am I supposed to get out of that?"

"I'll wait for you then. You can come here on your school breaks and stay during the summers. Then once you've graduated—"

"What? Move out to a rock in the middle of nowhere with a huge degree that I can't use?" He wilted under my words. "I'm sorry, I just... I want to be with you, but before we met, I had plans. I can't just throw that—"

"I'm not asking you to throw anything away. I'm telling you I want to make this work. What makes you happy, Ginny?"

"You. Of course, you. Ray. I want to be with you. Hey, I know! Maybe you can move to Iowa? Places are more affordable there, we can move in together, make a life—"

"In middle America? On a farm?" he laughed. "What would I do in Iowa? I'm not a farmer, Ginny, I'm a fisherman." He pulled me in tighter. "You don't have to commit right now. I know this is a lot but just say you'll consider it, staying here, with me. Or at least, come back. I'll have everything ready for you when you do."

"You'd wait for me?"

"I'd die for you, Ginny, I would. I didn't know what love was, now I do—it's wanting to sacrifice anything in the world, no matter what, to make a life with that person. You're my person, Gin. My forever. My always. What can I do to make you stay?"

His certainty was steady, almost too steady, while my thoughts circled in quiet resistance, searching for something I wasn't sure I'd find.

"Ray—you can't ask me that."

"Yes I can. I don't want to spend a single day without you, Ginny. Not one day."

"I don't want to spend a day without you either. But—"

The unspoken questions weighed heavy on my heart.

What happens when reality comes crashing down on this dream?

What happens when the summer ends and I had to leave?

I didn't see any way that I could stay.

"We don't have to talk about it anymore right now," I said. "We still have the rest of the summer to figure this out."

Or at least that's what I thought.

That evening as the boat carried us back to the mainland, I laid my head on Ray's shoulder as our island faded into the distance, but the promise of it stayed with me.

# Chapter 28

Over the next month, we became experts at launching his boat onto the shore of Isla Virginia. Each time, I sped toward the sand, he'd cut the engine and pull up the motor before anyone got hurt. We'd slide in, the hull skidding to a stop where the water kissed the shore. Every time we arrived, the island's untouched stillness welcomed us like a secret, as if the world itself had forgotten this place, and left it just for us.

Ray taught me how to fish right off the shore. We argued about how to cast the rod—he'd try to show me the right way, and I'd insist on my way.

Those small arguments became part of our dance—the way he'd step behind me, his arms guiding mine, his breath against the back of my neck. Tension always lingered between us, everything unspoken, simmering beneath the surface.

Like somehow, we both knew it would end yet every moment we spent on the island, I could feel Ray's dream coming to life, unbridled and full of promise. I can't explain it. I just knew what I felt. It was crazy—his idea—but some part of me realized that deep down, if anyone could make it happen, it was Ray who just might pull it off. He had that kind of determination, the kind that could turn dreams into living breathing beings.

We'd walk the beach, fish, and laugh. Every touch felt like something electric, like we were living inside a dream too beautiful to end. The way Ray looked at me—like he saw only me, like I was the center of everything—made the dream feel more real, more ours with every passing day.

Each time we skidded in, we brought more supplies. Blankets, pillows, a cooking pot, firewood. Eventually, we pitched a tent on a grassy overlook with a view of the waterway between us and the other islet across the way.

It was a world apart from everything else. We were hidden in the trees where no one could see us. The first time Ray zipped that tent closed, cocooning us in, he told me every detail about his dreams for us, about the kind of home and life he wanted to build. For me. Right here in this very spot.

"A place that feels like it belongs to the earth," he said, running a hand along the canvas wall as if he could already see the wooden beams, the stone hearth. "Big windows, set just right, so the view is framed better than any painting ever could—morning sun pouring in, moonlight stretching across the floor at night.

"A porch, just big enough for two chairs, maybe three. Small, but enough. And these trees—one day they'll grow thick and tall, wrapping us in, so no one will ever know we're here unless we want them to."

I laughed, tucking myself closer to him. It sounded crazy I know. A huge part of me that never believed that he'd do it. But there was this other part of me that knew, with Ray, anything could happen. And it did. And he built this cabin. And lived this life.

He just did it without me.

That wasn't his fault of course. It was mine. And I'll get to that. I suspect there will be plenty of tears shed between us. But what came before that—oh, dear, those are the parts you don't want to hear. And trust me, I wouldn't dream of telling you.

But if I have to drag up the most wonderful and terrible summer of my life, then I'm entitled to relive every bit of it—the heartbreak, the longing, and all the other parts no grandmother would ever share with her granddaughter. So let an old woman get some sleep already. Then maybe, if I'm lucky, I'll get to relive one of those moments in my dreams.

I stretched my legs, shifting against the couch cushions, and give Kassidy a knowing look.

That's when she groans, pressing her hands over her ears.

"Oh my God, Grandma. Stop. Please. I said nothing gross. Alright. Time for bed." Kassidy stood up.

I chuckle, pushing myself up too. "I said I'll spare you. But trust me, sweetheart—it was something."

"Stop. For real, Grandma, before I vomit on the few clothes I have here."

I laugh, swatting at her knee. "I would never dream of telling you. That story is way too juicy for an innocent girl like you."

She shakes her head, still making a face, and I can't help but smile. Then Kassidy wraps me in the hardest, biggest hug of my life. The whole world is in that hug—my daughter, my granddaughter, the daughter I lost. The love that slipped away, both a long time ago and just a few years back. She is everything.

"Thank you for that, dear. And I want you to know that you've been the best gift of my whole life."

I squeeze her wrist, look into her beautiful face, and say goodnight before turning toward the bedroom.

Sitting on the edge of the bed that night, in the dim light listening to the house settle around me—was both familiar and unfamiliar with the echoes and ghosts of a past that never seem to fade.

I should be tired.

I should close my eyes and let sleep take me away. Yet, I can't. It feels as though my mind is restless and showing me the story of my life, refusing to power down even if I try to switch it off.

I can't help but wonder if he kept it.

If I were a betting woman, I'd wager that he did.

I reach for the bottom drawer of the nightstand, where I last saw Ray tuck away my journal—the one that holds all the stories I'll never tell Kassidy.

My hand trembles as I open the drawer. Then I gasp. There it is. Right where I left it. The cover is worn soft. The spine creased, the pages inside are stiff and yellowed. But the ink is clear, like a tattoo on my bones that will never fade.

I pull it onto my lap, run my fingers over the pages.

I wonder how many times he'd read it.

How many times he relived those moments—of pleasure, of a love we had known only with each other.

I ran my fingertips over the pages, the scent of ink and salt stirring something deep inside me—like the past had been waiting for me to return. I exhaled, already knowing how deep the words would pull me under. Then I turned to the first page—my one and only entry.

Written just before the sea turned red.

There it was, the highest point of the most unforgettable summer of my life. Right before everything changed.

*August 1970*

*The first time I touched him he held his breath.*
*Like he hadn't expected it.*
*Or like he'd been waiting forever for it.*
*And the way he looked at me—God, that look could have set fire to water.*

*We spend our days wrapped in the quiet of this tent, the world outside shrinking until it's just us—talking, dreaming, and listening to the wind move through the trees. Nights are even better. Just the sound of his breathing beside me, his warmth so close, yet never close enough. I want him as much as he wants me.*

*The island is wild and untamed, and in this tent, we are the same. Tangled together in heat and laughter and the kind of passion I've only ever read about.*

*I feel safe here.*

*I never want to leave.*

*The rain falls softly against the canvas in a relentless rhythm, like it's keeping time with us. Ray lies beside me, his fingers tracing slow, lazy patterns on my skin. Every touch sends a shiver through me. The air inside our tent is tense and the heat between us scorching.*

*Ray watches me, teases me, those intense, dark eyes know exactly where to touch and what to do to make me writhe in pleasure. He lingers, waits for permission, savors me. I lean into his touch.*

*Ray is deliberate and slow with me, as though he is memorizing every inch. Hours. Days. Nights. Filled with passion. But no matter how much time we spend in that tent, it will never be enough. We both want more. Don't want a single heartbeat to slip away unnoticed.*

*The way he smiles against my skin, the warmth of his naked body pressing against mine—the heat and smell of salt and skin and desire—this is the most erotic summer of my life—filled with a longing I've never known before.*

*When the sun bakes the sand, we break free from the heat of our passion, sprint naked down the beach, and plunge into the Pacific. Every single time, the cold shocks my system, and steals the air from my lungs. Every single time, it's worth it.*

*Ray waits waist-deep, his hand outstretched, grinning like he owns the whole damn ocean. And the moment I reach him, our bodies collide, pulled together like we're made of the same thing.*

I wrap my legs around him, feeling the hard lines of his waist between them. Water swirls around us as his hands roam over me, gripping, teasing, pulling me tighter, and his mouth finds mine, hungry and desperate. Each kiss feels like I'll never get enough.

If I could freeze time and stay here forever with Ray and no one else for the rest of my life. I would.

We talk about the future, whisper about it like it's something we can reach out and grab. I let myself dream out loud—ask him if we can build a dock, so we won't have to beach the boat like maniacs every time we come back. He tells me he'll build one. Says he wants this place to be ours. Says he wants a house, too—one with windows placed just right so the sun and the moon will always light up the walls.

And he means it. He means every word.

At night, with the fire flickering out and the stars hidden behind the trees, it feels like the future is something we can shape with our own hands.

I tell him I'll work at the restaurant in town, let him pick me up every night so we can return to the island together. He likes that idea. Says when the babies come, we'll make a life here, raise them wild and free, let them grow up with the ocean at their feet. Can you believe it? Ray wants babies with me? I laugh, tell him we can't raise babies on an island with no running water or electricity. He just pulls me closer and tells me he'll make sure we have everything we need.

I believe him.

Every morning, I wake to the sound of waves, the mist rising off the sea, the sunlight filtering through the trees. But one morning, I sit up, wrap the blanket around my shoulders, and the thought slips out before I can stop it—what will I tell my parents? That I met a fisherman, and we're going to be castaways on an island forever?

Ray knows what to say. That we'll invite them out, let them see it, let them fall in love with this place—and with him, too.

He makes it sound so simple.

He kisses my temple and whispers that it is simple. He doesn't need anything fancy. He just needs me. Ray tells me he loves me. He looks me in the eye, laces his fingers through mine, and tells me he loves me. Says he wants to marry me! Grow old. Right here. Says it like it's the easiest thing in the world.

I think maybe it is.

Then he asked me if I would marry him.

Yes means giving up the life I've planned, the future my parents have worked so hard to give me. Yes means disappointing them. Saying no—

*I can't bear that either.*

*I know what I want more.*

*Yes.*

*When I look into his eyes, I see everything—the life we're about to create, the risks, the certainty that this is the only path I can choose.*

*Yes. I say, yes.*

I stare at the words on the page, my own handwriting frozen in time. The ink is faded, but the memory is not. I can still feel the way my heart pounded when I wrote those words, still hear the whisper of the waves outside the tent. I had believed it—every word, every promise, every dream we made that summer.

Almost six decades have passed since that night I said yes.

I let out a slow breath and closed the journal, resting my palm on the worn cover as if holding it shut might keep the past from creeping any further into the present.

I had believed, with all my heart, that he was everything.

That love was enough.

But life has a way of unraveling even the surest of dreams.

# Chapter 29

In the morning, I wake and stretch, feeling the stiffness in my bones before pushing off the blankets. The past clings to me like the scent of old paper—impossible to wash away without erasing every single memory.

Last night, I let myself return to a world that no longer exists. But today, I'm here. And so is Kassidy. Somehow, I'll find the courage to finish telling her this story.

She's already awake when I walk out, curled in the armchair by the window, a steaming cup of tea cradled between her hands.

She doesn't speak right away, just lifts one perfectly manicured eyebrow. She's been waiting.

"Don't look at me like that," I say, tying my robe at the center. "I haven't even had my tea yet."

She smirks. "Tea is on the table. And don't even try to weasel out of this. We're not going anywhere until you finish telling me what happened here."

I sigh, shaking my head, but I can't help the smile tugging at my lips. I want to tell her. To finally confess. Maybe, just maybe, it will bring me some small morsel of peace.

We settle into our places—the same as the day before. Kassidy is waiting for answers. The past is waiting to be reconciled, right where I left it. And, like always, it pulls me under.

If you want to know what happened to me and Ray. First I need to tell you what happened to me and SaLita and the orcas.

SaLita was the first person who made me see the orcas through different eyes. The one who sang to the whales from the lighthouse and who taught me to hear them. She was the woman who believed the orcas were her ancestors and made me wonder if maybe she was right.

I sat beside SaLita on the jagged rocks near the lighthouse. The wind whipped through our hair as the orcas moved gracefully along the shore, skimming across the water like ancient shadows. The early morning light was a pastel haze of pinks and blues set as a backdrop to their sleek black bodies and towering dorsal fins.

Some of the pod stopped to play and frolic in the bull kelp nearby.

Watching them never got old. Every time I went to the lighthouse and they showed up, giving me a glimpse into another world—one older, wiser, and more connected to one another than humans ever could be.

SaLita's eyes were dark and serious, fixed on the whales, but that morning there was also a heaviness, like she was looking through them and into something much deeper.

For all her beautiful youth, SaLita also carried the air of a woman much older than her twenty-something years. I was as mesmerized by her as I was by the whales, something seemed to linger in her that stretched back generations, a spiritual connection to the land and her people that I'd never fully understand.

We sat in silence for a long time, watching as they foraged nearby. After a while, SaLita spoke, as if she'd finally trusted me enough to share something of true substance.

"They're not just whales. To me, to my people, they are the qwe'lhol'mechen—our ancestors. The people who live beneath the sea." The look in her eye told me she wasn't just using the word ancestor as a metaphor. "We believe the spirits of those we lose live on in the whales, swimming alongside us, watching over us."

I turned toward her, studying her face. The depth in her expression and in her words made my chest constrict.

SaLita continued, her voice barely rising above the sound of the waves. "When the white men came to these islands, they didn't just take the land. They destroyed generations of my family and their traditions. They pillaged the salmon, cut the forests, poisoned the water, and slaughtered our family beneath the waves, as well as those who walked on land. Now, the fisherman, the whale hunters, the power companies, are still waging war on the people under the sea."

Her voice faltered for a moment, then sharpened with resolve. "Three dams in other rivers have already choked off their food supply, and there's another set to be finished in seventy-five, on the Swift. If we allow that dam to go up, there will no longer be enough salmon for my ancestors to survive. And what we let happen to the whales, will happen to all of us."

It felt like a warning. A prediction that carried the burden of a dark history and a fragile future.

"Is there still time? Can we help them?"

"Can we stop the fishermen from killing them with harpoons and bombs? Or stop the power company from putting up more dams? Can we stop the tide from rising when the storm rolls in is what you're really asking, and the answer is maybe."

The corners of her mouth pulled into a grim line. "These men are motivated by greed and power. They want land and money and status, and for those things, they will never stop, no matter who or what's in the way."

Her eyes hardened as she turned to me, her voice lowering as if she was sharing something sacred. "Greed is the evil destroyer of worlds, whether those worlds are made of water or air. Until there is no need for greed, those people who crave it will destroy the people under the sea, the way they destroyed our ancestors on this land."

Her words lingered next to a truth I couldn't fully grasp. A knot twisted in my stomach, guilt creeping in like a shadow.

I was the color of the enemy. My ancestors didn't live under the sea, they were the pillagers of it. The ones who took and destroyed without discrimination and I didn't know how to atone for that.

"Have you seen the helicopters?" SaLita asked, her eyes darkening. "Circling the bays, looking…Vultures hanging out the sides with binoculars. And bombs."

The image sent a chill down my spine. I shook my head.

I hadn't seen any helicopters. But knowing that she had was terrifying.

"They're chasing them." She turned to me, her eyes blazing with something fierce, and dangerous. "If I see him again, I will stop him. Send their machines falling from the sky." Her voice trembled with barely contained anger.

She was talking about more than just the whales. She was talking about her own survival, and dignity—and freedom.

"Five years ago, I watched a crazy white man capture an orca from the North," she continued, her voice growing quieter with each word.

"With a harpoon through its back, he hauled it down the coast all the way to Seattle, where he put him in a pond of sludge and poison and forced him to do tricks for an audience—a sea circus. Since then, I've had dreams of this man coming back. Taking my grandmothers and their daughters with him, enslaving them too."

I watched her face tighten, her eyes glistening with an emotion too strong to hide. "I've had dreams about you too, Virginia. Only it's not really you in my dreams—it's a girl who looks like you. A girl with hair as dark as the deepest ocean, and who carries something more powerful than the white man's harpoon."

Every tiny hair on my body stood up, and a cold chill ran down my spine. SaLita's gaze drifted back to the horizon. "Something's happening. I can feel a shift in the wind. That man is coming back, and this time it isn't just him, but an army who is more organized. They have eyes in the sky now," SaLita's voice cut through the air, sharp as the wind.

I stared out over the water.

Something in my knotted gut told me that she was right. I had no idea how it related to me, only that somehow, it did. I had only known her for a short time, but I could feel it—like I felt it with Ray—something powerful had brought me here, to that moment, to those whales, to her.

No matter what, I'd stand with her, and help to protect those magnificent creatures.

What happened the following week was one of the greatest tragedies of our time. A disaster whose effects would ripple through generations—for me, for Ray, and for the very heart of the sea.

# Chapter 30

I was the only one at the lighthouse that morning. I leaned my bike against a new sign someone put up that read: "Don't shoot seagulls or water birds—they are protected by law! And don't shoot a whale! You might wing it, and it will wash up on the beach!"

The irony wasn't lost on me. It wasn't a warning out of reverence for the whales, but practicality. Protect them not because they're sacred, but because they might cause too much trouble to remove when they die on the shore.

Undercurrents of anger toward the orcas were everywhere—more than I first realized. People in the restaurant would talk about them. The tourists were fascinated. Half of the locals were indifferent, and the other half wanted them gone—driven far out to sea where they couldn't compete for salmon. The fishermen especially loathed the black-and-white behemoths, blaming them for the dwindling fish stocks, and for the loss of their livelihoods.

Most people didn't give a damn about the real reasons salmon were in decline. It was easier to blame what they could see right in front of them—the vile creatures that haunted these waters—the blackfish— rather than confront what was really happening upstream from the dams.

Nobody talked about the dams choking the rivers back then, or the massive fishing boats hauling in more than their share, or the pollution that was poisoning the waters in Puget sound. By the time anyone really started paying attention, the worst of it was already done.

But the tribes knew. The coast Salish people knew. Even if their voices were silenced by the industry as quickly as they were heard.

That morning, I stayed on those rocks long enough to see a family of whales come by, gliding beyond the kelp. There were three of them this time. Their sleek black shapes were a stark contrast against the pink and blue morning sky. The largest one had a dorsal fin unlike any I'd seen. It wasn't the straight-edged blade the others had—it was bent, almost wavy, like a long-serrated saw. He moved along the shore with another large orca in the lead, and a smaller tucked between them.

I watched as they rubbed against the bull kelp, playful and free. They weren't vile to me—they seemed like part of the ocean. If the whales ate the salmon to survive, then that was the way of the ocean. And if there wasn't enough for us humans, then so be it. I'd gladly give up my share if it meant the whales could swim in peace. But the people in charge didn't care about any of that.

I climbed down closer to the water, my boots slipping on the wet rocks as my eyes locked on the whale's. I'd never been that close to them before. It was like witnessing creatures from a forgotten time—a force so powerful, too old for this world, and yet here they were, alive, against all odds.

For a brief moment, everything stilled.

The water.

The air.

The earth itself seemed to hold its breath with me as they swam by. But I suppose I should have known. It was the calm before the storm.

An evil voice shattered the stillness.

"Get back!" he yelled, startling me, snapping me out of the trance. I spun around to see a man barreling toward me, his face twisted with both anger and panic. "Get away from the shore!" he shouted again, flailing his arms as he scrambled down the rocks toward me.

Before I could react, his rough hands gripped my arm, yanking me backward with such force I nearly stumbled into the jagged rocks. If I'd have fallen, I might well have hit my head and needed help.

"You crazy or something?" he spat, his breath heavy with the smell of tobacco and brine. I wrenched my arm free from his grip. His eyes were wide, wild.

"What's wrong with you?" I said.

"Me? Ain't nothing wrong with me. Are you a dimwit or something? Those beasts will jump out of the water, snatch you by the shoelace, and drag you under. They'll peel the flesh off your bones like butchers! You're lucky I got to you first! You hear me? Or you'd be done for!"

His voice pitched higher, the words tumbling out as if he'd rehearsed this madness a hundred times.

"Didn't you see them stalking you? Circling, waiting for you to fall in like some stupid prey that don't know what she's doing? I've seen those things tear a man to pieces." His head shook with a tremor as he said it. "Shred him limb to limb and play with his body parts. Damn blackfish should be wiped off the face of the earth! Eradicated! We'd all be safer that way."

The man's words came fast, furious, and full of nonsense. I glanced toward the sea where the orcas swam, their sleek black bodies reflecting the morning light, their wide, toothy smiles looking anything but menacing. They ignored us completely. It looked like they were scared by the shouting on the shore and starting to swim away, not closer.

"They don't eat people," I said, and it came out as a half-laugh. His absurdity made him impossible to take seriously. "Those ones eat fish—salmon," I added, hesitating. I wasn't sure how to explain to someone so entrenched in hate what little I knew. "They're not monsters. Watch them. They're—beautiful and intelligent."

"Beautiful? Intelligent? They're not beautiful. Those vile creatures are the spawn of the devil. Would you stand that close to hell if you knew it was lurking right there under that water?" he scoffed, shaking his head as though I were the foolish one.

I sidestepped him, hoping to avoid more of his delusion, but he wasn't done. I didn't know whether to laugh or scream. The man was dead serious, his paranoia so thick it prevented him from seeing clearly.

I did the only thing that made sense—I turned around and walked away. Mounted my bike and headed down the road, his crazed rant echoing in my head. As I peddled away, sea on one side and pine trees on the other, I was jolted awake by a sudden crack that shattered through my thoughts—gunfire.

The loud snap tore through the air and rattled my bones. My hands jerked the handlebars, and my bike wobbled dangerously close to the edge of the road. A second shot rang out, and I didn't need to look back to know who was responsible. Fury surged inside me, burning away the fear.

I spun my bike around, pedaling as fast as I could back to the lighthouse. There he was, rifle raised, shooting into the water where the orcas had been.

"STOP!" I screamed. The word ripped from my throat, fueled by the rage building inside me.

He barely glanced at me, his focus still on the whales as they tried to flee. My legs shook as I charged toward him. Before I could think, I grabbed the barrel of his rifle. The gun went off, the shot ricocheting off the rocks with a sharp, metallic crack that sent a high-pitched ringing through my ears.

"You ignorant tramp!" he roared, shoving me to the ground with his free hand.

Pain shot through my palms as they scraped against the rocks, but I didn't care. All I could think about was the whales—the way they couldn't fight back, the way they didn't deserve a world filled with hunters and harpoons.

"Leave them alone!" I screamed, trying to keep his attention on me. "They didn't do anything to you!"

The man's face twisted in rage, his finger twitching on the trigger. For a split second, I thought he was going to shoot me.

Instead, he turned back to the water, ready to fire again. The whales were swimming further out, but they had a calf with them. They couldn't escape fast enough.

Desperate, I searched for something—anything—to stop him. My hand landed on a jagged rock. I didn't hesitate. I hurled it at him, hitting him square in the side of the head. Blood started pouring out of the wound, down through his hair and face and neck. He touched it with his fingers, looked at it then grunted and turned toward me with murder in his eyes.

He stormed forward, blood gushing down, and the butt of his rifle raised high above his head. My body froze with terror. I threw my arms up to protect myself, bracing for the blow. Then I heard tires on gravel coming to an abrupt stop.

"Ginny!" The voice came from behind—strong, commanding. Ray.

In an instant, Ray was there, pulling me to my feet and stepping between me and the crazed fisherman. "She doesn't know what she's doing, Gunter," Ray said quickly. "She's not from here."

My chest heaved, both from fear and anger. "You're on his side? He was shooting the whales!" I shouted, my voice cracking.

Ray's face hardened. "Everyone shoots at the whales," he said, and the words stung more than the fall. How could he be so callous—so…one of them?

Ray turned to the man. "What are you doing out here, Gunter? You're gonna miss the window if you keep wasting time on land."

"Miss the window?" His voice was rough like sandpaper. "I've been missing the window every damn day, thanks to those blackfish." He jabbed a finger toward the ocean, where the whales had disappeared beneath the surface. "There's no catch left. Those vermin just keep multiplying, eating all our stock! I'm going out of business because of them. We all are."

Far out on the horizon, a large boat appeared, its engine a low hum over the sound of the waves. I watched, horrified, as the men on board began tossing something—canisters of some sort, into the water.

Then came a loud explosion, water shooting into the air like a geyser. The man ran toward his truck, then sped off, gravel flying. I could tell Ray was relieved, so was I.

"What are they doing?" I gasped, looking back at the boat.

"Trying to scare the blackfish away," Ray said flatly, as if it were the most natural thing in the world.

"With bombs?" I repeated, my voice rising in disbelief.

"It's not going to hurt them. It'll just move them along. All the fishermen use them," Ray's voice was calm, indifferent. He glanced back at the water. "Those things have the whole ocean. They can go hunt salmon somewhere else. And Ginny, you shouldn't have done that. Gunter's family owns a lot of property and businesses around here. They keep guys like me in business. They're helping with this next job I've got. We're lucky he—"

"How can you say that?!" I felt my throat tighten, the rising anger making my voice shake. "You really think bombs don't hurt them?" I said, my mind racing. "And I don't care about that man or his family or his businesses, he was shooting at them Ray—shooting."

Ray sighed, running a hand through his hair. "Ginny, please. You've got to stop caring so much about those whales. It's gonna get you in trouble. You shouldn't come here anymore."

His tone struck me, sharp and cold.

"What? You can't tell me that. And what if I don't stop coming here, Ray?" I shot back, the words tumbling out before I could control them. "What if I care more about them than I do about catching some stupid fish we don't even need?"

Ray's expression darkened, his face tightening in frustration. "Stupid fish? Those fish are how I survive. How my whole family has survived. This whole island relies on those stupid fish, Gin. Those whales are nothing but pests. Like rats in a restaurant. Either they exist or we exist, can't you see that?"

I stared at him, stunned. How could we be so in love and yet stand on opposite sides of something that felt so clear to me? It wasn't just about the whales—it was about what we valued, and what we believed in. If we couldn't agree on this, what else could break us apart when it really mattered?

"Well I've heard it's not the whales that are causing the problem with salmon. People are talking about the dams. There's more going on here, Ray."

His laughter cut me off. "The dams? Now you're starting to sound like one of those kooks, one of those…radicals."

"It's not radical. It's true. And those whales deserve better."

"Deserve? They're not intelligent humans, Ginny. Those are big fish, acting on instinct. Like sharks, they're killing machines. They kill other whales for sport, rip out their tongues, and leave the rest to rot. They're not killer whales. They're whale killers. Don't you see? They're not even eating what they kill. They're wasteful. And you're acting like they're gods." He laughed then, but it was sharp and bitter. Ray's voice grew harder, "I've lived here my whole life, Gin. I know what those things are. You can't just come here and think you know it all, not about this."

I felt a surge of frustration rise inside me, anger clashing with sadness. I looked at him, searching for any sign of understanding. But there was none. It was like I didn't recognize him anymore.

"How can you not understand," I said softly, the fight leaving me, the words sinking into the quiet between us.

Ray's jaw tightened. "Understand what? That you want the whales left alone so they can eat all the fish and we starve?"

"We're not going to starve," I snapped, frustration getting the better of me. "I never even had salmon until I came out here. You could always…do something else?"

"Do something else? What the hell else am I supposed to do, Ginny? Fishing is all I know. And look around, there's not much for opportunity here. And I'm not going to college, didn't you see what just happened at Kent State? You think I want to take my chances out there in middle America? No thanks."

"So what? You'll stay here, and kill whales for the rest of your life?"

Ray's face hardened. "I don't kill whales, Ginny. I stay as far away from them as I possibly can." His shoulders dropped, and the man I knew—the Ray I loved—was back. "Ginny, I didn't come here to fight."

"Then why are you here?" I asked, exhausted. "You hate the whales. Why did you come to the lighthouse?"

"For you. And I'm glad I got here when I did. Gunter is…well, he doesn't lose. He doesn't back down. And he sure as hell doesn't like being made a fool of. You don't want to be on the wrong side of his temper."

I looked away, unable to fully process the shift in his tone, my emotions still too raw.

"Look," Ray continued, stepping closer, his voice softening. "Remember that job I told you about? The big one that pays enough to get the deed to our island?" He smiled, reaching for my hand. "It starts tomorrow, so I'll be gone for a few days, maybe more. And today, tonight—I want us to be together. No fighting. Especially not about those whales."

I blinked, my anger softening, but not disappearing. "You'll be gone for a few days? What are you doing?"

Ray shrugged. "Deep-sea fishing. Not my usual work, but they're paying me big time. Like I said, Gunter's family is putting up the money for it, so please try to stay away from him.

A knot formed in my stomach. Something felt wrong, but I couldn't put my finger on it.

Ray leaned in, pressing a kiss to my forehead. "I don't want to leave with us like this, Ginny. No more arguing, okay? Let's never talk about the whales again. You do your thing out here—just...don't fall in. Promise?"

I nodded, feeling the warmth of his arms around me, but something wasn't right. His words, his smile—they felt like a bandage over a wound that hadn't even begun to heal but was still being ripped open. And talking about the whales brought out a side of him I hadn't seen before. Or ever wanted to again.

"Come on, I'll throw your bike in the back and drive you to work. I'll be there when you're done. There's somewhere I want to take you."

"And you think I'm just going to go with you without even knowing where we're going?" I said, echoing the same teasing tone I'd said before. I didn't want to fight with Ray, yet trying not to feel angry was nearly impossible.

Ray played along. "I'll tell you if you want to know. But it'll be more fun if I keep it a surprise."

"Fine. I'll be surprised."

"Ginny, trust me. Most people go their whole lives without seeing this. They don't know where to look. They don't even know it's there—right under their noses, just beneath the surface. But I promise you, tonight will be like nothing you've ever seen before."

# Chapter 31

After my shift that night, Ray was waiting for me, leaning against his truck with that casual smile of his—the kind that made my heart skip a beat. I wrapped my arms around his neck, pulling him close, and our lips met in that familiar, magnetic way.

We could barely pull our lips apart long enough to get out on the water. But by some miracle, we did. And once that happened, Ray was right. He unveiled a wonder I didn't know the world could hold. Nothing before or since has rivaled the spell of that night.

Ray took us farther than I'd ever been before, even beyond Isla Virginia. The night was dark, the moon entirely hidden, and the boat moved effortlessly through the still water. There wasn't another boat or person anywhere in sight, not a single beam of light. The silence didn't feel eerie—it felt sacred.

"What are we doing out here, Ray?" I laughed. "You're not going to chop me up and toss me overboard, are you?" I teased, leaning back against the side of the boat.

"You've been watching too much of that television. All they talk about are those Manson murders. Yet another reason to stay out of the city and live out here with me." Ray grabbed an oar, dipping it into the water. "Come here, watch this," he said, and I leaned over the side of the boat, peering into the inky blackness. He stirred the water slowly and at first nothing happened. As he moved the oar back and forth, a faint glow began to trail behind it. Ray grinned as the water lit up, casting an ethereal shimmer across the surface.

"Ray—" I gasped, "what is that?" I could barely breathe as I watched the glowing tendrils spiral through the dark. "They look like fallen stars."

"Sure looks that way, doesn't it?"

Ray swirled the oar again, creating glowing shapes—hearts, circles, and spirals. He turned the night into something magical, like we'd stepped into another universe.

"What is it though?" I asked, transfixed.

"Nature showing off."

"It's like the ocean is lighting up from the inside."

Then, a shadow carved through the bioluminescence.

Ray stiffened and pulled in the oar, standing up quickly. He grabbed the sleeve of my coat and pulled me back from the edge. Another shadow followed, streaking through the glow. Then another. And another.

The orcas. They were feeding. Their dark bodies sliced through the iridescent water, chasing salmon, leaving trails of light in their wake. Each time they streaked passed, the light flared brighter, more vivid.

"Don't get too close," Ray said, stretching his arm over my chest. His voice was quieter than usual though. "If I'd have known they'd be here I wouldn't have brought you out."

He had his reasons for not liking those orcas, and I knew he was serious about what he said, but on that night, he was as entranced by them as I was. Both of us inched back to the edge to watch.

The smallest orca, a baby, had a distinctive white saddle patch that sat behind her dorsal fin, curving slightly like a crescent moon.

Ray shifted, uneasy. "I think we should—"

"No. Just stand here with me," I pleaded. I couldn't tear my eyes away. "I don't want to go. This is incredible. Thank you."

Slowly, I moved closer to the edge, the boat tilting slightly with my movement. I peered over into the glowing water. "They're just doing what they know," I said, then stretched my hand out.

Ray tried to stop me, but I couldn't help myself. I dipped my fingers into the water, swirling them around in the liquid light.

"Look how they move?" I whispered, my eyes following the graceful arcs of their bodies as they cut through the water deep below.

I sucked in a sharp breath as a larger one glided past. Its slick, black body momentarily breaking the lighted pastel surface before disappearing into the depths. Ray had his hands on my hips ready to pull me back. "They belong here, Ray. We're the visitors," I said, almost in a trance over how magnificent they were.

Even Ray was softer now. We watched in awe as the quiet lap of water against the hull was the only sound between us and the orcas.

"It's like…they're dancing," I murmured, my eyes still locked on the mesmerizing display beneath the surface.

My chest rose and fell with the rhythm of their movement, completely lost in the magic of the moment. Ray stayed close, ready to pull me back at the first sign of danger.

"They're feeding, Ginny. It could be a frenzy. And we don't want to be on the menu."

I leaned farther over the edge, dunking my whole hand in, my hair dangling dangerously close to the surface of the water.

"We're not on the menu," I said.

"Get back in here Ginny, we're leaving. This isn't smart." Ray put his hands on the controls. "Come on Gin, you're leaning too far over. This is out of hand now."

I was mesmerized, in a trance, I never wanted to look away—I wanted to be part of it, to swallow the ocean, to hold its magic and that moment inside me forever. To dance beside them in the glowing water.

"You're flirting with suicide, Gin!" Ray's voice was strained, pleading. "Don't lean over that far, what are you doing?"

I was lost in the glow. "They won't hurt me," I whispered, just as my grip on the boat's ledge slipped and I felt myself falling.

The last thing I remember was Ray shouting my name before the icy water swallowed me whole. The shock of the cold stole my breath and turned my legs into useless slugs. My soaked shoes and clothes dragged me down, heavy as anchors, but it wasn't blackness that surrounded me, it was light. Pastel, swirling light.

Ray threw out a life preserver, I saw it on the surface, but my arms were too slow, too heavy.

Above me, everything was disorienting—confusing. But beneath me, the water was bright and alive with shapes moving below my feet, like living shadows.

Then, the smallest orca appeared beside me. Her crescent-shaped patch right in front of me, her curious eyes watching me. Her teeth flashed, and she made strange sounds, but I wasn't afraid.

It was more like she was just trying to communicate.

Maybe it was the first stages of hypothermia. Maybe it was the magic of the orcas, but flashes of images filled my mind. The lighthouse. SaLita. Her voice, like a lullaby carried on the air.

Her message to me: "A descendant will come with something more powerful than any weapon."

The orcas surrounded me, an ancient force that felt more like guardians than killers. They weren't what Ray said they were. They weren't what anyone said they were. They were more intelligent than any of us realized.

I didn't know that I'd blacked out. When I came to, Ray was over me, dripping wet, shaking my shoulders. I coughed up water and shivered like I'd been locked in a cooler.

When Ray pulled me out, he said I wasn't breathing so he put his mouth over mine and shared his breath. He saved my life, Kassidy. He brought me back. But the orca saved my life too. Ray jumped in after me. But my body floated down. He said the littlest one, with the white crescent markings, nudged me back to the surface, held me there just like a mother orca would do for its young.

Under the water that night I experienced something transcendent.

Ray's fear for my safety had outweighed his terror of the whales, but if the orcas hadn't guided my body to the surface, I would have floated to the bottom of the sea.

Ray was holding me in his arms, his voice trembling with relief.

"You could've died, Ginny," he choked out, his face pale. I was still shivering, still lost in the experience.

"They're not killers," I coughed out. "There's more to them... something we don't understand."

And what he said next shocked even me.

"Maybe you're right, Ginny. Maybe you're right."

The orcas didn't tear me or Ray apart that night.

In fact, they saved my life.

But what happened next—I've never spoken of it.

Not to Stanley. Not to anyone. What I saw, what I did, was too painful to revisit. Until now. You deserve to know, Kassidy. Why I left this place and never wanted to come back. I'm sorry I waited this long to tell you, but I had my reasons.

Lord knows if there is anything I've learned it's that we can't turn our backs on the sins of the past—we must bear witness to them if we hope to change the future.

It was August 8th, 1970. The day started like any other. Ray was off on his big fishing job somewhere, and I made my way to the lighthouse. The weather was predictably grey and gloomy—but as soon as I got there, something different was in the air.

A strange stillness settled around me, heightening my senses and making the little hairs on the back of my neck stand up like the moment before lightning splits the sky. I couldn't see it, but I could feel it—an invisible force awakened my skin, telling me something was coming.

SaLita was already in her usual spot, sitting on the rocks like she was anchored to them, staring out over the water. It misted enough to leave tiny, glistening raindrops in her dark hair and the fog was so thick I could barely see my shoes resting on the boulder in front of me. The water beneath the bluff felt unnaturally calm. There were no orcas anywhere in sight.

Maybe they were out in the open ocean, or maybe they were right in front of us, hidden by the fog. I couldn't tell. But SaLita, who seemed to have some primal connection with them—always knew where they were before they appeared.

"What's wrong this morning?" I asked SaLita. "You can feel it, can't you?"

She didn't answer at first, just looked at me with eyes that seemed to see through the present and into something far away. Something ominous. Before she could speak, I heard the noise that was keeping her silent.

The faint hum of a helicopter, its blades slicing through the stillness. Then the sound of far-off explosions—one after another, relentless, like gunfire cracking apart the sky.

"They're here," SaLita said, voice trembling.

"Who?" I asked, my heart hammering against my ribs.

Fear coiled tight in my chest, cold and sharp, like the world was teetering on the edge of disaster—as if at any second a nuclear bomb would drop, vaporizing her and me and everything. And for some of us, that's exactly what happened that day.

"The qwé'lamats," SaLita's voice cut through the air like a drumbeat against the rising storm.

"SaLita what does that mean? I don't understand."

She turned to me, her eyes burning with an intensity that reflected generations of anger in her gaze. I'll never forget the look in her eyes for as long as I live. "Spirit thieves," she answered.

The words slammed into my chest like a fist.

Before I could even think. Before I even knew exactly what was happening. Before I knew what I was saying, the words came out.

"How do we stop them?"

I felt something deep in my bones—call it a mother's instinct. Call it compassion for all creatures. Whatever we needed to do, for the orcas, I would do it. I'd throw myself in front of a harpoon, jump onto one of those helicopters, gouge eyes out, anything to stop them. I turned to her, my breath shaky, but my resolve clear. "SaLita, what can we do? SaLita—" my voice pleaded. I tried to shake her out of her trance.

"We're going to stop them," she said, her voice stronger now.

Her eyes were filled with the kind of determination that makes you believe in the impossible. That was the day the world changed.

The day I stopped chasing carefree dreams and found something worth fighting for. And someone to fight against.

The Whale Collector.

# Chapter 32

David Ruby was a man with dollar signs in his eyes—the kind of man SaLita called *OhQwal'ah'oo*. It was a word I took to mean "greedy bastard." He was the type of man who claimed his evil deeds were done for the right reasons.

He was the original Orcatick if there ever was one. Except his obsession didn't stop with watching them in the wild—he had to have them, possess them, conquer them—put them in a tank so the whole world could see his prowess over the great beasts of the sea. It was one man's obsession that cost those families countless lives and their eventual extinction.

Of course, it wasn't just about the orcas. It was about money. Every blackfish he fetched for the budding aquarium industry brought in twenty thousand dollars—and those were just the ones they gutted and hung from the ceilings.

He got a cool seventy-five thousand for each orca he delivered alive, and that made it a deadly business. Dozens of those magnificent creatures were killed senselessly while those *OhQwal'ah'oots* figured out how to transport them.

It might not seem like much money nowadays, but back then, that kind of money was a payout men dreamed of and dozens of them got a piece of the pie.

After that damn fool swam around with his harpooned orca in a Seattle sludge pond, the public's hunger to see them up close grew insatiable. With no regulations in place—the waters were open for plunder.

The Whale Collector and his team were free to take as many as they could catch. Sell them, kill them, or condemned them to rot in a tank—there were no rules, no limits, and nothing in place to stop them.

It was the dick-measuring contest of a lifetime—a chance to show the world which man could dominate the fiercest creature on earth and prove, once and for all, that his courage—and his appendage—was the biggest. And I was right there to witness the ruin the OhQwal'ah'oots carved into the history of this land—leaving behind blood and a silence that still lingers.

There was another man responsible for the kidnappings, too. Gunter Amon. A fisherman turned self-made, money-hungry tycoon— with all the resources he needed to help The Whale Collector take as many as he wanted. Gunter had a personal vendetta against the orcas for eating salmon. Pretty sure the bastard was born without an amygdala. No empathy. No limits. Just carnage in a tailored suit.

If he'd been running the whole show that day, there wouldn't have been any captures. It would have been a massacre. A genocide of the entire population. To this day, I wish I'd killed him the moment I cracked his skull with that rock. Or at the very least, left him with more than a scar.

While the capture team was in full pursuit of the whales, SaLita and I were scrambling to figure out a way to stop them.

Her grandmother's garage smelled of oil and mothballs as SaLita rummaged through a toolbox. I stood by the workbench, gripping a rusty crowbar I'd picked up on a whim, thinking it might come in handy.

SaLita glanced over her shoulder, raising an eyebrow. "What are you going to do with that?"

I shrugged. "I don't know. You have a better idea?"

"Yeah," she said, holding up a screwdriver and a pair of pliers. "We need a car if you're going to get to use that crowbar."

She crouched by the driver's side door, scanning the driveway to make sure no one was watching. "Hold this," she said, tossing me the screwdriver as she used the pliers to jimmy the door handle. With a soft click, the lock popped, and she smirked. "Easy."

"You've done this before, haven't you?" I whispered.

"Just get in."

We slid into the front seat, the cracked vinyl squeaking beneath us. SaLita ducked under the steering wheel, twisting wires together with quick, practiced movements.

The engine sputtered to life, and we looked at each other, grinning like we'd pulled off the perfect crime straight out of a bad heist film. But the stakes were real, and neither of us had a car to borrow.

It was a small win, but as we backed out of the driveway, undetected, the reality of our situation sank in. We had no plan, no way to get on the water, and no clue how to stop the capture team. All we could do was listen to the sky, and hope for a sign of where to go next.

I glanced at the crowbar resting on the seat between us. It was absurd, really, but it was all we had.

No plan. No idea what we were up against. But one thing was certain: we weren't going to let those bastards get away with it.

It was easier to spot the capture team than we had imagined. They were well-organized, with several helicopters and a dozen speedboats. We sped through the island roads, trying to follow them and figure out a way to stop them.

Everything unraveled on Whidbey. An island adrift in Puget Sound, cradled between the Salish Sea and the Washington coast.

They surrounded the whales like mosquitoes, encircling the entire Southern Resident population. It looked like they were attempting to herd the pod into Holmes Harbor, but the whales were too smart for that.

What we didn't know at the time was that this wasn't the orcas' first encounter with the Whale Collector, his helicopters, speedboats, or explosives. The men had spent the entire week trying to corral the whales further down the coast, and the orcas had learned their tactics. Now, the whales weren't just fleeing—they were strategizing.

The orcas dove deep, resurfacing miles away from the team, but with only half the pod. That group headed toward Holmes Harbor, as the men had planned. But there were no calves in that group—only large males.

The whales had created a decoy pod. While the men chased the decoys, the mothers and calves slipped away, heading toward Deception Pass.

SaLita and I raced around Whidbey Island, following the sound of helicopter blades and the flashes of speedboats across the water. We were completely in the dark about what was really happening—or what we could do to stop it.

The KaWaltish people say the maiden of Deception Pass emerged from the sea that day, walking the shores with tears of saltwater and blood streaming down her face. They say she was guiding the whales into the open sea, where even the sea sprite was ready to aid in the family's escape.

I know it's just a legend, but as SaLita and I crossed the bridge that morning, I swear I saw her—a woman with seaweed tangled in her hair, walking beneath the arches. The sunlight glinted off the water, and for a moment, it felt like the line between myth and reality was gone.

The capture team cut off the mother-and-calf group before they could escape into open water—tossing explosives and scaring them back the other way. Blasts rang out in the air, a violent fracture against the hush of the sea, echoing across the islands.

SaLita and I watched in glimpses, our hands gripping each other so tightly it hurt as the capture team tried to corral a calf. The mother was frantic as her sleek body cut through the chaos. A speedboat lurched forward, forcing her away. The baby hesitated, spinning in the water, its tiny frame shuddering against the waves, confused.

Another explosion. The mother dove deep and so did the calf. But the little ones couldn't stay under for very long.

I pressed my knuckles against my mouth, stifling a cry I didn't recognize—an anguish I'd never felt before. A fury burning hotter in me than anything I'd ever known. Beside me, SaLita whispered a prayer or plea, I couldn't be sure. Her voice was strangled by the kind of grief that alters the core of who you are. I knew the world had cracked open—and that nothing we did would ever put it back together.

This was wrong, how could we stop it?

When the whales surfaced, panic spread among them, their vocalizations growing frantic as the water churned violently. Explosions rocked the sea, cutting off their escape and forcing them to turn back. From there, the team deployed their bombs strategically, driving the orcas into Penn Cove on Whidbey Island, where the spirit thieves had already set up their nets.

With the mothers and calves trapped, the decoy group arrived on the scene, swimming straight into the chaos, and allowing themselves to be captured.

That morning, the Whale Collector managed to trap the entire Southern Resident orca population—a superpod. He herded eighty of them into a massive seine purse while the others remained outside the netting, refusing to abandon their family.

SaLita and I stood on a rocky ledge overlooking Penn Cove, the scene below erupting into madness.

The water swirled as boats closed in, orcas thrashed, helicopters circled, and the cries of the whales echoed across the cove—raw and haunting, imprinting deep into my soul.

We searched for a way to stop what was happening, desperate for a plan—anything—to end the nightmare that was just beginning.

# Chapter 33

The Whale Collector released the largest orcas from the net after he realized they were too big to transport. That left the mothers and calves inside the purse style net while the males and larger females hovered on the other side in the open water, refusing to leave.

There were more than one hundred orcas in that bay, eighty inside the net. Kassidy, can you imagine the sight? I'd never seen anything like it. Never even imagined something like it. I was so far in over my head, it's a miracle I didn't drown right there on land.

SaLita and I camped out on the bluff overlooking Penn Cove, the damp chill seeping into our bones. For hours we watched as the men built the docks, their silhouettes grotesque against the mist. They moved in with long catchpoles trying to slip lassos around the calves. It was like watching hunters pick off the youngest, weakest of the herd.

The spirit thieves—the Qwé'lamats—were cold and methodical. They didn't care about the families they were destroying; all they saw were dollar signs. Watching them separate the babies from their mothers, indifferent to the devastation they were causing, was the most gut-wrenching sight of my life.

The whole scene was one gigantic, chaotic mess. No one knew how to handle so many whales at once. At one point, the men tried to release some of the mothers, but they refused to leave their calves. Then, they freed the larger juveniles, and those orcas wouldn't leave the bay either.

The fact that those whales didn't rebel—didn't bite, attack, or kill those men—was a testament to their nature. Though many times, SaLita and I wished they had.

Through the soul-shattering ordeal, the whales never stopped calling to one another. Their frantic cries pierced our ears, reverberating off the islands, and sinking into the sand, the bays, and the very air we breathed. It was a chorus of desperation that burrowed deep into my being, a sound so haunting it still echoes in the silence of my mind.

Even now, I can hear their voices—trapped—as if the sea swallowed their grief and releases just enough to remind us of what those men took, and of what the world lost that day.

You could tell by the pitch of the orca's calls, and the desperate way they thrashed around, that they were in extreme distress. They were pleading, crying, begging, and wailing. Even now, it's heart-breaking to think about what we saw that day.

I've heard those cries a thousand times when I close my eyes at night and try to sleep. Mothers screaming for their babies, the calves responding with terror in their voices. There is no other way to describe what happened except that it was utter horror for those orcas.

By mid-afternoon, the men had already taken two calves out of the water, ripping them from their families like they were nothing more than a stupid fish to be put in a tank. They hoisted those babies thirty feet into the air, their massive bodies dangling helplessly from the crane, then flopped them onto flatbed trailers.

My breath caught in my throat as I watched. Can you imagine? A creature that massive being taken out of the weightless water, flopped on its belly, dry and terrified, covered in a dark tarp. The sounds and smells so foreign to them it would be like aliens snatching a human and hauling him light years away to another planet.

As soon as they took a calf, the men worked fast to get its angry mother out of the net where it stayed with the others in the cove. The whales on the outside of the net seemed to be searching. They were spy hopping as if trying to find a way to free their trapped family before another life was stolen.

Some other locals had come out to see the commotion. People gathered on the shore farther down, watching in morbid fascination. No one had ever seen orcas up close before.

You have to remember, Kassidy, that this was before the rise of orcas in tanks all over the world. What we witnessed that day in Penn Cove wasn't just a tragedy—it was the birth of a dark industry. The moment orcas in captivity became business, and their wild innocence was sold for profit.

Folks marveled at their sheer size, amazed by how easily men could wrangle such power. Others watched with anticipation, eager to see wild creatures tamed by small men. And some, bitter over dwindling fish stocks, thought the whole lot of them should be slaughtered to bring back the fishery.

I scanned the shore, searching for a familiar face. Surely Ray had heard about what was happening. No fishing job was bigger than this. The island was not massive in size and word traveled fast. I searched the shoreline and the road, looking for him.

He wasn't there.

Just clusters of men with hands in their pockets, watching, pointing. Fishermen, wives, children perched on their fathers' shoulders.

It was a spectacle.

Even some of the elders—those who had lived long enough to see the tides shift in unnatural ways—stood in silence, weeping, watching history unfold, unsure of what to do or unwilling to intervene.

There were people like us out there too, wanting to fight back, but the Whale Collector had guards, armed with guns and batons and they turned anyone away who got too close. Some families that lived on Whidbey Island sent telegrams to state officials, begging them to intervene—but that took too long.

We stayed out there all day watching, trying to figure out the best way to help the whales. Aside from killing all the men—which we'd discussed—the only way was to somehow set the orcas free. But that would have been impossible during the day with so many guards.

We had to wait for the cover of darkness and hope that by the time we could act without being seen, it wouldn't be too late to save the ones that were left.

"We need wetsuits and something to cut the net—see that shed?" SaLita said, pointing to a fishing cabin nearby. "I know the people who live there. They won't help us, but I know that shed has the tools we need. We'll get in there once it's dark, then slip into the water and cut the net. We'll have to be quick and quiet. And we'll have to swim out far, and deep, coming around from the horizon side, so the guards on the shore don't see us."

My hands trembled thinking about it. The enormity of it all— swimming next to the whales, cutting the nets in the dark, the cold open ocean—the thought of it all was terrifying. But doing nothing to help them was not an option.

"What if the whales think we're the bad guys?" I asked.

SaLita turned to me, her eyes reflecting the sadness beneath the water. "They don't see us as good or bad. To them, we're lost. We've forgotten them. Forgotten the language of the sea. We've broken our pact. But they haven't. They remember what we once were and what we can be again. They're waiting for us to return. They'll see that in you."

I swallowed hard, SaLita's words sinking into my stomach like stones. I shoved my fear down with them, burying it deep.

What we had to do was more important than my fear.

I thought of Ray—wondered if he'd help us if he knew what was happening, or what I'd tell him when he found out. But even my thoughts of Ray were fleeting in the urgency of what we had to do.

The minutes crawled by as we waited for the sun to disappear behind the veil of fog. Then, as the last of the light drained from the sky, SaLita nudged me.

"It's time."

We slipped down the backside of the bluff, careful not to make a sound, and headed toward the shed. SaLita moved as if she'd done this a hundred times, but my heart was hammering in my chest, giving away that I hadn't done anything like this before in my life.

We got to the shed, but it had a padlock, and my heart sank. SaLita didn't hesitate. She walked around to the back where the metal was rusted, splintered at the bottom.

She wrenched away a piece of the rusted metal bending it upward, making a hole barely big enough to crawl through. Then she lay on her back, inching her way under the boards. The metal scraped against her torso tearing at her clothing and skin, but she didn't stop.

I crouched beside her, feeling utterly useless.

"I can't get through," she said, stuck halfway, her voice a frantic whisper. I tried to push her through, pull the metal away, but it was too strong, and she was too stuck, nothing worked.

Panic surged in my chest. "SaLita, what do we do?"

She didn't answer right away. Then, her body went still. "Push my feet," she whispered, her voice tight with pain. She took a deep breath, exhaling slowly as she made her torso as small as possible and began to wiggle through the narrow gap.

The jagged metal scraped her skin.

She forced herself forward, whimpering with each inch she gained. A light flicked on in the house nearby, and a dog barked. SaLita made one final shove, I heard her cry out—a sharp edge cut deep into her thigh. Blood gushed down her leg as she disappeared into the shed.

I fled for the cover of darkness as the homeowners flipped on the outside light. A man scanned the darkness but when he saw nothing he went back inside.

"SaLita, are you okay?" I whispered.

She opened the shed door a crack, then hurried to where I was hiding in the brush. I saw the blood before I saw her face. Her forehead was scraped, her forearm cut open. There were tears in her shirt and a deep gash on her thigh where her skin flapped open from the metal that had carved into her skin.

She held tools in her hands and a wetsuit draped over her arm.

"These will work to cut the net," she said, "but there is only one wetsuit." She looked down at her bloody leg, her voice wavered. "I can't go in the water like this. You'll have to do this alone."

# Chapter 34

If you feel tense just from me telling you this story, Kassidy, imagine how I felt, living it. Even now, decades later, I can still feel it—fear, sharp and suffocating, squeezing my chest.

Terrified doesn't even begin to describe what I felt that night.

But I stuffed all of it down into a deep, dark pit, blacker than the water in front of me, where I hoped it would stay long enough for me to get the job done.

So many calves had already been taken. Stolen. And the ones still trapped in the net? No one was coming to save them. We were their only chance. SaLita knew it. I knew it too.

The night air was thick with the scent of pine trees and seaweed. I could hear the low murmur of men's voices carrying over the water. The wetsuit must have weighed a hundred pounds in my hands.

"Put it on. Fast." SaLita's fingers trembled as she helped me into the thick wetsuit.

There was pain in her eyes and blood dripping down her leg.

"SaLita, you need to get to a hospital."

"I'll be fine," she said, taking off her button up shirt. She winced as she tied it around her thigh, then she turned back to me not letting anything slow her down.

"SaLita, what if—"

"No what-ifs," her voice cut through my panic. I had so many what-ifs. "You have to do this. Swim. Cut. Don't think."

She handed me the bolt cutters. They were heavy. Unwieldy. Like an anchor tied to my wrist. I nearly dropped them as their weight pulled my arm down. How was I supposed to swim with them?

What if I couldn't? What if I drowned? What if—

But most of all—how was I supposed to go into that black water with all those killer whales?

I knew they were smart, not the monsters the fishermen made them out to be. But they were in distress—trapped, traumatized, their world shattered by humans like me.

How would they know I was there to help?

What if they thought I was one of those evil men trying to steal their babies?

Suddenly, everything we were doing teetered on the edge of disaster. I might end with my limp body clamped between the teeth of an angry mother orca.

My hands trembled as I zipped up the wetsuit. The sticky, musty material clung to my skin, warm at first, but I knew that would change the second I hit the water. Hypothermia. How long did I have? I didn't know. It didn't matter. I had to do this. I had to somehow find courage I didn't yet have.

I followed SaLita down to the shore. She crouched at the edge, scanning the cove. The orcas inside the net were dark shadows on the surface, massive bodies that barely moved, as if the battle they fought had worn them down.

Men with flashlights and guns tucked into their waistbands patrolled the docks, their shadows long and sinister in the dim light. I hated them. Every single one of them. With every cell in my body, I wanted to tear each one of them apart like they had done to those whales. It was that rage and anger I felt toward those men that cut through my fear and kept me moving forward.

SaLita turned to me when our feet hit the water, her voice steadfast. "Stay low. Swim silent. Steady your breath and your mind. It'll be cold at first but as you move your body will warm up. Cut the nets at the far end where they're weakest. It won't take much after you get started. Just follow a straight line all the way to the bottom. Dive as deep as you can. Use these."

She handed me a mask with a rubber nosepiece that was flexible in my hands.

"How am I supposed to see?"

"Your eyes will adjust. Feel your way through."

"What if they think I'm food?"

"They don't care about food right now. And they eat salmon. By echolocating its swim bladder, remember? So unless you look like the swim bladder of a salmon, they won't mistake you. Now go. This is our only chance. If the whales are still in the net tomorrow, they'll take all the calves. You know they will. You must do this, Virginia."

"I know," I said, every ounce of me trembling.

SaLita clutched her leg, blood seeping into the water around her ankles. The sight of it only made my heart pound harder, my pulse raced in my ears. I waded into the freezing water, the bolt cutters like lead in my hand. The cold bit into me when it reached my stomach, stealing my breath, but I didn't stop. I couldn't stop.

I dove in but the wetsuit wasn't enough to shield me from the cramping cold. Every nerve in my body screamed to turn back.

I pushed forward. Ate my fear. Swallowed it whole.

The net stretched out in a giant circle creating an underwater prison. I hid behind a boat moored to one of the makeshift docks, its hull barely concealing me from the guards on patrol. I hung there, catching my breath. Waiting for the guard to walk away.

I saw the orcas on the other side of the net, their tall fins rising out of the water. Being that close—they were massive—too massive even to comprehend. I could even feel their presence all around me, their sheer size sending waves through the water with the slightest movement. When the guard disappeared, I took my opportunity.

I made the first cut to the float line on the surface of the water. Three guards patrolled farther down, their flashlights bobbing in the dark. I took a huge breath and went under. Everything inside my head hurt as the cold seeped in. My ears, my teeth, even my hair seemed to cramp from the cold.

My hands shook as I cut the net under the surface, kicking carefully so I didn't make a splash but to also stay afloat. The more I moved, the warmer my body became and the more my adrenaline kicked in. The first cuts were the hardest, but once I was a few levels down, they became easier, and every cut was a small victory that pushed me farther.

The farther down I dove, the more the currents sloshed me around throwing me this way and that. Then I realized it wasn't the oceans' current pushing me. It was the movement of the water displaced by the massive bodies that were swimming mere feet away from me.

I could hear their sounds. Whistles, chirps and clicks. I didn't turn around to see them for fear that I might scream or freeze with terror.

SaLita's words echoed in my head: *Swim. Cut. Don't think.*

I went up for air then dove back down and cut some more. Over and over. SaLita was right, my eyes did adjust, but just barely.

Then I felt it—a brush against my leg. A rush of water, that almost left me somersaulting. Followed by the unmistakable presence of something enormous moving behind me, so close the water around me swirled and I had to kick to stay upright.

Then I saw its body, a white slice, massive in size, swim by. Then another flash of white. A swirl of water. I kicked, desperate to find the surface, but I couldn't tell which way was up or down. The currents were disorienting. My lungs burned. I began to panic as I couldn't find the surface. There was only one thing I could do.

The lack of air in my lungs made the decision for me. I released the grip on the heavy weight I'd been carrying. As the cutters fell to the bottom, my body instantly became lighter and floated to the top.

The second I broke the surface, I gasped for air, the sound of my breath like a megaphone ripping through the quiet night.

And then I saw her—still trapped on the other side of the net. The largest of the mothers. Staring at me. Her calf next to her. One of them letting out a sharp whistle.

I froze as they evaluated me, my intentions, her dark eyes locked on mine. Her innocent baby at her side and I knew, like all mothers know, she'd do anything to protect her young.

"You're free," I whispered, my voice trembling. "You can swim through now."

A moment passed—an eternity—before the giant orca dove under, the calf following her.

"HEY! Stop right there!" a voice shouted from the dock.

Flashlights swept the water as the guards ran toward me, their footsteps pounding on the wood. I ducked under, but it was too late—they'd seen me. I had no choice but to swim away.

I swam underwater as fast as I possibly could. I closed my eyes as the terror creeped in, the tremors rolling through me, and the cold water burning my scalp. When I was forced to surface for air, the spotlight blinded me, but I didn't stop. I took a huge breath and dove back under, swimming away from the cove.

When I stumbled onto the beach, SaLita was there, limping toward me. "They saw you," she said, out of breath. "I tried to distract them, but—"

"I cut the net," I gasped, collapsing onto the sand. My body was exhausted, more exhausted than I'd ever been. "There's a hole big enough for the calves to slip through. But I dropped the bolt cutters. I couldn't dive any deeper. SaLita, did they swim out? Did the whales get away? Did you see them?"

SaLita looked out at the open water, her face unreadable. "I can't tell," she said softly. "We'll have to wait until morning to know for sure."

I closed my eyes, my body trembling from the cold, exhausted beyond anything I'd ever known. The whales were still out there—maybe free, maybe not.

But I had done everything I could. At least for now.

Whatever came next, I knew one thing for certain: I'd keep fighting for them—no matter the cost.

# Chapter 35

Kassidy was staring at me, her expression unreadable. For a fleeting second, I thought I saw something flicker behind her eyes—doubt, sorrow—maybe it was something else.

"You were just a kid," she murmured. "You were younger than I am right now." Her fingers tightened around the edge of the blanket. "And if you could do that—" She hesitated, swallowing hard, something sad settling in her gaze—a shadow. "Grandma, what you did was heroic."

I shook my head. "Before you say anything further, I need you to know that I am not a hero. What I did was not heroic. I wasn't even brave. I was terrified. And stupid."

"What? That wasn't stupid. It *was* brave. You saved them."

A sharp pang cut through me. The words came out harder than I expected. "No, Kassidy. I didn't."

Her brow furrowed, lips parting as if she was about to say something more.

I held up a hand. "Let me finish, then you can wield whatever judgments at me that you want, and I'll accept them."

Kassidy's mouth pressed into a straight line, but she nodded. I could see it though—that uncertainty. Something was truly bothering her, but now was not the time to stop. She had to know the truth.

She thought I was a hero.

Nothing could be farther from the truth.

The room settled into silence, and I began again with everything I'd left unsaid.

SaLita and I stayed on the beach until morning, huddling together, our eyes fixed on the cove as if we could will the whales to appear, and swim free. The sky was still midnight blue, with only the faintest sliver of light on the horizon.

The cold had settled deep into my bones, each breath a shaky reminder of how long we'd been waiting. Still, we refused to leave—we had to know they were safe. Had to be sure they made it through.

"Did they swim away? Are they free? Can you see anything?" I asked, my voice hoarse from the cold, and my eyes blurry from exhaustion.

SaLita, always clearer, calmer than me, scanned the water. "I can't tell. There are divers in the water now. I think they're trying to repair the nets. They've got men with oxygen tanks."

My jaw clenched, and a bitter laugh threatened to escape. "Oxygen tanks? That would've been nice," I muttered under my breath, thinking of the cold, the darkness, and how I'd gone down alone.

Pride mixed with a fear that I couldn't shake lived in me. I still felt as desperate as I had in the water, needing to know if I'd done enough to set them free.

SaLita squinted toward the cove. "I don't see any calves in the net. Only the big orcas. I think you did it, Virginia."

I wanted to believe her. I wanted to feel relief, but instead I felt nothing—just an empty hollowness where hope should have been. Something gnawed at me. The silence in the air, the stillness across the water. The whales weren't calling to one another the way they had been. No frantic cries. No thrashing. They were docile, gloomy…as if they knew something we didn't.

"The water. The whales. They're too calm," I said, barely able to get out the words because my shoulders were shaking so violently with the cold. The unnatural silence crawled under my skin, making me feel a deep unease. It was as if the sea itself knew something was coming. "They should be calling to each other. What's going on?" I asked.

SaLita stood. "I'm going to get closer, try and get a better look before the sun comes up. Before they see us."

"I'll go with you." I pushed myself up, my legs stiff and shaky, but I needed to see. I had to know.

We crept along the rocky shore, keeping low, moving closer to where two men worked in the pale dawn light. As we approached, a figure on the shore caught my eye—one of the men, pulling something from the water.

My heart began to race, a sharp pounding in my chest. I squinted, trying to make sense of the scene. They were dragging something heavy. Something large and…lifeless.

No. My stomach churned.

When we reached a vantage point where I could see clearly, I stopped, my breath catching in my throat.

Two calves. Dead.

Their small, lifeless bodies lay on the shore, their tails limp in the men's hands as they dragged them out of the water.

The bile rose in my throat, sharp and bitter. I clutched SaLita's arm, needing something to anchor me, to pull me out of this nightmare.

"They killed the calves," she whispered, disbelief thick in her voice.

We watched, paralyzed with horror, as one of the men pulled out a knife and slit the belly of the first calf. Blood seeped into the water, a dark stain spreading into the cove where its mother still swam, trapped. I stood frozen, unable to look away as he stuffed the calf's body with large rocks. My vision blurred with tears.

The man with blood up to his elbow signaled to another on the water, and a smaller boat approached, tossing a rope to the man on the beach. That's when I realized that I knew that boat.

I rose to my feet, no longer caring if anyone saw me.

Then I saw him.

Ray.

It was his boat—the boat I'd been in all summer, the boat I never wanted to be away from—and the man I never wanted to be without. There he was, sitting at the helm, complicit in these vile atrocities.

My world collapsed in on itself, the ground beneath me splitting open as everything I knew fell into the void. It couldn't be. No. Not Ray. Not the man who felt as essential to me as the saltwater running through the sea. Not the man who'd sworn he loved me, who'd described this place with reverence, as though the land and sea flowed through him.

A sharp ache gripped my chest, each thought unraveling, leaving nothing but a bitter truth as I tried to deny what was right in front of me, though there was no mistaking it. It was him. It was Ray.

He sat in the driver's seat, expressionless, as the man on the shore secured the rope around the calves' tails. Then he signaled to Ray. The boat lurched forward, dragging the dead orcas through the shallows and into deep water behind its wake.

"How could you?" I whispered, though my voice barely made it past my lips. My hands shook uncontrollably, the trembling spreading through my entire body. "I loved you." I couldn't stop the tears as they spilled silently down my cheeks.

My mind spiraled into disbelief and horror as I watched, my heart breaking as the boat moved farther from shore, the calves' bodies bobbing in the water behind it. Each moment I stood there watching, a knife sliced deeper into me, shredding my heart, piercing my soul, and tearing apart my insides the way those whales had been torn apart.

SaLita stood beside me, her face ashen, her hand gripping my arm. "He's sinking them," she whispered. "He's going to sink their bodies."

I shook my head, tears streaming down my face, unable to process what I was seeing. How could Ray—my Ray—be part of this? How could the man I loved, the man I thought I would spend the rest of my life with, be capable of such cold, brutal cruelty? I knew he hated them, the fishermen all did, but this wasn't just hatred. This was...monstrous. Evil. If he could do this, what else was he capable of?

I watched, helpless, as Ray stopped the boat far out on the horizon and cut the lines, letting the bodies sink into the depths of the cove. With them, the last pieces of the future I had dreamed of, the future I had with Ray, sank too.

The men on shore pulled in their nets, releasing the mothers.

The cove was silent as the last whale swam away.

The men dismantled their docks, as if nothing had happened. But the silence they left behind wasn't peaceful. It was hollow, filled with the ghosts of the calves they'd slaughtered, and all the ones that had disappeared down the road—kidnapped, enslaved.

"I'll never forgive him," I whispered, my voice trembling. "Never."

# Chapter 36

An entire generation of orcas was stolen from the sea that day. Locals say one hundred orcas swam into the cove. Eighty were corralled into the net. Seven calves were lifted out of the sea and sold into captivity. Five others drowned during the madness.

It was those stolen orcas who launched what would become a multibillion-dollar entertainment industry. Their capture ignited a ruthless demand that spread like wildfire, leaving orca pods across the world hunted, fractured, and forever changed. But here in Puget Sound, the terror for those families was only beginning.

What started in Penn Cove became a blueprint for devastation.

By 1976, 270 Puget Sound orcas had been captured, and fifty of their youngest were sold into captivity for the live orca show industry.

It all happened so fast, Kassidy—faster than anyone who cared could fight back or protest against it. At the time, more people were fascinated with the whales and wanted to see them up close, than were willing to fight for their right to live wild.

The last calf taken out of the water in Penn Cove was four years old. She was sold to an aquarium overseas, then passed from one tank to the next all over the globe. She was the only one to survive the kidnapping for many years after. The rest of those calves died in transit, or soon after in their new alien homes.

Millions of dollars have changed hands for that one whale who survived being passed from tank to tank, and park to park. Billions more were made in ticket sales from her exploitation.

I went to see her, Kassidy. The infant orca that was stolen from Penn Cove that night. The one who survived captivity.

It had been nearly 20 years.

Stanley and I were on vacation in Mexico. You were just a little girl and stayed at home with your auntie when I took a flight into the capital. I had to see for myself if it was really her. If she was still there.

She was.

Not the small calf from the wild Pacific, but an enormous killer whale with a collapsed dorsal fin, trapped in a tank so small she could barely turn around.

I stood there, watching her—languid, wasting away alone, without another of her kind, without anyone who spoke her language. Sunburned and lethargic, she was a shadow of what she should have been. The sight of her cut me deep. There was nothing I could do for her. Coupled with the grief I felt over your mother's death, I couldn't talk about what happened with Ray or the orcas with anyone.

To this day, Kassidy, seeing what happened to Keelah's family that night—firsthand—and then watching her trapped in that tank remains the most tragic thing I've ever witnessed.

If not for the crescent-shaped saddle patch, I wouldn't have recognized her, but when I saw that, I knew.

My suspicions were right.

Not only was she in the net at Penn Cove. She was the same whale I saw that night with Ray. When I went under the water, she was the one who guided me to the surface, or I might have drowned.

...

Kassidy's sharp inhale shattered the silence.

The memory moved further into the distance as Kassidy stared at me with glossy eyes.

"Yes, you heard me right," I said softly. "Keelah was the one who saved my life all those years ago. She was just a baby then, four years old. Even so, she would have weighed three thousand pounds. But she was the one."

Tears ran down Kassidy's cheeks now and her fingers clutched the blanket in her lap, knuckles white. She was trembling.

"Sweetheart, you're shaking." I leaned forward, concern in my chest. "Have I said too much? I've just gone on and on—this must be so hard to hear."

"Grandma—" Her voice carried sad emotion.

But whatever she wanted to say, whatever was clawing its way to the surface, never came out. Kassidy pressed her lips together, and a line of tears rolled down her cheek.

I reached for her hand, smoothing my palm over hers. She sucked in a breath, shaking her head as if willing something to stay back. The moment passed quickly though. She exhaled, swiping at her cheek, steadying herself the way she always did when she was upset.

"Go on, you finish. And then…" Her voice trailed off; she was almost… whimpering. "I have something to tell you."

I nodded. Then with a quiet breath, I picked up where I left off.

"That's why I never took you to an amusement park, Kassidy. To watch those poor creatures do tricks for treats. I couldn't do it. I knew what happened to them, how it all started because I was there. I couldn't support their prison sentence.

"I believe that if everyone knew the truth—if they'd seen what I saw that night in Penn Cove—there wouldn't have been tickets to sell at all. There would have been outrage. Action. Eventually there was but not after those greedy power and money hungry bastards decimated those poor creatures.

"The last time I looked it up, Keelah was still alive. Sold again to some fancy new corporation. She is fifty-seven years old. Fifty-three of those years spent in a tank, performing for audiences who clapped and ate their cotton candy while millions of cheering families looked on— unknowing, or refusing to admit what they felt in their hearts. That they had paid to keep her there.

"The Southern Resident whales of the Salish Sea never returned to Penn Cove. Locals say they've avoided that side of Whidbey Island ever since. Not one sighting on the books. Smart creatures. I never went back there either.

"I did come back to Isla Virginia, though. The day after the captures. I came here to confront Ray about what he'd done. And to tell him I was pregnant. And then to tell him that I was leaving."

…

That morning, I made up my mind.

I knew what I had to do.

At first, I thought I was sick from everything I'd seen, everything I'd done—the adrenaline, the stress, the lack of sleep.

I threw up several times before it finally hit me.

I had to be sure, so I went to the store that morning and bought a test. I should have known, considering, well, all that we'd been doing that summer.

I was pregnant.

It couldn't have come at a worse time.

I borrowed a small fishing boat and went out to confront Ray. I pulled up to the island where we had once dreamed of building our future, devastated but unwavering.

Whatever Ray and I had ended the moment I saw what he was capable of. There was no unseeing it, no pretending he hadn't played a part. After what I witnessed, staying with him wasn't just impossible— it was unforgivable.

You don't raise a child in the shadow of something like that. I couldn't build a family with a man who helped tear other families apart. There was no future left to build with him—not one I could live with.

Part of me wanted to kill him for what he'd done. Another part of me—the part that still loved him—hoped that what I saw was all one big misunderstanding. That somehow it wasn't him on that boat. But I knew it was. Isn't it strange how our mind clings to a story we know is a lie, to avoid the heartbreaking truth?

When I pulled up to the shore, Ray was there chopping firewood like it was any other day, as if the last twenty-four hours hadn't shattered our world. The consistent rhythm of his axe cutting through the wood should have comforted me. Instead, all I could see were those whales. Their blood in the water. The horror he and those other men inflicted on them.

Ray turned when he saw me, surprise and joy flickered across his face. That quickly melted, giving way to something else—guilt. He ran down to the shore, his steps hurried, eyes searching mine.

"Gin, what's wrong? You're shaking."

I stepped out of the boat. My legs felt weak. Every part of me trembled and not from the cold. I couldn't look at him. Not after what I'd seen. Not after what he'd done. But even more so, I couldn't look at him because I couldn't bear the loss of him—of the love we shared— all of those beautiful moments that would live on in my memory not as the best summer of my life, but as the most heartbreakingly cruel.

Ray's hands reached for my shoulders.

I jerked away.

He froze, his face falling as if I had struck him.

Maybe he'd known the moment he saw me, or maybe it was the look in my eyes right then that tipped him off.

His voice cracked, "Gin. Talk to me."

"I saw you, Ray. I know what you did."

His expression shifted—faint recognition.

And then…fear.

I watched as a shadow of something unspoken tightened his features—but he didn't speak. I pressed on, anger and rage spilling out of me now.

"You weren't fishing, Ray! You were killing!" I screamed. "You and those other monsters killed that family after you stole what you wanted from them. You stole their calves. Their babies. And then you murdered them. I saw you, Ray," my voice cracked, my throat raw from tears.

His eyes dropped, as if he couldn't bear to look at me. He couldn't hide, or explain it away, still, he tried.

"Ginny…I didn't know what was going to happen. I swear. I didn't even know the job had anything to do with those whales."

"It doesn't matter," my voice broke. My chest heaved with the effort of holding back sobs. "You murdered their babies. You helped to steal them, and murder them. I watched as those men slit open their bodies and fill them with rocks, and then you…you dragged them out to sea. I was there when their blood stained the water where their mothers were still swimming. I was there, Ray."

His eyes snapped up to mine, wide with shock. A flicker of recognition, putting it all together.

"You were there?" His brows knitted tight together. "Where?"

"On that beach. And in the water. I saw everything."

He took a step back, shoulders sagging, his eyes filling with something that might have been regret. Or maybe it was shame.

"You were in the water. What were you doing there, Ginny? What did you do?"

"Me? What did I do? I tried to help. What did *you* do?

"I didn't know it was going to happen like that, Ginny. You have to believe me. I didn't know those men were hunting orcas to try and trap them. No one in their right mind catches orcas. I thought I was hired to help catch big fish. That's what I was told. I swear to you. I had no idea, Ginny, I swear. But how—what do you mean you were in the water?"

"It doesn't matter! You didn't try to stop them, you helped them. I tried to stop it, Ray."

"Ginny, I couldn't have stopped what happened. Those men were prepared," he pleaded.

"You hate those whales. You don't care if they live or die or suffer," my voice trembled. "I tried to push that fact aside but now I can't. Not after what I saw you do."

"Hold on. Wait a second. I don't know what you think you saw, but it's not like that. And I didn't have a choice. Those whales were already dead." His voice broke, desperation creeping in now. "Ginny, I have the money now, enough to buy this land. You can stay. You don't have to go back. I can take care of us now."

"It's blood money!" I screamed.

He took a step toward me.

I took a step back.

"I can't stay. Here. With you. On this stupid island. With a man who claims to love the sea but who will kill the creatures that belong to it."

"You have it wrong, Gin. Let me explain what happened—"

"You hate those whales. You can't tell me you don't."

His face crumpled like he'd been slapped.

And the face of the man I loved was gone. The man who had held me and told me stories of the sea, who had promised me a life together alongside it. That man was gone in my eyes.

"I hate you for what you did," I said, my voice barely above a whisper. "I'll never forgive you. And I hope you never forgive yourself. You and all those other men deserve to suffer for what you did."

He took a step back, his hands falling to his sides.

"I know, Ginny," he said, his voice shaking now. "I wouldn't have gone had I known. But once I was there, I couldn't walk away. Gunter wouldn't have let me. Their cries were awful; it was heartbreaking. Those whales calling to one another. I don't hate them. I know that now. Those aren't just fish. But there's nothing I could have done to save them. Nothing. Ginny, we can put this behind us. We can still do everything we planned. I'm not a murderer. Please, you don't have to leave. We can make this work. We have too. Ginny, I love—"

"No."

He reached for me again, but I stepped back. I couldn't bear to be near him, but it hurt to be so cold to him, too. I was just so angry, and young and impulsive.

I'd made my mind up.

Looking at him was heartbreaking.

He was everything I loved and was about to lose. But I didn't see any other way. I couldn't live with him after what I'd witnessed.

Ray kept on talking, it was like he was in a trance. "We can buy this land. We can be together. You don't know what happened."

But I didn't hear him. I was in shock.

Tears blurring my vision. "You're not who I thought you were. It's like…it's like I don't know you at all. Like I never knew you. You tore us apart when you tore that family apart. And I won't let you do that to me, to our family. I'm pregnant, Ray. I took a test this morning."

He collapsed into the sand like the air had been stolen from his lungs. He just stared, wide-eyed, unblinking, like the news had shattered something in him. There was desperation in his eyes. Then hope.

"I'll do anything. Please. Please don't leave," he whispered, his voice breaking. "You do know me. You're the only person who ever has. Please, you have to believe me—I didn't kill those whales. I swear to you."

He pressed his palm to his chest. "I can't live without you, Ginny. Without our child. Please, I'll do anything." His voice was raw and pleading. "All I want is for you to be happy. To prove to you how much I love you—please, just tell me what to do—" Tears welled in his eyes, spilling over. "Anything you say, I'll do it. Please."

"Let me walk away."

"No." His voice was barely more than a breath, but I felt it, the way it broke against the air between us. His chest rose and fell in a shudder, his breath escaping in a sharp, hollow rush. "Anything but that. Please." His head shook, his eyes pleading, raw. "Please, anything but that."

But I was already turning away.

I couldn't stay. I couldn't look at him. It hurt too much.

I walked back to the boat, my steps fast, each one painful as tears spilled down my cheeks. I felt the loss of every dream we had, every hope, every bit of the future we'd imagined together.

But I didn't look back. I couldn't.

No matter how much I loved Ray. He wasn't the man I thought he was, and I couldn't be with a man who had any part in that. Because if I did, I knew I might break in half.

The next time I saw Ray was sixteen years later on that very shore.

It was the day I returned to tell him that our daughter, your mother, had died. And that's when he told me the truth about what happened in Penn Cove.

How those calves had really died.

How *I* had killed them.

# Chapter 37

Kassidy wiped at her cheeks with her sleeve. Her voice cracked as she shook her head and tried to speak. "I—I don't even know what to say, Grandma. I guess I understand why you never told me. It's just...so sad."

I let out a slow breath, the kind that carried years with it.

"It was sad. It still is."

I traced the edge of a dog-eared page on the table, feeling the worn paper beneath my fingertips.

"It's not the kind of story that gets easier with time. And I won't blame you for being angry with me for keeping the truth from you all these years. I was wrong to deceive you, Kassidy. To let you believe your mother was anyone other than mine and Stanley's. But Stanley was a good man—he would've gone along with whatever I wanted. It was me who didn't want to tell you. And that was selfish."

I swallowed hard, my throat tight. "But I didn't keep it from you to hurt you. I did it because saying it out loud, admitting all of this, was unbearable. Even now."

Kassidy shook her head, her eyes glassy. "I'm not upset with you, Grandma. You raised me when your daughter died. You were a great mom. Still are."

Kassidy glanced around the cabin, at the stacks of books, the pages filled with notes and careful handwriting, all bathed in the golden light. She gestured to the scattered papers. "All this, doesn't look like a man who hated whales. It looks like he revered them."

I leaned back, staring out the window at the endless blue beyond.

We sat surrounded by Ray's life's work—data on orcas, photographs of the pods, their family trees, their matriarchs. It was all there, documented with painstaking precision.

"He spent more decades of his life devoted to them, than he did despising them, Kassidy. That counts for something, doesn't it. It was wrong what I did to him. So hurtful. I was so young and stupid."

"What do you mean?" Kassidy asked. "No one would blame you for leaving after what you saw. After what he was a part of. But—what happened when you came back here after mom died? You said—"

I cut her off, not quite ready to admit it.

"Would you go be a darling and fill up my cup? There's a chill coming through."

Kassidy unfurled the blanket she'd been wrapped in and walked to the kitchen to pour me another mug of hot tea.

When she came back, steam warmed my cheeks as I cradled the mug. But the heat did nothing to steady my hands, or my nerves. There was no softening the blow, no gentler version. What I had to admit next would land like a fist.

"Grandma..." Kassidy's voice was quiet but insistent. Her wide eyes locked onto mine, searching. She knew me too well. She could feel what I wasn't saying.

"Tell me," she said, hesitating. "And then...there's something I need to tell you." She swallowed hard, her fingers curling into her sleeve.

I exhaled, readying myself. "Alright. Here's the rest of it. And then, I promise—you'll know everything. And whatever's on your mind, sweet girl, whatever you need to say—I want to hear it."

I set my mug down and leaned back, bracing myself to finish what might be the hardest part of this whole mess. Kassidy tucked in her legs and curled up in her blanket again.

...

When I left this island, I thought I was doing what was best for everyone. I told myself that Ray wasn't a good person. That our baby was better off without him in our lives. That the little girl growing inside me would be better off never knowing he existed at all.

God, how I was so naive and angry and stubborn and wrong.

When I told my mother I was pregnant, she was devastated, naturally. It was a different time back then. Parents weren't as accepting of those types of things like they are now.

She never told my father, instead, she shipped me off to college in Wisconsin instead of staying near home like I'd planned. Sent me away where no one could see my growing belly.

I lost my scholarship to the prestigious STEM program I planned to attend. My mother made me enroll in school to become a nurse. She said they'd be more accepting of my position. She made me promise to give up the baby, then return home like nothing had happened. We'd never tell my father and then everything would be right with the world again.

That was my plan too, at first. So, I did what was expected. Mind you, I was devastated. And depressed. I'd just lost the love of my life, was pregnant with our child, alone, heartbroken, and I couldn't tell anyone what had happened that summer. I kept it all inside.

I went off to college in a strange town. My heart wasn't in any of it—not my pregnancy, my schoolwork, not even my life. I didn't want to be in Wisconsin. I didn't even want to be on the earth. Unless it was with Ray. But that wasn't an option either. And I sure as hell didn't want to be a nurse. Can you imagine? Me, a caregiver?

And then, by some lifesaving miracle, I met an angel. When Stanley came into my life, he was a senior, I was a freshman. And he loved me and your mother growing in my belly instantly. Instead of running off, Stan ran toward me like we were meant to be together.

You see, Stanley had an accident when he was a child, and could never have kids of his own, so when he found me, he believed our life together was his fate, and he did everything in his power to make me happy and keep me by his side. For that, I am eternally grateful.

I loved how kind he was. The most accepting man I'd ever known. The world could use a lot more Stanleys. It was like God himself came down from heaven and handed me your Grandpa Stan on a silver cloud. He was that heavenly. He was much too good to let go. So, I held on to him with my life and the one that was growing inside of me.

I told him up front that the father wasn't ever going to be in our lives. I promised him that and I never told him who Ray was, never even mentioned his name. Not at first anyway.

Ours wasn't the kind of love I'd had with Ray—not wild, and passionate, but it was real, Kassidy. Mine and Stanley's love was the kind that grew over time—like a thoughtfully tended garden.

We raised Karleen and Stanley never treated her as anything but his biological child. Your mother was stunning. I imagine she'd look just like you if she lived to be your age.

But she wasn't as gentle as you, she was wild like Ray. So it shouldn't have been a surprise when she came to me with a growing belly just as she was becoming a woman.

She had so much life in her...from the time she was a toddler she was a firecracker with bright eyes and dreams bigger than her body could hold.

When she came home that day and told me the same thing I told my mother—that she was pregnant, I hugged her and told her that everything was going to be alright. That Stan and I loved her and would love her child and that we'd all get through it just fine. She refused to tell us who your father was, I promise you I honest to God don't know. I figured in time, we'd find out, so I never pushed her on it. And then—well, you know what happened.

Stan turned your mother's bedroom into a nursery, even took a different job so he could be home more with us and help raise a new baby. He was thrilled. All he wanted was to be a father and grandfather as many times as possible.

On the day she had you, I knew something was wrong. She was lethargic all week. When she went into labor, she wasn't in pain like a woman usually is, she was apathetic, already slipping away before anyone knew something was wrong with her heart.

No one could have known. They didn't test for anomalies like that back then, didn't even know what they were. She crashed before we could even cut the umbilical cord.

Her death...I don't have words for the kind of devastation it brought. It shattered me. Shattered Stanley too. Bringing home a granddaughter, without your daughter? There are no words for that kind of pain.

But we grieved differently.

Stan became preoccupied with raising you and thank God he did. There was no better person for the job. He bottle fed you around the clock and was over the moon with joy that we had you. It was like the stork had rang the doorbell and dropped off the most perfect little pink package just for him, to help him get through his grief.

I loved you too, don't get me wrong. He took it upon himself to be your full-time caregiver. Took time away from work for months when other husbands and fathers stayed out of the house so the women could raise the children. He was modern like that, even back then.

He was also like that because I was destroyed—sunk into a depression so dark I couldn't see a way out of it. I didn't know what to do with myself, or if I could even go on living. It's like a switch turned off in my head and I couldn't feel joy even when it was right in front of me or swaddled in my arms.

Weeks went by, then months, and by the time we threw you your first birthday party I'd tried medications, talking, journaling, walking, but nothing I did helped to lift me out of the utter despair I was trapped in over losing your mother.

It was a kind of black grief I can't even explain, Kassidy. Something deeper and darker than I could bear on my own. But I had no idea how to come out of it—or if I even could.

All these years later, I see it more clearly. Losing your mother didn't just break me—it unearthed everything I had buried. The grief of losing Ray. The life we dreamed of but never had. The life Stanley and I wanted with Karleen but never got. The trauma of what I'd seen on that cold dark night. It all came crashing down on me, tangled together and pulling me under.

You see, I never let myself process any of it. Never worked through what happened. I just stuffed it down. Had Karleen, committed to Stanley. I never told Stanley about Ray or what happened. I hadn't told anyone. I'd barely admitted it to myself. It was just…too painful.

Stan and I talked about trying everything to try and pull me out of it. Inpatient treatment, shock therapy—nothing was off the table. Not even coming back here to face my demons.

Eventually, I realized what I could no longer ignore. Until I told Ray what happened to our daughter, I wouldn't be able to live with myself. I had to make peace with him, even if I couldn't forgive him. Even if I told him and he couldn't forgive me.

Something in me just said that he deserved to know.

And deserved to know about you.

Maybe I was doing it for Ray. Or maybe it was an excuse to try to make amends with our past. Maybe I just wanted to see him again. Or maybe I wanted to hurt him. I don't know what I was thinking. I was depressed. Reaching. Grasping for anything to lift me from the dark.

Feelings are complicated. People are complex. They do things that don't make sense. I wasn't in my right mind. I wasn't in any mind. I was just lingering in this gray space, trying to find a spark of life again. I suppose some part of me knew that Ray might bring that back.

When I told Stan I needed to come back to these islands and tell Karleen's father what happened, by that time, he was willing to do anything to help me. And instead of being devastated, he understood. He gave me his blessing to do whatever I thought might help.

Like I said, Stanley was truly a good-hearted man.

He understood that I needed to deal with my past, in order to have a future together. He was worried about me, of course, but I kissed him goodbye, and I promised to come back to him. For everything that he'd done for me, and Karleen, and you, I would never break my promise.

Still, I needed to leave. So, I came back here, to the only place I could think of that might heal me somehow.

I came back to Isla Virginia.

And I came back to Ray.

# Chapter 38

When I showed up on the dock outside, it was like Ray had been waiting there for me for sixteen years. He'd been building this cabin for when I came back to him. And he'd been praying, that I would.

Ray even tried to find me in Iowa, but Stanley and I were in Eau Clair by then. Ray left the only world he knew, drove clear across the country in that beat-up Ford, asking around bus stops and diners—anywhere someone might've seen a girl with a baby.

When I walked back into his life, into this cabin, it was like stepping into a different world—and it was a different world.

This was Ray's new world.

He'd spent his entire life trying to make up for what happened in Penn Cove. Devoted every second to saving the orcas that were left, hoping that maybe he wouldn't go to hell for what he'd done. And maybe, somehow, if I ever came back, he could prove to me that he'd changed his heart about them.

Ray was what you might call a citizen scientist. He documented their lives, their whereabouts, their markings. He made observations about their lineages, their behavior, and their food, and took thousands of photographs to catalog them.

He knew everything there was to know about the chinook salmon, too. But even back then, it was too late, the dams were already built, there was nothing anyone could have done to stop them.

After Penn Cove, and the countless captures that happened in the years after, the resident orca population was decimated. Then after the Deville dam doubled down and held back more water, their food source disappeared, and the river systems went to shit.

Eventually, in time, everyone forgot that Ray had been a part of the roundup that day and he became a local legend for helping with the orca conservation efforts. Him and SaLita even found each other and joined forces. They created the Salish Sea Orca Conservation Center together. Can you imagine that?

He cried when he saw me pull up that day.

I cried too.

The boat rocked gently as I stepped onto the dock, Ray waiting a few paces away. The years had settled into him—lines around his eyes and streaks of silver in his hair—but his presence, the unwavering warmth of him, hadn't changed one bit. He stood still, his eyes never leaving mine, and in that moment, it was like no time had passed at all.

I wanted to say something, but my voice caught in my throat. Instead, I walked toward him, and when I reached him, he wrapped his arms around me.

It wasn't tentative or polite—his embrace wasn't just warmth and welcoming either—it was a belonging I hadn't realized I'd been missing.

For a long time, neither of us spoke. The waves lapped at the dock, as the sound of gulls overhead filled the silence we didn't want to break. When we finally pulled apart, he looked at me, his voice soft but unwavering.

"I never stopped waiting for you."

In that moment, I knew—we still loved each other.

Ours was the kind of love that doesn't disappear; it only waits in quiet agony until it's found again. It wasn't the kind of love you can grow in a garden either. Our love was like a whole universe that could sustain itself—one moment, there's nothing, and the next, an entire world is born that can never be destroyed.

Ours was the kind of love that heals even the darkest despair—it survives over distance and time. And it was exactly what I needed to want to keep living.

Ray and I were meant for one another in this life, and in all the ones to come. No matter what happened or how much time had passed between us, nothing can change that.

But our world was complicated.

We both knew it. Just because we were two sides of the same coin didn't mean we'd land face-up together.

This cabin Ray built was more than a home. It was a love letter to me. These wooden walls hold the memories of his hands. These smooth beams and the intricate carving he spent years perfecting—are imbued with the very essence of his soul.

It looked the same back then as it does now. Only there are more books and papers and photographs, if that's even possible.

"I built it for you. For us," he said.

I knew what he wanted.

I wanted it too.

"Ray..."

"I know," he said quickly, cutting me off. "I know you have a life. Our daughter. I'm not saying—I'm just..." He looked down, then back at me, his voice softer now. "It's just ...I want you, and...to have a place where you always belong and come back to, no matter what. Whenever you're ready. If, you ever become ready."

That first night, we stayed up late talking about everything we hadn't said in decades. Of course I told him about Karleen—how brilliant she was, how her laugh could fill a room.

Then I told him about her death, about how her heart stopped and no amount of extraordinary measures could bring her back. I told him about her funeral and the darkness I was in after losing her. About the darkness I was still fighting back.

I told him all about Stanley, and how wonderful he was, and of course, about you. Ray listened, sometimes his face was a blank wall, other times it crumpled. I watched him take it all in—the years he'd lost, the daughter he never held—and I felt something break open between us. There were things too heavy for words, but we sat with them anyway.

Through it all, his hand never left mine, his eyes never turned to anger or hate. Once all the truths were out in the open, it was like I was finally set free. And maybe, so was he.

I was still sad, but not in the depth of despair that I'd shown up with. Ray said he forgave me long before I showed up on the dock. And I believed him. We talked until the morning sun came up, holding each other in the quiet stillness of the cabin.

The next day, Ray introduced me to a charming little boy named Shephard. A family lived on the other side of the island by then, and Ray looked after their son like he was his own. Seeing him with that boy healed and broke my heart in equal measure.

After that, Ray took me out on the boat—the same boat we'd fallen in love on all those years ago. The wood was weathered now, its surface faded and worn by time, but as I ran my hand along the railing, the memories came rushing back.

It was as if they had seeped into the grain itself, tucked into every groove, etched into the very soul of the boat, a testament to everything our love had once been.

Ray's voice pulled me out of my thoughts. "They're still here, you know. The orcas. The same family is still out there."

"How many are left?"

"Twelve," he said, his voice heavy. He swallowed hard. "Their numbers never recovered. The spirit thieves kept coming. Then the dams. The noise. Cargo ships. Vessel strikes. Oil spills. It was all too much. But that night in the cove—that was the beginning of the end."

We spent the morning in silence, letting the rhythm of the water guide us. Ray cut the engine and closed his eyes, the boat rocking gently as he stood, a small speck among the expanse of the sea.

"They're close," Ray said, his eyes distant at first, then focused on me.

"How do you know?" I asked.

"You ever feel tied to something you have no business being connected to—and yet, you still are? No matter the distance, the years, the miles of water or land between you, there's still a thread connecting you—invisible, but unbroken.

"I can feel them now, in my heart, the same way I still feel you. Just as strong as the day you left. My love for you never faded, Ginny. Not for a second. It didn't even dim. It just… shifted. I had to put it somewhere. So I gave it to them. I love them as much as I still love you."

I didn't know what to say.

Part of me wanted to reach for him—touch his face, anchor us both to the moment—but my body stayed still. My voice too.

And then, it wasn't more than a moment later that they appeared— first one dorsal fin slicing through the surface, then another. Six of the last twelve members of the Southern Residents swam gracefully, their movements fluid and deliberate, as if the water itself bent to their will.

The ban on whale watching had already gone into effect so there were no other boats around. Fishing was based on lottery systems even back then. But it was all too late. Too much damage had been done.

I sobbed when I saw them. Circling our boat, as if they were saying hello to an old friend. Ray was no threat to them. He took out his camera, capturing their lives with his lens.

Ray spent his entire life trying to make up for what happened in Penn Cove. He thought if he devoted his life to saving the whales that were left, maybe he wouldn't go to hell for what he'd done. Instead of finding a wife, raising a family, Ray stayed on his lonely island, with his whales, and with his memories, and lived out his days doing what he thought might save them, and save his soul.

Ray took my hands in his, his grip steady but weighted, as though he were holding more than my fingers.

"There's something I've never told you. Something I've carried alone because I thought it might protect you. But if you were to hear it from someone else…" He exhaled, his voice trembling. "It's also the one thing I need to tell you—for my own soul." He paused, his eyes locking onto mine, raw and unguarded. "If I don't say it while I have the chance, it may haunt me forever. Or worse, it might find its way to you someday, when I'm not here to protect you the way I can now."

"Ray, what is it? You can tell me," I said. But his words didn't land—they detonated, tearing through me in a way I hadn't thought possible.

Then he told me the truth.

The night the whales were trapped in Penn Cove, someone cut the nets. Two calves drowned in a tangled mass of nylon because of it.

It was me, Kassidy.

I killed those calves.

I cut the nets to try and save them, but instead, I killed them.

Ray knew. He knew that morning, before I left him. When I told him I'd been in the water, he knew.

But he never said a word. He spared me the truth, let me believe it was him, or the crew he was with, that slaughtered them.

It doesn't make what they did any less horrible. But I was so quick to judge, so sure of what I saw, that I never let him speak—never gave him the chance to tell me his truth. Youth does that to us. Makes us think we know everything when what it should do is make us shut up and listen.

SaLita told Ray she was there when the nets were cut, but she never revealed that it was me, she never gave anyone my name.

Ray knew it was me.

After I left, the Whale Collector wanted blood. He went on a hunt for the people who had cut the net and robbed him of two calves, and the forty thousand dollars that was lost.

But those calves didn't die because of Ray that night.

They died because of me.

My days on the island with Ray blurred together after that. We spent quiet mornings on the water in his boat, long talks in the cabin, with stretches of silence that spoke louder than words ever could.

We talked about the whales, about Penn Cove, about all the regret that haunted him, and all the regret that was killing me.

There are some things that happened on this island that I never told Stan. Because they would have broken his heart, and he didn't deserve it. But the week I spent with Ray…if I hadn't opened up to him, hadn't let myself feel, reveal, and heal all at once, I don't think I'd have come out of the grief I showed up with.

I know how strange this must sound, but being here with Raymond was the only way for me to get back to Stanley. Time doesn't heal old wounds. It buries them. Healing only happens in a relationship—with someone who not only loves you, but loves you enough to help you heal. Those wounds we try so hard to forget, have to be reopened. But only just enough, so they can be stitched back together by someone who knows how to hold the needle.

Ray was the only one who could understand my pain and know what to do with it—because he carried the same pain too. Being together that week was the only way either of us could finally begin to heal. And not just heal enough to live, to love, to breathe. But heal enough to one day die—with peace.

That's what we gave to one another in that week. Or at least, that's what he gave to me. And I can only hope that when it was his time to go, he felt the same.

Unraveling nearly twenty years of buried pain—laying it bare for someone to see, to hold, and having them forgive you—was the most cathartic, transformational, transcendental thing I've ever done. And offering forgiveness in return? That changed me just as much. Without it, I don't know who I'd be. And I couldn't have done that with anyone but him.

Being with Ray healed me in a way nothing else could, and I have no regrets about that. He helped me become whole again—whole enough to be the mother you deserved.

But if Stan had known the truth, about how I felt about Ray—it would have destroyed him.

So, I kept what I'm about to tell you to myself.

Ray and I never shared our bodies with one another that week. We didn't. Even though it felt natural—right even—we didn't. I slept in his room. He slept in that little bed in the back.

That boundary somehow made every moment we spent together even more intimate than if we'd have given in to physical desire.

What we shared wasn't passion; it was something deeper, something raw and profound. In this cabin, out on that water, we gave each other something no physical connection could have offered. A kind of intimacy that changes a person—that strips you down to your barest self and leaves you completely open to bonding with another in a way you otherwise can't. In that vulnerability, we forged a love that became unbreakable.

I loved Ray in a way I could never love Stan. That's not to say it was less. It was different. You might even say I loved Stan more, since I went back to him. Or maybe it was my love for you, Kassidy, that I came back for. But Stan gave me a life when I thought mine was over. He deserved every bit of respect and love I could possibly give him. So every day, I lived for him, for you—except for that week with Ray. I lived for me.

I wanted to stay. God, how I wanted to stay here with Ray.

But I knew I couldn't.

Stanley had saved me when I was drowning, and he didn't deserve to be left for a man I loved in another time and galaxy. I owed him more than that. I owed our daughter's memory more than that.

When the week was over, I stood on the dock with Ray, the boat waiting to take me back. His face was calm, but his eyes betrayed him.

He didn't beg; he knew it too—what we had to do.

"I love you, Ginny."

I reached up, cupping his face in my hands. "I love you. But I can't stay."

"I know," he said finally, his voice breaking. "I'll wait."

"No. You can't wait."

"I don't have a choice."

"You do have a choice, Ray. Please don't wait for me. I can't come back or I might not be able to… Ray, I won't be strong enough to walk away and lose you one more time."

He smiled—the saddest one I've ever seen. "Don't you understand? The love in my heart for you is like the tides. It can't be told what to do. It doesn't live by anyone's rules. It can't be stopped, or changed, or broken. It can only be what it was created to be. And so I have to wait. That is my fate. My *Maqluna*. I am tethered to you. And you are tethered to me."

The words tore something inside me.

I knew they were true.

I also knew what I had to do.

As the boat carried me farther from the dock, I turned back one last time. I felt our hearts tethered together—like he'd said—by an invisible rope, stretched taut to its breaking point, until it finally snapped, leaving us both shattered on opposite ends of the divide.

I wanted to jump off the boat and swim back, tell him I'd changed my mind. But I didn't. I couldn't.

Then my tears came, hot and relentless, as I realized I had left the love of my life behind—for a second time. I cried like my body itself was a dam that held back the ocean. It hurt, but I knew it was the right choice and somehow, someday, some part of us would be together again. Some loves are meant to last a lifetime. Others are meant to last forever.

Ours…well, Kassidy, I hope you're lucky enough to find a love like ours—one that stays with you through every turn. A love so profound it doesn't end with this lifetime but follows you into whatever comes next.

Me and Stanley found a way to keep living—to move on and survive. Ray did too, in his own way. We all healed.

At least on the surface.

Everyone, except the whales.

Their loss was too immense, too irreversible. Extinction leaves no room for recovery. And these orcas—these whales—are unlike any others on the planet, Kassidy.

Once they're gone… there's no bringing them back.

In my lifetime, *Maqluna* has revealed herself in all the ways she promised. Except one.

SaLita once spoke of a girl with hair as dark as the deepest ocean, who would come bearing something more powerful than any weapon.

A descendant.

My descendant.

I've spent countless hours pondering who and what could be more powerful than any weapon. And I believe I know the answer.

Someone to remind the world what it forgot.

That it's not too late. That some things can still be saved.


Now, Kassidy, it's your turn, dear. What do you need to tell me that's got you nearly coming out of your seat?

# Chapter 39

When her grandma stopped talking, Kassidy needed a moment alone and headed into the kitchen to make a cup of tea. The cabin fell into a quiet hum as shadows stretched long across the walls and the last light of day faded through the windows.

Kassidy's whole world felt different, like the ground beneath her cracked open and what she thought she knew about her family, about herself, fell into the earth, leaving her in a strange land alone and untethered.

There was the world she knew, where she grew up with Virginia and Stanley. And then there was Raymond, Shephard, the island, and the whales—filling her heart and mind in ways she never imagined possible.

Kassidy sat on the sofa, still trying to process the cascade of secrets she'd learned. She stared out the window, her eyes fixed on the shimmering waters beyond. Kassidy couldn't tell how Virginia was doing, if she was the steadfast woman of steel, she knew her to be, or if her armor had cracked. Her senses were off, on overload. She needed a break from the cabin—she needed some air.

Before she could move, a knock echoed through the room, steeped in fading light. Kassidy's pulse jumped. It could only be one person, and she was grateful he'd come.

She pressed her palms flat against her jeans, smoothed a few loose strands of hair. A pointless effort—she felt completely unraveled.

When she opened the door, Shephard stood there, framed by the last slivers of sunlight. His presence filled the space between them, warm, steady, and completely disarming. The pull between them was as strong as ever, an unspoken chemistry neither of them had ever needed to name.

They stood there, eyes locked, her world shifting in a way it only did when he was near.

"Shephard," she said, her voice quieter than she meant it to be.

"Are you okay?" His lips curved into something just shy of a smile, but his eyes—his eyes were searching, as if he could see past whatever mask she might try to wear. "I've been thinking about you. Nonstop actually. I haven't heard from you, so I stopped to check in. Did your grandmother make it? You need anything?"

Her thoughts were scattered, her pulse tripping over itself. It wasn't just everything her Grandma had told her, or how her whole world changed in the space of an afternoon. It was him too.

Not seeing this man for a mere two days felt like two years. She wanted to fall into him, to be enveloped in something she knew, something she felt was real. He belonged to her in some unspoken way. It was like this place, this moment, had been waiting for them, even if everything else felt like it was spinning off its axis.

"Kassidy," he interrupted her spiral.

"Virginia is here. She's fine…I'm—" She swallowed hard. "Shep, it's true. About Ray. And there's so much more I can't even—"

Before she could explain, Virginia's voice cut through the air behind her.

"Now who on earth would be knocking on your door all the way out—"

Virginia blinked, pulling herself back when she saw them.

Kassidy stepped aside, motioning for Shephard to come in.

"Virginia, this is…Shephard."

Her grandma's eyes narrowed, her sharp gaze assessing the man in the doorway as recognition flickered.

"Well, I'll be damned," she muttered. "You were just a little boy last time I met you. You used to sneak over here to go fishing and go on all sorts of adventures with Ray." Her voice softened, "Haven't you grown up to be quite the catch."

Shephard smiled, the mature wrinkles framing his eyes. "I'm sorry, have we met?" he said, his tone polite but guarded.

Kassidy looked at Shephard and smiled, imagining the adorable little boy he must have been, and what his life with Ray might have looked like growing up there.

Virginia chuckled. "Of course you wouldn't remember. You were just a little boy. We only met once. When I came out to visit Ray." Shephard looked at Kassidy who shrugged as if to say—I'll fill you in later.

"Your family still live on the North side?" Virginia asked.

"Actually, it's just me now. Everyone else moved inland."

"You live out here—alone?"

Shephard nodded once.

Kassidy shifted uncomfortably and cleared her throat.

"Virginia," she said, "will you be alright if I go into town with Shephard for a little while? Or do you need me to stay and make sure you don't get into trouble."

Kassidy's grandma folded her arms, her sly smile returning. "I can manage just fine. But Shep, before you go, do me a favor and get this old TV working? *Jeopardy's* on soon, and I'll be damned if I miss it."

Shephard smiled and nodded, moving toward the TV. He knelt and rolled up his sleeves, Kassidy's gaze roamed over the curve of his forearms, the strength in his hands. She felt her cheeks flush, and that soft ache of vulnerability followed, the way it does when someone shows up and excites your whole world. She felt tethered to him in a way she couldn't explain.

Ginny's voice broke the spell as she moved shoulder to shoulder with Kassidy. "So," she said, under her breath, "this is what you've been doing out here for two weeks—*all alone*. He's quite the catch, and it seems like you've hooked more than just his attention."

Kassidy bit her lip, trying to fight off the nervous heat rising in her chest. "Mind your own business, *Isla Virginia*."

Virginia raised one eyebrow but didn't press, though the corner of her mouth twitched like she was enjoying this a little too much.

Kassidy knew she'd been had. Virginia's gaze drifted back to Shephard, who was busy fiddling with the TV.

"Mm-hmm," she mused, folding her arms. "And I'm sure checking on Kassidy was the only thing on your mind when you came over."

Shephard stilled for half a second before continuing to adjust the antenna, and Kassidy felt her face heat.

After a few moments, Shep turned the TV on, and the screen flickered to life. But it wasn't *Jeopardy*. The local news blared across the screen, the anchor's serious tone grabbing everyone's attention.

"Breaking news today about orcas from around the world—first off, the investigation into the slain orca, Marie, in the Gulf of Alaska last week continues. New evidence has surfaced, connecting a luxury yacht in the Pacific Northwest to the shooting incident…"

A picture of a yacht filled the screen, sleek and remarkable. Kassidy's heart dropped into her stomach like a rock. She looked at Shep, who stood there, staring at the screen, his jaw clenched tight, eyes fixed forward. He didn't look at her. Didn't meet her gaze.

Her mind raced, but before she could even begin to form the question, the news reel changed again.

"And some other heartbreaking news tonight coming out of the Salish Sea, as the last reproductive female in the vanishing Southern Resident population has given birth. The calf survived only thirty minutes. The mother has begun what scientists call a 'tour of grief.'

"She's been seen throughout the islands for the last two days carrying her dead calf on her rostrum. In 2018, the orca known as Tahlequah, swam for 17 days over one thousand miles with her dead newborn. The longest tour of grief recorded in history. No one knows how long this funeral procession will go on.

"The only other surviving Southern Resident, Ocean Sun, now in her nineties, is swimming beside the grieving mother, taking turns holding the deceased calf when the mother becomes too exhausted. Ocean Sun's daughter, Keelah, is perhaps the most famous Southern Resident, and still remains in captivity after being taken during the infamous Penn Cove roundup in 1970.

"The population has suffered catastrophic losses over the last few decades pushing their numbers to imminent extinction. Washington officials have put measures in place to try and bring their numbers back, but critics say the efforts have come much too late."

"Oh my God," Virginia whispered. Her ashen face stared at the screen. "After all these years, that family is still paying the price for what we did."

Kass could hardly breathe, the truth squeezing tight around her. The orcas. Their history. Their pain. What was still happening. Still repeating. What she had done. Nothing had changed.

The final blow came as the news anchor's voice grew sharper, more pointed, as she covered another local story.

"In a landmark deal between an aquarium in the U.S. and Mexico, Keelah, the captive orca at the center of a decades old debate, has landed in her new home at the Capri Son Aquarium and theme park. Capri Son has just announced her arrival and is launching a new global campaign around her to try and bring back business to the once booming industry.

"The park has found a new and stunning way for participants to be up close with the famous killer whale. For a hefty fee, participants can dawn a mermaid costume and swim underwater in an adjacent tank from the whale."

Kassidy's body went stiff as her face filled the screen.

Virginia gasped.

Kassidy slapped both hands over her mouth, but it did nothing to stop the sob that tore from her throat. The sight of herself—next to the whale, frozen in time—made her stomach twist.

And then it changed.

There she was, underwater. Palms pressed against the invisible barrier, suspended in the aqua haze. Her hair floated in all directions, weightless, as she stared into Keelah's eyes.

The nausea hit so hard she thought she might faint.

She swayed on her feet, Shephard gripped her elbow and waist holding her upright.

There was nowhere to run from this moment, this truth.

Keelah. The whale that had been stolen. The calf that had been ripped from her mother's side. The ghost of a life that never should have been taken.

And her own family—Virginia, Ray, the past she barely understood—woven into that same history. She wasn't just part of it. She was an accomplice. She dared a glance at Virginia.

Her grandmother stood frozen, her lips parted, eyes locked on the screen. Her breath came shallow, almost absent. And then, she stepped back.

One step. Then another. As if putting distance between them. Shephard stood on guard ready to catch either one of them if they fell down.

When Virginia finally spoke, her voice was paper-thin, raw with something Kassidy didn't recognize and had never heard before. Not anger. Not rage. Worse. Disappointment.

"Oh, Kassidy…" Her throat bobbed as she swallowed. "What have you done?" Kassidy couldn't stop the tears—they fell hard, fast, blurring her vision.

"I didn't know they had her," she choked out. "I swear, I didn't. Billy signed me up for this job. Once I got there, I—" She swallowed hard. "I was under-water when I discovered the truth. By then it was too late, and I felt like I didn't have a choice."

Virginia exhaled a broken sound, but she still didn't look at her.

Kassidy turned toward Shep, desperate for something—anything—but his face was unreadable.

She felt alone. Desperately. Hopelessly alone. This was her fate. The woman had predicted it, told her this would happen.

"We needed the money, Grandma. I was going to tell you. I used what they paid me to pay off the farm so you could stay there. I didn't know that's what I was signing up for with Keelah. I swear it. I was supposed to be doing this stupid mermaid thing and when I showed up, there were protesters. And a whale. I don't know how to fix this. I don't know if I can."

Virginia's expression softened, but the pain was still there, etched into her face. She was talking, but Kassidy could barely hear what she was saying. She'd betrayed her grandma. She knew how her grandma felt about the orcas in captivity. Even if she didn't know why at the time. She knew. And now, she knew exactly why. Exactly how personal it had been.

Now, people are going to buy tickets to Capri Son because of her. And in doing so, not only support Keelah's captivity, but support everything that family has been through without even knowing the truth about their history. What they'd lost. What they were still losing.

Others would hate her for what she promoted—as they should. She'd lose her sponsors. Lose her business. She knew all along this is what was waiting for her, she just couldn't bear to stare it in the face until she was forced to. She felt like the worst kind of coward and had no idea how to make it right.

She glanced at Shep, his eyes still averted. Something unsaid lingered between them. She pulled away from Shep as if backing away from him before he could push her away himself.

She didn't think her heart could take his rejection.

Kassidy's heart pounded so hard she could barely hear her own voice over the rush of blood in her ears.

"I don't know how, but I will fix this."

Her grandma's gaze was steady, unreadable. "Capri Son is powerful, Kassidy. Dangerous, too. Some things can't be fixed."

Kassidy swallowed, shaking her head. "I was a coward. I came here and stuck my head in the sand. I distracted myself." She hung her head, feeling Shephard's gaze on her.

"I knew this day would come. And I knew that I would have to be the one to fix it—if that's even possible. And I still ran from it anyway."

She exhaled sharply.

"I lied to you, Shephard. I didn't tell you that Ray wasn't the only reason I was here. I didn't tell you that I was running. From this. From myself. I'm so sorry."

She slumped, then straightened, forcing herself to stand taller, stronger.

"I didn't try to fix this before. But I'm going to try now."

She turned to Shephard, her chest tightening like it might cave in. "I understand if you don't want to be here. You're not a coward. Why would you want to be with someone who can't even stand up for herself?"

Her voice cracked, but she didn't look away.

"You grew up here. The whales aren't just animals—they're part of this place, part of you. I know that. What I promoted—my cowardice for not walking away, and giving the money back—it's shameful."

She sucked in a shaky breath as her own words sank in. "It's unforgivable. I'm going to take a water taxi to town. I need to make some calls where the cell service is good."

She turned to leave but Shephard grabbed her elbow, holding her back, other hand flexing at his side.

For a second—one unbearable second—she felt the loss of him. Then he closed the space between them.

"Jesus, Kass." His voice was rough, strained. He reached for her shoulders—slowly, carefully, as if she might bolt. Then he cupped her face, his calloused fingers warm against her damp, salty skin.

"Don't you think you're being a bit too hard on yourself? You really think I'd walk away? Because of this?"

Her breath stuttered. "I just assumed—"

"I won't leave you to face this alone. I can help you find a way to make it right." His thumb brushed a tear from her cheek, and something inside her tore open. "You showed up here for a reason. And I'm so grateful you did. I'm not walking away from that. From us."

His voice was wrapped around her, reassuring and calm, unshaken by the storm between them.

"You're standing in front of me, owning this. That takes courage. You're not a coward. Don't say that. If you're willing to fight for this place, for them—then we're meant to stand next to one another and fight together."

A sob clawed up her throat, but she bit it back, gripping the front of his shirt like he was the only thing keeping her upright.

Then she turned back to her grandma, desperation in her voice. "Grandma, I'm going to find a way to fix this. I'll find a way to make you not disappointed in me."

Virginia shook her head, her eyes softening—but not relenting.

"Kassidy," she said quietly, "you know better. I will stand by your side through this too. You do need to make it right. But I'll support whatever that looks like. If there's a way, I'll help you find it."

Kassidy blinked and a tear ran down her cheek as Virginia reached out and took her hands.

"We don't fix our mistakes by tying an anchor to them and hoping they never surface. We fix our problems by dragging them out into the light, where the people who truly care about us join hands and keep us out of the darkness."

Virginia gave Kassidy's fingers a squeeze before letting go, pulling her shoulders back, her chin lifting with quiet resolve. Then, with a pointed glance at Shephard, she huffed.

"The only thing I'm disappointed in, Kassidy, is that you let Shephard here touch your cheeks with his bacteria-covered hands and didn't even tell him to keep his germs off you."

Shephard looked down at both his palms, flipping them over and back again with a confused grin.

Kassidy smiled—then laughed, big enough to flash a glimpse of white teeth.

Virginia smiled too. "You'll probably get a staph infection now. And then a pimple. And ruin your beautiful complexion."

Kassidy let out a breathless laugh, the knot in her chest and stomach finally loosening.

Shephard rubbed his chin, still looking slightly lost.

Virginia shrugged. "Oh, you're alright, Shep. Just keep your grubby hands off her face, that's all."

# Chapter 40

Kassidy stared at a black screen in her hand as she waited for Shephard to taxi his float plane up to her dock.

The moment her phone powered back on, it exploded—chimes, notifications, alerts—one after the other, like a storm hovering offshore that had been waiting to pummel her.

Voicemail full. 12,348 new messages. 208,214 new comments.

The numbers felt surreal, but the pit in her stomach told her exactly what they meant. She didn't need to open them to know. Her career was in shambles. She'd be canceled. There would be enough controversy to bury her in the court of public opinion for the next century.

Her hand shook as she pressed play on the most recent voicemail. Billy's frantic voice filled her ear.

"Kass, where in the hell are you?! I can see you moving in the ocean—I've been tracking you so unless you're inside the belly of a whale, why aren't you answering?! This is a Code SPARKLE! Do you hear me? Code SPARKLE! Obviously, you haven't been watching TV or checking your feed, or you'd have called me by now!"

Billy's voice rose an octave, teetering on hysteria. "Your face is everywhere! Not just the U.S., Kass—Shanghai, Paris, *everywhere*. Capri Son plastered your photo on their billboards, magazine ads, and TV commercials! This is bigger than we could have ever dreamed!" He squealed with excitement. "I'm opening Chablis. Call me!"

Kassidy's stomach dropped. Her fingers hovered over her screen and she opened her account on RippleHub. The numbers were overwhelming—tens of thousands of tags, hundreds of thousands of comments—some of them adoring, but others—-filled with hate.

The hashtags alone, were enough to bring tears to her eyes.

#CaptivityQueen #MermaidOfMisery #WhaleJailor #SellOutToTheSea

Memes of her face spliced beside oil rigs, crumbling seawalls, rusting tank enclosures, even scenes from the Penn Cove captures— circulated faster than she could scroll. She was the face of a movement she didn't believe in, branded a symbol of cruelty and extinction.

She hadn't just lost control of her image and her platform—she'd lost her identity.

The headlines gleamed.

"Orca Encounter Back!"

"Chinese Orquariums on The Rise."

"Kassidy Karlson: Mermaid or Murderer?"

The nausea in her stomach churned as she heard footsteps on the dock. She turned to see her grandma, rushing toward her.

"Does that thing have room for me?" Virginia hollered over the sound of the plane's engine pulling up. Kassidy nodded. "Good. I'm going with you."

The roar of the engine intensified as Shephard pulled alongside the dock, the plane hovering on the water. He helped Virginia in the back, then Kassidy into the seat beside him. She felt a momentary reprieve when Shep's hand found hers, warm and strong. When their eyes met, he didn't avert his gaze.

"How can I help you? I have connections. Resources. Anything you need."

"I don't know if this can be fixed by any of that."

Shephard swallowed hard and gave her a reassuring squeeze. "It's not our mistakes that define us. It's what we do after that matters."

She sat in the co-pilot's seat next to Shep, trying to ground herself in the presence of his confidence—something real amid the turmoil. But even his warmth, his steadfastness, couldn't untangle the cyclone building inside her. She couldn't live with herself, knowing that no matter what she did, her face was out there—circulating, forever—promoting something she didn't want any part of.

Kassidy knew she'd stuck her head in the sand after that day at Capri Son. She knew she was running from a truth that would catch up with her. Now that it was here, she still had no idea how to fix it.

As they soared through the air, the water stretching far below them, Kassidy's mind reeled. She had to figure out if there was a way to get out of the Capri Son contract. Get her face taken down from their ads. Her mind raced so fast the ground was slipping away beneath her.

The plane touched down in front of Shep's grandfather's sprawling estate.

"Who owns this place? The Grand Sheik of Dubai?" Virginia drawled.

"No. This is my grandfather's estate. I keep a car here. We'll take that into town."

"What does your grandfather do, sell kidneys?" Virginia asked. Shephard looked at Kassidy who was too distraught to even laugh at what they both knew was the apple not falling far from the tree.

The yacht was gone.

Neither Shephard nor Kassidy mentioned it as they shuffled out. By the time they reached town, her anxiety was a living, breathing thing, clawing at her insides. As soon as Shephard parked the car, she jumped out and rushed into the nearest coffee shop where she'd have a solid signal—her fingers fumbling as she dialed Billy's number.

"Billy," she gasped when he picked up. "You have to fix this. It's so much worse than I imagined."

"Kass, calm down," Billy said, with a note of condescension. "I know losing half a million followers seems bad, but it's not. It's just the initial wave—it'll level out. All publicity is good publicity, remember? And look, you've already gained over 400,000 new ones, and they're climbing by the hour. These people are excited about your campaign. This is the start of something bigger than you ever imagined. You don't need those old followers. You're going global, Kass. GLOBAL."

"Billy, no." Her voice cracked. "You don't understand. I don't want my face to be on those ads. I don't want any of this. I should have said no that day, I'm such an idiot for going along with it. You don't know what I know about that whale. Where she came from, where I'm standing right now…They're all going extinct because of people like us. Because of *you* and *me*, promoting this, Billy. I have to get my face off those ads. I thought maybe I could ignore it. Or that it might drift away but this is so much worse. I can't support this, Billy. I'll find a way to give the money back. All of it."

Billy scoffed. "This campaign has launched you onto a worldwide stage. Do you know how many other aquariums have contacted me since your ad came out? They all want you."

"No." Kassidy whispered, almost to herself.

"This is fame, baby! Of course it'll come with criticism, but so what. Go get yourself a massage, or manicure, or hire a man to take care of your needs. You're a celebrity now, you can have and do anything you like. Trust me, you'll thank me later."

"I don't want fame, Billy. I want out. I want my face *off* those ads, and if you won't help me, I'll find someone who will."

Billy sighed, the sound patronizing. "Kass, whatever you're feeling now is a little bump on the road to greatness."

She hung up.

Billy wasn't going to help her.

He wasn't going to stop the runaway train that was her endorsement plastered next to a captive whale.

The chimes on her phone rang out again. More notifications. More comments. And then—her stomach dropped—posts Billy had been making on her behalf for the last two weeks. They were all wrong. Photos of her with the whale, captions written as if they were coming from her: "The most magical experience of my life. #MermaidLife #OrcaMagic." Then she scrolled to the next one: "I can't wait for everyone to experience this! #OceanDreams #CapriSonAdventures." It was all wrong. The words felt like poison.

Kassidy didn't know how to fix it, but she knew how to put a hold on it—at least for now. She changed her passwords, locking Billy out of her bank accounts and social media. She deleted everything he had posted in the last month.

Shephard, watching over her shoulder, nodded. "That's good. But maybe turn off the comments too. The last thing you need is a flood of trolls keeping this alive."

Kassidy hovered over the settings. "Right."

"You should take down that 'Sunrise on the Dock' post too."

She frowned, glancing up. "What? Why? That one has nothing to do with this."

Shep stared at her with an intensity she hadn't seen before. "I know. I just don't like other guys looking at you the way I do. And that photo. Wowzah."

Her pulse stuttered, she shifted her weigh to one hip, "Shephard Maddox are you the jealous type?"

His gaze lingered for half a second longer, unreadable, before he straightened and cleared his throat. "No. Of course not. But you could take down the boob tape video, too."

Kassidy snorted. "No way. That one paid my bills for nine months."

Shep's brows lifted. "Wow," he mouthed.

She whipped her head toward him. "How many videos of mine did you watch?"

He rubbed the back of his neck. "Enough to pay your bills for another nine months." He shrugged. "When I didn't see you for two days, I couldn't stop thinking of you so I watched them."

"All of them?" She stared at him, heart stuttering.

Shep rubbed the back of his neck, a sheepish smile tugging at his lips as his eyes darted away. "Only once or twice. Okay maybe three times. But five times max." His face flushed a deep shade of pink. "I also know how to fish braid now. So, if you ever need an extra set of hands..." he held his up and fluttered his fingers.

Something warm flickered to life in her chest. God, had she lucked out finding this man.

Someone up there must have played matchmaker because damn—Shep was made for her.

She turned back to the screen, her fingers lighter on the keys. "Alright, fish braid expert, what else should I do?"

Before he could answer, the sound of a gathering crowd turned their attention. They walked out of the corner coffee shop and saw a large group gathering near the stage.

The chatter fell to a quiet mumbling when WeNala Seawalker took to the podium wearing the same traditional regalia she always wore at these gatherings.

"The salmon are the lifeblood of this ecosystem," WeNala said, her voice firm, powerful. "Without them, the rivers will run silent. The forests will starve. And the whales will disappear—forever." The crowd clapped. "We cannot turn a blind eye to what's happening beneath our feet and in our waters. We cannot expect industries to check themselves, we must keep ourselves and our systems in check if we want to see life in the ocean tomorrow."

Kassidy, Virginia and Shephard stood at the back of the crowd, watching the scene unfold. She moved closer to him, standing shoulder-to-shoulder, lacing her fingers through his.

"If we allow the salmon to disappear," WeNala said, her voice filled with conviction, "the whales will disappear too. And what happens to the whales…will happen to all of us. It's not just the corporations that are causing their extinction—it's anyone who turns a blind eye to what's happening to them. Anyone who *pretends* not to see that we are killing our ancestors with our noise, with our vessels, and with our appetites for their food.

"Our greed is what is killing them. It's time that we sacrifice small comforts now, so that they can swim in these waters tomorrow!" Applause erupted, once it quieted, she continued. "Each of us bears the responsibility to save the wild that can still be saved. And to bring back the salmon if we want to bring back the orcas of the Salish Sea."

The crowd murmured in agreement.

Kassidy's stomach churned.

WeNala continued, "Only when our stolen child is returned to the Salish Sea can we begin to heal. We must insist that Keelah be returned home, so that she may live out her days in the ocean and not in a tank. Here, she can feel the tides, hear familiar calls, and be reunited with her mother who still swims in these waters today."

WeNala's words felt like they were aimed directly at her. She couldn't shake the feeling that the crowd's eyes were beginning to find her, too.

"Now, it is with great honor and *tal'shen* that I introduce a woman who has spent her entire life fighting for these orcas. A woman who was there during the capture era. Who was there, in Penn Cove when greed stole our family under the waves and sold them into slavery. She is a champion for all those who have been stolen, and for those still trying to survive in our crowded waters. She is my mentor, and grandmother, SaLita Seawalker."

Virginia gasped, her hand flying to her mouth as SaLita took to the stage amid roaring applause. Kassidy looked first at her grandma, and then to SaLita who gripped the edges of her long skirt in clenched fists as she ascended the stairs.

Her silver hair, woven with beaded strands that resembled seaweed, cascaded down her back, glinting as though the ocean itself flowed through her. SaLita reminded Kassidy about the legend of the Maiden of Deception Pass.

Weathered by decades of sun and salt, SaLita bore the resemblance of her ancestors—lines etched deep with stories of the land and sea, her presence commanding the crowd like the swell of the ocean commands lost ships at sea. Generations of wisdom reflected in her eyes as she scanned the crowd, and the strength of an entire people seemed to exude from her, every inch a queen of her people.

When she spoke, the wise woman's voice filled with decades of fight and defiance.

"I have not forgotten what happened in Penn Cove," SaLita started, her tone strained.

Kassidy cupped her hand around her grandma's elbow ensuring she wouldn't fall.

"Children were ripped from their undersea home while their families stood by helpless and were forced to watch. They cried to one another over the young ones lost. Our people have not forgotten. Now, it's time to return the stolen one to her home."

The crowd erupted in applause, but Kassidy barely heard it over the pounding in her ears. She looked at her grandma, who was pale and motionless, her eyes locked on SaLita as if she were seeing a ghost, as if seeing her brought Virginia back an unthinkable pain.

The crowd's energy was shifting, growing more intense by the second. Someone shouted, "Free the Swift! Bring the salmon back!" Others took up the chant, their voices growing louder, angrier.

"We have the power to change the course we're on," SaLita continued, her voice rising. "Our actions. Our deeds. Where we spend our money and energy and time matters!"

Kassidy's breath quickened. The world around her closed in, the pressure of the accusations, the guilt, the crushing fear—all of it consuming her. Shephard gripped her hand, grounding her.

Someone tapped WeNala on the shoulder. A whisper passed between them, and WeNala's gaze followed the outstretched hand of the person on stage, pointing toward Kassidy and her grandma.

The world seemed to slow.

WeNala's eyes narrowed, her focus shifting from the crowd toward them. She took the microphone from her grandma.

"I agree with you, Grandmother, we do have the power to change our fate and the fate of these whales. Some of us have more power than others." Kassidy felt like she might throw up. Her knees were weak, and she held her stomach. "Shephard Maddox, President and CEO of Deville Power, literally has the power to save the Salish Sea. Shephard Maddox, would you like to come up to the podium and tell us your plans for fixing the damage your company has done, and for saving our ocean home and all its creatures?"

WeNala's words echoed through Kassidy's head.

*President and CEO? Shephard?*

A wave of disbelief crashed through her. She turned to Shep, her eyes wide, searching his face for any sign of denial, for something to tell her why he hadn't been honest with her. He was an engineer. Yes, he worked for his grandfather but, he didn't tell her he ran the company.

Shep's expression was set in stone. His eyes darkened—no longer the playful, brooding man she thought she knew.

He looked...hardened.

Like a man who had a vault filled with secrets.

Virginia stood frozen on the other side of him, confusion written across her face. The crowd's murmurs grew louder, like the building swell of a tidal wave. All eyes were on Shephard.

Kassidy's breath came in short bursts as she waited for Shephard to explain what was happening. But he didn't. He dropped her hand.

Slowly, Shephard stepped forward, a polite smile the only reaction to an increasingly hostile crowd as he made his way through.

His gaze met Kassidy's before he walked up on the stage—a brief look, full of something she couldn't quite place: guilt? Regret? A plea for understanding?

Who was he, really? What had he done? Why did they hate him? But she already knew.

The dam.

But who was she to judge him after what she'd done? Maybe that was why she didn't feel afraid of his past, or his future. Now, both of their secrets lay bare.

# Chapter 41

Shephard stood tall, his jaw set, as if he had known this moment was coming. The quiet was dense, like fog rolling in from the sea, impossible to ignore. His eyes swept over the crowd, but his calm demeanor did nothing to quell their energy that was turning volatile.

Shephard stepped up to the podium, SaLita and WeNala stood behind him, arms crossed, faces stoic like ice. Their refusal to shake his hand, a clear statement—Shephard was the enemy.

He remained calm, his demeanor polite.

"Did you know about all this?" Virginia muttered, her voice tight with concern as she gazed toward the stage.

Kassidy shook her head but didn't take her eyes from the man she was so clearly falling in love with. A man who was also wrapped up in this complicated mess she couldn't even begin to unravel.

Shephard adjusted the microphone and cleared his throat. He offered a warm smile as he began. Angry murmurs rippled through the crowd. The kind that grew into a full-blown wave of fury as soon as Shephard spoke.

"Hello and thank you, WeNala, SaLita, for inviting me up." He glanced at the woman behind him and smiled but his charm did nothing to defrost the ice. "We appreciate every opportunity to connect with the community and hear your concerns. So, if you have questions for me, I'd be happy to answer."

It took only seconds for the crowd to erupt with anger.

"Free the Swift, you lying bastards!" someone yelled.

"You're starving our whales!" another hollered. The anger spread like wildfire, voices overlapping, drowning each other out. It wasn't just the usual restlessness or frustration—it was something much darker, much more dangerous. They were out for blood, and Shephard stood at the center of it.

His eyes darkened as he glanced at Kassidy—steady but distant. Then he interrupted the angry crowd.

"Your passion for the river and the whales is commendable. Believe me when I say I share that same desire to have clean rivers and a healthy population of all marine life in our waterways. Deville Power has hired an independent agency to do a thorough assessment on the dam's impact of the salmon runs," he said, his voice firm against the growing angry din.

But the crowd collectively groaned.

Someone shouted again, "We've heard it before!"

"You're stalling!"

"Free the Swift!"

Shephard kept his composure as he continued.

"The assessment includes a feasibility report that I will make public, detailing steps to remove one, or more, of the dams, *if* that is what is recommended."

"More excuses!" someone yelled. "The dam is killing the fish and the orcas, and you know it!"

"The studies have already been done!"

SaLita stepped off the stage with a microphone in her hand.

"Mr. Maddox has been kind enough to speak with us today," she said, her voice commanding silence. "If you have a question, please step up to the stage and ask it. There's no need to shout at Mr. Maddox like he's a feral animal." She shot him a glance and muttered off microphone. "Even if he may be exactly that."

Shephard stiffened but looked unaffected by the jab. Kassidy didn't understand why people hated him so much. She didn't understand why they were so against the dam. It wasn't just anger—it was loathsome, disgruntled, guttural...hatred.

Shephard might have been their target but being associated with him made her part in the problem bigger than it already was.

People began to line up. Kassidy's stomach churned as the first audience member spoke, their tone sharp and filled with accusation.

"Everyone knows that dam is useless. Why won't Deville Power face the truth and do the right thing? Take it down before it's too late."

Shep's expression tightened. A rustling of agitation spread through the crowd like dry grass catching fire.

"It's true that energy production from the dam has declined," he said, voice composed. "But the power generated there still provides critical energy for homes and businesses throughout the Pacific Northwest."

A few voices rose at once, overlapping—frustrated, skeptical.

Someone from the back called out, "There are other sources of power that won't kill the salmon!"

Shep lifted a hand, palm out, cutting through the noise before it could spiral.

"Please—let me finish." His tone was firm but calm, his gaze sweeping the crowd until the voices quieted. "If production stops, those families and businesses will have to get their power elsewhere. And right now, there is no elsewhere. The economic impact on those families and small businesses would be catastrophic."

Another voice came through the mic SaLita was holding.

"Tell us—was it your yacht anchored off the coast of Alaska the day the whales were shot? Don't pretend the orcas matter to you—they don't fit your business model, and they never did. Your family's legacy is blood in the water. Decades of abduction. Slaughter. Captivity. Why should anyone believe you're not just the next polished predator in a long line of them?"

Kassidy felt a chill run down her spine as the accusation hung in the air. He leaned into the microphone, his voice uneasy, but steady.

"It's true. I was in Alaska at the time of that tragedy."

The crowd erupted—a cacophony of shouts and rage echoing through the space. "But I did not hurt those whales. I grew up here, in the Salish Sea, like most of you. I care about our waterways and estuaries, our salmon, and our orcas." Shephard pressed a palm against his chest. "I will do everything that is advised by the experts—" The crowd began to groan again, Shephard hurried to finish his sentence. "To protect the land and water and marine life in the Salish Sea."

The next person at the microphone stepped up, her voice trembling with fury. "We can't wait for another study. All the studies have been done. Our whales are starving while you sit on your hands. We've all seen their peanut heads. And that mother, carrying her dead baby, parading it in front of us, crying for help, begging us to stop what we're doing. Enough is enough, Mr. Maddox. You're the only one who can save the orcas that are left. If you have a heart, you'll do the right thing."

Shephard nodded and tightened his lips. "Deville Power has worked with the state of Washington to enforce bans on salmon fishing, to reduce vessel noise and re-route traffic. We believe those efforts have helped. It could take a decade to remove a single dam. Even if we take them all down, in ten years, it might be too late. We need to focus on other measures to protect them right now—"

The crowd spoke over one another. They'd heard it all before a million times.

"Boo!" The crowd cut him off with a chorus of boos and jeers.

Each shout was a stone hurled in Shep's direction, but he stood his ground, absorbing the blows with barely a flinch.

Kassidy's heart pounded in her chest; her throat tight with the unknown of it all. She'd come here thinking the scrutiny would be on her, but the crowd had turned their full fury toward Shephard, and with each passing second, more accusations flew.

"We don't need more of your lies. We need your action!" someone shouted from the middle of the crowd.

Shephard didn't waver. "I will do everything in my power to reverse the damage—"

Before he could finish, a black town car screeched to a halt beside the stage, the back door opening with a slow, ominous creak. A man in the backseat, locked eyes with Shep. His expression was displeased—demanding. Shephard stretched his neck as if there was a noose tightening around it. Then he spoke into the microphone.

"Thank you," he said, then stepped off the side of the stage and walked toward the town car.

WeNala seized the moment, her voice carrying across the chattering crowd.

"We have another visitor here today who has inserted themselves into the politics of the Salish Sea. Someone who, in her own way, also has power. To help. Or to harm." WeNala turned, her eyes narrowing as they landed on Kassidy. "Kassidy Karlson," she called, her voice carrying over the crowd like a sentence being passed. "Would you care to come up and explain your new partnership with Capri Son, Ms. Karlson? Can you justify your recent promotion of orcas in captivity, with our orca, Keelah, that we are working hard to return to her home, while you are working hard to keep in a concrete tank?"

Kassidy's heart stopped. For a split second, the world narrowed to her name, reverberating through the air. The crowd turned as one, their eyes sharp, predatory, hostility crackling in the atmosphere like electricity before a storm.

"Whale jailor!" someone yelled, their voice ringing out.

"Captivity queen!" another person hissed.

These weren't extremists, nor were they shouting for sport. They'd just been quiet long enough—long enough to watch the whales vanish, the salmon run dry, and billionaires keep smiling for the cameras. They were locals who'd watched their coastline bleed for decades—and they'd finally had enough. Theirs was heartbreak, hardened into rage.

Kassidy's pulse thundered in her ears. The hostility aimed at Shephard was now rapidly shifting toward her, like a pack of wolves turning on fresh prey. Kassidy felt hatred in their eyes, each one a dagger piercing through her skin.

She couldn't even blame them for how they felt. She'd felt it too—powerless, betrayed, and sick of pretending everything was fine.

This wasn't supposed to happen. She'd wanted to be a voice for change—use her platform for a higher purpose than herself, for something good. Now, the world was turning on her and somehow, she had become the villain in her own story.

She looked to Shep, her eyes pleading for some kind of lifeline. But his eyes too, were filled with something she didn't recognize.

The crowd's shouts grew louder, and more frenzied. Kassidy could feel their anger rising, swelling like a tidal wave about to crash over her.

Her legs felt weak, her body frozen in place as the mob's fury threatened to drown her. Insults were hurled. Whispers of betrayal. Calls for justice. Demands that she answer for her actions.

Before the crowd could spiral further, Shep stepped in, his body a barrier between them and the chaos. His hand was suddenly on hers, firm, grounding. His grip was tight, almost desperate, as he pulled her out of the crowd, carving a path for the three of them.

Virginia clutched Kassidy's other arm, her breath uneven but her grip strong. She wasn't speaking—Kassidy could feel the tension in her, the way she moved stiffly, like she was holding something in.

Her grandma wasn't afraid, but she was angry. And maybe, deep down, she was also heartbroken by what this had become.

But it wasn't over. Kassidy's heart pounded, a sharp, jagged beat that echoed in her ears. The crowd's fury didn't wane as they hurried away—if anything, it thickened, pressing in on them like a living breathing thing.

Shep's grip stayed firm as he ushered them toward his car, his eyes constantly scanning, always ahead. But behind them, a voice sliced through the noise.

A woman followed close, her words cutting through the angry chatter. "Running won't save you Kassidy Karlson."

The words hit like a slap to the face. Shephard opened the car doors, guiding them both inside without a word. Then he slid into the driver's seat, fists clenched tight around the wheel, eyes fixed ahead as he pulled the car away.

The noise from the crowd faded in the rear window, but Kassidy still heard their shouts in her mind. Her body trembled, she turned to Shep, her voice barely a whisper.

"They don't understand. I'm trying to fix this."

But that's not what the crowd saw.

They saw her as the status quo. Another smiling face cashing in on the same system that caged the orcas—polished branding, different promises, but the same cruelty in a new disguise.

It didn't matter that she hadn't known.

It didn't matter that she regretted it now.

Or that millions of people had clapped and cheered and paid for a ticket without ever asking—at what cost. It didn't matter that they too, needed to share the blame.

None of that mattered—not when grief had hardened into distrust, and every new face looked like the same old lie. Because when people are that hurt, that betrayed, they don't look for the good anymore—they just look for someone to blame.

For decades, marine parks had controlled the narrative, convincing the world that orcas were safer in tanks than in their own ocean. That concrete walls and choreographed tricks were 'education.' That the ones born in captivity could never survive in the wild—because captivity had already stripped them of that choice.

Now, she was standing in the aftermath of those lies, caught between what she had been and what she wanted to be.

They saw her as the enemy.

They saw Shephard as the enemy. And maybe he was. Kassidy didn't know how he really felt about any of this, or what his intentions were—he hadn't been fully honest. But neither had she.

That crowd saw both Kassidy and Shephard as the people standing between them and saving the last fragments of their dying world.

They wanted action.

They wanted answers.

And she was starting to realize that neither she, nor Shephard, had either. At least, not any she knew about.

She stared at Shep, waiting, hoping, praying for him to say something—anything—that would make it all make sense.

# Chapter 42

As they pulled up to Shep's grandfather's estate, the garage door groaned shut, sealing them in alongside the black town car that followed them home.

Kassidy fidgeted nervously in her seat, glancing toward the other car. Her fingers brushed against the door handle, her mind racing, then Virginia's voice shattered the heavy silence.

"Your grandfather is Gunter Amon? The man who single-handedly strangled the river with that god-awful dam?" Virginia's voice was so matter-of-fact, it was hard to tell if she was calm or in shock.

Kassidy's stomach churned at the realization of what Shephard commanded with Deville Power.

"You have all the power," Kassidy said, whispering it out loud, as the realization hit her.

"I don't," Shephard sighed, shaking his head slowly in resignation.

"But you're the CEO. You can breach the dam."

"It's not that simple. And I'm not the CEO. Not fully. Not yet. Gunter has to step away first."

"It has to be that simple, Shephard. There's no other way," Kassidy insisted.

Shep's jaw tightened as he glanced between Virginia and Kassidy, his shoulders tense with burden.

"Yes. My grandfather owns Deville Power," he said, firm but with a hint of desperation. "And yes, I will be the CEO. And I'm trying to make things right. I just need more time. There are things I need to put in place."

Kassidy's eyes met his, searching for something to hold on to, but all she saw was a man caught in an undertow with no way out.

If she stood by his side, she'd be in a relationship with the power tycoon who destroyed whole ecosystems and caused the extinction of a species. And did nothing to stop it.

Shephard leaned forward, his voice dropping as if someone might overhear. "Whatever he says, just agree with him, okay? We can sort it out later, please, just trust me."

Virginia snorted from the back. "Agree with him? I'm not some gullible kid. I was right here in the summer of '70, watching your grandfather and his family throw their money at ripping whales from the sea like they were bath toys. And that's not even half of it. He didn't stop with whales—he decimated the salmon, and he's still at it, pretending the blood's not on his hands."

Kassidy felt the air leave her lungs. She turned to Shep, her grandma's words sinking in.

"How long have you worked at Deville Power?" she asked, her voice barely more than a whisper.

Shep's gaze dropped, shame creeping into his expression.

"A long time."

Kassidy slumped back in her seat, her world tilting on its axis.

Virginia's voice broke through sharp as a blade. "That's long enough to be part of every dirty, backwater deal Gunter has made to keep his power empire afloat."

"It's not like that," Shephard said, suddenly defensive. "And I don't defend him." He looked at Kassidy, eyes pleading. "There are things you don't know. Things I can't tell you right now. Not yet." Please, just go along with this. It's the best way. Do you trust me?"

Kassidy's emotions felt tangled in a knot she couldn't undo. She wanted to trust him, to believe he was different from his grandfather, but how could she when he wouldn't even tell her the truth until it was forced out of him?

Virginia leaned forward, her eyes narrowing at Shep. "If you want to make it right, tear down the dam. Everyone knows it's the problem. You do too. I can see the guilt in you. You think you're hiding it, but it leaks out in the pauses, in the way you look away when the truth gets too close. That guilt won't go away until you do the right thing."

Shep's sigh was barely audible, but Kassidy saw the way his hands tightened into fists.

His voice was taut with tension. "I can't just deconstruct hundreds of millions of dollars of concrete overnight. It's not that simple. Like I said, I need time."

"They should have never been built," Virginia snapped. "That man is a tyrant. The devil of the Pacific Northwest. People call him The Chain King, you know."

"Is that what your planning? To deconstruct it?" Kassidy asked. If he was, that would change things. Change her mind about him.

But if he wasn't—if he was just going to keep holding the solution in his hands and refuse to act—then what did that make him? A coward? A bystander? Just another man who let the world burn while pretending his hands were clean?

Shephard ran a nervous hand through his hair. Kassidy felt a distance between them that hadn't been there before, the gap widening with every second of silence that passed.

She had been right there, standing on the edge of something with Shep—something real—but now it all felt like a lie.

She'd admitted what she'd done. Albeit not right away—and maybe not until she had no other choice—but she owned it now. And she was determined to do something about it.

If Shep wasn't going to act, if he was just going to uphold the status quo, she wasn't sure she could stand by him. That's not who she wanted to be. At least, not anymore.

Shephard opened the car door without another word, stepping out as if the conversation had drained him of all energy.

"I'll get you back to your cabin before dark," he said over his shoulder as he stepped out.

Beside him, his grandfather struggled to get out of the black town car, his movements slow and unstable. Shep was there in an instant, catching him by the elbow, steadying him.

But Virginia wouldn't be silenced so easily.

"You murderer," she spat at Gunter, who was hobbling up the stairs into the house on the arm of his long time driver. Gunter turned, his age showing in the sag of his skin and the shrewdness of his eyes. He looked ancient and malicious at the same time, a monster drudged up from the depths of the sea.

Shephard shot Virginia a look, as if begging her to stop. But he didn't know Virginia. She'd stand her ground in a hurricane.

"You killed those whales decades ago, and you're still killing them now. I was there when you started all of this—your pathetic little power company, inherited from your father. You might have built something, but you destroyed so much more. You're nothing but The Chain King they say you are."

Gunter's face twisted into a cruel grin as he turned to Shep, his expression dark with amusement. Then his gaze shifted to Virginia, lingering. At first, his eyes flickered with curiosity, but as the seconds passed, something changed. His smirk faltered, his brow furrowing as recognition slowly crept across his face, like a shadow overtaking the light.

"I remember you," Gunter said, his voice a low growl as he pointed a crooked finger at Virginia. "You're old now, like me," his lip curled with disdain as he spoke. "But I know that face. Saw a picture of you once—after you cut my net and killed those calves. You and that KaWaltish witch in the costume. Cost me a fortune with that stupid stunt." His voice rose with every word, his tone sharp enough to draw blood.

Shephard frowned, confusion clouding his face. Kassidy's breath caught, her hand instinctively clutching her chest.

But Virginia stood firm, her face an unreadable mask.

"You two cunts sabotaged my operations!" Gunter snarled, his lip curling as his gaze bore into Virginia. "I looked for you. To get my money out of you and look at this—all these years later—my prodigal grandson delivers you right to my door. How poetic," he chuckled, a dark, hollow sound. "I'll have my lawyers draw up papers to take everything you own for what you took from me. Every last penny."

"You're insane," Virginia's voice was steady as steel, her laugh sharp and cutting. "Those weren't your whales to take, and you know it."

"I did those stupid creatures a favor. I freed them from the pollution and sludge being pumped into their home."

"Nothing has ever been freed by being enslaved," Virginia seethed. "How much blood do you need on your hands before it's enough?"

Gunter's grin twisted into something more sinister.

"It's not my hands dripping with blood. Now, is it?" He leaned forward, his cane tapping the floor with a deliberate rhythm before jabbing it in Virginia's direction. "Where's that pathetic twat of yours? The one who couldn't even go on with his life after you fled from what you did? What kind of man gets so hung up on a woman he can't even live for himself?"

Gunter barked out a cruel laugh, shaking his head. "Only a dimwit imbecile, that's who. He deserved to rot alone on that island. Damn lucky my family was there to keep him company."

Virginia's shoulders tightened, but she didn't flinch. Kassidy felt the air shift around her as Gunter's words slammed into her like a fist.

"Looks like even Ray's precious efforts were too late." Gunter pounded his cane against the floor with a crack. "Shephard!" he yelled. "Get this woman off my property. Get both of them out of here." He jabbed the cane toward the women like a weapon.

"I don't want to see her—or that fame-thirsty little tart you've been traipsing around with. Just another attention parasite who's never done a real day's work in her life. Sells her skin, struts like she's God's gift to men, and peddles cheap crap made halfway across the world like it means something. There's nothing there—no substance. Just whatever she's selling that day, and I don't want you to be seen with her, Shephard. You hear me?"

He turned his glare at Shephard again, who looked in physical pain. Gunter's voice was cold and cutting.

"I can forgive my grandson for being blinded by your looks—but now that I know what scum runs in your blood, it's over. You're not to be seen with this trash ever again, boy. You hear me!? Or I'll tear up those papers you're about to sign."

His cane struck the floor with a sharp crack, his anger radiating like a lightning storm. "Answer me when I talk to you, son, tell me you won't associate yourself with this trash or so help me I'll undo—"

"I won't, Grandfather," Shep said, eyes down, cold, as distant as they had ever been. "You have my word."

"Good. Now I won't tolerate these kinds of insults under my roof," he snarled. His voice dripped with venom as his eyes bore into Kassidy and Virginia. "Get them out of here!"

Kassidy felt like the air had been sucked out of the world. The poison in his words coursed through her.

"Yes, Grandfather," Shephard said quietly, his voice barely more than a whisper.

She wanted Shephard to defend her, to stand up to his grandfather, but he didn't. He simply nodded. Agreed.

She had been hoping for something—anything—that would make her believe Shephard was different. That he wasn't who the crowd said he was. A puppet. But he wasn't different.

He'd agreed to never seeing her again. It didn't even feel real.

Shephard ushered them out of the hangar-sized garage and down to the dock where the floatplane bobbed gently on the water, the silence broken only by Gunter's voice calling out again. "Shephard! Once you take out the trash get back here and sign these papers you hear me! I won't have those damn protesters walking all over my company! Get back into town and make your announcement and break it up! Someone's going to pay!"

Virginia narrowed her eyes at Gunter, but Kassidy's focus was on Shephard, who just nodded. Agreed with Gunter. To take out the trash. And then get back to business.

He'd done the right thing at the protests. He'd been kind. He'd explained the situation, and tried to bridge the gap between both sides.

But now? Now he just stood there, complicit in the mess, and in the greed and hatred his grandfather perpetuated.

Kassidy had seen the way his whole body tensed. The way he ground his teeth, silent as Gunter's words lashed at her like a whip.

She saw the flicker of pain in Shephard's eyes before he masked it, before he lowered his gaze and said, I won't, Grandfather.

Those three words were an agreement to never see her again.

A vow to stand with Gunter and everything he stood for.

Kassidy wanted to believe he was different, that he wasn't the man the crowd accused him of being. A puppet. A coward. A man who stood on the wrong side of history.

But in this moment, how was he any different?

He couldn't even stand up for her. Or Virginia.

Let alone himself.

Getting Virginia to leave was like trying to pull an old anchor from the ocean floor—stubborn, rusted in place, refusing to budge. Kassidy had to drag her away, her sharp muttering and pointed glares doing nothing to shake Shep from his silence.

Inside the plane, the quiet was unbearable. Virginia mumbled and ranted but kept her volume to herself—at least at first.

Kassidy sat with her hands clenched in her lap, her thoughts a whirlwind of anger and hurt. She wanted to reach for Shephard, to talk, to feel his comfort and closeness, but after what he said…

And her grandmother wouldn't. Shut. Up.

"He's a bad man," Virginia ranted, staring out at the massive estate and trophy room you could see from the moon. "Only cares about himself. And I'd bet my life he doesn't give a damn about you, Shephard. Even if you are his grandson. I don't know why you agreed to what he said, but I don't even blame you for not standing up to him. The man is cruel and not afraid to destroy everything in his path. Even his own family."

"Grandma, please." Kassidy's voice was shaky, pleading.

"I will not remain quiet!" Virginia's voice was fierce, her eyes blazing. "The man's a liar. A dirty politician and the worst kind of narcissist. I've followed his destruction for fifty years."

Shephard didn't say a word, his silence cutting deeper than any argument. Kassidy couldn't bear to look at him, her heart breaking with every second that passed.

As soon as the plane touched down at Shep's dock, Kassidy threw the door open and leapt out, her breath coming in sharp, ragged gasps. She didn't want to hear excuses. She didn't want to see the look in his eyes and not know if she could trust him.

"Kassidy!" Shep's voice was desperate as he ran after her. "Please, wait. We need to talk."

But Kassidy didn't stop. She couldn't stop. She needed to get as far away as possible.

Virginia's voice called out from behind them, light but distant. "Don't worry about me! I'll walk around the shore. I know the way!"

Kassidy stopped, turning to face Shep. Her eyes were cold now, hard as stone. "Where's your yacht?"

Shep's face fell. "Being stored."

"Being stored where? Why?"

But all he had for her was silence.

Kassidy's heart pounded in her chest as she stared at him, the pieces of the puzzle slowly coming together.

"Did you have anything to do with the shooting of that orca?"

The guilt in his eyes was louder than any words.

"It's not what you think," Shephard said, his voice desperate. "I would never—" He looked at her, eyes pleading for understanding.

"How could you agree to never seeing me again? Why didn't you stick up for us? For yourself?"

He reached for her, but she pulled away. Shephard's eyes were filled with confusion and pain. "I can't tell you. If you could just…I need some time Kassidy."

"No. Our magical two weeks of hiding things from each other is over. You know my secret. Now, what are you hiding?" She didn't blink. "I'm done pretending. I've been quiet, careful, afraid—and it got me nowhere. I'm ready to face it all now, whatever comes. But I won't stand next to someone who's still hiding in the dark, hoping no one sees." Kassidy's voice trembled, her anger bubbling to the surface. "Why do you put up with him? If he's as bad as my grandma says, why do you stay by his side like his loyal pet?"

Shep's eyes darkened, his frustration boiling over. "It's complicated. There are things you don't understand. Things that have been going on for decades. Sacrifices made. I can't just walk away."

Kassidy shook her head, the tears finally spilling over. "You're right. I don't understand. I don't understand how you could be so—so complicit. I don't understand how you could stay silent. How you could have as much power as you do and do nothing with it and just agree with him. And I don't understand how you could ask me to trust you when you didn't stand up for yourself."

"You kept secrets from me too," Shephard said. "And I let you reveal them on your time. All I'm asking for is the same. I have every intention of telling you everything you want to know. Like I said, I just need a little more time—please."

She had to leave. Now. She didn't know if she could trust him and all signs pointed to that she couldn't. Kassidy didn't want to stay and let herself fall even harder for something that could never work. Fall for someone who wasn't what he seemed to be.

Shephard took a step toward her, his hand reaching out again, but Kassidy stepped back, her heart breaking.

"I've spent my whole life letting people take advantage of me," Kassidy said, her voice shaking. "I've built a business that should have made me happy, but it didn't because I did what I thought other people would be proud of. I've let people walk all over me. And I'm so stupid for it. But now, I'm done with it. And I can't be associated with you, or your grandfather after what I know he's done. And how he continues to ruin lives."

"Kassidy, please," Shephard whispered, his voice broken. "You don't understand. I'm trying to make things right."

"By taking down the dam?" Kassidy said, her voice cold. "By doing the right thing? By not bowing down to that monster? Even if he is your family. He's a tyrant."

"If you are who I thought you were—if you're one of the good ones—then say it. Show me. Let me see the part of you you've been hiding. Let me in. But if you're not… if you're just another man protecting himself at any cost, then keep your secrets. And your distance. Just don't ask me to stay in the dark with you."

He didn't move. Only whispered, "I can't tell you."

She gasped. And something inside her tore open.

"Then I guess we're done."

Then Kassidy turned her back on the man who had once held her heart in his hands.

Waves crashed violently against the shore as she made her way toward the cabin, the salty breeze stinging her eyes.

Kassidy felt the hollow ache in her chest grow deeper the further she got away from Shephard, but she couldn't stay there any longer. That man wasn't who she thought he was.

She had to stand up for what she believed in, even if it meant walking away from the one person she thought she could love forever.

# Chapter 43

Kassidy felt her heart cleave in two. One part clung to Shep's goodness, to the sense that he was different. The other half warned her to guard what was left of herself—that the battle ahead would take everything, and standing next to Shephard when it happened would only reinforce every judgment the public had already passed on her.

The wind whipped through her hair and waves crashed against the shore. A sudden salty spray forced her to close her eyes, as water clung to her lashes and settled cold on her cheeks. When she opened them, the sea stared back, a cold, uninhabitable wilderness.

This wasn't her home.

She couldn't live on that island any more than she could live under the sea. She hadn't grown up there, hadn't known it's tides. She wasn't connected to those whales or the fight to save them. There were people who cared more, who'd been fighting their whole lives. Whatever connection she felt was shallow with roots that could be torn free in a single tug.

Who was she to think she could make a difference?

Or that anyone wanted her to try?

She saw the hard lines of hate on their faces, and the scorn in their eyes. The people that belonged there despised her as much as they despised Shephard, who'd lived there his whole life.

There was a time when she hadn't felt so helpless, when she had a say over the direction of her life—and sometimes, even influenced the lives of others. How foolish she'd been to think she could accomplish something with a higher purpose than serving herself. Any chance of that had slipped away before it started.

After what she'd done, it felt as if her voice had been swallowed.

Maybe it should be. Maybe she deserved to be silenced if she couldn't add something meaningful to people's lives instead of just creating more noise.

Everything she wanted to change in her life, now felt out of reach.

There was no good reason to stay a minute longer. Kassidy yanked open the screen door and stormed into the cabin.

"Grandma! Let's go! We're leaving." She dropped her bag on the floor and stuffed it with the few things she'd brought.

Kass paused, her attention caught on the stacks of papers and the faded photos—a lifetime devoted to the orcas. She tried to ignore the tug she felt, the connection that linked her to the man who had brought her here.

But this wasn't her life. It was his, layered in ink, carved in wood, stacked with memories that weren't hers. She was a visitor in a strange place, nothing more.

"Grandma!" she called, louder this time. "Chop-chop. We're leaving in five minutes!"

Virginia emerged from the bedroom, her finger trailing along the carved map on the wall, her eyes softened by a smile that held decades of memory. She looked out the window at the narrow channel between the islands.

"I'm not leaving, dear. I just got here," her voice was steady enough to calm a churning sea. "I've spent a lifetime dreaming about this island, this cabin—wondering if what happened here was even real. Sometimes the memories blurred into a dream, other times twisted into a nightmare. So I buried them in order to have a good life—with Stanley—and to raise you in a happy home.

"Now I'm feeling things I haven't allowed myself to feel in half a lifetime. Ghosts I've never laid to rest surround me. I need to stay and hear what they have to say.

"You go do what you need to do. I'll be fine. Strangely, I feel less alone on this tiny rock than I do back home."

"But Grandma…you love the farm, and it's yours now. It's paid off. There is nothing there to worry—."

"The farm was Stanley's dream. It's time for me to chase my own now," Virginia cut in. She gave a small, wistful laugh.

"I'm an old widow. And that means I can do silly, impractical things and no one can tell me I can't. So, I'm staying here—where a part of my heart has been all along.

"There is nothing I need to go home for. Not even the farm. You can sell it and everything in it for all I care. My time at that place has come to an end. Everything I need is right in front of me, and in my memory. As odd as it may seem, standing here, in this cabin, I feel whole in a way I haven't in years."

Kassidy wrapped her arms around her grandma, pulling her close enough to nearly topple them both. She pressed her face into Virginia's shoulder and whispered, "I love you, Grandma."

"I love you too, sweetheart. And I'll be right here when you come back. Go do what you need to do. Go make things right. There's always a way. And that Shephard—I know what I said about his grandfather and it's the truth, but that doesn't mean he's a rotten egg too. I was quick to judge, but I think there is something more at play there. But you'll have to determine that for yourself."

Kassidy swallowed hard, knowing that even if the storm passed, things would be different, but there was too much she didn't know about him, and about herself. How could she trust him—when she barely knew who she was anymore?

Finding a love like the one she thought she felt with Shephard wasn't meant for people like her. People who had spent their lives running from their true selves. And yet, she wanted so desperately to believe anything could be possible.

Kassidy turned to leave, her hand resting on the door, when Virginia touched her arm.

"I ran from this place once, too. I thought leaving would be easier than facing everything that happened. What that left me was a lifetime of unanswered questions and a heart that never quite healed.

"I don't regret my life with Stanley. But I never got a second chance at a life with Ray. Sometimes, you don't get a second chance. Just remember that. Maybe Shephard is not the obstacle you think he is—maybe he's the path forward."

Kassidy's throat tightened as her grandmother's words sank in.

She gave a faint nod, pushed open the door, and stepped into the biting wind.

On top of the rocky outcropping, Kassidy held up her phone and waited for a signal strong enough to call for a taxi. Waves crashed against the shore sending up plumes of salty spray. In a lull she heard the crunch of gravel—footsteps.

She didn't have to turn around to know who it was.

"Kassidy."

She closed her eyes, tears spilling over her lashes. Behind her, Shephard's words tumbled out.

"I can't tell you what you want to know," he said, his voice low, careful. "Because they're not only my secrets to tell. But if you could trust me—just trust me—when I say I'm not trying to deceive you…"
He exhaled sharply. "I'm trying to do the right thing. For everyone. And keep the promises I've made. Even if, on the surface, it looks like the opposite."

He reached out, his hand settling gently on her shoulder.

"Please, don't leave," he whispered, his voice hoarse. "Whatever this is between us—it's real. You see me, Kassidy. The real me. Even if you don't know everything about me yet."

She turned to face him.

"From the moment I saw you on the ferry, and then when you showed up here, I knew something bigger than us was at work. I just knew something was pulling us together. This place has a way of tearing people apart, but you and me—we keep finding each other here. Please stay. Please?"

Kassidy bit her lip, struggling to hold back the sob climbing its way up her throat. "What you said—what you promised. About never seeing me again. Why would you say that?" She shook her head. "Even if it wasn't true, what reason could you have? How can I stay here with you after what you said—and not knowing what's really going on?"

"Kass, I know I let you down back there. I won't make excuses for that. But I need you to believe that what I did wasn't out of cowardice. There are things I can't explain yet, but that doesn't change how I feel about you. What we show on the surface doesn't always reflect who we are underneath. You can feel my heart—I know you can. Just like I can feel yours."

Shep's words filled the space between them but didn't quell her unease. Kassidy swallowed the lump in her throat, turning her gaze away from him, her heart twisting painfully. She took one last look at the endless horizon beyond the waves, blinking back the last of her tears. She pulled out her phone.

"I need a water taxi to Friday Harbor, please. Yes. Now." Her voice was calm and steady. Her mind made up.

When she glanced back at Shephard he was walking away.

Half of her broken heart wanted to chase after him.

The other half told her she should walk away, too.

The water taxi dropped her off in Friday Harbor, but the ferry to the mainland wouldn't arrive for another two hours. Kassidy decided to take a cab to the lighthouse, where she'd wait.

She walked toward the relic that remained—still strong and standing firm against the wind and waves. A witness to the lives lived and lost in the surrounding sea.

Kassidy sat perched on the boulders and took out her phone, eyes flicking between the comments flooding in. The teaser video posted by Capri Son was everywhere—a perfectly curated clip of her diving elegantly under the shimmering dome with Keelah beside her. Capri Son's marketing slogan said: "Magic is coming to Capri Son this summer! Are you ready to dive in?"

The video had been live for less than a few hours, but the engagement was off the charts. She should've been thrilled. This was exactly the kind of buzz Capri Son had paid for. But her stomach churned as she skimmed the comments—on news articles, in reposts, in threads she hadn't even been tagged in. Even with her own comment section locked down, the conversation had spread like wildfire.

"Kassidy, I used to love you, but this is so disappointing."

"Mermaids are fake. Exploiting animals is real!"

"Do better. This is not magic. It's cruel."

"Animal abuse at its finest."

"This isn't 1995, Kassidy. Orcas in tanks are not okay. Educate yourself. #Canceled."

"Kassidy Karlson = part of the problem!"

"Is this what you stand for now?"

#FreeTheWhales #KassidyKarlsonExposed #ProfitOverCompassion #StopAnimalExploitation #NotYourPhotoOp #BoycottKassidy

Her phone buzzed with a notification. A name she recognized instantly flashed across her screen: Taylor Sinclair. Kassidy's heart dropped into her stomach.

"No, no, no," she whispered as the video appeared.

Taylor was a powerhouse, her eco-focused vlog, *Call It Out* regularly hitting the top charts. She had a knack for dismantling brands—and people—who didn't align with her views.

Kassidy's thumb hovered over the screen as the video auto played. Taylor Sinclair appeared, her sharp features lit dramatically in her podcast studio.

Her voice was surgical, deadly as she spoke to her audience.

"Let's talk about Kassidy Karlson," Taylor began, leaning in. "Yes, *that* Kassidy Karlson. The one who tells you how to use boob tape to create perfect cleavage. Or how to contour your face to perfection and which yoga leggings will give you a dreamy booty. Looks like she's had a moral overhaul and is turning her sights from body shaming to animal exploitation. She's now the face of Capri Son's so-called 'Mermaid Metamorphosis'—but what's she really selling here? Let's, Call It Out."

The screen cut to Capri Son's video, her graceful dive juxtaposed with the ominous sound of whale cries echoing faintly in the background. Taylor's voiceover continued.

"What the video conveniently doesn't mention is the five-ton, fifty-seven-year-old orca trapped inside that exhibit. Her name is Keelah. She's spent her entire life in captivity, stolen from her family in the wild decades ago. And now she's being paraded around as some kind of sideshow attraction—again, and they're all discussing it as "rescuing her." But don't worry, because Kassidy looks stunning while Keelah swims in agonizing circles in a concrete tank while no one is talking about the massive efforts underway to retire the whale to her home waters off the coast of Washington State."

Kassidy felt a wave of nausea roll through her, her stomach churning as the tightness in her chest grew unbearable. Tightness from her heart breaking, but also because all the air had been squeezed from her lungs, crushed beneath the mountain of problems on her shoulders.

The video cut back to Taylor Sinclair, her piercing blue eyes locked on the camera.

"Kassidy Karlson, you built your empire selling women a dream—that with enough money, they could be as beautiful, as desirable, and as extraordinary as you. And now, the message hasn't changed. For a fee, you, too, can swim with a natural wonder of the sea, and become part of the machine keeping her in captivity.

"Kassidy Karlson, how can you stand by while a company profits from the suffering of this magnificent creature? Is this really what you believe in? What you want to represent?

"So, before you, out there in *Call It Out* land, get swept up by a beautiful photo you can buy into, ask yourself this: What is the real cost of your six minutes under the water?"

The video ended, but the damage had already begun. Kassidy refreshed her feed. Taylor's video was spreading everywhere, reposted by eco-influencers, activists, and even a few celebrities.

New hashtags like #FreeKeelah and #MermaidHypocrite trended within minutes.

Her phone buzzed again—a text from Billy.

Damage control ASAP. Call me.

Her RippleHub profile stared back at her, mocking her with its now-familiar bio: "Empowering women to live boldly." The follower count below it ticked downward like a broken stock market ticker.

19.4M Followers.

She refreshed the page.

12.2M Followers.

Her stomach tightened. She refreshed again. Another hundred thousand gone. A new comment. One that hit harder than the others.

"What a fake. I can't believe I ever looked up to you."

Her phone vibrated violently—Billy's name flashed on the screen. Reluctantly, she answered it.

Kassidy pressed her phone to her ear.

"Billy. This is so much worse than I imagined," she said, her voice strained, teetering between panic and denial.

"No. It's just trolls. They'll move on in a week, they always do. However, we have lost a few brand sponsors. But we anticipated this."

"Which brands?"

His voice softened, but only slightly. "BreezyGlow pulled the makeup collab. BlissFit wants to pause the leggings campaign. And Vata—"

"Vata?"

"They're claiming you've violated their ethical partnership clause."

"What ethical partnership clause?" Kassidy clutched her chest.

"The one you signed. It was in the paperwork."

"Billy, you said Capri Son was airtight. You said this gig would be huge for my career."

"I was right, wasn't I? All celebs have major setbacks that ultimately propel them forward. This is no different. I'm with Jonah now, we have a plan. Don't worry about anything! I promise, this will blow over and we'll be better for it. Wait—hold on. Something's weird with your RippleHub login. I was going to tweak your bio, but I can't get in."

Kassidy's pulse spiked. He hadn't realized yet.

Billy kept talking, unfazed. "Must be all the hits on your sites. We'll figure it out later."

"No. I need to fix this," she said, her voice firm, without a speck of hesitation.

"Kass? Wait. Stop. Don't do anything until I call you back with the details of our plan. You don't want to ruin this. We need to play our cards right here and ride this out, otherwise no more makeup deals, no more brand trips to Ibiza, no more six-figure paychecks. You'll go from Kassidy Karlson, global icon, to a cautionary tale in a TED Talk. Don't do anything stupid Kass—"

"I already did the most reckless thing I could have ever done. I let someone else take control of my career—of me—because I was too blind, too caught up to see what truly mattered. You're fired, Billy. I love you, but you're fired."

Her hand trembled as she ended the call, the screen fading to black. For the first time in years, Kassidy felt completely untethered, the polished facade of her carefully constructed world slipping away. It was terrifying and surprisingly liberating all at once.

She could start over if she had to, but more importantly, she had to find a way to undo what she had done.

Kassidy scrolled through her list of contacts and dialed the number she had for Ted Moore.

"Hello? This is Kassidy Karlson," she said into the phone. "Yes, we met…yes, that's me, and yes, it's why I'm calling. I need your help." She held her breath listening to Mr. Moore, finally sighing in relief. "Thank you. I'll be right there."

The drive to the lawyer's office unraveled in a blur—too many thoughts chasing too little time.

Now Kassidy sat uncomfortably stiff in the chair across from Ted Moore, gripping the edge of the table as if it might anchor her to the earth.

"Ms. Karlson," Mr. Moore began, flipping through a folder of documents. "I reviewed what you sent me. Your contract with Capri Son, the penalties for breach. They include repayment of your advance plus damages for reputational harm."

"How much?" Kassidy asked.

Mr. Moore pushed a piece of paper toward her. Her eyes scanned the total at the bottom: 3.5 million dollars.

She felt the air leave her lungs.

"That's...more than I have. A lot more."

"My suggestion is to start liquidating assets."

Kassidy sat across from Ted Moore, her hands clasped tightly in her lap as they discussed the steps needed to sell the farm she'd just paid off—but every word was a nail driving deeper into her uncertainty.

Was she honoring Virginia's wishes? Or was she dismantling something sacred to the only father and grandfather she'd ever known? Was the farm really the burden Virginia claimed it to be, or had those words been spoken in a moment of frustration?

Kassidy's mind raced with doubt, terror flickering in her eyes as she tried to convince herself this was the right thing to do.

This plan—risky and uncertain—was the only one she could see that might save them all.

# Chapter 44

Just as she stepped onto the sidewalk outside Mr. Moore's office, Kassidy froze, her heartbeat quickening as SaLita Seawalker slid out of a car in front of her—eyes locked on Kassidy.

Kassidy took a deep breath and tried to stand with her shoulders back and hold onto what little dignity she had.

"If you're here to tell me what a horrible person I am, save your breath. I already know." She held up her phone. "The world has already weighed in, and I only have myself to blame."

Kassidy faced the older woman, whose deep lines and piercing gaze seemed as timeless as the islands.

SaLita's voice carried on the gusty wind. "I'm not here for that. My name is SaLita, I knew your Grandmother Virginia, and your grandfather, Raymond."

"I'm aware. Grandma told me everything."

"We were unlikely friends once. Your grandma and me. We shared an adventure that was both wondrous and terrible."

"She told me about that too."

SaLita's gaze grew sharper. "Your grandmother risked her life even though neither of us knew what would come of it. I believe that spirit lives on in you."

Kassidy straightened, nerves jangling. "What do you want from me, Mrs. Seawalker?"

SaLita's eyes narrowed, glinting like the dark waters churning behind them. When she spoke, there was a hint of urgency in her voice. She glanced back toward her car.

"I'd like you to meet my granddaughter."

Kassidy's shoulders tensed. "We've met. She's not a fan."

"No, she's not."

Kassidy sighed, guilt gnawing at her. "I didn't know they had Keelah. It was supposed to be a promo for a new exhibit. I should have read the whole contract before I signed up for it. I know what I did was horrible. I'm trying to make it right." Kassidy glanced back at Mr. Moore's office.

SaLita nodded, her gaze unyielding. "Yet here we are. And what happened cannot be changed. But because of it, now you have an opportunity. Something that wasn't possible before." SaLita held Kassidy's gaze.

"What opportunity?"

The woman's voice was low and steady. "There are currents in life just as there are in the sea, pulling us this way and that, for reasons we don't understand until we arrive where we're supposed to be. Your grandfather brought you here for a reason. Don't you see? You're not here by coincidence. And you've been given a great opportunity. For redemption. Maybe even freedom. These islands are asking something of you, and I think it would be wise to listen. They've been waiting for you. As have I."

"I don't understand."

SaLita motioned toward the car where WeNala was waiting in the driver seat. "Will you come with us? There is something we'd like to show you."

Kassidy felt the pull of a great and vast force—something she couldn't walk away from, no matter how much she wanted to leave it all behind. Yet she had no idea how she could help them or even undo the damage she'd done.

WeNala drove, hands steady on the wheel as Kassidy sat silently in the back seat of the SUV beside SaLita. The rhythm of the road felt hypnotic as she stared out the window at Fidalgo Island. The seascape unfurled in shades of green and misty blue, both rugged and serene. The coastline disappeared then reappeared like a daydream, glimpses of gray water dotted with tiny islands wrapped in fog.

As they approached the Deception Pass Bridge, rocky cliffs jutted out toward the sea, and the sky above felt endless and intimate. Kassidy remembered the expansive bridge that stretched between two islands from when Shephard flew them over.

But now, crossing it felt different, like she was entering its world rather than just looking down at it.

Deep water churned beneath the bridge, currents twisting in every direction, a reflection of her own tangled thoughts—the revelations that had led her here, the unexpected bonds forged with people, creatures, and a place she never expected to feel connected to.

SaLita's voice finally broke the silence. "That is Penn Cove," she said, calm and knowing.

The tranquil stretch of water was framed by forested hills and dotted with bobbing boats. Kassidy imagined what it must have been like with one hundred orcas in the water, their sleek black and white forms moving as one organism.

The women didn't speak about the captures, or what that night cost the families above and below the sea. The sight and stillness of the water seemed to speak for itself—as if it was forever marked by the history it carried, and haunted by lives lost and futures that were stolen.

After another ten minutes along the winding roads that snaked beside the sea, WeNala finally turned onto an unmarked dirt path. It led them down to a small inlet nestled between steep, pine-covered hills.

"This," SaLita said, her eyes reflecting the gentle shimmer of the water, "is Seagrass Bay."

She opened the door and stepped out, Kassidy following as the brisk air filled her lungs. Before them stretched a serene, crescent-shaped bay—darker and deeper than the others, ringed by tall pines and rugged, rocky shores.

"When Qilalugaq comes home, this is where she will live out her days," SaLita said, her gazed fixed on the water. "She can never be returned to the wild. It is too dangerous for her now. Qilalugaq is too habituated to humans, and she's never learned how to navigate boat traffic, avoid toxic algae blooms, or find food without it being handed to her in a bucket.

"Had she grown up with her family, she would've been taught these things. But that was taken from her. The ocean isn't safe for her now. This bay is all she has left. Here, she will live in a sea pen where she will feel the tides move through her body, chase the giant silver salmon, and hear her family's calls.

"The cove is deep. She'll be able to dive and forage, rub against the bull kelp and swim fast if she chooses to. Here, she will have as much freedom as humanity can offer her.

"For all that she has lost, this is what we must do for her. Give her a place to live out her days in peace. And die with what dignity she has left."

A jolt of pain struck Kassidy in the heart, a tangle of guilt, remorse, and a flicker of impossible hope. She could see it—Keelah gliding through the bay, moonlight caressing her at night, sunlight warming her sleek black skin by day.

"I can almost see her there—like this place was made for her," Kassidy said, her cheekbones catching the silver light off the water as she stared out. "How come no one knows about this? How come she isn't here already?"

WeNala stepped forward and let out a soft, bitter laugh—a sound that carried more anger than Kassidy expected.

SaLita held up a hand, silencing her granddaughter. "People do know," she said, "but not enough of them, and not the right kind of people. Ca PRISON," she emphasized the words, "won't give up their billion-dollar slave without a fight. We need more voices that care about the plight of this orca. About all the orcas. We need more people to use their voices and their buying power to fight for them." She turned to Kassidy and smiled, a whole universe of plans behind her eyes. "That's where you come in, Kassidy Karlson."

Kassidy felt her chest tighten. "I don't know what I can do to help...after what I've done to harm her. But I'm willing to try. What can I do, SaLita? Why did you bring me here?"

A wide grin spread across SaLita's face as if she'd been waiting for this moment all along.

"Qilalugaq's mother, Ocean Sun, is still alive, still swimming somewhere out there. Once we bring Qilalugaq home, she will come home to reunite with her daughter. When she does, there is nothing for her to eat—"

"Yet," WeNala finished the sentence.

"There is something else you need to see," SaLita said. "So that you understand what we are fighting for. This is not a fight to save one whale. It's a fight to save them all."

SaLita reached into her pocket and pulled out her phone. As she dialed the number her eyes twinkled with amusement.

"Hello," SaLita said. "I have someone with me who needs to see the Elwha. Can you take us up? Yes. We're at Seagrass now. Three of us." SaLita's face lit up with a satisfied smile. "Wonderful. Thank you." She nodded, then hung up, her gaze resting on Kassidy.

The women stood on the dock, talking and shivering until the distant hum of a plane cut off their conversation. Kassidy looked up and saw a pale-yellow float plane coming over the tops of the trees.

"Shephard?"

WeNala's voice drifted over Kassidy's shoulder, playful.

"Nothing is what it seems around here now, is it?" Kassidy glanced over her shoulder at the wise young woman then back to the unmistakable yellow plane.

It seemed that secrets were woven into the landscape. And even if she walked away, she was tethered to those secrets. As unsettling as it felt, she also sensed the importance of the secrecy, too. As if keeping things hidden in plain sight was the last fragile shield protecting the very thing it concealed.

"I thought you hated him," she said, turning to the women.

"We *did* hate him." WeNala's lips curved into a sly smile. "Until he gave us a reason not to."

"We never hated him," SaLita reprimanded, casting a glance at her granddaughter. "Well…maybe you did, a little…but that was a long time ago. You can't judge a fish who learned to swim in another stream." SaLita paused, her gaze fixed on the sky. "His grandfather is a wicked man—one who should be cast into the *Maqluna-Karrak*, the dark mouth, where only the worst souls are swallowed. A fate worse than death. But Shephard is nothing like his grandfather. He is a warrior for the land, and the orcas. He is like us."

"He's a different breed alright, a real *Nalukai,*" WeNala said in the way a sister might tease her little brother.

"He's the right kind of different," SaLita continued, a finality in her voice. "A man with integrity. And patience." Kassidy shook her head, feeling torn between hope and doubt. SaLita must have sensed her skepticism. "Maybe you don't see it…yet, but you will. I have seen both of you in the waves."

A gentle rumble filled the air, and the women looked up as Shephard's plane cut through the clouds.

"There is no use trying to deny it," SaLita murmured, eyes closed, chin high. Kassidy waited for her to elaborate. "The pull of this place. The threads connecting all of us." She opened her eyes and looked at Kassidy. "You will regret running from here, and from him. This is where you are meant to be. Raymond knew that too. That's why he called you here."

As the plane descended, it left a wake in the water below. Kassidy's emotions swung from shock to excitement. She didn't know what awaited her or if Shephard would bring more questions than answers, but one thing was certain, she couldn't turn away. She wanted to be part of whatever they were doing. And deep down, she knew SaLita was right—about everything.

SaLita and WeNala watched the plane land, their eyes filled with the wisdom of countless years spent defending their home and all the creatures that lived there. They were admirable and beautiful and everything a human should be. They lived with purpose and courage and Kassidy felt inspired to do the same.

She didn't know how, but she vowed to redeem herself, repair her mistakes, and be as courageous as the women that surrounded her. If they believed in her to do something good. Then she was going to believe it was true.

Shephard brought the plane to a smooth stop at the end of the dock, his gaze meeting hers instantly. He looked as surprised to see her as she was to see him. Then surprise quickly faded into a warm and welcoming smile.

Whatever lay ahead, she'd find a way through this tangled knot of history, love, and duty—with her new allies by her side and a man who felt like both a challenge and a promise of something uncharted.

# Chapter 45

A flood of emotions swirled inside her—surprise, relief, and an unexpected sense of clarity. In Shephard's presence, surrounded by the quiet reassurance of SaLita and WeNala, Kassidy felt the walls she'd kept around her trust begin to fall away.

Whatever Shephard was hiding, why he was acting that way in front of his grandfather, what he'd said…She hoped he must have had a good reason. Perhaps she didn't need to know every part of him to trust him completely, but she needed some answers. Kassidy had a feeling she was about to understand more of him than she ever had.

SaLita opened the passenger door to the floatplane with practiced ease, as if she'd done it a thousand times. WeNala stepped forward, ducking as she slid into the back, her palm finding Shephard's shoulder. A low chuckle passed between them; a shared laughter filled with a silent history like two friends exchanging an inside joke.

Kassidy watched as these women, who once seemed wary and distrustful of Shephard, now treating him as one of their own. When SaLita leaned in and kissed his cheek with the same warmth her grandma showed her, more of Kassidy's doubts melted away, giving way to something new.

Shephard was bonded to these women in a way that ran deep.

Once the Seawalkers were settled in back, Shephard turned to Kassidy, extending his arm with a charming smile, the kind that made her feel as though she'd been let in on a secret. And she had.

She wondered how many more secrets were still waiting—what was real, what was fake, and who was aligned with whom anymore. The ground beneath her felt as fragile as the air between them. So she did the only thing she could: she moved forward, choosing blind trust in a man she was falling for despite the risks.

She slipped her fingers into his warm, firm grip, and as he helped her into the seat beside him, her heartbeat faster—half in fear, half in hope.

Kassidy wrapped both arms around him, her senses filling with his scent—like the forest after a storm. In his embrace, all her defenses faded.

She could feel his heartbeat against her own, constant and true, and whatever questions she had about what he might be hiding dissolved, replaced by the certainty that, whatever it was, he kept it close to protect, not deceive.

Shephard chuckled softly, his eyes meeting hers with a gaze that held a thousand unspoken words, then he looked over his shoulder at SaLita.

"You should have told me you were bringing my favorite person on the planet," he said to SaLita, though his smile turned toward Kassidy.

SaLita's laughter rang out, brimming with life. "If I had, would you have hurried up and gotten here sooner? We almost froze to death out there."

Shephard laughed. "Fifteen minutes from door to door *is* sooner. Probably a record," he grinned, hand resting on Kassidy's knee. "But if I'd have known she was with you, I'd have been here in six."

Kassidy observed their easy interactions and WeNala's sly smile. They were all in cahoots. That much was clear. Bound by a connection she was only beginning to see. A connection that felt authentic and as real as any could be.

Kassidy's voice held a note of curiosity through the headset. "Would anyone care to tell me what is going on? And who is Elwha?"

Shephard's eyes sparkled, but he only smiled wide.

"We *can't* tell you who she is," WeNala said, an excited gleam in her eyes. "But we can show you."

With a firm grip, Shephard eased the throttle forward, and the plane skimmed across the bay before lifting off. They soared over the deep cove leaving behind Whidby Island and the glistening expanse of the Salish Sea. He banked hard over the coastline, the rugged edge giving way to an endless stretch of green forest as the ocean faded behind them.

Each mile was filled with a quiet rhythm, knowing glances and the gentle brush of Shephard's fingers against Kassidy's hand. Half an hour passed this way, as a silent language built between them, until Shephard nodded toward the river below.

"That's the Elwha," he said, voice filled with reverence.

WeNala leaned forward, her hand tracing the path of the river. "For over a century, two dams blocked this river," she began, her voice resonating with pride and sorrow. "They choked the flow of salmon and disrupted the natural cycles that sustained our people."

Kassidy's gaze shifted to the winding river below, carving its way through the forest—wild and unbroken, its banks alive and vibrant with new life.

Kassidy recalled the suffocated river Shephard showed her, the Swift. Where stagnant water covered in algae was locked behind the masses of concrete. Compared to this place, his grandfather's dam looked like it was suffocating every breath of life around it.

"My grandma has been fighting for forty years to convince the government to remove those dams. A decade ago, they came down. Now, for the first time in generations, the salmon have returned."

Kassidy stared, captivated by the sight of the river alive with motion, its banks lush with renewal.

The plane glided lower, giving her a glimpse of the ancient forests reclaiming the edges. WeNala pointed to a thicket of green where tall pines stood proud among budding alders.

"Look there—sediments, and seeds buried beneath the dams have risen up and given life to a new forest," WeNala said, reverence in her tone. "The trout have come back, and the brown pelicans, too. The Elwha's recovery is bringing life to the entire forest and river ecosystem."

The scene unfolding below was a living canvas—silver flashes of fish leaping in the currents of the Elwha, their scales catching the light like scattered stars. Pelicans glided above the water's surface, dipping into the river with powerful, sweeping dives, while eagles circled high above. Along the banks, otters scampered and played, a reminder of the life that pulsed through every ripple and shadow.

It was as if the river itself was breathing.

Kassidy felt a swell of emotions—hope and awe.

She turned to Shephard, knowing why they were there. "I thought you said you could never take the dam on the Swift down?"

"I said what I needed to say in front of the company. I wanted to tell you the truth, but there was too much at stake to share the truth with you." Shephard's hand tightened on hers, their eyes meeting with a fierce intensity. Then he looked down at the river, and his voice carried the immensity of their struggle.

"Without Chinook, the orcas will die," WeNala cut in. "Their bloodline will be lost, their language, everything they know and what make them who they are will die too."

"Can't they find another source of food? Seals or other fish?"

"Qilalugaq's family doesn't eat seals or other mammals—it's their code," WeNala said. "Orcas aren't all the same. Each pod is unique in how they speak, what they eat, the knowledge they share, and where they roam. They never mix families, and they never eat food their pod isn't trained to hunt and eat.

"They might be able to adapt with enough time, but with so few individuals left, that's unlikely. Change is happening too fast for them to keep up. It could take decades for them to find another family, learn a new language, integrate into a new culture." She paused, her gaze holding Kassidy's. "This is their home. We have destroyed their only food source with the dams. We must fix it. We must help them, before there are none left to help."

The truth landed like a hard blow to her heart——the rivers, the sea, the salmon, and orca connected as one. Taking out the dam, restoring the river wasn't just about preserving a place.

It was about bringing back a world that had nearly been lost.

And the truth was, they might still lose it—even if they fought like hell, even if they did everything right.

Kassidy turned to Shephard, whose expression was unwavering. He met her eyes as he spoke. "I signed the final papers this afternoon. There are still a few steps I need to take. But we're almost there. We have a plan. So, Kassidy... do you still want to know my secrets?" He held her gaze. "Because the real question isn't if I can trust you to hear them. It's if I can trust you to keep them."

Kassidy gave a silent, steady nod.

For Keelah.

For the orcas still out there.

For SaLita—for everything this land had lost and survived.

She would fight with them for what was right.

This was where Shephard's true allegiance lived—where his heart had always been. Even after all the fear, all the reasons she'd given herself to walk away, the truth was carved into her now.

He was one of the good ones. The rare kind.

The kind you don't get twice.

He was her *Maq*.

The plane veered back toward the sea, tracing the river's winding path. Below, the Elwha shimmered in the light, a testament to what could be, yet Kassidy felt the anxiety for what lay ahead—her role in this fight was unclear, but the reason for the fight was irrefutable and she knew she had to help.

They touched down in Seagrass Bay, the floatplane gliding to a smooth halt at the dock. SaLita and WeNala stepped out, exchanging a look of solidarity with Shephard.

Before they parted ways, WeNala locked eyes with Kassidy. "We won't stop until the Swift is free and Qilalugaq is home."

"Even if the orcas never return," SaLita added, "we'll know we did all we could to make amends and give hope to future generations."

Kassidy felt the strength of their determination. These women were fierce, honest, and driven for all the right reasons.

Shephard exhaled beside her, shaking his head slightly as he glanced between them. "I grew up watching my grandfather measure power by what he could take from others," he said. Then his eyes moved across the three of them—calm, unblinking.

"But this?" he said. "Unity, wholeness, commitment. This is real power. And I'm damn grateful to stand beside all of you in this fight."

The new friends exchanged goodbyes, and the plane lifted once more, carrying Kassidy and Shephard over the chain of islands until they landed at Isla Virginia.

Inside his home, Shephard poured Kassidy a glass of water, then sat beside her on the couch, his expression thoughtful as he gathered his words.

"I didn't want to keep anything from you," he began, "I also didn't want to drag you into something you didn't ask for. This fight...to remove the dam is dangerous, Kassidy.

"My grandfather is a dangerous man. He's ruthless and cunning and will not bend no matter who or what he destroys. He has a way of silencing anyone who threatens his control."

He looked away; jaw clenched. "It's terrifying, what humans can do when they don't understand." His eyes changed now. "I've spent my life staying close to him, sacrificing every relationship I've ever had, with everyone I've ever loved—my family, my own mother, to keep on the mask.

"It was the only way to take control of Deville Power. The only chance anyone had of taking him down and tearing out the dam."

Kassidy reached for his hand, her fingers tightening around his, his revelations shocking and terrifying, clarifying all in one.

"I had no idea how much you've sacrificed. Tell me how to help. What can I do?"

"Today was a huge step," Shephard said, his voice resolute. "Made my role official. Airtight. And I think I've found a loophole to put Gunter out of business for good." He met her gaze, the intensity of his mission burning in his eyes.

"Will you stay with me?" he asked.

"I'm putting everything on the line. My name. My blood. My future. You. All I ask is you don't walk out before you know what I've risked for this."

# Chapter 46

Friday Harbor had seen its share of protests—marches for the vanishing orcas, vigils for the collapsing salmon runs, outrage over the oil-slicked, engine-churned sound. But nothing like this.

Since news broke that Capri Son's newest exhibit would feature Keelah—and that no one had been held accountable for the brutal killing of the last female orca from the AT1 pod in Alaska—the crowds swelled beyond anything the town had seen.

The outrage reached further than just whale lovers. It united everyone who had ever cared about clean water, marine life, habitat destruction, or corporate corruption.

Less than a week had passed since Capri Son's ad campaign went global, featuring Keelah and Kassidy—the orca and the mermaid.

Public reactions were instantly fractured.

Some praised the company's decision to 'rescue' Keelah from a crumbling tank in Mexico City, calling it an overdue act of compassion. Others condemned it as nothing more than corporate rebranding—arguing that captivity in any form was still captivity.

A third group, led by the KaWaltish First Nation and the SOCC—SaLita's family and coalition—demanded Keelah be returned to her native waters, to live in a sea pen or, if possible, be rewilded.

Skeptics said she'd never survive the transport. Scientists, marine biologists, activists, and former Capri Son orca trainers flooded the airwaves, debating her survival odds: Could her immune system handle colder waters? Would she recognize wild prey? Could she withstand the stress of transport—or adapt to a life with fewer human cues?

But none of that seemed to matter. Capri Son wasn't about to relinquish their most valuable asset—not after unveiling the half-a-billion-dollar AquaDome built specifically for her, a state-of-the-art enclosure they touted as "the ocean, reimagined."

Tourists were already booking out months in advance. Keelah had become more than a whale. She was a spectacle. A symbol.

A dead industry, resurrected—marketed as rescue, engineered for profit. Sleeker now, dressed in compassion and gleaming tech, it was captivity rebranded so smoothly that even well-meaning people didn't see the chains.

Some were thrilled, lining up to buy tickets, while Kassidy's follower count soared with every mermaid post Capri Son put out.

Others saw right through it—Capri Son, doing exactly what corporations like it had done for decades: monetizing marine life behind glass and hashtags. And in a world that couldn't agree whether to save the orca or set her free, Keelah had become everyone's commodity.

A sea of voices rose together—louder, more determined than ever—as people poured into Friday Harbor from across the country for another rally.

Faces stretched from the stage to the edges of the square, pressing shoulder-to-shoulder, buzzing with a shared urgency. People encircled the orca statue that loomed in the background—a somber reminder of all they had lost and still stood to lose.

Camera crews and journalists captured sound bites from attendees who had traveled from as far as Alaska to stand in solidarity with the Orca Conservation Center. The quiet coastal town had become the center of a powerful movement.

Kassidy took in the scene, standing near the stage, Shephard by her side as the crowd's raw energy pulsed, a potent mix of hope and outrage. She felt nervous about speaking after running off last time, but she also felt like this was where she belonged.

Now, she had a plan—together they had a plan—and she was on the right team and fighting for something that mattered. No more using her voice to promote the fleeting trends that used to shape her life and work.

Now, she'd found a cause she wanted to fight for, and would use her voice and her platform to help save it at any cost.

Shephard wrapped his hand firmly around hers. His quiet smile and gentle squeeze anchored her to him—giving her all the support she needed to survive the coming chaos.

On the stage, SaLita stepped forward in full regalia. Her traditional KaWaltish attire a reflection of the ocean itself. Layered blues and greens rippled like water with each step she took, and atop her head, an orca headdress rose up like a cresting wave.

SaLita's voice broke through the murmur. She spoke in a language that seemed so ancient and foreign it was a miracle it survived through time.

Kassidy didn't understand a word SaLita was saying, but she didn't need to—she felt them. Felt their power thrum through her, connecting her to the woman speaking and to everything living and breathing around them.

The crowd grew silent as SaLita's native language and the story she told with her eyes, and hands and body carried everyone back through time into a forgotten culture. A time when her language was the only one spoken in these islands. A time when the Southern Resident orcas roamed in the hundreds, moving freely through uncrowded waters. A time when giant Chinook made their epic migration from the open ocean up the winding rivers and back again.

The words were guttural and the dynamic movements and gestures told the tale of a lost world that existed in harmony—a place without fish farms, or dams—before the relentless hum of boats and noise fractured the peace. SaLita's story was about a time before the capture era—the kidnappings and captivity—a glimpse into a lost culture.

While Kassidy understood there was no going back to that time, she also had hope for a better way forward that might save the place she'd come to love. When SaLita shifted to English, the syllables felt short and hollow cutting into the present moment and the harsh reality of all that had happened to get there.

"The SSOCC has worked tirelessly to bring Qilalugaq home." SaLita's voice rose, claiming the crowd's attention. "Qilalugaq is our kin, our nation's child, stolen from us—taken from her home when she was a baby. Now, it is time that she is returned to that home. Seagrass Bay is a sacred stretch of water to the Coast KaWaltish people, and it is ready to receive Qilalugaq and keep her safe until her last day."

Her words echoed across the square and for a moment, there was silence, and then a wave of cheers surged, a tidal roar that rippled through the gathering. The unity, the collective force of their voices, was electric and further confirmed that this is what Kassidy wanted to be a part of.

SaLita wasn't done, she held up a hand silencing the crowd. "Ca PRISON has profited billions of dollars off the backs of our ancestors beneath the waves," her voice was unbreakable.

"Despite what they've profited from enslaving our orcas, Ca PRISON refuses to spare a single dollar to retire Qilalugaq into the waters that call to her. But now, I'm here to announce that we don't need their money to transport her home or take care of her.

"It is with great honor that I stand here today to announce that the SSOCC has raised enough money to prepare Seagrass Bay as a sanctuary for Qilalugaq—to transport her back to her home waters and care for her, where she will thrive for the rest of her days as a great killer whale of the Salish Sea!"

A thunderous wave of applause and shouts of joy rose to meet the sky, cheers mixed with tears of relief and triumph. Kassidy felt a lump in her throat. The sight of so many people, gathered with hope and bound by determination, struck something deep in her—a feeling of belonging.

She reached for Shephard's hand, her fingers lacing with his, joining them together with the islands and the mission.

Cheers quieted as SaLita's hand lifted again, her expression growing serious. "But…" She let the word hang in the air, a single note of warning that shifted the crowd's energy from elation to apprehension. "Ca PRISON will not let Qilalugaq leave without a fight.

"They want to keep her in their tank, and profit from her enslavement until the day she dies." A murmur of anger stirred through the crowd, voices echoing their indignation. "We must come together and fight for her return."

Just then, a sleek red car glided through the throng of people, stopping short of the stage. Dark, tinted windows gleamed like a warning, reflecting the curious, anxious faces around it. When the door opened, a poised woman stepped out—her expression sharpened to a point as if daring the crowd to look away.

Kassidy's stomach tightened. The sight of Jonah Thorne rekindled every bit of guilt, anger, and shame she'd been trying to reconcile. Shephard stiffened beside her. A low warning grumble emanated from his throat as if he'd turned into an attack dog.

"Jonah? What is she doing here?" Kassidy whispered as if her words could somehow ward off the woman's ominous presence.

Jonah stepped forward, dressed in a striking crimson suit and impossibly high heels, her every movement was deliberate and unyielding. As she cut a path through the crowd, the air grew colder in her wake. Without waiting for permission, she walked up the stairs, heels clicking like a countdown.

SaLita crossed her arms in a stance of quiet defiance. Jonah extended her hand, her expression controlled. But SaLita only stared, keeping her arms firmly tucked, refusing to engage with the captor. The hostility between them was apparent from even the farthest watcher in the square. The crowd held a collective breath as they waited, like everyone sensed the threat this woman posed.

SaLita lifted her chin, then gestured to the microphone with a slow wave of her hand. Jonah's smile was thin, almost brittle as she stepped up to the mic. When her voice came, it was well-practiced, and entirely unruffled.

"So *this*…is the famed Salish Orca Conservation gathering." Jonah's tone had a polished veneer of politeness that barely masked her condescension. She looked around the crowd as though assessing a room of unremarkable folk. "Forgive my intrusion—I simply couldn't resist stopping by to show my support and, of course, offer my assistance to this noble organization and it's many causes." Her lips curved in a smile as hollow as her words.

Then, from the red car, another figure emerged, his silhouette tall, dressed in a tailored suit of corporate armor.

"Billy."

Kassidy's hand flew to her mouth, a gasp escaping as she struggled to process the sight.

"You know him?" Shephard asked.

"Yes. He's my manager. I fired him this afternoon."

"For those unfamiliar, I'm Jonah Thorne, CEO of Capri Son Industries," Jonah said. Some of the crowd looked on in suspicion, others in open disgust as whispers of disapproval spread like a ripple. "I was there the day Keelah was rescued from that decrepit tank in Mexico City—a pool so cramped she could barely turn, so shallow she couldn't dive.

"Capri Son Industries saved her and in doing so paid a substantial sum to remove her from that decaying tank. We've since invested hundreds of millions of dollars and built her a sanctuary where she can live out her days in an environment that mimics the ocean."

Jonah spoke with graceful, sweeping gestures, her manicured fingers conducting the narrative.

"Our beloved Keelah is no longer forced to endure the scorching sun or consume rotten fish once forced on her. At Capri Son, we provide her with only the finest care. She isn't made to perform or interact with trainers; on the contrary, she lives freely, choosing where to swim and what to eat. People come to see her and take photos, yes, but they do so only to marvel at her majesty—not to exploit her."

The crowd's mood shifted, a mix of confusion and discontent rising. A voice cut through, loud and indignant.

"She's a slave! Set her free! Bring Keelah home!"

The chant grew as other voices joined in, gaining momentum.

A flicker of irritation crossed Jonah's face, her mask slipping. But only for a moment. Jonah straightened, her polished calm never faltering even as the crowd's anger swelled.

"I'm aware of what Ms. Seawalker has planned at Seagrass Bay," she said, her tone patronizing. Murmurs rippled through the crowd. "That is why I'm here. To let everyone who loves Keelah as much as we do know the truth about her return." People shuffled, brows furrowed. "I want Keelah to come home as much as you do. It's romantic to think of her in her home waters after all these years, but to bring her back, would sentence her to death."

The crowd stilled, held a collective breath as her words settled.

"Let me remind you of the grim reality of orcas that try to get returned to the wild. There has never been a success story. Keelah can never be returned to these polluted, lifeless waters."

A sigh moved through the crowd like a wave, as if everyone knew it but didn't want to believe.

"Her family starved to death here in your bays," she went on, "and by all scientific assessments, they will never return. Extinction is imminent for Keelah's family.

"Since she is the last of her kind, bringing her here—to poisoned waters, empty of food and plagued by the noise of reopened shipping would mean death for the orca we've all come to love."

A strange silence fell over the crowd as her words sank in. It was as if no one knew whether to agree or resist. And yet, the argument wasn't new. And the cruelest irony was that the captivity Capri Son defended was the same captivity that had destroyed the world Keelah could never return to.

"Keelah will never be released back into the wild," Jonah went on, her word sharp and distinct. "She deserves better than what this land can offer her, and Capri Son is committed to giving her a safe, controlled environment where she can thrive for the rest of her days."

For a moment, there was only stillness. A weary agreement. Then, as if their initial feelings flooded back, the crowd erupted.

"You're not saving her—you're holding her hostage!"

A chorus of agreement rose with voices calling for Keelah's freedom. Their anger grew to a defiant wall of sound against Jonah's chillingly composed front.

WeNala stepped up, her presence as commanding as her grandmother's, forcing Jonah to step aside. Then she lifted her hand, calling for silence and the crowd stilled.

She spoke with unwavering pride. "We are right to fight for her return and we will not give up until Qilalugaq is home!"

She raised her arm in the air, fingers spread wide, and moved it slowly from side to side. A swell of cheering rose from the crowd as arms lifted in unison, a thousand hands stretching skyward, fingers fanned like fins, swaying back and forth in the wave-like gesture Kassidy had seen once before.

But this time, it was different. This time, the motion rippled through the crowd like a tide—undeniable, unstoppable. With so many arms raised, it became a living signal—bold, defiant, and unified. More people than ever were on Keelah's side.

"What Mrs. Thorne said is right. Keelah cannot come home to these waters as they are now. But that is changing. Now, we have a plan to bring back the salmon, and to bring Keelah home.

"A new force has joined our mission and tipped the scales in our favor. Although she is new to us, she is a voice many of you already know." WeNala paused, letting the crowd simmer. "Please welcome and give her a chance to speak. Kassidy Karlson."

A ripple of recognition and confusion swept through the crowd. Kassidy took a deep breath.

"Kass," Shephard murmured, lifting his hands to cradle her face. "Everything you gave up—you'll get back tenfold for what you're about to do." His thumbs brushed her cheeks, his voice steadier now. "You've got this. Like you've already got me." He leaned in, his forehead resting against hers. "Once they see who you really are, they are going to fall in love with you. Just like I have."

Kassidy's breath caught. She searched his face, stunned. Her heart stuttered like it wasn't sure what to do with the words. He didn't give her space to say anything back. Instead, he just leaned forward, pressing a soft, steady kiss to her forehead.

She nodded, a small, grateful smile crossing her lips. His words wrapped around her like armor, solid and true.

The crowd was split as she walked onto the stage. There were scattered claps from fans, but also eyes of distrust and disappointment. Not that she could blame them.

Kass took a shaky breath, preparing herself, then stepped up to the microphone. SaLita and Nala stood behind her on the right. Jonah stood stage left, clapping for Kassidy, and when she came close Jonah leaned in and spoke quietly enough for only Kassidy to hear.

"Your contract prevents you from saying anything disparaging." Jonah smiled and kept clapping. "If you do, you'll be eating out of garbage cans for the rest of your life."

A voice pierced the quiet. "Captivity Queen!"

Another voice joined, sharper. "Sellout!"

Kassidy's gaze flicked to Shephard, who nodded, his expression calm, urging her to keep going.

Kassidy knew what had to be said, and she knew what she had to do. She stepped away from Jonah and up to the microphone.

"When I agreed to a partnership with Capri Son"—Kassidy glanced at Billy, still standing by the car—"I didn't know they had Keelah. I should have, and that's my fault. But I truly thought I was endorsing an exhibit that would support ocean conservation, not orcas in captivity." Her voice gained strength as she continued.

"It wasn't until I arrived on the job and was under the water, that I learned Keelah was held there. I felt trapped in a contract. If I'd known the truth sooner, I never would have joined the campaign. Seeing my face beside Keelah, as if I endorse everything that has happened to her will haunt me forever. She deserves to come home to unpolluted waters, free from noise, and filled with fish. I made a grave mistake, but I'm here to make it right. From now on, I'll use every resource I have to help make it happen. To bring Keelah home. And to hopefully, bring them all back home."

Half the crowd erupted in applause, while the rest remained quiet, still skeptical.

Kassidy nodded to the side of the stage. "Mr. Moore?"

Ted Moore stepped up, clearing his throat as he approached the microphone. "Hello," he began, his voice crackling slightly. "I represent Ms. Karlson."

He looked out at the faces, pausing briefly as if aware of how fast everything had unfolded.

"And I can confirm that Kassidy Karlson has donated every dollar from her work with Capri Son to the Salish Sea Orca Conservation Center." A ripple of murmurs passed through the crowd—things had moved at a staggering pace, faster than anyone could have expected.

He glanced at SaLita, who gave a small nod of approval. "The sum is significant—millions—and it's been earmarked to bring Keelah home and support her care once she arrives."

He paused, then continued, his voice steady. "Ms. Karlson has not profited from the Capri Son campaign. In fact, it has come at a tremendous personal cost. In less than a week, she's sold her childhood home and everything she owns to repay Capri Son in full—plus the substantial penalty she incurred for breaking her silence."

He looked out over the crowd. "She did it to speak out against the return of a cruelty we all agreed belonged to the past—orca captivity, long banned and globally condemned. I can also confirm that Ms. Karlson has donated every dollar of her remaining personal wealth—leaving herself only a six-month emergency fund—to the SOCC, to ensure Keelah's return becomes a reality."

A ripple of surprise followed by slow claps moved through the crowd as Ted stepped back. Kassidy returned to the microphone.

"Money alone can't make up for my mistake or convince Capri Son to help bring Keelah home, but I can, and will, do everything in my power to make things right. Starting now, I'm partnering with SSOCC, donating my time, and all of my resources, and connections to their cause. Tomorrow I'm launching a global initiative in partnership with the SSOCC, and we will fight Capri Son until they release Keelah to her Coast Salish family. Beyond that, with SaLita and Nala, we will fight to protect marine habitats across the globe that are on the brink of collapse, and about to lose their beloved orcas like the ones you've lost from this bay."

Kassidy stepped aside turning over the stage to Nala, who approached with quiet dignity. Nala lifted her chin, and when she spoke, her voice was clear and reverent.

And, just as they had planned it, Kassidy took out her phone and began a live recording on RippleHub.

"There are worlds within worlds. And there is a deep crisis beneath the water. Our unique population of orcas is on the verge of extinction. The last few individuals may already be gone—and with them we will lose their knowledge, their language, their songs and their bloodline forever.

"The dams have starved them, vessels have struck them, pollution has poisoned them, and our noise hinders their hunting. We must fix what we have done, and this isn't just happening in the Salish Sea. What's happening here will happen to the creatures along your coasts too. Only with the rescue and repatriation of the stolen one, can we begin to heal our lost sea."

Nala's gaze swept the crowd.

"What this woman"—she gestured at Jonah— "said is true. Qilalugaq's family is gone, thanks to corporations that kidnapped and sold their young into captivity nearly sixty years ago. This family has never recovered, and those responsible have never been held accountable. Not for the calves stolen from Penn Cove. Not for the ones who died in the nets, and not for the ones whose bodies were dumped to hide the damage. "Justice was never served—not in the courts, not in the culture, and not in the conscience of those who made it happen." She paused, then lifted her voice. "We must pursue justice and restore our sacred sea."

The crowd fell silent, captivated by her words.

"Bringing Qilalugaq home isn't just about justice for one whale," she continued. "It's about justice for all the atrocities our ancestors beneath the waves have been forced to endure. Bringing the stolen one home is the first step in repairing what was broken—above and below the water—and honoring the legacy of the Salish Sea."

Nala looked into Kassidy's camera, her words streaming live. The viewer count rose rapidly—before she knew it, fifty thousand viewers joined the live-stream in real time, then one hundred thousand, then more.

"We don't need signatures. We don't even need your dollars. We need your commitment. Protect your waters before it's too late. Protect your habitats before we lose them all. Don't let what happened to us happen to you."

Her voice rose. "If we fail to act, everything the people under the sea have endured will be forgotten—vanished like dust. Their fight, their extinction, will be erased from memory, leaving nothing for the future to learn from the past."

Nala scanned the crowd then looked back at the camera.

"Everything my family warned of came to pass. We predicted the extinction of the salmon when the dams were built. We warned of oil spills when these sacred waters were opened to cargo ships and global markets. We foretold the fall of the oldest family in the sea with the rise of corporate greed. But our voices were drowned out by people and companies with more power than we could overcome."

She paused. "Don't let that happen in your communities. Or what happened to our orcas will happen to the lands and creatures you love."

She let it sink in. "Learn from us—that when the easy solutions fail, we must rise and do the hard things." A beat of silence passed.

"Our orcas may not survive," she said. "But yours can. Look to the past. Learn from what we did—and what we failed to do. Our mistakes, our triumphs—they are the blueprint for a more unified future."

A surge of applause rolled through the crowd, echoing across the bay as Nala lifted her hands in thanks, embodying the ocean's strength and determination.

"We have a plan," she continued, "and if enough people join us, we believe we can save the wild orcas that still remain." She turned to Kassidy, and their eyes met.

Their hands clasped, a silent pact between them.

Nala returned to the mic. "There's no more time to waste. Tomorrow, we will show those who are not paying attention what it will feel like if we let our oceans die and our whales vanish. If you stand with the orcas of the Salish Sea, or the whales in Valdez whose home was filled with oil, or the North Pacific Right Whales, of which only thirty remain, or the blue whales struggling to survive after near extinction, then join us. Stand with us as we fight for our oceans."

Jonah huffed and walked off stage, while Shephard clapped in solidarity. Kassidy returned to the microphone, her gaze catching on Billy just as he turned away, climbing into the car.

She faced the crowd.

"From this moment, I'm dedicating my platform to this cause. I'm stepping down from all sponsorships that don't align with my values. If you must unfollow or cancel me, so be it.

"But if you're with me and want to make a change, tomorrow, turn your profile photo into a deep blue sea and use the hashtag #SilenceForSurvival. Join me in a 24-hour blackout. Our silence will echo the silence that looms if we let our oceans and creatures die. Let's show the world that we are one, and that they too can join our cause, and fight together."

She paused, her gaze strong and unyielding.

"Who's with me?"

# Chapter 47

When Kassidy was done speaking and Shephard gathered the press for his announcement, a wave of silence fell over the crowd, sensing that this moment was more than just a public decree.

It was a reckoning.

Shephard adjusted the microphone, his face focused. Cameras flashed, and chatter rippled through the audience, but Shephard remained steady.

"On behalf of Deville Power, I am here to announce a pledge of ten million dollars." A gasp came from the crowd. "This money is to be used in whatever manner necessary to ensure that Keelah is brought home, and cared for in the sanctuary the Orca Conservation has provided."

Surprised murmurs, claps and cheers spread. Shephard smiled into the news cameras, and when the applause quieted, he spoke again.

"In addition to supporting Keelah's safe return"—he took a deep breath, his tone grounded and clear—"as of this moment, Deville Power has deployed engineers to the Swiftcreek Dam where they are beginning the process of a phased removal, starting with a notch. A large cut in the dam that will begin to restore natural water flow and allow us to clear decades of sediment. This notch will allow salmon to migrate freely again while we work to remove the entire dam structure over the coming years."

A wave of cheers rippled through the crowd, the excitement palpable. Kassidy felt the thrill of it too, and a powerful realization settled over her as she witnessed a moment on so many fronts. Just as the crowd's cheers reached a crescendo, a furious voice rang out.

"Shephard! This is madness!" Gunter Amon stormed up to the edge of the stage, his face contorted with anger. He pointed a shaking finger. "You cannot make decisions like this that will destroy everything I've built!"

Shephard turned, his expression calm as he faced his grandfather, a man who had trusted him and tried to shape his path for years. Their history was complicated, but today, it was simple. Shephard was his own man. Always had been, no matter what he led Gunter to believe.

"This isn't about *you*, Gunter," he said, his voice steady and cold. "This is about doing what's right. And yes, I do have the authority to make these decisions. You appointed me as CEO, remember?"

Gunter's face twisted, a look of betrayal shadowing his eyes.

"I will not let you sink my company, boy! Now, get off that stage so I can fix what you've done before you ruin everything."

A slight smile tugged at Shephard's lips, one devoid of warmth. He stepped aside from the microphone so only Gunter could hear.

"Thank you, Gunter, for teaching me everything I know about business. You taught me how to play the game, how to fight for power, and most importantly, how to win." Shephard leaned in slightly, his voice unwavering. "You showed me exactly the kind of man I never want to be. I spent fifteen years making you believe I was exactly what you wanted—a loyal protégé, someone who would continue your destruction. But I'm not you, Gunter. I never was and I never will be. So I'm giving you something you never extended to anyone else."

Shep's jaw tightened. "I'm giving you a choice. Step out of Deville for good, right now, or watch everything you've built crumble from the inside out." His voice dropped lower, cutting like a blade. "I've spent years stacking evidence—every deal, every dirty dollar. Extortion, blackmail, fraud, tax evasion. Enough to bury you so deep you'll rot before you ever see daylight again."

The crowd watched, riveted by the confrontation but only a few people could hear the interaction. The shock on Gunter's face was evidence enough of the dawning horror as he realized how thoroughly he'd been deceived.

"You think you can turn against me?" Gunter's voice cracked, a rare vulnerability slipping through his fury.

Shephard's gaze hardened; his voice filled with resolve. "I'm not turning against you. I'm standing up for what I believe is right. Deville Power will no longer be a tool of destruction. Today, we start being a company that unites and leads a new generation into a smarter future. Now, which will it be? Step aside, or—"

"Jail? Ha!" Gunter laughed. "You ain't got nothing on me. I'll destroy you for breaching your contract. You're fired!"

But Shephard didn't flinch. He turned to the police officers standing nearby, the crowd falling silent as he prepared to make the final, irreversible revelation.

"Officers," he said, his voice carrying across the crowd. "I have information related to a crime that took place in the Gulf of Alaska."

The whole town seemed to stand still, as if sensing the gravity of what was to come.

"I witnessed the killing of the AT1 orca, Marie. I was there when Gunter Amon fired the shots that ended her life."

A gasp rippled through the crowd as Gunter's face went white, his eyes widening with shock and fury.

"Lies!" Gunter shouted, his voice cracking with desperation. "You have no proof! This is a pathetic attempt to ruin me." Shephard didn't blink.

"I have the weapon," his voice was calm, lethal. "And the crew will corroborate." Shephard's gaze didn't waver. "I regret that there was nothing anyone could have done in time to save the animal."

Another officer stepped forward, his presence foreboding. "Mr. Amon, we'd like to ask you a few questions."

Gunter's savage gaze darted between Shephard and the officers, panic flaring in his eyes.

"You're a traitor—a damn fool! No wonder your whole family walked out on you! I'll see to it that you lose everything you own and love. Anything that's left, I'll destroy it myself. You hear me Shephard! You won't get away with this. No one can take me down. Especially not some snot nose entitled little piss ant like you!"

One of the officers stepped closer, his hand raised in a placating gesture. "Mr. Amon, we're going to need you to come with us."

Another officer addressed Shephard. "You too Mr. Maddox."

"Yes, sir." Shephard said.

But Gunter was far from cooperative. He swatted the officer's arm away with surprising force. His face contorted, years of anger and entitlement blazing as he turned on his grandson. "I built this empire!" he roared, shoving a second officer who moved to restrain him. "You owe me, boy! I won't be brought down by the likes of you."

The officers exchanged a tense glance.

"Sir," one said firmly, moving to restrain him. But Gunter pulled back, swinging a fist wildly and narrowly missing his mark.

"Get your hands off me!" he shouted, his voice echoing across the crowd as he struggled against their hold, his movements erratic and defiant. "This isn't over—you hear me, Shephard? Those whales will ruin you like they ruined me. All of you stupid, small, feeble-minded algae loving idiots! You'd rather shit in the woods than have power to your homes!"

The officers overpowered Gunter, pinning his arms behind his back. "Mr. Amon, you are under arrest for disorderly conduct and assaulting an officer." They pulled his arms into place as he continued to resist, muttering a stream of curses, his face red with rage.

As the cuffs clicked into place, Gunter's body slumped slightly, though his eyes still burned with defiance. "You will all regret this. I built this place into what it is today!" he snarled, his voice venomous. "Now, I'll make sure this whole pathetic place crumbles."

Shephard held his gaze, unflinching. "I'm not afraid of you anymore, Gunter." The words were calm, clear, and final. "And neither is anyone else who lives here. You've done nothing but destroy this place, not build it up. Your rein of destruction and power is over."

The officers led Gunter away, his muttered threats fading into the crowd's buzz of whispers and gasps.

The once-powerful man was now shackled, his control shattered in full view of the people he'd sought to dominate.

As Gunter was escorted into the back of the cruiser, Shephard's hands unclenched, as if years of deception and silent guilt were starting to dissolve.

Kassidy rushed to his side, her face bright with admiration and relief. She wrapped her arms around him.

"I knew your heart was good," she whispered, her voice filled with pride and awe. Shephard looked down at her, his hands gently cradling her face as if to ground himself in this moment, to feel the reality of it.

"This is just the beginning, Kassidy," he murmured, a quiet determination filling his gaze. "We've got a lot more work to do. But we can get to it now."

A flicker of excitement passed over her face, mixed with a hint of disbelief. "Is that it? Are all your secrets finally out?"

Shephard held her gaze, his expression softer than she'd ever seen it. She searched his face, waiting for the other shoe to drop. For some shadow of doubt to slip through. But it didn't.

"Yes," he said simply, his voice confident, sure. "No more walls. No more hiding. Just you and me, Kass."

Emotion swelled in her chest as he reached for her, threading his fingers through hers—solid and real. A bridge between everything they had been and everything they still could be.

She let out a breathless laugh, shaking her head. "I don't know what to do with all this honesty."

He grinned. "Get used to it."

As she felt the warmth of his arms, a new resolve took root within her. Together, they would inspire change, calling on the world to protect the wild and bring Keelah home. They believed in what they had witnessed today, people coming together, and were ready to fight.

This journey was just beginning. With Shephard by her side, Kassidy felt the pulse of something unstoppable—a movement fueled by their shared hope and unwavering love for nature.

Tomorrow, they would step into uncharted territory, ready to awaken the world and lead the charge across oceans and borders.

SaLita stepped back after whispering something into Shephard's ear. His face went pale, his expression frozen.

Kassidy looked between them, "What is it? Everything okay?"

He drew in a breath, steadying himself. "Yes, everything is fine. But we need to get back to the island."

"Is Virginia okay? Shep, what's wrong?

Panic coursed through her.

"Your grandma is fine. She's waiting for us."

Relief hit her like a wave, but the adrenaline still thrummed beneath her skin. Minutes later, they were in the air.

Sunlight spilled across the water, casting silver threads that danced on the surface.

The yellow floatplane soared through the mist, its wings grazing the open sky. Kassidy felt the rush of something new coursing through her: freedom.

She felt unbound from everything that had once defined her. The days of promoting hollow causes were over. What lay ahead was hers to build—something real, something that mattered. She already knew what was next for her.

She'd get involved with advocacy and awareness.

Kassidy had big ideas on how to help SaLita, the SSOCC and other places around the globe who were facing similar patterns.

Capri Son would probably retaliate, slap her with a lawsuit—but that was a battle she was willing to face—and she had a plan for what to do if they came.

Beside her, Shephard flew with an ease she hadn't seen before, his gaze was peaceful, his jaw relaxed, his smile…sultry. The man beside her, who had carried a secret for so many years, was finally unburdened. With Gunter gone, he was free. She smiled, realizing they both were, and together, they were heading home.

Kassidy reached for his hand, and as their fingers intertwined, a rush of heat filled her heart. He was everything she hadn't known she was waiting for—determined, strong, and the missing piece that made this life feel whole. Together, they could shape something true and lasting in a world that so often felt beyond the reach of anything good.

Ahead, Isla Virginia rose from the water, etched with evergreens and shadowed by secrets. Its lofty cliffs and hidden coves had already begun to feel like home—a place that held the memories of her family's past and the promise of her own future. Yet, as they drew closer, and it came into focus, she felt a pang of anticipation, as if the island itself held one last story it was waiting to reveal.

The floatplane touched down, skimming the water before gliding to a halt. They stepped out onto Shep's dock, then Kassidy followed him, hand in hand, along the familiar trail to her cabin where the air smelled of cedar mulch.

Laughter drifted through the air, mingling with the rustle of the trees. She paused, listening.

"Was that…laugher? Shep, who's here?" she asked, feeling Shephard's hand tighten around hers.

He met her gaze with a knowing smile and took both of her hands in his. "Your grandfather."

# Chapter 48

The cabin was warm inside and bathed in the golden light of early evening. Virginia sat by the fire; her face softened with a joy that Kassidy had rarely seen.

Beside her, a man stood, like a figure from another lifetime—his hair the color of ash, his posture solid yet worn. And his eyes were the same shade as hers—pale blue, edged in silver, kissed by the faintest trace of violet. When his eyes met hers, they held both joy and sorrow.

"Kassidy," Shephard said, releasing her hand. "Meet Raymond."

Ray's eyes filled with quiet awe as he tilted his head and stared at her. Kassidy felt her breath stall in her chest, as she struggled to understand why and how he could be there.

Her gaze shifted from Raymond to Virginia, who wiped at her eyes, as if she still couldn't believe what she was seeing. And Virginia just stared at Ray, like she was memorizing his face, or too afraid that if she blinked, he might disappear. If not for Virginia staring at Ray and Shephard introducing him, Kassidy would have thought the man in front of her was a ghost.

But how could he be there? Kassidy searched through everything she'd been told. What had she missed? Raymond had vanished. The man who had given his life to the sea and the whales—was dead.

"But... I thought... you were dead."

"I'm sorry about that." Ray nodded, his smile faint but sincere. "I hope you're not disappointed. I did have a whole grand exit planned," he said. Then lifted his hand, forming a noose above his head, stuck out his tongue, and let his eyes roll back dramatically.

Virginia gasped and slapped at his arm. "Raymond!" she hissed.

Shephard groaned, muttering, "Jesus, Ray," under his breath.

Kassidy stood frozen, wide-eyed. a strangled laugh catching in her throat.

Ray just grinned and dropped his hand. "I thought my time here was done. And I'd made peace with that." Then he turned and his eyes found Virginia. "Except now... turns out I need a little more time. And I'm damn thankful to have it."

Kassidy's mind reeled, fragments of his life rushing at her—the faded photographs, the journals, the pieces of a man who had lived for two things: redemption and the woman he'd never stopped waiting for.

Now here he was, standing before her.

"But... where have you been? Why are you here? Why am I here?"

Beside her, Shephard chuckled quietly, shoved his hands in his pockets, and glanced at Ray with a crooked grin—like they were both in on something she wasn't.

Ray's eyes twinkled with mischief as he looked at Shephard.

"I've been camped out at that new inn overlooking the square. You know, the one with the rooftop patio that makes you feel like you can spy on the whole town. Got a good view of the harbor from up there. Spent my days watching the tourists come and go, keeping an eye on the protesters too.

"Good thing I got there when I did—almost didn't get a room, seeing as I didn't have a reservation and all. I couldn't come back out here. Would've foiled my own plan to give you two a little space. Some time to figure each other out. Without me getting in the way."

Her eyes darted to Shephard.

Ray smiled, almost sheepish. "I had a hunch about the two of you. Any granddaughter of mine surely has a heart for the sea. And Shep here, well, he's pretty much Poseidon himself, now isn't he?" Ray rocked back on his heels. "I had to stay away. How else was I going to get the two of you to meet and fall in love?"

Shephard laughed under his breath, the sound full of something closer to gratitude than humor. He shook his head slowly, looking at Ray like he was seeing all the years stacked behind him.

"You old romantic," Shep said. "You just couldn't help yourself now, could you? Had to give Maq a little shove."

Ray's face softened, voice dipping into something quieter, something true. "Only because I knew," Ray said, shaking his head. "I just knew you two would be perfect together. I had to make sure you found each other. Before it's too late." His gaze drifted between them, something knowing in his expression.

"Some folks spend a lifetime looking for the right person. I knew you two were meant for each other. Figured I'd make sure you got all the time I never had. And I was right, wasn't I? You saw it the second you met. Didn't you? I knew you would. I knew it because I was lucky enough to have that kind of love once. And that kind of love—you don't question it. When it shows up, you hold onto it. Even if all you get is one moment. One year. Or one summer."

Kassidy's heart stirred with a thousand questions, but she held back, sensing that there would be a better time and place.

Ray walked to Shephard and cupped his hands around his shoulders, his eyes filled with pride.

"You did it," Ray said, his voice rougher than before. "I'm proud of you. More than you'll ever know. SaLita called me. Told me everything. All these years you stayed the course when it would've been easier to walk away. Took the hard road. Paid the price. And because of you, everything that should've never been destroyed has a fighting chance to come alive again."

There was a quiet triumph in Shep's eyes. "It's not over yet."

"Yes, it is," Ray said. "Now that you're in charge, whatever can go right, will. You're a good kid, Shephard. It has been one of the greatest honors of my life to have you call me grandfather."

"I knew you were up to something," Shephard said quietly. "Couldn't make myself believe you were really gone."

Ray raised an eyebrow, a glimmer of humor in his eyes.

"Oh yeah? How's that?"

"Because you never leave a job unfinished." Shep's eyes darted around the room, at the massive amount of projects and work Ray had done in his lifetime—the photo identification, the mapping, the carvings. "I knew you'd need to find out if the notch we put in the dam worked."

Ray lowered his chin and raised his eyebrows, hands still on Shephard's shoulders. "It did, didn't it?"

A wide smile slowly grew on Shephard's face. "It did. Exactly as we intended. Phase two will start soon."

Ray's face softened with a bittersweet smile as he looked toward the island's shore, the place he'd been tied to his whole life.

"Good work, Shep. Good work. You've sacrificed your whole life to make this happen. You're a selfless, noble man and the world is a better place with you at the head of it. So...I'm officially done here." He took a step back. "You two can take over now. This land is yours," he said to Kassidy. "And I have something more precious than all of this that needs my attention." Ray looked to Virginia, his gaze tender. "We have less days ahead than we've been apart, so I can't let a single moment pass without that woman by my side. If she'll have me."

Virginia smirked, brushing a tear from her cheek.

Ray took a breath, his gaze shifting between Shephard and Kassidy, his voice soft but resolute.

"Kids, this is your fight now." He reached out, clasping each of their hands, bridging the already undeniable connection between them. "You two are everything this place needs and could hope for. Together, with SaLita and her family, you'll be unstoppable. And finally fix what we were never able to."

Kassidy's heart swelled, a wave of admiration rushing through her as she saw Shephard's quiet pride and the bond he shared with Ray— closer than family.

Ray turned his gaze back to Kassidy, his eyes filled with decades of unspoken words. A flutter of emotions rose inside of her—wonder, gratitude, and the promise of something wondrous and new.

"Kassidy, please accept my apology," Ray said, his voice almost hesitant. "For bringing you here without giving you the whole truth."

Kassidy crossed her arms and arched a brow. "Well, it's a little late for a refund... so I guess I'm stuck with this. And all of you."

Ray looked at Virginia. "You and Stanley raised her right."

"We did indeed," Virginia nodded.

Ray turned back to Kassidy. "And I'm forever in debt to the man who was your father. Ginny told me how wonderful he was."

"Yes, he was," Kassidy said, quiet tears in her throat.

"This place is yours," Ray said. "But your grandmother and I were wondering if perhaps you'd let us stay here a while longer? We were thinking that since Shephard has a big spread over there, maybe he could put you up at his place for a while, so Ginny and I can, get... reacquainted."

Both Kassidy and Shephard took a step back. Shephard cleared his throat. Kassidy grumbled, something that sounded a lot like—gross.

"Oh, get your minds out of the gutter you two!" Virginia hollered from her spot next to the fire.

Kassidy smiled. "This is your home, Ray. Thank you for letting me be part of it. If you still want me to look after it someday, down the road, I will take care of it the way you intended."

Ray nodded as his face filled with quiet pride. "I know you will."

Virginia stood and placed a hand on Ray's arm. "Kassidy looks just like her mother," she said.

Kassidy felt her breath stop.

The sorrow of her mother's absence settling in.

"I didn't get the chance to know her, either," Kassidy said. "But maybe..." She reached out, her hand hovering over Ray's heart. "Maybe we can talk about her sometime, and I'll tell you what I know."

Ray's hand covered hers and he pressed her palm to his heart. His touch warm and steady and his eyes full of water. "I would like that very much. You have made an old fisherman so happy today. I may never have known your mother, but..." His voice was thick with emotion. "I can feel her presence in you." He hesitated. "May I—" and before he could ask the question Kassidy hurled herself toward him, hugging him so hard he almost took a step back.

Kassidy's heart swelled, a bittersweet ache spreading through her as the solemn truth settled between them—they had both lost someone they'd never known.

She looked at Ray and saw more than just the man standing before her. She saw quiet strength, and the resilience to move forward against cruel odds.

When she and Ray finally pulled apart, Shephard was beside her grandma, his arm wrapped around her shoulders in quiet comfort.

Ray stepped toward them, holding Ginny's gaze for a long moment before taking her hand. Then, without hesitation, he pulled her into his arms. His voice was barely a whisper against her hair.

"I may not have been there for every moment," he said, "but I never stopped loving you. Not for a single day."

"You're my favorite adventure, Ginny, and I never want our journey to end." There was a lifetime of love and loss trapped in his words. "Even after all this time I love you like it was the first day we met. You make me feel young again. And if you'll have me, I'd like to hold your hand until my last breath."

The words, filled with sorrow and promise, hung in the air, and seemed to transcend the years. Kassidy felt the tug of tears in her eyes as the depth of their bond settled over the room, as real and timeless as the place that surrounded them.

Shephard wrapped Kassidy in his arms, and a new purpose took root within her. Tomorrow would bring challenges and battles, but today, they were a family—unbreakable and bound by a love that had withstood both time and distance.

In that moment, Kassidy realized Virginia had been right when she said time didn't heal wounds. It only hid the hurt. True healing came from being seen, from being loved by someone willing to mend what had been broken, guiding every stitch with a steady hand.

And maybe, just maybe, she'd found someone who knew exactly how to thread the needle.

"We should all go to Shephard's tonight though, just in case the power goes out again," Kassidy suggested, her voice carrying a note of urgency. "It looks like there is one of those storms coming in again."

Ray raised an eyebrow, looking puzzled. "The power has never gone out. I've never been without heat and lights for a single night. There's a generator for that and I made sure it's in perfect working order before I left."

Kassidy blinked, her brow furrowing in confusion. "But it did go out. The first night I was here." She turned to Shephard, her voice trailing off as realization dawned on her.

Shephard, standing nearby, shifted on his feet, his expression caught somewhere between sheepish and guilty. "Yeah…about that," he muttered, rubbing the back of his neck.

Kassidy's eyes widened. "Shephard? You did not cut the power on me, did you?"

He shrugged, a reluctant smile tugging at his lips. "I may have. Accidentally, of course."

Ray snorted, shaking his head. "See? I knew it. I knew you two would be perfect together. I should've had my own TV show. Like that Millionaire Matchmaker lady. I would've had you two married off by lunchtime."

Kassidy stared at Shephard, equal parts flattered and flustered. "I can't believe you cut my power."

Shephard raised his hands in surrender. "Hey, it worked, didn't it? I just had to see you again."

Kassidy groaned, threw her hands up and let them fall back to her thighs with a slap. "Unbelievable."

Virginia chuckled; her voice tinged with amusement. "Well, Kassidy, I guess you can't say the man doesn't take any initiative."

# Chapter 49

Ray and I spent the next six years on Isla Virginia, and I swear, they were a lifetime unto themselves. Ray opened his arms, and I ran into them—like a kid bursting out of school, racing toward the only place that ever felt like home.

He loved me without conditions, without hesitation, as if all the years between us hadn't left a single scar. And this time, I didn't have to push my love for him down the way I'd done for nearly fifty years. My love for Ray surged to the surface, fierce and unrestrained, like the very first day he'd stolen my breath away.

Some might say we were too old for another passionate love affair, but they'd be wrong. What we had, was a second chance. It was deeper now, layered with the years, the losses, and everything we'd lived through without each other.

They say time apart makes the heart grow fonder, and I once thought that was a lie—that I'd already loved him as much as anyone could love another. But time, it seemed, had only deepened that love, rooting it in places tragedy couldn't touch. What we shared hadn't been erased; it had endured and was waiting for us to come home.

We spent our days in passionate work—mostly on his fishing boat, the same clunker we fell in love on back in the summer of seventy. We tracked different kinds of whales, birds, and worked to pull out invasive species that threatened to overtake the islands. The nights were just for us, stargazing from the shoreline. Ray made bonfires, and we talked about things we'd never dared to share with anyone else. Things I'd never even shared with Stanley because I couldn't tell him how I truly felt about Ray.

We bickered and laughed like we were twenty again and loved one another fiercely, kissing as passionately as two old fools could. We knew each night when we laid down next to one another that it could be the last, so we never wasted one second of the time we had left.

Ray called it *our reckoning*—a time to confront our pasts and make amends. We were two souls trying to make right by the world before it was too late. And in that tiny sliver of time, we found something some people never find—a love that lit up every corner of our lives, even the ones we'd kept locked in the dark.

My years with Stanley taught me that love is a choice—an unwavering commitment that can be deep, fulfilling, and safe if you keep choosing to make it that way. But Ray…Ray showed me that some love isn't a choice at all. It's a force that sweeps through your life and leaves you changed, no matter how hard you try to hold it back.

He also taught me that love isn't about never saying you're sorry; it's about being forgiven—after you apologize. Ray forgave me long before he ever forgave himself. He forgave me for leaving him, for running from the life we were meant to have. And somehow, in the years that followed, he found a way to forgive himself too—for the things he could never undo. In ninety-six years, he'd done a hell of a lot more good than he ever had to apologize for.

It was citizen scientists like Ray and SaLita whose patience and reverence contributed immeasurable knowledge to what we know about the orcas we love. It's the information and photographs they gathered from observing them in the wild that made us fall in love with the killer whales. Not those bigots who enslaved them and took all the credit for making the world fall in love with them. It wasn't seeing them in captivity that made us fall in love with them. I believe it was whatever is in that fourth lobe of theirs that is responsible for that.

Watching the orcas in their rightful habitat, not in captivity, is what opened people's hearts and minds. Learning the truth about their families, and their intelligence is what turned the public to support them. Not their slave routine in the pool. How they mourn their dead, that their mothers and grandmothers live to be one hundred years old, and spend their whole lives teaching their family how to survive, is why we love them. They go back for their wounded, like us. They save their sisters by holding them on the surface giving them a chance to stay alive. Watching and learning about the whales in the wild is what makes people empathize with them and want to protect them.

There are countless faces who no one will ever know that contributed to protecting the whales—contributed to saving whatever was left.

Shephard's family never understood why he stayed close to Gunter all those years, and frankly, I don't know how he did it. But in the past few months, they've started to see the depth of his sacrifice. His mother was the first to visit, telling him how proud she was, even if it took time and distance to understand his greater purpose. His father came around soon after, recognizing the burden Shephard carried by stepping into Gunter's shadow.

Shephard took over Deville Power and was more determined than ever to clean up the mess. And his niece, Sophie—well, she's thrilled her uncle ended up with a RippleHub celebrity. When she visits, it takes all they have to get her to leave.

One by one, Shephard's family returned to his life, their bonds mending as if some strange tide were pulling them all back together. Alongside Kassidy, they've become a family again—stronger and more united than ever.

And Kassidy…I didn't realize how much she was like Ray all along. In more ways than determination and creativity, she brings people together, igniting hope and compelling them to stand for something greater. She's not just Ray's granddaughter; she's his legacy. In her is the future of a new generation—a force that's already begun to shake the world. And what has come from that shake up has been nothing short of a wave of miracles.

Kassidy's work with the SSOCC has reached heights I can barely comprehend. She didn't just organize protests and rallies. What they've done is unprecedented—sparked a movement that spanned continents, bringing people together from all over the world in ways no one had ever done.

It began with what I thought was that silly twenty-four hour silence. Turns out millions of young people unplugged and turned their profiles ocean blue.

It was a stunning reminder of what the world would be like if we let our oceans go silent—a silence that couldn't be ignored. From there, people lined coastlines across the globe, from Washington to Norway, Japan to Argentina, forming human chains.

Millions stood shoulder-to-shoulder, drawing a literal line in the sand, calling for the protection of marine habitats for the world's most vulnerable populations. Their stand, arm-in-arm, disrupted ports, halted shipping, and cost millions in commerce over just a few hours. Just enough to bring the right people to the table to discuss real change.

As the movement grew, so did Kassidy's voice and vision. Turns out if you ask millions of followers to donate five dollars, you can raise enough money to get the government's attention. Together, they created the largest wildlife preservation fund the world has ever seen. Kassidy insisted the money raised go only to Indigenous led conservation projects working to restore ecosystems, remove dams, and clean polluted waters. It was a ripple that became a tidal wave, a force no one could ignore. The fund supports the creation of Marine Sanctuaries—places where orcas, and other endangered species, can live and thrive without human interference. Her vision is a testament to Ray's dream—a dream she fought for with every ounce of strength she had.

Shephard donated his ridiculously obscene yacht to the SSOCC, and now it sails under SaLita and Nala's care, with a team of researchers traveling the globe to document how habitats recover when left in peace—like the Elwha and the Swiftcreek Rivers. Each time they send word, I feel a pang of pride. Shephard could have sold that yacht, used it for his own gain, especially since he dismantled the dam and put himself out of a job, but instead, he gave it back to the ocean, a piece of himself carried on the world's swells.

Not every victory went our way though—on the day we hoped to bring Keelah home, she took her last breath in that tank. Capri Son blamed it on age, but we knew better. There were whispers of infections, of water quality problems they couldn't fix. Keelah lived longer in captivity than any other orca, and in a way, her suffering changed the way people saw orcas. People loved her up close, but love and captivity should never go hand-in-hand.

Jonah Thorne refused to give her up. It didn't matter what anyone did or could have done, not enough people stopped buying tickets, so Jonah never had a reason to return her to the sea.

Not even in death did Capri Son return Keelah home, despite the pleas from her living ancestors who begged for the chance to grant her a *Saqumata*—their sacred rite of return. WeNala, SaLita, and SSOCC fought with everything they had to see her remains carried back to the waters that once cradled her.

Capri Son chose instead to discard her like refuse, burying her in a garbage dump and hoping the stench of betrayal would stay buried with her. But when the truth surfaced about the cheap way they disposed of her massive body, it broke something. People who had once stood behind what they were doing, finally saw them for who they really were. Capri Son hadn't just buried a whale. They buried whatever was left of their own soul, and profits. Jonah was chosen to fall on the sword for their decision. Capri Son fired her, pinned the blame on her, and washed their hands of all culpability.

The loss of Keelah struck hard in the islands. It sparked a kind of mourning I'd never seen before. People who'd never given a thought to an orca's life suddenly felt her absence, and they raised their voices, demanding that it never happen again. Keelah's death became a call for change—for orcas, and for every wild creature held captive. A reminder that some things are meant to remain wild, and that real love means knowing when to leave something untouched, while we still have the chance. And that some places were never meant for human feet.

Believing we need to leave our fingerprints on every inch of this world is to forget the beauty that thrives without us—the wilderness that needs no interference, no taming—only reverence and respect.

And as for that little piss ant Billy—well, he and Kassidy made up, 'cause she's much nicer than I am. He comes out to visit sometimes, but his path is still alongside boob tape and shapewear. Fitting for him, I suppose. Some people don't care about anything other than what's in front of them and that's okay, as long as they stay out of my way, anyway.

Oh, and Gunter…Gunter was charged with the murder of that poor orca near Resurrection Bay. They locked him away in Spring Creek, right by where he shot that poor animal.

A maximum-security prison where he sees nothing but concrete walls instead of the beauty that surrounds it. His reign of greed and destruction is over, and if he ever steps foot in the Pacific Northwest again, he'll find himself an enemy of the people.

They say the universe is the only thing that is truly infinite, and that it's expanding farther and farther each day. But there is something else that's as infinite as the expanding universe too—love. I've come to see that you can stretch it over everything—as thin, and far, and wide as you can possibly imagine—and still love expands, grows bigger, can encompass everyone and everything, and is all renewable: boundless, unyielding. You could stretch it across oceans, continents, and across a thousand lifetimes, and still, it never runs thin. Love can pull everyone and everything under its wings, and still, it keeps on going. Which is why I can almost hear Ray's laugh in the wind that rushes past these trees and see him in the salt-gray waves that lap against the shore.

Six years, three days, and eleven hours—that's how much time we had together before he slipped away like the tide. It wasn't enough. But no amount of time could ever have been enough. I find comfort in knowing that my love for him in those few years was as deep as any love could be—and he felt it, too. Sometimes I wonder if it was better that way, to have a passion and love so fierce, yet be limited by time so that its heat never has a chance to dwindle.

The doctors said Ray died because he had an enlarged heart. After Ray, I had a hunch that's what killed Karleen too and after some digging, I was right. I wished Stanley were alive so I could tell him there was nothing we could have done to save our beloved Karleen, but that conversation will have to wait until I see him again.

Some legacies are simply too big to be tied to one person or even one lifetime. Ray left behind more than memories; he left a legacy woven into this land and into the hearts of those who carry on his fight to protect it. I find peace in knowing that nothing is ever truly gone—not his passion, not the love we shared. Ours was the kind of love everyone hopes to find. The only kind Ray and I ever knew.

Deep. Real. Endless.

The kind of love that could fit inside a whale-sized heart.

# Epilogue

The afternoon sun bathed Isla Virginia in warm light, casting a familiar golden glow that had become part of Kassidy and Shephard's life together. They sat side by side on a weathered wooden bench outside Ginny's cabin, overlooking the sea while their youngest, Kalina, played in the sand under Ginny's watch.

A decade had passed since Kassidy first came to the island—and four years since Ray was gone, too. Everyone had grown—except the island itself, which seemed to be aging in reverse, the land more pristine, the sea clearer, quieter than ever before.

Living on Isla Virginia, surrounded by its remote beauty and isolation, deepened the connection to the land and sea for everyone who lived there—and made Kassidy and Shephard's love for each other grow deeper still. They could thank Ray for that; he'd been right to play matchmaker. They were a seamless fit in every way that mattered.

Kassidy leaned into Shephard, one hand laced in his, the other resting on her very pregnant belly. He was more her rock than ever. Husband, father, protector. A man of unshakable character, devoted to Kassidy, Kalina, Virginia—and, of course, to the black-and-white giants of the sea, who would forever need people like Ray, SaLita, and Shephard watching over them. All while guarding his own family and home, too.

Shephard made good on his promise to dismantle the Swift Creek Dam. Freed from its confinement, the river roared back to life, its revival even more dramatic than the Elwha's. The wild salmon, resilient and determined, did the work nature intended. With the flow of water restored, their ancient cycle of birth and death resumed, carrying vital nutrients and minerals from the ocean, through their bodies, and releasing them into the river basin where they spawned and died— nourishing the earth, igniting new life, and restoring balance to the ecosystem once more.

The river and surrounding land were now part of the Salish Sea's protected habitat—the largest the Northwest had ever seen. In a historic shift, the coastal First Nations had taken their rightful place in its stewardship, caring for the earth and waters with traditional practices passed down through generations.

Shephard stepped down as CEO, appointing someone who understood the rivers and oceans in ways he never could, as her ancestors had been here for generations. TaLeya Nahale's family was native to these lands, and her resolve to protect and restore them was as fierce as her family's connection to them. Shephard watched with quiet pride as she took the helm, her intentions grounded, her spirit unyielding in her commitment to preserving the waters they both held dear.

In her hands, Deville's mission was no longer corporate; it was personal. With each project she championed, a new legacy took root—one guided not by profit, but by an enduring, ancestral duty to care for the land and water as faithfully as one would care for family. TaLeya's unwavering commitment to leading Deville in a new direction allowed Shephard to step into an advisory role, freeing up more time for him to be with Kassidy and their growing family.

Kassidy's work with the SSOCC had taken her across all seven continents, often with Shephard by her side but since the birth of their little girl, everyone stayed closer to home.

The world around them had changed rapidly in those ten years. Some dreams had come true, while others remained just out of reach. The Southern Resident orcas hadn't rebounded or returned, but they held on to the hope that somewhere, a few individuals were still out there, adapting in their own quiet way.

Even in her nineties, Ginny was a force—fiercely independent and, in her words, "soft, yet formidable as a smack of jellies." When she wasn't tending to the island's small garden or fishing off the rocks, she was doting on Kalina, telling her stories about Ray and the days they'd spent together on this very island. She kept his memory alive, and Stanley's too, often saying how lucky she was to have found two great loves, each different and deep in their own way.

Kassidy yelled from inside the cabin, "You guys! Come here! Quick!"

Shephard grabbed Kalina, and the three of them hurried in.

Kassidy pointed toward the television.

The local news was on, a bright-red News Alert banner scrolling across the bottom of the screen. They stood watching as the broadcaster spoke over video footage taken off San Juan Island.

"Three orcas were spotted today off the west side of San Juan Island," the anchor announced, her voice carrying a note of excitement. "Initially believed to be a rare sighting of transient orcas passing through, researchers at the Salish Sea Orca Conservation Center have now confirmed that the female in this group is indeed J61—Mira—who was formerly presumed dead, but who is not only alive but in remarkably good health. Even more astonishing, she's traveling with a newborn calf and another orca believed to be a male, and perhaps her mate."

The screen cut to an interview with a NOAA Marine Fisheries biologist, who seemed barely able to contain her amazement. "This is truly unprecedented," she said. "We're still gathering information, but thanks to the extensive photo cataloging conducted by Raymond Hawthorne and the dedicated work of the SSOCC, we've identified that J61 has likely adapted into the family of a different ecotype. She was seen traveling with an offshore male. If the calf is indeed their offspring, it represents a new lineage—one carrying the genetic strengths of both salmon-eaters and shark-hunters, a combination that could be uniquely resilient in our changing waters."

Kassidy felt her breath catch, her hand instinctively reaching for Shephard's. He turned to her, a look of awe in his eyes and they shared a long, meaningful gaze. One that held all the understanding of the years they'd spent fighting for the sea and each other. Mira had survived, adapted, and returned with a new family. It was an enormous win—for orcas, and for all the people who had fought to save them—after years sustained by little more than hope that their efforts wouldn't come too late.

As the newscast concluded, Virginia stepped up beside them, reaching to hold her great-granddaughter, her eyes misty. She wiped a tear from her cheek, gave Kassidy a small smile. Shephard put his arm around the women in his life, the ones who had become his heart and home.

That night, with Virginia settled in her cabin and Kalina asleep in her room, Shephard and Kassidy sat on their bedroom balcony overlooking the sea as the sun dipped low, casting a warm, golden glow over the island. Shephard pulled Kassidy close, pressing a soft kiss to her temple. She closed her eyes, leaning into him, feeling the strength of his embrace—the same strength that had carried her through the last ten years.

"Thank you," she whispered, her voice barely audible over the tightness in her throat.

"For what?" he asked, his voice gentle.

"Keeping your promise," she replied, a faint smile playing on her lips. "For taking me places I never could have imagined."

Shephard's arms tightened around her, and she felt the constant beat of his heart, a rhythm as familiar to her as her own. Together, they had built a life that honored their families' legacy in the best way they knew how—and honored the love they shared.

As they sat together, watching the waves lap against the shore, Kassidy felt the steady, enduring pulse of their love—a force that had sheltered them through loss and grief and carried them toward a future bright with hope and possibility.

Theirs was a love built to last, like the generation before them that had grown there. It felt as if the island itself nurtured a unique kind of love—one vast and deep, inspired by the land and sea—a love untethered and ocean-bound.

# AUTHORS NOTE

On September 30, 2019, I was on a kayaking trip in the San Juan Islands. Our guide warned us that our chances of seeing the Southern Residents were slim—they were endangered, starving, and rarely spotted. At the time, I didn't know their history or the ongoing struggle for their survival.

As with many of the places I've been fortunate to visit, I chose to arrive with just enough knowledge to be safe—but not so much that it filled my mind with secondhand images or expectations. I wanted the experience to unfold in real time, unshaped by what I'd seen or read before. I choose to discover the world through my own experiences, just as much as I choose to learn about its history and struggles.

Halfway through the trip, we stood on the shore of Henry Island where our guide let out a shout and pointed to the water.

There, gliding through the water undisturbed, were dozens of orcas moving together. Later, through the extensive daily logs and sighting records, I confirmed that what we had witnessed was a rare gathering— J, K, and L pods together in a superpod.

Tears filled our guide's eyes. I felt the awe of seeing them in the wild too, but I didn't understand the significance at the time. I didn't know that witnessing the Southern Residents all together like that was a rare and precious gift, like winning the conservation lottery. Nor did I know that what I was privy too that day, was at real risk of disappearing forever.

When I got home, I plunged into a deep dive on who these orcas were and ultimately uncovered the harrowing plight of the Southern Residents. I learned about the capture era and the brutal realities of wild captures around the world, the suffering of orcas in captivity, the decades of atrocities inflicted upon them, the depth of human speciesism directed at marine life, the salmon crisis, the profound cultural significance of this particular ecotype, and the relentless fight to save them.

My kayaking trip was nine months after my animal rights book, *Rescue Matters* had been released and I was deep in the world of helping to save stray and unwanted animals in the state that I grew up in. The thought hadn't even crossed my mind to write this book. I was simply hooked on reading everything I could about the subjects included here. I quickly became an orcatick of my own making, devouring every bit of research I could.

Somewhere along the way, a story began to form in my mind that I couldn't shake. An epic sweeping tale of romance and drama set in the capture era that spans generations. Like all my other books have, the story picked me, hounded me, harangued me, and wouldn't let me sleep until I sat down and started putting words on paper.

In 2022, I started writing the first draft of this novel and soon after, I was paralyzed with a crippling self-doubt: Who was I to write this emotional story about a place I'd never lived? There were experts in the Pacific Northwest and writers who could tell this story far better than me. These orcas are the most documented on the planet. Everything that needs to be said has been said—by people far wiser and more equipped to help them than I am. Writing about captivity and habitat conservation in this region wouldn't change anything; that fight was already well underway, and I had nothing new to add.

Those doubts, along with a million others, said that I couldn't do a story like this justice. So, I abandoned this project and gave up writing this book. But the book didn't give up on me. It tugged at my covers while I slept, it rubbed at my conscience like a blister in my hiking shoes.

So, I did the only logical thing: I ignored the pain. Instead, I asked the universe for a sign—a specific, undeniable sign that if shown to me, I would have to believe that this was the next story I needed to write. I gave said sign a deadline then continued to ignore this one and work on other projects.

As my sign deadline approached, I confided in my friend Aliah about my unfinished manuscript. I told her how the story wouldn't leave me alone, yet I questioned my right to write it. It wasn't my story to tell. What if I got things wrong? What if I stepped on toes or unintentionally offended the very people fighting for the cause I cared deeply about?

Thirty minutes later, Aliah and I were in an Uber on our way to a concert. Our driver, Tahir, originally from Pakistan and a twenty-year resident of Minneapolis, Minnesota informed us that he and his brother had just bought a gas station in the San Juan Islands (1,800 miles away) and would be moving there soon.

'*The* San Juan Islands? Like, the Pacific Northwest, San Juan Islands?' I asked.

He nodded.

We proceeded to talk about my work in animal rescue, my book about saving thousands of dogs in North Dakota, about life, fate, and about orcas.

Tahir shared words with me that felt like a prophecy and a calling, and perhaps, a sign. Wrapping his fingers around my wrist, forcing me to look him in the eye, he said that....well I can't remember *exactly* what he said here, it gets kinda foggy, there were drinks involved, we were, after all, on our way to a concert, but it had to do with writing, my 'calling' and something about those orcas.

What I *do* know, is that when we got out of the car, Aliah looked at me, eyes wide, and said, "What the hell just happened?" I looked at the hair on my arms, standing straight up like I'd just been hit by lightning. She looked at her arms, also hit by lightning. We both felt it. Whatever *it* was.

"Do you think it's a sign?" I asked Aliah.

She slapped her forehead, looked at the hair standing up on her arms again and said, 'You need to write that fucking book."

So, I did what any writer filled with perpetual crippling self-doubt would do. I analyzed the encounter to death and concluded that it was all just some strange coincidence. That Tahir was just being nice or perhaps was schmoozing me for a nice tip. Which he got. So, once again, I pushed this manuscript aside.

Five months later off the coast of Lahaina, Hawaii, I was on a boat in the Hawaiian Islands Humpback Whale National Marine Sanctuary when a voice—call it an instinct, call it fate, or *the universe*—or call whatever you want, implored me to "Go stand over there! RIGHT NOW!" The strange voice inside my head pushed me SO HARD, I literally almost fell down the stairs on top of which I was standing.

I argued with the strange voice stating that, "No. I'm comfortable right here. I don't want to lose my seat and go and stand somewhere else. There are no whales, over there. Everyone is on the other side. Why would I go stand right there, at the back of the boat, where nothing is going on?" But the voice insisted, yelling louder a second time. "Go. There. NOW! (You dumb broad!)"

So, I called my husband over and instructed him to, please just stand right here and don't ask me any questions. I don't know why, but just turn on your camera, okay? To which he replied with silence and stared down into the empty blue water. I aimed my own phone into the great blue where absolutely nothing was happening, and no one was looking and my patient husband stood beside me, making sure I didn't try and jump over.

After a few seconds, an enormous whale unfurled its arms in a slow, graceful circle, like some giant creature out of *Avatar*. It rose up from the deep, circling and staring then surfaced just a few feet in front of us. The ancient creature looked me in the eye, gave a stern warning *perhaps*, then slowly sunk back down, disappearing under the water before lumbering away.

Yes, we both caught it on video. It's on my social media if you want to watch. And it's a damn miracle I caught it at all, because I held my phone to my chest and didn't look through it, because I didn't want to miss the moment in front of me with my own eyes, knowing it was indeed, a rare gift. Our encounter wasn't a whale breaching in the distance photo op. It was an intimate moment where the universe screamed, "Believe me now? Bitch?"

Or perhaps, if you don't believe in such fated things. It was simply another confidence in my life.

So, I did what any writer filled with crippling self-doubt would do. I analyzed said encounter to death, watched my video back three thousand four hundred times and concluded that since we were in a whale sanctuary, during peak season, in what is known as "whale soup," my encounter was, in fact, not magical, nor rare, or a "a sign from the universe that I should write this book." It simply was my lucky day.

Indeed, it was—as the harbor we frequented and loved, along with far too many innocent souls that lived there, was wiped off the face of the earth just a few months later.

Back home, I decided that—on the off chance something bigger had been trying to speak to me that day—I'd listen. I got back to work on this manuscript and vowed that if—no, when—doubt crept in, I'd slam the door in its face and keep going.

I reminded myself that writing this book wasn't about changing the world. The fight to keep cetaceans free and out of captivity is already in the hands of braver, more committed souls than me.

Writing this story—at its core—was something I simply couldn't not do. It wouldn't leave me alone. I wrote the book I would want to read, and I was obsessed while writing it. If it reaches just one reader like me, someone who loves it as much as I loved creating it, that's enough. Novels are, if nothing else, entertainment. And if for nothing else, I wrote this to entertain myself and anyone else who might enjoy it.

If anything good comes of it beyond that, I welcome it. If anything bad comes, I'll face it knowing my intentions were pure, my heart is not iced cold, and I'll never stop learning from my mistakes and trying to be a good citizen of this planet.

I realize that many who find this story may have, at some point, visited an orca show, paid for a dolphin encounter, or supported captivity in ways they didn't fully understand at the time. I get it—because I've been there too.

I was a '70s baby and an '80s kid. Back then, orca shows and dolphin encounters were everywhere, and I was young, impressionable, and dreaming of being a fairy princess-mermaid-marine biologist. I've been to an orca show when trainers still swam in the tanks. I stood on a dock in Mexico at twenty-four, watching as my youngest daughter won a dolphin encounter, and though I hesitated, I allowed us to redeem it.

I've been to zoos, rescue centers, and wildlife rehabilitation facilities. I've visited Steve Irwin's zoo in Australia and watched alligators be lured in for entertainment and 'education.' I've drunk 8,000 year old glacier water from Vatnajökull and then prayed I didn't just give myself some ancient bubonic plague when I didn't feel well after.

I've purchased a dog from a breeder. I've eaten animals raised and killed for food, salmon from the Pacific, and ice cream like a glutton. I've made mistakes, bad choices, and decisions I would undo if I could.

But when we know better, we do better.

I sit in judgment of no one. This is a work of fiction. Good fiction can hold up a mirror. If Virginia's words—or anyone else's—stir something in you, it may be worth asking why.

Again, I sit in judgment of no one who has visited orca shows for entertainment. I promise to keep learning, questioning, and doing better when I know better—and I hope we all do the same.

While writing this book, Tokitae, died at the Miami Seaquarium. There was an oil spill in the San Juan Islands, the Southern Residents were spotted for the first time in Penn Cove since 1970, and the lower four snake river dams are no closer to a notch than they are of being torn down.

This story may be fiction, but its roots are real, and extinction is forever. While I did write this for entertainment, I'd be remiss if I didn't admit that my hope is that some part of this story moves you to help protect wild habitats, near or far.

I believe that through habitat conservation we can preserve life's essential and beautiful diversity and that without those sanctuaries, far too many of our world's most precious creatures will not be able to adapt quickly enough to our evolving ways. Help protect the habitats you love, and together, we will never have to wake up to a headline that says, *"GONE FOREVER."*

Thank you for going on this journey with me.

-Charmaine (C.J.)

# The Truth Behind Whale-Sized Heart

While *Whale-Sized Heart* is a work of fiction, the reality beneath it is far more haunting. Below are *some* of the real events, statistics, and stories that shaped this novel—many of them are heartbreaking. All are true.

**Fact:** Before the capture era of the 1960s and 1970s, the Southern Resident orca population was estimated to be over 200 individuals. By 1976, following these captures, the population had declined to about 71 individuals.[6]

**Fact:** In October 1965, Ted Griffin, owner of the Seattle Marine Aquarium, and his partner Don Goldsberry captured the original Shamu in Puget Sound, Washington. Born around 1961, Shamu was a member of J pod, part of the endangered Southern Resident orca population.

During her capture, her mother was harpooned and killed as she tried to protect her calf. Shamu was then sold to SeaWorld San Diego, where she became the first "Shamu" to perform, marking the beginning of the orca entertainment industry.

Later, in August 1970, Griffin and Goldsberry led the infamous Penn Cove capture near Whidbey Island, supplying more orcas to marine parks.

At the time of Shamu's capture, there were no legal protections in place to prevent or restrict these activities. The lack of oversight allowed capture operations to proceed unchecked.

The Marine Mammal Protection Act of 1972 provided federal protections, but it was Washington's decisive legal action in 1976 that specifically terminated orca captures in the state's waters. The state's lawsuit against SeaWorld led to a federal restraining order, halting further captures. [26,27]

**Fact:** The Penn Cove orca capture in August 1970 was a significant event with lasting impacts on orca populations. Seven young orcas were taken from the wild and sold into captivity during this event. Each orca was sold for approximately $20,000.

Five orcas drowned during the capture process. To conceal the deaths, the capture team filled the carcasses with rocks, tied anchors to their tails, and sank them. Three months later, a trawler inadvertently brought the carcasses to the surface, and they washed ashore on a nearby beach. [16,17,18]

**Fact:** Leading the Penn Cove capture, Ted Griffin (Seattle Marine Aquarium) and Don Goldsberry (Director of Collection for SeaWorld) have been "credited" for changing public perception of killer whale from savage killers, into the beloved black and white orcas we revere today. [2]

**Fact:** In the 1976 documentary "The Killer Whale Hunters" Goldsberry acknowledged the deaths of orcas during capture operations, stating:

*"At that particular time, we had other animals in the net. We were busy, I was sorry that we did kill animals. But there was nothing I could do they were already dead and I had to be concerned about the live animals. So, we slit open their stomachs, put anchors on 'em and sunk 'em. Because no one else would take them and, and—that's what happened. I did not advertise the fact that I lost them. I don't like to lose animals. But, eh, I did lose 'em and, eh, no one would take them, so I wasn't going out and put up a big billboard, I killed x amount of animals. I did it, and eh, that was it. It was just that simple."*

In the same documentary, Goldsberry expressed his belief in the positive impact of their work. *"I care more about these animals than all the environmentalists put together. I think my ex-partner and myself have done more for these animals than all environmental groups put together. We've showed the public what they are like. They are beautiful animals."* (YouTube link in the recommended reading section to this actual interview and video footage of the captures).

**Fact:** Between 1965 and 1973, at least 45 Southern Resident killer whales were captured and delivered to marine parks. This significant reduction in their numbers has had lasting effects, and the population has not fully recovered since these captures.[8]

**Fact:** In 1974 there were 71 Southern Resident orcas in the wild.

**Fact:** In 2024 there are 74 Southern Resident orcas in the wild.

**Fact:** Since being enlisted as endangered in 2005, their numbers have not rebounded.

**Fact:** In March 1976, Ralph Munro, then an aide to Washington Governor Dan Evans, witnessed a distressing orca capture by SeaWorld in Budd Inlet, Washington, recalling how the capture team used explosives to herd the whales, causing them to scream in panic. Munro's account highlights the traumatic nature of these captures, which led to significant public outcry and legal actions to protect orcas in Washington waters.

After witnessing the operation, Munro collaborated with Attorney General Slade Gorton to file a lawsuit against SeaWorld that ended live orca captures in Washington's waters.

Later, he joined environmental groups to secure the Endangered Species Act protections for the Southern Resident orcas, leading to their endangered status in 2005. [20,21]

**Fact:** Tokitae, also known as Lolita or Sk'aliCh'elh-tenaut, was captured during the Penn Cove Roundup, in August 1970 at approximately four years of age. She was the last surviving Southern Resident orca in captivity until her death on August 18, 2023, at the estimated age of 57. She spent 53 years in captivity.

**Fact:** After her capture in 1970 from Penn Cove, Washington, Tokitae (Lolita) was transported directly to the Miami Seaquarium, where she remained until her passing in 2023.

Her tank, known as the Whale Bowl, measured approximately 80 feet in length, 35 feet in width, and 20 feet in depth, making it one of the smallest and oldest orca enclosures in North America.[3] (Follow the link in the citation for photos and video spanning decades.)

**Fact:** Between 1962 and 1976, approximately 270 orcas were captured in the Salish Sea, the transboundary waters between the U.S. and Canada. Of these, at least 12 died during capture operations, and more than 50, primarily from Puget Sound's critically endangered Southern Resident population, were kept for captive display. Tokitae (Lolita) was the last surviving orca from these captures.

**Fact:** Wild orcas swim 100 miles a day and male and female offspring stay with their mothers and family their whole lives.

**Fact:** The Miami Seaquarium's Whale Bowl lacked adequate shade to protect Tokitae from direct sunlight and heat. A 2021 report by the U.S. Department of Agriculture noted that the facility failed to provide sufficient shade for the animals, including Lolita.[4]

**Fact:** Tokitae was given medication daily to manage stress ulcers, eye conditions, sunburns, skin rakes and infections. In 2016 she tested positive for e. Coli and MRSA and was considered "super-infested" with pathogens.[5]

**Fact:** As of November 2024, SeaWorld's U.S. parks house a total of 18 orcas across three locations. In 2016, SeaWorld announced plans to end its orca breeding program and pledged that the orcas currently in its care will be the last generation.

Corky, (as of this writing) is the oldest orca in captivity, is still alive at SeaWorld San Diego. Captured in 1969 from British Columbia's Pender Harbour, she has spent over 55 years in captivity. Corky is a member of the Northern Resident Orca community's A5 pod. Advocacy groups continue to campaign for her retirement to a seaside sanctuary in her native waters.[9,10]

**Fact:** Between 1976 and 1989, at least 54 orcas were captured from Icelandic waters and sold to marine parks around the world. Among them was Keiko, the orca who later starred in the film "Free Willy."[19]

**Fact:** The work of the China Cetacean Alliance has established that in 2021 there were 85 facilities holding whales and dolphins in captivity with a further 34 parks currently under construction. It is estimated that a total of 1,082 cetaceans are held, which is an increase of 80% over five years.

The number of captive orcas in China has increased in recent years. In 2021, there were 15 wild-caught orcas held in Chinese facilities. By 2024, this number rose to 22, comprising of 15 wild-caught individuals and seven captive-born calves. This growth reflects China's ongoing expansion of marine parks and orca breeding programs.[11]

**Fact:** The Exxon Valdez oil spill in 1989 had significant impacts on killer whale populations in Prince William Sound, Alaska. The AB pod, a resident group, lost 14 of its 36 members following the spill, approximately 39% of the pod. The AT1 transient pod lost nine out of 22 whales within a year, about 41% of their family.

The AT1 pod has not had any calves since the spill. Its population has remained at seven individuals. The key breeding females have been lost. With no reproduction and recruitment, the AT1 population is not recovering and their eco type will go extinct.[14,15]

**Fact:** Between 1955 and 1975, the U.S. Army Corps of Engineers constructed four dams on the Lower Snake River: Ice Harbor, Lower Monumental, Little Goose and Lower Granite. These projects were authorized by Congress to enhance hydropower generation, navigation, and irrigation in the Pacific Northwest.

Their construction faced opposition from environmentalists and local communities concerned about potential ecological impacts, particularly on salmon populations and river ecosystems. Critics argued that the dams were unnecessary and posed significant environmental risks.

Now, seventy years after the construction of the first dam, the initial critics of the Lower Snake River dams, a mix of environmentalists, local fishing communities, indigenous tribes, and conservation groups who warned of the environmental harm, were largely correct. The dams have had significant, adverse impacts on the river's ecosystem, particularly on salmon populations.

The dams obstruct salmon migration routes, which has led to substantial declines in wild salmon and steelhead populations—a major issue for the ecosystem, local fisheries, and indigenous communities that rely on salmon as a cultural and economic resource.

The decline in salmon has also affected orcas in the Pacific Northwest, as they rely heavily on salmon as a primary food source. Despite mitigation efforts like fish ladders and spillways, these have not fully counteracted the ecological damage. There is an ongoing debate about breaching or removing some of the dams to restore river health and salmon populations.[12,13]

**Fact:** On October 4th, 1954, 74 American servicemen in the United States Navy assisted the Icelandic government in "saving the fishing industry" they reported was being decimated by black fish. With machine guns and bombs atop an anti-submarine warship and assisted by a dozen Icelandic fisherman in their boats, the men killed approximately 100 killer whales in a single operation calling them "savage sea cannibals" and noting that the sea was "red with blood."

(While researching this particular event—initially out of curiosity to verify its authenticity—I encountered numerous sources that either dismissed it as false or provided no verifiable information. The truth was difficult to uncover, as reliable sources were not readily available through standard searches.

However, after extensive research, I located and cited the original sources, including Naval Aviation News (December 1956), which documents the special taskforce VP-7 involved in this operation. Screenshots of these original records have been included for fact-checking and transparency.)

**Fact:** There are no documented cases of wild orcas killing humans.

**Fact:** As of November 2024, China remains the only country actively breeding orcas in captivity. Chimelong Ocean Kingdom in Zhuhai continues its breeding program, with multiple orca births reported since 2017.

In contrast, other nations have ceased such practices: United States SeaWorld ended its orca breeding program in 2016. In 2017, France banned the breeding of captive dolphins and orcas. In 2019, Canada passed legislation prohibiting the breeding and captivity of cetaceans, including orcas.[29,30]

**Fact:** Orcas have a unique and highly developed part of the brain called the paralimbic region, which plays a major role in processing emotions. Unlike in humans, this region has an extra lobe of tissue, hinting that orcas might experience emotions in ways we don't fully understand, possibly combining emotion with complex thought.

This advanced brain structure supports the orcas' deeply social lives, which we see in the close bonds within their family pods. Scientists believe orcas may have a sense of self that extends beyond the individual, encompassing their social group. Their behaviors—like communicating through distinct sounds, coordinating hunts, and caring for injured pod members—suggest an emotional depth and social understanding that is rare among animals and possibly unmatched by humans. [22,23]

# ACKNOWLEDGMENT OF INDIGENOUS LANDS AND CULTURES

*Whale-Sized Heart* is a fictional story inspired by true events that unfolded on lands and waters sacred to the Coast Salish people, including the Lummi Nation and other Indigenous nations of the San Juan Islands, Vancouver Island, and the Fraser and Columbia River Basins.

This story draws from the tragic history of the Penn Cove orca captures and the installation of dams that reshaped life for the rivers and salmon. These events and actions have caused irreversible harm, not only to the ecosystems, but to the cultural lifeways of the Coast Salish nations, whose ancestors walk the lands and whose orca kin live on under the waves.

With profound respect, I recognize that my work draws from the legacy of those who have long protected these lands, waters, and creatures. With profound gratitude for the people who continue to care for these places, thank you for sharing your wisdom and passion with all of us who listen.

I commit to deepening my understanding of Indigenous cultures in the places I call home and to those I visit nationally and when abroad, knowing that my learning is a lifelong journey and a necessary part of being a respectful guest on these lands and as a citizen of this planet.

With respect and reverence,

Charmaine English (C.J.)

# IF YOU ENJOYED WHALE-SIZED HEART

Please consider leaving a review.

Your thoughts help other readers discover the story and make a huge difference for authors like me. Whether it's a few words or a full review, I appreciate every single one. Thank you for reading!

If you'd like to be notified of upcoming sales, new releases, and special offers, sign up for my mailing list at:
www.cjlovejones.com/mailing-list

I'd love to stay in touch!

— C.J.

Amazon Review QR

Goodreads Review QR

If you enjoyed this story, here are more books by C.J. English & C.J. Love-Jones (Fiction Pseudonym) you might love.

Nonfiction by C.J. English:

*Rescue Matters*
4 Years. 4 Thousand Dogs. An Incredible True Story of Rescue and Redemption.
Amazon #1 Best Seller – Animal Rights

*WTF Am I Supposed to Eat?*
A Dieter's Manifesto.
Amazon Kindle Best Seller – Weight Loss

Fiction by C.J. Love-Jones:

*Becoming Mistress Maye*
For any woman who has felt the pressure to conform to society's beauty standards.
Amazon Kindle Best Seller – Women's Fiction

*The Replacement Husband*
One decision. One lie. And a love that refuses to stay buried.

*Affairytale*
A Novel.
Amazon #1 Best Seller – Diaries & Journals

## Conservation Organizations and Advocacy Groups

### Orca Conservancy
A Washington State 501(c)(3) non-profit organization dedicated to the recovery of endangered Southern Resident killer whales and their habitats. Website: **www.orcaconservancy.org**

### Center for Whale Research
Conducts scientific research on the Southern Resident killer whale population to inform conservation efforts.
Website: **www.whaleresearch.com**

### Whale and Dolphin Conservation (WDC)
A global charity committed to the conservation and protection of whales and dolphins worldwide. Website: **us.whales.org**

## Support Indigenous-Led Conservation Initiatives

### Se'Si'Le
Utilizes Indigenous ancestral knowledge for the benefit of Mother Earth and future generations. Website: **www.se-si-le.org**

### Sacred Sea
Dedicated to protecting the Salish Sea through Indigenous-led conservation efforts. Website: **www.sacredsea.org**

### Indigenous Environmental Network
Supports Indigenous communities in protecting their environments and achieving sustainable livelihoods. Website: **www.ienearth.org**

## Participate in River and Habitat Restoration Projects

### American Rivers
Works to protect wild rivers, restore damaged rivers, and conserve clean water for people and nature. Website: **www.americanrivers.org**

### Elwha River Restoration Project
A landmark project that removed two dams to restore the Elwha River ecosystem. Information: **www.nps.gov/olym/learn/nature/elwha-ecosystem-restoration.htm**

### Save Our Wild Salmon
A coalition working to restore abundant, self-sustaining populations of wild salmon and steelhead to the rivers, streams, and marine waters of the Pacific Northwest. Website: **www.wildsalmon.org**

## Protect Wild Salmon Populations

### Pacific Salmon Foundation
Focuses on the conservation and restoration of wild Pacific salmon and their ecosystems. Website: **www.psf.ca**

### Wild Fish Conservancy
Dedicated to the recovery and conservation of the region's wild-fish ecosystems. Website: **www.wildfishconservancy.org**

## Advocate Against Captivity

### The Dolphin Project
An organization dedicated to the welfare and protection of dolphins worldwide, advocating against captivity. Website: **www.dolphinproject.com**

### Whale Sanctuary Project
Aims to establish a sanctuary for whales retired from entertainment facilities. Website: **www.whalesanctuaryproject.org**

## Engage in Citizen Science Projects

### Orca Network

Promotes awareness of the whales of the Pacific Northwest and supports their conservation through educational programs and citizen sightings. Website: **www.orcanetwork.org**

### Happywhale

Allows individuals to contribute whale sightings to a global database used for research and conservation. Website: **www.happywhale.com**

### Get Involved Locally

Participate in local river clean-up events, conservation groups, or volunteer opportunities focused on waterway preservation, habitat restoration, and educational outreach near you.

# ACKNOWLEDGEMENTS

Thank you to my long-time editor, Nicole, who helped shape and polish this story into the best one I could write—who tackled time jumps and story structure that other editors would have tossed in the slush pile, knowing it was my vision and my gamble to take. Your insights and expertise have always been, and still are, invaluable. I'm forever grateful for your help.

Thank you to Erica Rapp for working with me behind the scenes on so many projects, in whatever way I need. But mostly, for your eternally candid honesty and authentic friendship.

Thank you, Brenda—my cheerleader—for always encouraging me and believing in every project I take on. I am eternally grateful for your unwavering support and faith in me. Thank you for reading through the early, messy drafts and helping me shape them into the best stories I can tell. I write for me. But I write for you, too.

Thank you, Aliah, for taking me to Kenny Chesney and letting me ramble about some book about whales that I might write. For having the same sense and intuition at the exact same moment when Tahir spoke his foggy, prophetic words. Your encouragement kept this project alive when I needed another push.

Thank you to Penny for your willingness and time to proofread and for your keen eye and attention to detail.

Thank you to all the early readers who agreed to help launch this book on day one so that other readers might find it.

Thank you to my husband, the absolute greatest love of my life. Without you, I'd only be fantasizing about love stories and writing about romantic dreams—instead we get to live them out together. Thank you for tolerating me, allowing me to hibernate, ignore, disappear, and tune out our life so that I may chase my tiger.

I am forever indebted to you for the gift of noise cancellation airpods, Delta upgrades, airline drink vouchers, and accumulated Sheraton points.

Without you I'd be forced to work a real job for a lot more money, while flexing optimism but secretly dreaming about writing.

Because of your support, I get to live this era of my life, not as the extrovert I inherently am, but as the introvert I choose to be—creating worlds, living without noise, and finding a peace I otherwise wouldn't have known. Lastly, thank you for being okay with a wife who puts on her uniform at 9 p.m. and doesn't take it off until 1:30 p.m. the next day. I know our life is a team effort. But I nominate you as MVP.

To the readers who have been with me since 2015 and have followed me into fiction—thank you for spending your precious time with me. I am grateful for however you found me and for whatever reason you stuck with me. Don't be a stranger. I won't be either.

Until next time, dear friends. Eat plants. Drink wine. Save animals. Read great books. Try to be a good human—and raise good humans too. I'll do the same. -C.J.

RECOMMENDED RESOURCES AND READING:

Throughout my research for this book, I explored numerous books, articles, studies, and podcasts on these topics. Many of these resources provided invaluable insights and inspiration. While it would be impossible to list every impactful source here, I have curated a short list of references that I found especially moving or thought-provoking. This selection is not meant to diminish the importance of other works not mentioned. I am deeply grateful to the journalists, researchers, scientists, ecologists, marine biologists, orca enthusiasts, naturalists, and Indigenous nations who dedicate their lives to understanding and protecting these extraordinary and vulnerable beings with whom we share this planet. Their work informs and inspires this story with the utmost respect. These are my personal recommendations and acknowledgements.

Audible Original: Tokitae
https://www.audible.com/podcast/Tokitae/B09KWZKK24
https://www.bonnieswift.com

Incredible, well-researched, sensitive, and truly heartwarming podcast by a writer, speaker, and journalist whose work I deeply admire.

Orca: Shared Waters, Shared Home,
https://www.amazon.com/Orca-Shared-Waters-Home/dp/1680513265

It is with great respect and admiration that I recommend the work of Lynda V. Mapes, whose in-depth reporting and storytelling at The Seattle Times offer profound insights into the Pacific Northwest's natural world. For those without access to The Seattle Times, her book, Orca: Shared Waters, Shared Home, provides an exceptional look at orca conservation and the interconnections within our ecosystems.

For anyone seeking a deeper understanding of the Penn Cove orca capture, I highly recommend viewing the remarkable photographs taken by Wallie V. Funk. His images are a powerful and moving documentation of this event, capturing moments that words alone cannot fully convey. Funk's work, available through Western Washington University's archives.

MABEL Digital Collections: Western Washington University's MABEL platform hosts a selection of Funk's photographs. View the collection here: https://mabel.wwu.edu/funk-wallie-v-papers-and-photographs

*Beneath the Surface: Killer Whales, SeaWorld, and the Truth Beyond Blackfish* by John Hargrove.

*Endangered Orcas: The Story of the Southern Residents* by Monika Wieland Shields.

Documentaries:
*Blackfish*
Examines the consequences of keeping orcas in captivity.
*The Breach*
Investigates the decline of wild salmon populations and its impact on ecosystems.
*Dammed to Extinction*, a documentary by Michael Peterson and Steven Hawley. https://www.dammedtoextinction.com/

The following link goes to a ten-minute clip features restored 16mm footage of the actual 1970 Penn Cove orca capture. Baby Wild Films Presents: The Killer Whale People is a nationally syndicated, Emmy Award-winning television special from 1999, produced by Michael Harris and hosted by Nancy Wilson of Heart. https://youtu.be/ho2-WFC7j6U?si=BOQq_58Et2_jFQ5V

1. Inspired by Lummi legend, adapted for this work. San Juan Journal. (n.d.). *Southern Resident killer whales given Lummi name in a traditional ceremony.* Retrieved from https://www.sanjuanjournal.com/life/southern-resident-killer-whales-given-lummi-name-in-a-traditional-ceremony/

2. *Time* Magazine. (1954, October 4). *Iceland: Killing the Killers.* Retrieved from https://time.com/archive/6795010/iceland-killing-the-killers/

3. Anon. (1956). War against killer whales near Iceland. Norsk Hvalfangst-tidende, 45(10), 570—573.

1956: Iceland asked the US Air Force for some help in blowing up killer whales, and the US obliged by dropping depth charges on killer whales until they left the fishing grounds.

### War against Killer Whales near Iceland

According to a notice in the Danish Fishery Gazette, repeated in «Fiskets Gang» of May 24, killer whales have appeared in large numbers in the last 3 or 4 years outside the south-west coast of Iceland. Experts have assessed the number at several thousands.

In view of the prominent place of the fishing industry in Iceland's national economy the Ice-landic authorities decided that they could not allow this dangerous competitor to enter Iceland's chief fishing grounds. As the killer whales did not content themselves with eating the shoals of fish, but also began to plunder the fishermen's nets, to devour the catch and tear to pieces the fishing tackle, with the result that last summer the total damage was reported to be two million kroner, the situation became extremely serious.

The authorities commenced action by promising a reward for each head of a killer whale brought in, but it was very soon found that this measure was inadequate. In the next round whole fleets were therefore fitted out which put out to sea to fight the enemy in veritable naval battles. But this did not prove effective either.

The Icelandic authorities then applied to the United States Air Force asking for the loan of an aeroplane which could drop depth charges. The American authorities stated their willingness to do this. The operation was started in October and went on for some time under the direction of Agnar Gudmundsson, formerly whaling gunner in Whale Ltd. Not very many killer whales were killed, but after depth charges had been thrown down for 2 - 3 days the killer whales disappeared from the fishing grounds.

Citation: Anon (1956) War against killer whales near Iceland. Norsk Hvalfangst-tidende. 45(10):570-573

4. Naval Aviation News. (1956, December). Killer whales destroyed — VP-7 accomplishes special task. Naval Aviation News, 19.

" Killer Whales Destroyed - Page 19 - Naval Aviation News - December 1956 - WebSite: http://www.history.navy.mil/nan/backissues/1950s/1956/dec56.pdf [09AUG2004]

**Killer Whales Destroyed**
**VP-7 Accomplishes Special Task**

Adm. Jerauld Wright, Commander in Chief, Atlantic Fleet, has announced the completion of another successful mission by VP-7 against killer whales off the coast of Iceland.

Killer whales annually plague Icelandic fishermen by damaging and destroying thousands of dollars worth of fishing nets. Last year VP-18 destroyed hundreds of killer whales with machine guns, rockets and depth charges.

Before the Navy lent a hand last year, killer whales threatened to cut the Icelandic fish catch in half. This created a crisis because fishing employs about 20% of the population and accounts for the majority of Iceland's foreign currency income.

The Icelandic Office requested help, and Capt. W. A. Sherrill, Commander of the Naval Forces in Iceland, assigned VP-7 to the task of ridding the coastal areas of killer whales. Ranging from 20 to 30 feet in length, they are feared as one of the deadliest of ocean creatures.

19

5.      King Television. (1976). *The Killer Whale Hunters* [Documentary]. Seattle, WA.

6.      World Animal Protection. (n.d.). *Lolita: What happened to the orca who lived at Miami Seaquarium?* Retrieved from https://www.worldanimalprotection.us/latest/blogs/lolita-what-happened-to-the-orca-who-lived-at-miami-seaquarium/

7.      KPCW. (2021, October 30). *For 51 years, this killer whale has lived in a tiny tank. Now her health is at risk.* Retrieved from https://www.kpcw.org/npr-news/npr-top-stories/2021-10-30/for-51-years-this-killer-whale-has-lived-in-a-tiny-tank-now-her-health-is-at-risk

8.      Retire Lolita Campaign. *Lolita's Health Issues and Advocacy for Retirement.* Retrieved from https://www.retirelolita.com.

9.      Georgia Strait Alliance. *A Brief History of the Southern Resident Orcas.* Retrieved from https://georgiastrait.org/work/species-at-risk/orca-protection/southern-resident-orcas/brief-history-southern-residents/.

10. Marine Mammal Commission. *Southern Resident Killer Whale Population*. Retrieved from https://www.mmc.gov/priority-topics/species-of-concern/southern-resident-killer-whale/population/.

11. Natural Resources Defense Council. *Penn Cove Captures: Why Southern Resident Orcas Need Us*. Retrieved from https://www.nrdc.org/bio/giulia-cs-good-stefani/penn-cove-captures-why-southern-resident-orcas-need-us.

12. National Geographic Society. (2016, March 17). *SeaWorld ends orca breeding program, focuses on conservation and education*. National Geographic. Retrieved from https://www.nationalgeographic.com/animals/article/160317-seaworld-orcas-killer-whales-captivity-breeding-shamu-tilikum

13. Double Bay Sanctuary. *Corky's Story: The World's Oldest Captive Orca*. Retrieved from https://doublebaysanctuary.org/corky/.

14. Animal Welfare Institute. *Orca Captivity in China: A Regressive Path*. Retrieved from https://awionline.org/awi-quarterly/spring-2024/orca-captivity-china-chooses-regressive-path.

15. U.S. Army Corps of Engineers. *Lower Snake River Dams*. Retrieved from https://www.nww.usace.army.mil/Missions/Lower-Snake-River-Dams/.

16. National Oceanic and Atmospheric Administration (NOAA) Fisheries. *Snake River Dams and Salmon Recovery*. Retrieved from https://www.fisheries.noaa.gov.

17. NOAA Office of Response and Restoration. *Exxon Valdez Oil Spill: More Than Two Decades Later, What Have We Learned About Killer Whales?* Retrieved from https://response.restoration.noaa.gov/oil-and-chemical-spills/significant-incidents/exxon-valdez-oil-spill/more-two-decades-later-have-kil.

18. NOAA Fisheries. *Killer Whale (Orcinus orca) AT1 Transient Stock.* Retrieved from https://www.fisheries.noaa.gov/s3/2023-06/KILLERWHALEOrcinusorcaAT1TransientStock.pdf.

19. Whale and Dolphin Conservation (WDC). *The Penn Cove Orca Captures.* Retrieved from https://uk.whales.org/end-captivity/the-penn-cove-orca-captures/.

20. KING 5 News. *Timeline: Tokitae, the Southern Resident Orca's Tragic Journey from Puget Sound to Miami Seaquarium.* Retrieved from https://www.king5.com/article/news/local/timeline-tokitae-southern-resident-orca-tragic-journey-puget-sound-miami-seaquarium/281-208c8f05-cb35-47ed-abae-26466eda52fd.

21. Orca Network. *Tokitae's Story.* Retrieved from https://www.orcanetwork.org/tokitaesstory/blog-post-title-two-6scey.

22. Whale and Dolphin Conservation (WDC). *Orca Captivity.* Retrieved from https://uk.whales.org/end-captivity/orca-captivity/.

23. Earthjustice. (n.d.). *Puget Sound orcas recognized as significant* [Press release]. Retrieved from https://earthjustice.org/press/2003/puget-sound-orcas-significant

24. We Are Puget Sound. (n.d.). *Sound Champion and steward: Ralph Munro.* Retrieved from https://www.wearepugetsound.org/blog/sound-champion-and-steward-ralph-munro

25. Smithsonian Magazine. (n.d.). *Understanding orca culture.* Retrieved from https://www.smithsonianmag.com/science-nature/understanding-orca-culture-12494696/

26. Victoria Whale Watching. (n.d.). *Insights into the whale brain.* Retrieved from https://www.victoriawhalewatching.com/insights-into-the-whale-brain/

27. Animal Welfare Institute. (n.d.). *Infographic: Orcas in captivity.* Retrieved from https://awionline.org/content/infographic-orcas-captivity

28. Whale and Dolphin Conservation. (n.d.). *Orca captivity.* Retrieved from https://us.whales.org/our-goals/end-captivity/orca-captivity/

29. Whale Sanctuary Project. (n.d.). *The first orcas captured and sold to marine parks.* Retrieved from https://whalesanctuaryproject.org/first-orcas-captured-sold-marine-parks/

30. NOAA Fisheries. (n.d.). *Marine Mammal Protection Act.* Retrieved from https://www.fisheries.noaa.gov/topic/laws-policies/marine-mammal-protection-act

31. Dolphin Project. (n.d.). *The dark era of orca captures in Iceland.* Retrieved from https://www.dolphinproject.com/blog/the-dark-era-of-orca-captures-in-iceland/

32. BBC News. (2017, May 8). *France bans captive breeding of dolphins and killer whales.* Retrieved from https://www.bbc.com/news/world-europe-39834098

**33.** Vice. (2016, March 17). *SeaWorld says the current generation of captive orcas will be the park's last.* Retrieved from https://www.vice.com/en/article/seaworld-says-the-current-generation-of-captive-orcas-will-be-the-parks-last

www.ingramcontent.com/pod-product-compliance
Lightning Source LLC
Chambersburg PA
CBHW070906260626
47162CB00007B/2576